The Good Things of Sicily

Alexander Lucie-Smith

The Catania Novels

I The Chemist of Catania

II The Nymph of Syracuse

III The Feast of the Dead

IV The Castle of the Women

V The Gravedigger of Bronte

VI The Good Boys of Sicily

Chapter One

The telephone call came late. He had been expecting it, hoping for it, and as he picked up the receiver, he looked at his watch, and thought the timing convenient. It was nine thirty. The children were in bed. His wife was watching television. He exchanged a few brief words with the person at the other end, and then went to the bedroom to change and get what he needed from the drawer that he was careful to keep locked. Then he looked in on his wife who, seeing him in his suit, knew that he had something to do, something she should not ask about. He read the disappointment in her face. In Catania, he had been out every night; since moving to Palermo, he had become a changed man with a changed way of living. Every day after breakfast, he left the flat in the small square named after Ignazio Florio and walked to the office in the viale della Libertà; he would have coffee out, come home for a light lunch, return to the office and go to the gym in the early part of the afternoon, but would always be back in the evening to see her, to see the children, to have supper and then go to sleep at the usual hour. He was such a devoted family man.

His car was kept in a garage in the square, and the man on duty waved to him as he drove out; the garage was owned by the Santucci family, and the men who supervised it knew better than to look even remotely surprised to see don Traiano at any hour of any day, let alone this hour of 9.30pm on a Thursday night in January. No doubt his business was completely legitimate. The garage, unusually, had no twenty-four-hour CCTV.

His destination was a restaurant and small hotel in the hills above the city of Palermo, an agriturismo that produced lemons and wine; the Santucci family had been involved in the export of wine and lemons for a hundred years. It was a family business, though the restaurant and the bed and breakfast side of it were recent additions to the citrus groves and the vineyard. He had already been there himself, anonymously, to check out the lie of the land, and he had read about the place; he and Elena Santucci, the boss's sister, married to Renzo, the nominal head of the Palermo operation, had spent some time looking at the accounts. Accounts were terribly boring, and he liked to think of himself as a man of action; but accounts repaid careful study, and after looking at what felt like thousands of details of profit and loss, it was this place that he had fixed upon, the Mattarella agriturismo, a place that he felt might well be the weak point where the first attack should be made. One should always try to find where the enemy was weakest.

He did not have much difficulty negotiating the evening traffic or in driving up the narrow steep and torturous road. When he parked the car, he looked out at the lights of Palermo gleaming beneath him and the sea beyond, and thought how pretty the place was, remembering how splendid the view had been in the daylight. He walked across the gravel of the carpark to the bright lights of the restaurant. There were not many cars, but that was not surprising for January, even if it were a Thursday.

He walked in and spoke to the young man at the desk, a young man, perhaps slightly older than himself, who took in the details of the visitor with sharp and suspicious eyes: the suit; the neatly cut, short, dark hair; the confident expression. Traiano was aware that he was being looked at, judged, appraised. He was aware too of Tonino and his girlfriend Petra, on the other side of the room, but he did not look at them, and gave no hint that he was aware of them. He saw the young man look at him with something approaching distaste, asking him if he had a booking.

'I have no booking,' he said. 'I would like to see the boss.'

He did not add that he would like to see the boss at once, but his tone conveyed as much.

'I will see what my father is doing,' said the young man.

The way he said it indicated that he thought his father would have better things to do. He left his desk and went through a door that led down a corridor to a room at the back.

'Dad,' began the young man, but his voice trailed off, as he realised that the visitor had followed him.

His father, who had been looking at something on his desk, looked up in annoyance at the interruption.

'It's OK, Antonello,' he said to his son. 'You can go.'

Traiano sat down without invitation in the comfortable chair opposite the desk, and said:

'Get me a Cinzano, no ice, Antonello.'

Antonello, hesitating by the door, looked at his father, who nodded, and then left. Traiano stared at the man behind the desk, and then said:

'Well, signor Mattarella, it is nice to put a face to the name.'

Mattarella felt immediately that he was at a disadvantage. He could not ask who his unexpected visitor was, because, though he had never knowingly seen him until now, he knew it could only be Trajan Antonescu. And Trajan Antonescu, now sitting so comfortably in his favourite chair, having penetrated the inner sanctum, knew that he had no need to introduce himself. After all, ever since he had arrived in Palermo the previous January, he had become known. All the suppliers knew that don Antonio Santucci had long retired, and that don Renzo, his nephew, had taken over, and that this newcomer from Catania, Antonescu, was there to provide the necessary backbone that Renzo lacked.

The two men looked at each other.

'I gather there has been some trouble,' said Traiano easily.

'I was not aware…' said Mattarella. 'But if there has been some trouble, I am only too happy to do everything I can to sort it out. And sort it out to your satisfaction, don Traiano.'

'I am pleased to hear it,' said Traiano. 'I hope very much that everything can be resolved peacefully. We do not want any bones broken, do we?'

Antonello returned. He was carrying a tray with a glass of Cinzano and a glass of red wine. He proffered the tray to Traiano first of all, and then to his father, who took the glass of wine with a steady hand, and only betrayed himself by taking too large a sip too quickly. Of course, Antonello, seeing the way his father behaved, knew who this was too. Until two or three years ago don Antonio Santucci used to sit in the chair opposite his father; before don Antonio, either his deceased father or his uncle had done so, and in those days his father had been the one who had brought in the drinks, while his grandfather had sat behind the desk.

'Antonello,' his father now asked, detaining him. 'Did something happen in the restaurant this evening?'

Antonello, caught in the act of leaving, was rooted to the spot. He looked at his father. Then he turned to face the stranger, knowing that this was the real centre of power in the room.

'There was an altercation,' he said. 'The young gentleman and his companion… I presented them with a bill. Perhaps I made a mistake. Maybe I was not sufficiently respectful, sir.'

Traiano looked at him.

'I am very sorry, sir,' said Antonello.

'You realise who the young gentleman is? He works for me and I work for the Santucci family, your single largest client. We have been buying your lemons for decades, and I hear they are good lemons. We have been buying your wine, which, people in New York tell me, the Americans are not buying as once they did. Perhaps we should just drop you altogether, given that your produce is what it is, and how you treat us. Perhaps we should let you go....'

'Sir, it was an honest mistake,' said Antonello.

'Oh, was it? Do explain.'

Antonello looked at his father, and then looked away, when he saw no help would be forthcoming from that quarter.

'He looked a bit young, that is all. I did not understand that he was working for the family. Naturally, I gave him the bill. He told me he would not pay, and perhaps I did not understand properly and was a bit rude. Then he asked to use the phone, and I might have said... I don't know what I said,' said Antonello, aware that with every word he damned himself further.

'My son is young and inexperienced and perhaps a bit full of himself,' said Mattarella, now judging it right to intervene. 'He thinks he knows it all. Whenever a member of the family comes up here they eat and drink on the house. Antonello, come here.'

The young man approached his father hesitantly. Mattarella stood up and slapped him hard in the face. Antonello gasped and looked for a moment as if he might burst into tears.

'Now go out to the young couple in question and take them the very best bottle of wine we have with my compliments,' said his father. 'Tell them that you are very sorry indeed for your previous rudeness, and tell them that everything is on the house tonight, including the best room we have, if they want to stay the night. Now, just go and do it, while don Traiano and I discuss business. Oh, and prepare them a case of the same wine and another case for don Traiano as well.'

The young man withdrew.

'That boy is a fool,' observed Traiano.

'It was an honest mistake,' said Mattarella.

'There's no such thing. There are only mistakes. Which have to be paid for. And only one question, who pays. He insulted the wrong person. Tonino is young, and today is his birthday, that is why he came here to celebrate. He is young, but he is tough, and he does not like insults. He called me because he wanted my permission to take his revenge. Obviously, he knew that this establishment is one of our accounts, that is why he came here, expecting a warm welcome.'

'If we had known....'

'Well, you should have known. If Tonino wants to give your son a good kicking, how could I possibly tell him not to? If he wanted to stick a knife in his guts or put a bullet into his arrogant brain, do you honestly expect me to object?'

Mattarella took a slurp of wine and then spoke, knowing that what he said now would be important.

'Don Traiano, I love my son very much, but I am not blind to his faults. Please let me be the one to punish him. He is a stupid boy, as you say. I was once a stupid boy, but I learned my lessons and I remembered what I learned. I worked with don Antonio Santucci for many years, and always showed him the proper deference. My father before me worked with don Lorenzo, may he rest in peace, and don Domenico, and none of us have yet forgotten don Carlo, who we all liked so much, may he too rest in peace. The relationship with the Santucci family has been very profitable for all parties concerned.'

'Ah, but has it?' asked Traiano. 'For all parties concerned? You see, we have been looking at the books. Don Renzo is a very relaxed person, as was don Antonio before him, but don Renzo's wife, she is a trained accountant, and she looks at these things in the way other people look at, well, the things they like. She knows how much we pay for each lemon from this place, and how much we get when that lemon goes on the market in New York. It is really quite fascinating, the journey from tree in Sicily to bar in Manhattan. I am sure it is something you yourself have often wondered at. The lovely fruit growing on your trees... which ones will end up where? Which ones will have the honour of being in the bar of the Algonquin Hotel in New York, or the Waldorf Astoria? You see, even fruit has its hierarchy. Just like people. As it turns out we are making a decent return on your lemons. But your wine…. The joke is that if the vats of wine which we export to America were to fall into New York harbour, the very fish would die. Very soon we will have difficulty giving the stuff away to the sort of alcoholics who drink in the streets. Even they have some standards. And we are paying you for something better. They say that you are selling the good stuff here and giving us the rubbish. But you are getting paid what you were always paid, and we are getting less and less value for money.'

Traiano took a sip of his Cinzano.

'Frankly, signor Mattarella, the situation cannot be allowed to continue. Your son, as you have admitted, this Antonello of whom you are so fond, has his faults. The worst by far, which you may be ignorant of, is his tendency to be a chatterbox. He goes down to Palermo and boasts to all his friends how clever he is. He tells them that his father is making lots of money, and that his father is making money at the expense of the Santucci family, so clever is he. He says these things in bars which we own, and where the waiters and barmen are always keen to overhear the sort of stuff that will interest us. And we were very interested in some of the things your Antonello has been saying. He tells his silly friends, in the hope of impressing them, that you, yes, you, signor Mattarella, buy cheap wine in the provinces, the very cheapest, and sell that on to us, while your own product is sold in the restaurant. In other words, that you are cheating us, and that you think we are too stupid to notice. But now we have noticed. But this sort of boast is not clever, because it makes us look bad, and a company like ours trades on its reputation. And we do not like to appear the dupe of anyone. So, what is to be done, signor Mattarella? And denying it would not be wise. Because we know, not only because of your chatterbox son Antonello, but because of the accounts. We have seen the falling off in the last few years, we have seen the way the account we have with you has failed to yield the harvest we expected. We have calculated the exact sum of which you have cheated us over the last four years. Roughly four hundred thousand euros, give or take.'

Mattarella was pale, and it was clear to Traiano that he could see that the game was now over. Mattarella was now torn between fear of the future, anger with his son, and a desperate desire to negotiate.

'I don't have anything like four hundred thousand,' he said at last.

Traiano held up a hand to silence him.

'But you do not dispute the figure,' said Traiano. 'It is rather a round sum, I admit, but we think it is adjacent to the amount you have stolen from us. Perhaps more accurately it is not the amount you stole, but the amount we require of you so that we may be placated. Think of it as a fine. You don't have four hundred thousand? No? Well, it can be in kind rather than in cash.

We will settle for a 51% share in the property. Please do not look surprised. It is a good offer. We will own just over half, and we won't even charge you rent. On the day of your demise, there will be a surprise for your son and heir, but all this was little Antonello's fault in the first place. Really, it is a generous offer. You will go down to our offices first thing tomorrow and our lawyers will draw up the papers. You will sell us 51% for four hundred thousand euros, though naturally you will never see a penny of that. The alternative is that little Antonello gets a bullet in the back of his head some ten minutes from now. If I were him, I would prefer to lose my inheritance to losing my life. But you may think differently. You may decide you do not love him that much after all. But I think you will do as we say. As for the future, Antonello had better watch out. He is in danger of becoming a nuisance.'

'Don Traiano,' said Mattarella slowly. 'The blame in this matter is entirely his. As you say, he thinks he is so clever. But he is my son. I believe you have children. Family is everything, absolutely everything. You choose your friends, but not your relations. The boy thinks he is clever. This scam was his idea. In fact, I only went along with it because the boy is so ungovernable. He is not clever, as I say. I did warn him. I will willingly give you what you want and will be there tomorrow morning at 9am. But Antonello.... His mother is dead, and he is my only child.'

Traiano made a dismissive wave of the hand.

'I am not interested in Antonello. He is your affair. Let him discover the mistake he has made on the day of your funeral. May that be many years hence, signor Mattarella. But in the meantime, he should perhaps have a taste of your belt. You spoiled him, you know. In the end, it is your fault. Yes, yes, I know, an only child. But still....'

He got up and left. As he passed through the dining room, on the way out, he gave a slight nod to Tonino. Then he went to his car. Antonello followed him into the carpark with a case of wine. He drove down the mountainside. He would be home in good time, just as he had promised his wife.

The next morning, he was at the office at the usual time and asked the people at the front desk to let him know when Mattarella arrived; he did not have long to wait. Mattarella was there at 9am exactly, and was shown into the room where the lawyers were waiting for him. At about 11am, as he was on his way out to coffee at one of his usual bars, he was assured that Mattarella had left, and that all was now in order, and that the Santucci group of companies now owned 51% of the freehold of the Mattarella agriturismo. As he was standing in the crowded bar with his cappuccino and his mini cornetto, amidst the noise and the crowd of mid-morning, Tonino came up to him, as he had been expecting.

'They invited you to spend the night there. Did you?' he asked.

'No, boss. You told me to think strategically, and to make decisions based on the information of the moment. I took Petra back to her hotel, just as her mother had asked me to, before 11pm. But then I went back up the hill.'

'Go on,' said Traiano.

'He wasn't pleased to see me.'

'Antonello? I imagine not. Did you beat him up for insulting you?'

'No, at least not this time. I can save the pleasure for a later date. Something interesting happened. He was very eager to give me something he thought I wanted. Not another case of wine, either. Antonello has a friend called Simone Rota, about his own age. They have known each other a long time. This Simone has an uncle who works for us. Antonello says that is where the big fraud is. Antonello thinks that Simone will finger the uncle for us.'

'These people have no loyalty amongst themselves,' observed Traiano. 'It is the secret of their failure. You found something out about this Rota, the nephew, where he lives and so on? Good. Find out some more. I am interested. And leave Antonello alone for now. Maybe later, we will see. Maybe if we get the bigger fish, we will use Antonello for the message we want to send. But if this information is valuable, we might even spare Antonello. That is what his father expects, I presume. He has paid us enough to leave the boy alone; he does not deserve such a father; Antonello has no care for his father, or for his friends. He thinks only of himself. What a fool, but a useful one. What did you think of that place?'

'Nice. Good food. Excellent wine.'

'Did Petra enjoy it?'

'I think so, boss.'

'You think so?'

'Well, she said she did when I left her at her hotel.'

Traiano gave a low laugh.

'How is her mother? How is your friend Roberto and the other two daughters? They are a nice family. Good ordinary people. And you are like another son to Petra's mother, aren't you? How is your father, by the way?'

'Enjoying life,' said Tonino. 'Back home, with my mother. The new baby is cute.'

'But you are better off here, aren't you? With me and don Renzo and all the joys of Palermo?'

'Yes, boss.'

The reply was hardly confident. It was clear that the young man wanted to confide something personal.

'Boss, I am very happy to be here, and, much as I love my mother, not to be with her and my father and the new baby. He has wasted so much of his life in jail, perhaps I am right to let him live his life now. But she wanted that too, my mother. I should be grateful to don Calogero for securing my father's release.'

'Don Calogero's lawyers, you mean.'

He spoke with bitterness. He had spent so much time with lawyers of late. It was disheartening.

'But the thing is that Petra asks questions. I want to settle down one day, maybe with her, maybe not, but when I raise the topic, she says we do not have enough money, and I tell her we do, and she asks questions, where does it come from, and she asks about you, and my father, what was he in jail for, and about don Calogero.'

Traiano was thoughtful. This was not good.

'And what do you say?'

'I say as little as possible, and that upsets her. She says I am not telling her the truth, whatever that means. What is the truth, anyway, boss?'

'The truth is something complicated, better left unsaid, because it's too difficult to put into words. So, she is asking these things; I wonder why? You are who you are, isn't it obvious, so why ask? You are the friend of don Calogero, the friend of myself, no less. Is she stupid? Doesn't she know what that means? And you have plenty of money. Why ask? She should just accept it and be grateful.' He paused. 'Are you in love with her?'

Tonino shrugged.

'Well, if you were, you ought to go and get an honest job, or go back to school, or be a bit more like that nice Roberto, your friend. Though I doubt you are cut out for that any more than I am. You never know, she may come round; she may realise that you have good qualities that others do not have, and she should not probe too deeply; but perhaps not. Does one want a girl like that to come round? Perhaps you should find a nice girl, one from our quarter, though Petra's quarter is pretty close to ours, find another girl who is no trouble and who accepts you for what you are. There, that is my advice, not that I often give it, or am often asked for it. Petra may realise where her best interests lie; wait and see.' He paused, and changed the subject. 'Have you seen don Renzo recently?'

'Not recently, boss,' said Tonino.

'Seen any members of the family? I mean, apart from Beppe?'

'I see Sandro from time to time,' he conceded. 'I go up to the house. Beppe does not know.'

'Best keep it that way if you want to remain friends with both,' said Traiano. 'Beppe is a nice boy; I wish I could say the same of Sandro. Renzo is tearing his hair out about Emma, not that it is any business of his. I suppose you heard…?'

'I did, boss.'

'She still refuses to say who the father is; her mother is very upset. Her father, well, I have no idea how he is reacting, and no one much cares. Sandro says he will shoot whoever made her pregnant. My guess is that she does not know who the father is, given that she has slept with so many men, many of whose names she never caught. Is there anything you might want to tell me?'

'What does Beppe say, boss?' asked Tonino.

'Why are you answering a question with a question? Beppe, as it turns out, seems little interested in who knocked his sister up. That sort of thing does not interest him in the least, strange to say. But as I say, is there something you want to tell me? The baby was born on or around 30th September, and nine months previous to that is the week after Christmas. Now what were you doing then? Is it possible….?'

'Boss, there was this party at their house, and Sandro invited me to bring plenty of cocaine, and it may have been possible that… Boss, I can't lie to you. She and I… it was not the first time, and because everyone was so drunk and high, I forgot to be careful, I did not think… When I heard she was pregnant, I thought it might be me. When I heard the baby was born on 30th September, I was sure it was me. I went to see her, she does not deny it, but she says that she wants to bring the child up on her own, without me, and that she does not want to have anything to do with me. I have told Roberto, and I have told my parents, but I have not told anyone else.'

'How did they react?' asked Traiano curiously.

'Roberto told me I was a fool. We had a fight.'

'With fists?'

'Is there another type?'

Traiano did not need to ask how the fight ended.

'And your parents?'

'My mother was very upset. I am seventeen, but she doesn't quite understand that. She doesn't realise that I go with girls. My father was more understanding, but he could see my mother was upset and he beat me with his belt. I did not mind. It was the first time he was really able to play the father with me.'

'But you did not tell me,' said Traiano. 'I mean, you can, and no doubt do, sleep with whoever you like, but this is the former boss Santucci's daughter and don Renzo's cousin. Sandro says he will shoot you, but no one cares what he thinks. Renzo may kick up a fuss. Even Beppe may object. How long has this been going on with Emma?'

'Since the night of don Renzo's wedding. But we have not been meeting often. Just every now and then.'

'She has been a bit of an embarrassment for some time, that girl. Now… It strikes me that your mother will be very keen to meet her new grandchild, am I right? Yes? She will talk to her friend signora di Rienzi, who will mention it to her son.'

'Am I in trouble, boss?'

'You may be. You were born for trouble, Tonino. And so was I. When I met my wife, the reaction of her family was not favourable. But they calmed down. The money helped. Emma is a rebel. If she accepts you, and she might, so will they. They will have no choice. Well, I am glad you chose to tell me, as I can tell the boss if he mentions it, and prove that it was not a secret you tried to keep from him or us. Run along. Are you in trouble? I don't know, that is the answer.'

With a wave of his hand, he dismissed him. He went back to the office. He did not go straight to his desk, but took a detour to see Elena.

'Oh,' she said, looking up from her computer. 'You have discovered something?'

'I have. Clever you to spot it. Is Renzo in?'

'He will be in later,' she said, brushing aside any mention of her husband aside. 'Well?'

'One of our suppliers has had a little fraud going for some time, namely selling his own wine to his clients at his agriturismo and then giving us low quality stuff he buys somewhere else, and which is not worth exporting.'

'That is Mattarella?' she asked. 'The figures spoke for themselves.' She nodded. 'But there is more....?'

'Much more, I hope. The son of the owner has indicated that the real cheaters are to be found elsewhere. I am going to follow that up. In particular I need to know about a man called Rota. Is he on the payroll?'

She looked at her screen. He did not understand computers and had never used one, but he loved the way that a few taps could elicit the information he craved.

'Yes,' she said at last. 'We have two of them. One is Matteo Rota, who has worked for us for over twenty years, anyway since 1990, come and have a look here. He is well paid too.'

Traiano looked at the sum that appeared on the screen, the amount Rota took home every month. It was a nice amount, but not so very impressive, not enough to make a man rich.

'The other Rota?' he asked.

'Simone…. He just worked for one summer and was paid much less. I presume, from his date of birth, he is a student or something.'

'And what does Rota senior do for us?'

'He is team leader, whatever that means. Who is in his team, I wonder? It's Byzantine. Meant to confuse anyone who is too curious, I suppose, but confusing for you and me too. Given that he has worked for over twenty years doing what he does, and is team leader, and is paid so well, he is obviously a trusted man.'

'And my information indicates that we are wrong to trust him. I will find out more. Where exactly does he work?'

'I can't tell. Do you want to go down wherever it is and check up on him?'

'And warn people that we are suspicious? No. That is the last thing I am going to do. Rota will only discover he has a problem on his hands when it is too late for him to do anything about it.'

Elena nodded her head. She did not like Traiano, though she had known him for years, ever since her brother had taken up with him, when he had been a little boy doing his First Holy Communion. Her mother loathed him, her sister Assunta too. He was a foreigner and an interloper, and his mother, the former prostitute Anna, was a bold woman whom their brother seemed almost to fear. Elena was now married to a rich man, and wished that they could do without Traiano, this boy from the slums, even if he wore a suit. But her husband Renzo seemed to like him, even depend on him, and her brother certainly did. Though she sometimes wondered, after nearly two years of marriage, if her husband were a good judge of character. Anna Maria, the banker, her brother's wife, loathed Traiano, she was sure. Though he was attractive, Elena admitted to herself: she appreciated his muscled shoulders, his black eyes and his firm rear, which she often caught herself staring at, as now, as he turned to leave the office, jacketless.

The next day, on a side street off the Corso Calatafimi, one of the less than beautiful arterial roads that led into the heart of Palermo, Tonino was waiting. Standing around waiting on a winter morning was not per se enjoyable, but it was one of the things that he had got used to in his life working for don Traiano. He reflected on what had happened two nights ago: his deliberate provocation of Antonello Mattarella, the arrival of don Traiano, and what should have happened next, his taking out of Antonello to teach his father, and all the other suppliers, a brutal lesson. He had had his knife with him and been prepared to use it; he had not liked Antonello; but what had happened when he had taken Petra back, and then come back alone, changed everything. One used a small fish to catch a bigger fish. And he was now waiting for the bigger fish. Antonello, in his desperation to curry favour, to row back from his previous arrogance, had not only given him the name, but had shown him a photograph on his phone of Simone Rota, and he was sure he would recognise him. He had been told the address, and from the door of the apartment block, a shabby rundown building, even by the standards of Palermo, had already emerged several people who could not be him. So he waited patiently, as he had done since seven that morning.

The wait, he knew, would be worth it. The boss had promised him a fee for the Mattarella job, which had not quite come off in the way anyone expected; if this current job led to something bigger, then there would surely be a bigger pay off for him. He needed the money. He had his expenses, the cost of his motorbike, the cost of his flat, the cost of living in general. But he was building up quite a bit of cash in his various proxy bank accounts, and was the owner already not only of his flat, but a few tiny vineyards here and there. Ever since his father had been released from jail and gone back to Catania (and ever since he had taken the chance to come to Palermo, in part at least to avoid him) he had no longer supported his mother. He missed his mother, but she was happy with his father and with the new child.

He had a completely new life here in Palermo. Because the Santucci group of companies was facing falling profits, because of the poor management first of don Antonio Santucci, and then of don Renzo Santucci, Trajan Antonescu had been sent to try and sort things out; and with him had come Tonino, as a ghost worker, someone who did not exist, but whose work would be very useful. It was the sort of work one could not talk about, of course. Indeed, he was there to do the work that could not be talked about ever, and it was as if he did not exist.

Roberto Costacurta had come with him to Palermo, and the small apartment in the restructured block by the Casa Professa, a few paces from the via Maqueda, was on paper owned by him, and the only official resident was himself. Quite a lot of people passed each other on the stairway, not knowing who was who, not asking questions, and no one at all would have been able to say who he was, or whether he lived there or not. Roberto emerged from the place at regular intervals to go to the University (he had transferred to Palermo from Catania) or to go to his part time job in the viale della Libertà, where he worked as he had done in Catania for Assunta, doing paralegal work, but this time for her sister, Elena, don Renzo's wife. Having the entrée into the offices, he was the messenger between Traiano and Tonino, the man that Traiano did not know. He served in place of a text message, for no one trusted mobile phones. It had been Tonino's idea for them to share a place together, and for Roberto to continue his studies at the University here in Palermo.

There had been two reasons why Roberto had wanted to stay in Catania, and these were his friendship with Assunta di Rienzi and his love affair with Gabriella Bonelli. As for the University, he thought Palermo a better place than Catania, and the shift was a good idea. But these two friendships were important to him. He liked Assunta and she liked him; but it went further than that. He was ambitious, he wanted to get on, and Assunta was useful to him. That personal touch had led him into the world of business. As regards Gabriella, what man wouldn't enjoy the experience of sleeping with a beautiful older woman every week? He certainly did. He liked her, of course, but there was more. She was a way into a society that he aspired to join. But he did not see her that often, and their relationship was semi-clandestine, though her brother knew about it. However, in the end, important as they both were, the two women could not contend with the importance of Tonino. He wanted to be with Assunta and Gabriella in Catania, but he had to stick with Tonino, that was non-negotiable. He knew it, and so did Tonino. Tonino assumed he would be coming; and Tonino had assumed rightly.

The wait for Simone Rota to emerge seemed interminable to Tonino. What was it that don Traiano had said to him, something about the truth being complicated and better left unsaid? Well, that was true, he reflected. He never dwelt on the past, and particularly not on the people who had inhabited that past and who were no longer there. He never thought of don Gino, Pavel

Bednarowski and his mother; they were in an area that his thoughts never visited, an enclosed space that his mind never penetrated. They were too complicated to think about. As for Petra, his girlfriend, he could think of her quite easily, and he could think of his mother with delightful simplicity. The same thought, an uncomplicated thought, applied to the child he had with Emma, and to Emma herself. He loved the child, he liked Emma, and if only she would come round, she would prove to be a better girlfriend than Petra, with all her annoying questions that tried his patience. She was a boss's daughter too, albeit a failed boss; their coming together had been accidental, but it might have excellent consequences. One could see where things might end with Emma; he was seventeen, he was a father, which pleased him; perhaps he had a future with Emma.

But the truth, the complicated and unexamined truth, which he did not want to confront, lay in the question of his relations with Roberto. They had shared a flat for two years, and every week, once, or sometimes twice, they shared a bed, something they had first done that time they had gone to Enna on that mission from the boss. He had grown up in a milieu, it hardly needed to be said, where it was generally held that that sort of people should be shot, drowned, or at very best exiled to uninhabited islands and left to starve. Whenever the topic was raised, which was not often, he had heard these opinions expressed and given the impression that he fully agreed with the standard view. But it was not quite like that, was it? Ruggero Bonelli, though no one ever mentioned it, had inherited his art collection from Professor Leopardi, much to the horror of the Professor's relatives, and it was clear to him, he was not sure how, that the Professor had been Bonelli's - he couldn't quite bring himself to use the word – lover. Bonelli was respected, as a scholar, as a gentleman, and no one had ever suggested he be shot, or drowned or sent to Lampedusa. But the world of Bonelli and his sister was a different world to the world he had grown up in, even if Bonelli had grown up in Catania; his was a different Catania. In his Catania there were boys who went with men for money, but that was considered shameful, and those men should all be punished, though in fact they never were, though their weakness was fully exploited.

But the nights when he got into bed with Roberto, and Roberto wrapped his arms around him and kissed him with enthusiasm, and gave him more pleasure than he had experienced with any girl – what did that mean? When he found himself looking at Roberto, and Roberto looking at him, in that way, what did that mean? He told himself that it meant nothing at all, that he was not like that, though Roberto, despite his many experiences with women, might be; that he would get married, that he did not like men in the way Bonelli did, and he certainly did not belong to the tribe that ought to be shot, drowned or exiled to Lampedusa.

Of course, they never discussed it, he and Roberto. They never spoke about this, though they spoke about girls, about football, about the affairs of the office, about food, and about their mothers in Catania. They spoke about everything, except that one thing. Not to speak about it was to assert its non-existence. To speak about it would make it a thing. The truth, left unsaid, ceased to be the truth. And yet, standing here in the cold of a winter morning, near the Corso Calatafimi, one's mind went, unbidden, to the previous night, and the warmth of Roberto's bed. Oh, he treated Roberto with feigned indifference, even with contempt and hostility, but it was the picture of Roberto that came constantly into his mind.

He wondered - and this was a thought that kept on intruding - if Roberto, now at the university - the same university that Simone Rota went to - if Roberto was in fact this moment thinking of him? But he had no way of knowing, as to ask this question, even of himself, was to enter forbidden territory. On the one hand, why should he? He had come with him to Palermo, he seemed enthusiastic in bed, but there were other things in Roberto's life. There was Assunta, there was Gabriella, there was his mother, there were his sisters….

The wait on the pavement seemed never-ending. Numerous people had passed by who could not be Simone Rota, because they were too old, too young, or the wrong sex. Tonino was wearing a pair of jeans, with trainers, a scarf, and a corduroy blouson jacket of dark burgundy colour, which was perfectly tailored to hide a gun and a knife. The gun pressed against his side, and the feel of it was good.

Then at last he saw him, coming out of the door of the apartment block, the one who had to be Simone Rota. He was in his early twenties, and looked depressed, his expression no doubt evoking the home he had just left, the small apartment where he lived with his widowed mother and his sister. One saw it all in that expression. A bright man, a student, working on his degree, someone who would get on, if only the circumstances were right. Someone who depended on the rich and perhaps not particularly generous uncle for charity. Someone used to daily disappointment. Someone who, like Tonino himself, was ambitious, but unlike Tonino, frustrated.

He was walking towards the Corso Calatafimi and the bus stop which would take him towards the centre of the city, presumably on his way to university. Tonino resolved to stop him, and did so by the simple expedient of calling his name. Simone turned. He looked puzzled, not recognising the youngster in the burgundy jacket and with the short wiry hair.

'Hi,' said Tonino.

'Hi,' replied Simone a little uncertainly.

'Antonello Mattarella has spoken to me about you,' said Tonino.

He now had his attention.

'How is Antonello?' asked Simone. 'He is more a friend of my sister's than me.'

'He is alive, just. And the reason he is alive is that he told us about you.'

Simone looked puzzled.

'Us?' he asked. 'Who are you?'

Then he saw the gun. Tonino, while speaking, had taken out the gun and draped the scarf over it, and was pointing it at Simone. His eyes looked beyond Tonino, but there was no escape, even if the Corso Calatafimi was busy with traffic and pedestrians. Only he saw the gun.

'Let us go and talk,' said Tonino, gesturing with his head towards a bar.

They went in and sat at a pair of high stools at a table. He kept the gun in his hand, under the table, pointed somewhere between Simone's crotch and his knee, at the soft flesh of his thigh. No one had ever pointed a gun at Simone before now; he felt a mixture of terror, numbness and curiosity.

'Who are you?' he asked.

'Wrong question. You should ask what I want. I shall tell you. I want to know all about your Uncle Matteo and his job. I want information, and you are going to give it to me, or receive a bullet in the groin.'

'You must be keen to know,' observed Simone, with a bravado he did not feel, overcoming the dryness of his throat. 'I have information, but I will sell it. I want something in return.'

'What you get in return is not getting a bullet in the leg or worse,' said Tonino. 'Don't annoy me, I might just pull the trigger by accident.'

Simone took a deep breath, calmed himself, and considered. The moment of maximum danger was surely the moment of greatest opportunity. It occurred to him that the youngster would not pull the trigger. The gun was a threat designed not to be used. He wanted information, and so would not kill him. Moreover, there would be no malicious wounding either, as that would mean a trip to hospital, an interview with the police (not that anything would come of that) and above all a warning to Uncle Matteo. His uncle was the one they wanted to talk about, he was sure, and this was an opportunity for him. The last thing they wanted was to alert his uncle to the idea that they were after him.

'Shoot me, and the element of surprise is lost. My uncle will wonder what is going on. It will alarm him, and perhaps he will take precautions of some sort or other. I imagine this is about him, and that you do not want him to know.'

'And you do not want him to know either, do you, that you have been talking about him to your friend Antonello. We know you have. If this gets back to him, that you have been so stupid as to talk, your uncle, fond of you as he is, will not be pleased. In fact, you need to talk to us, because we are the people who can protect you from Uncle Matteo's anger.'

He saw this register.

'Just think how much he has been stealing over the years, and weigh that against how much he cares for you. Yes, he got you that summer job, but… when it comes to safeguarding his fortune, or his fondness for you, I am sure I know which he cares about most.'

'What do you want?' asked Simone.

'To get the money back, to stop the theft, to get to the truth. To deal with Matteo Rota. That last thing is something you don't just want as well, but you need.'

Simone was silent.

'He would sacrifice you. So you had better get your sacrifice in first,' said Tonino.

'I don't want to know anything about that,' said Simone. 'But if you let me speak to your boss, I will tell him everything.'

'That is not how it works. You speak to me, not him,' said Tonino.

Simone looked at him. He could feel the pressure of the gun's muzzle against his leg. He knew this was the moment. He had to be brave, daring. Everything depended on it.

'I only speak to him, not to you,' he said.

Then, putting down his coffee cup, he calmly got up and left. He walked down the pavement, and only when he had reached the corner of the street, did he break into a run.

The weekend came, and business gave way to family life. It was essential, absolutely essential, that they go back to Catania that weekend, or so Ceccina reasoned, but Traiano managed to persuade her that this was not necessary at all. Her sister Pasqualina was in Catania with her husband and her new baby, but he reasoned they could all come to Palermo for the weekend, rather than they go there; after all none of them had been to Palermo, at least not since they had moved there a year ago. They had not seen the new flat, the new city, and he might have mentioned, the new life they were living. The truth was, he did not want to go back to Catania, he did not want to see one person in particular, and that person was don Calogero. He had complicated feelings about him, ever since the death of Gino, and to see don Calogero more than he had to was not something he relished. Of course they communicated, but they very rarely met except for business meetings. He did not feel the need to socialise with him more than necessary. She, Ceccina, in truth, for her part, had no particular desire to go to Catania when her relatives could come here. Her parents were living in the flat that they owned, the one underneath the boss, where they had lived for such a relatively short time, so that was taken care of. But just as her husband had no desire to see the boss, she had lost the will to see her old friends, even if she could. Alfio's wife, Giuseppina, had gone with her husband to East Africa. Alfio's cousin, Catarina, Gino's widow, had disappeared. These had been her close friends, but both had left the scene. The rumours about Catarina abounded. It was assumed that she had found a new man and moved away to be with him. Who this new man might be, no one could be sure, though there had been a few guesses. He had to be rich, powerful, the sort of man one would want to disappear for. No one discussed this, but surely everyone knew, and the knowledge was there, dangerous, waiting to cause unutterable harm. This was something she would discuss with her sister, not her husband; but she was sure her husband would discuss it with Corrado, Gino's brother, her brother-in-law.

They were to arrive on Friday night, the entire family, from Verona. The two sisters had much to busy themselves with, not having seen each other for almost a year, and the two men went for a turn around the square in front of the Politeama, a short walk away, to take some fresh air and to talk. The eldest child, Cristoforo, insisted on coming with them, and walked between them. Cristoforo, now nearly seven, fifteen years younger than his father, loved his uncle obsessively, and held his hand. This made Traiano smile. He had similar feelings but kept them hidden. He was passionately attached to Corrado (it was something his wife joked about) but he knew Corrado viewed him with cool indifference which made him sad. He had been looking forward to seeing him a great deal, but he had found, on meeting, that Corrado met him, not like an old friend, but a not particularly valued acquaintance. He was not just saddened by this, but a little angry too; yet more feelings to be kept hidden.

'How is the case going?' asked Corrado.

'I thought you might ask,' said Traiano. 'I am glad you asked out here. We never discuss such things in the house or on the phone, as you never know who is listening. In case you think that sounds paranoid, just listen to this. The picture of the Madonna and Child; they say it is stolen; Bonelli says he sold it to me and he inherited it from the Professor. Fine. This is what the lawyers tell me; I myself leave it all to them. They said I could admit to receiving a stolen painting, and plead guilty and be sentenced to six months, which would be suspended. Well, that sounds like a trap to me, so it is out of the question. All we have to do is to find an expert who will say in court that the painting is a nineteenth century copy of a Mantegna and not a real Mantegna, which should not be hard. Well, we have done that, but for the experts we produce, they produce some other expert, so called, who contradicts our expert. They have got nothing on me, but they are fishing. It gets better, or worse. They are now talking of charging me with conspiracy to defraud, to money launder, as well as receiving stolen goods, and that could carry up to ten years in jail. And they are now looking for evidence of such a conspiracy. They have dragged in Piuccio, you know, the one who oversaw your brother's funeral. You might well wonder what he has to do with it. Piuccio took a coffin up to Rome the year before last, and I went with him. They know this. Did you know that there are cameras on all the motorways, that recognise number plates and photograph vehicles? Well, they traced Piuccio's hearse; and there was nothing untoward about this, as you have to do paperwork when moving dead bodies around the country, and everything was in order. But one of the photographs made it clear that I was next to the driver. So, there you have the conspiracy. Piuccio and I were smuggling something in the hearse. Except there was a coffin, to be buried in Rome the next day, in the hearse, and when they asked what I was doing there, I told them. I am a friend of Piuccio, I went to keep him company, as it was a long journey, and he needed more than the radio for company to avoid falling asleep at the wheel. And when we got there, Piuccio dropped me off at the shrine of Our Lady of Divine Love, where I spent the night. I said it was a place I had always wanted to visit. But you see, Bonelli was also in Rome at the time, and he had flown there, so that was traceable; so they claim that Bonelli, Piuccio and I were all there at the same time, up to no good, smuggling art works, stolen artworks. But the good news is that they have interviewed Piuccio, they have interviewed me, and they have interviewed Bonelli, and they get the same story every time. They have interviewed the people at the shrine, who say they remember me, and that I was not alone, with someone whose name, luckily, they did not record, by the greatest stroke of luck. The person was someone we are not admitting to, and so that is another stick they have to beat me with. Why was I at Divino Amore with someone whose identity I will not discuss?'

Corrado nodded.

'And?' he asked.

'Tonino was there with me, but they will never be able to find that out. He was in the back of the van, sitting on the coffin, so there was no evidence that he was with us, as he was not photographed by the cameras. And the people at the shrine did not mention his name. We did not ask them not to, they just didn't, and I assume they have no love for the police either. They can't prove I have conspired with Tonino as they have no hard proof I even know him, except most casually. But, yes, Tonino has enough information to send me to jail for ten years at least. Not that it is in his interest to do so. Of course, what they want is electronic evidence to back up their conspiracy theory, but they won't get it. I am very careful. I trust no one. I don't even discuss this with Ceccina. It is better not to worry her.'

'But you are worried?'

'I know what they are playing at. It will be interesting to see what they try next. Well, I know. The latest ploy is to drag in Volta, the mayor of Catania. He gave Piuccio his new job running the cemetery. But I have never met Volta, never communicated with him. They want to drag this on and on until I cave in. I won't. I have too much to lose.'

'And the other cases?' asked Corrado.

He laughed.

'How I hate lawyers. The other cases do not involve me, but they have the potential to make trouble. They worry Renzo sick, and he is always going to be the weakest link in the chain. I see a lot of Renzo, and this is the only thing we ever seem to discuss. It is all the fault of that sickening boy, his cousin Sandro. He refuses to admit he took cocaine at the weekend when your brother died. Well, not exactly. He admits he did but says it was not his fault, that he was young and led astray. Renzo admitted it, admitted culpability, and took the rap. Sandro will not. So, the case drags on and on, appeal after appeal, making out that he is the victim of myself, of poor Gino – blame the dead guy - and of Renzo. It is a load of rubbish, but it takes time. I have had to testify that I did not take cocaine that weekend and have never done so in my life. Renzo too had to confess to his longstanding drug use and the fact that he has completely changed. It has all generated a lot of unwelcome publicity. But Sandro will not drop the matter. But it is all part of a strategy, a strategy to influence the other case, that of the inheritance.'

'Was the will ambiguous?' asked Corrado.

'Of course not. Beppe got everything the old man had, and if he dies before his twenty-first birthday, it will all go to the Church. A good idea, as that prevents anyone, well, trying to settle the dispute via a short cut. Sandro's case is predictable, that Beppe and his mother influenced the old man unduly, as he lay on his death bed. He wants half, or a quarter, or something. Well, he wants a share, and if he makes enough of a nuisance of himself, then he hopes Beppe, or rather Angela and Beppe's lawyers, will offer an out of court settlement. It is awful, as the whole thing is a soap opera, and the publicity immense. Which, of course, Sandro wants; the more publicity the better. He thinks it will shame Beppe into coughing up. It is blackmail. He hopes, I imagine, that myself or Renzo will advise Angela to settle, just to shut him up.'

'And will you?'

'Never! If you had met Sandro, you would know why. But listen, tell me about Catarina and her baby Tino. What has become of her?'

'You have no idea?' asked Corrado. 'Neither have I. No one knows, not even her parents. She has disappeared from the face of the earth.'

'No one ever has before now, you know,' said Traiano. 'Not even she. As a matter of fact, I have known where she is for at least a year. It took a bit of time, but I managed to find out in the end. Someone did not want us to know where she had gone, and that intrigued me. There had to be a reason. And whoever arranged for her to disappear was a powerful and rich man, because these things cost money. At first, I assumed it was Alfio, but then when he went to East Africa, I realised it was not. He liked her, you know, in more than a cousinly way. No, he is happy and working hard in Africa, and Giuseppina is with him. He has been given that nice posting by the boss, perhaps as a reward. Eventually I hit upon asking some of our friends in the police where she might be; after all, they would know, and who should get back to me, but the person I had not asked, one Colonel Andreazza, asking me not to ask. I knew then that someone powerful had arranged it, and after a few months of persuasion, I got him to talk. He told me, and he wished he had not. It seems that it was organised by a proxy of Alfio's, Costantino, who arranged a new identity for her; she is living under her new name in Enna; she has two children now; and well, it must follow that Calogero is the one behind it all. Enna is a very convenient location.'

'Who else knows?'

'No one, apart from you and me. Oh, and Tonino. He was in it from the start, not that he has breathed a word. He is always going between Catania and Palermo. I imagine he carries the messages. Needless to say, I do not like it. Another man's wife… even if that man is dead. It is not good. And he did not tell me, because he knew I would disapprove.'

Corrado was silent. He saw the implications.

'My brother's death?' he asked.

'An accident, but it was a suspicious one. But that is in their arsenal, if they want to make further trouble.'

'Are they trying to pin the supposed murder of Gino on you?'

'They are hinting at it. They could arrest me for murder, let the case go on for years, and then drop it for lack of evidence. It's blackmail. The trouble with blackmail is that it works, most of the time.'

'Was it an accident?'

Traiano was silent.

'They may be trying to get me to tell them something I know, or something they think I know. They may be trying to get me to accuse someone else, provide evidence. It is a strategy. A clever one, but I am not going to fall for it. Maybe they want me to point the finger. From their point of view the perfect villain would be Renzo. They were great friends; they had a drunken fight, and Renzo pushed him over the edge. That is a good story, at least for someone who does not know Renzo. Sandro counts for nothing. But they were both upstairs watching a film, along with Alfio; they were half asleep…'

They walked on in silence.

'Have you discussed this with anyone else?'

'No.'

'Are you worried?'

'No. They have no hard evidence about anything. They are just trying to rattle me. It is not working so far. They will lose patience and go away.'

'But the other cases?' asked Corrado.

'They, we, all have the same lawyers. We are impregnable.'

He said this with a confidence he did not feel. They were far from impregnable. There was a weak link, and that link was Renzo.

Chapter Two

Ever since he had had his brush with the law and been reprimanded for his cocaine use and had voluntarily undergone a course of detoxification in the early months of his marriage, don Renzo Santucci had become a keep fit fanatic. The death of Gino, which had been caused by drink and drugs, haunted him. The idea of going to jail and getting a criminal record frightened him, and the voluntary course had been a condition for his accepting a record but escaping jail. As part of this health fixation, he had taken up running, and was training himself for the Palermo marathon, which he was going to run in aid of his Aunt Angela's drug rehabilitation charity, for which he occasionally gave speeches, outlining his own escape from addiction. Traiano encouraged this, as did Elena, thinking it was good for him to have outside interests, and that the less time he had to interfere in the real business, the better. Indeed, he knew very little about the real business, being too lazy to master the detail of how things worked. This he left to his wife and to the wife of don Calogero; and the things that needed fixing in the engine room, those were left to Traiano. And it was also Traiano's job to steady this nervous young man, the figurehead of the entire enterprise, to calm him down, and to stop him creating trouble. He saw his main task as to stop him panicking, to stop him ruining things for the rest of them. And this was what he did every Saturday morning.

It was their custom to meet at 7am on Saturdays at the sports centre that belonged to the Santucci group of companies, not far from the Politeama. Traiano would stroll there, as it was only a couple of blocks away from the piazza Ignazio Florio; Renzo would run from his house in the northern suburbs, a matter of three or four kilometres. They would meet to play squash, a game that Traiano had learned to play purely because Renzo liked it. The court was booked for them every Saturday at the same time, and the place was usually deserted. After the game - and Renzo was good, so one did not have to let him win, he usually won quite fairly - they would have a secret conversation in the changing room showers, the one place they were sure could not be bugged, being too wet and too noisy.

The paranoia about bugging was something that Renzo readily accepted, and Traiano was happy for him to accept, as, if he believed every phone, room, and computer was monitored, it made him less likely to say something indiscreet. This morning, he fed him the news about the Mattarella business, which interested him; he outlined how clever Elena was in spotting accounts that did not quite add up; and he said a little about the case of Matteo Rota who they suspected of longstanding fraud. It was important to give Renzo this information, as it gave him the impression he was being consulted and informed, that he was somehow in charge, and the last thing he wanted was Renzo getting the idea he was not important.

He told Renzo that Corrado had arrived, and that they would meet over breakfast later. Renzo was pleased by this. He remembered Corrado from the funeral. He had liked him. He still missed Gino. In fact, now Gino was dead, he seemed to have expanded into this wonderful figure who had dominated his life; but that was true of all dead people, Traiano reflected. Even he had forgotten how dislikeable and annoying Gino had been when alive. Now he was dead, he almost liked him.

'So, this Rota business…' said Renzo. 'When we find out what he has been doing, you will deal with him?'

'Of course, not just him, but the people he has had helping him. And the nephew who has informed on him.'

'Why him?'

'Loose ends need tidying up,' said Traiano.

'Of course,' agreed Renzo.

'I will run the names past you, when we know more, and you can give the nod. You may know them, as they are all longstanding employees.'

'You will do it yourself?'

'I'll use Muniddu and Tonino. They are good, you know.'

Renzo nodded.

'We need to get the core business back on track,' said Traiano. 'This should do it.'

Again, Renzo nodded, busily shampooing himself.

'You have a high opinion of Muniddu and Tonino?' asked Renzo.

'I do. Very. They are good workers. I trust them. We can trust them. There was something I wanted to tell you,' said Traiano. 'About your cousin.'

'Sandro?' asked Renzo, rinsing out his shampoo.

'No. Emma.'

'Oh, the embarrassing one,' replied Renzo. 'Wait. You have found something out.'

'I have,' said Traiano.

'The little devil,' said Renzo, after he had told him.

He was not sure whether he ought to be angry or pleased, Traiano could tell. On the one hand this reflected badly on his Uncle Antonio, Emma's father, whom he hated. That a newcomer from Catania had fathered a child with the former boss's daughter betokened a lack of respect, to say the least. Tonino had made a fool of don Antonio Santucci and his family, that was for sure. But at the same time, that was his family as well, and it meant that Tonino, a person of no importance, of whom he was much inclined to be jealous, could now make a claim to be a relation of his, and by extension, of Calogero, his brother-in-law. Everyone knew that to be a brother-in-law was a very special type of relationship; he did not like the way Tonino's relationship with Emma might intrude on his exclusive relationship with the boss; worse, it might make him the brother-in-law of Beppe. That would be intolerable, in a sense; but it might also lower Beppe's, the heir's, standing. And that would only be a good thing. He would have to reflect on this.

The moment of secrecy and confidences was over, and the thought of the planned death of Rota and his associates had been overtaken, in Renzo's mind at least, by the question of his cousin Emma and her child. They withdrew from the showers, and in the changing room someone was sitting on the bench, evidently waiting for them. It was Beppe. Renzo looked at his young cousin with a frown of distaste. He would like to have continued discussing the Emma question with Traiano, but that was impossible with her brother present, he realised. This annoyed him. The very same thing was a matter of relief to Traiano. It was best that Renzo had time to think about the matter on his own. He was glad to see the teenager.

'Have you come to play squash? Because if you have, you are too late,' said Traiano.

'I came for breakfast,' said Beppe. 'I knew you would be here. You told me, remember? My father is at Castelvetrano, my mother has gone on pilgrimage with the wives of drug addicted men to Cascia, and my sisters, I have not seen; Sandro is at home with someone, so I crept out, without disturbing him, on my bike. There was no traffic at this time, and it took fifteen minutes.'

He kissed Traiano.

'This boy loves everyone,' said Renzo with a touch of acerbity. 'Come and kiss me,' he ordered.

'And everybody loves him,' said Traiano.

Beppe had suggested to Tonino that he should come with him to the gym, to surprise don Renzo and don Traiano. He had made an excuse and declined the invitation. The Saturday morning meeting between the two was a sacred moment, he knew, the one time in the week the two men could talk without being overheard by anyone; he knew that, because Traiano sometimes referred to it, saying he would ask (or rather make a pretence of asking) don Renzo 'on Saturday morning, when we are alone.' If they wanted him, they would invite him. He assumed that Beppe had no idea of the nature of these Saturday morning meetings, and thought of them as purely social and sporting. They were not. They were moments to talk of murder and extortion, not that Beppe would know anything about that. He liked Beppe, who was one year his junior, but he thought him naive, even a little deficient in common sense. But he liked him, he liked him a lot. Beppe was a child who wanted to be loved, and he felt a strong pull towards him; in this he shared something with Traiano, but not, he thought, Renzo. More importantly, Beppe liked him, though Beppe seemed to like everyone.

Tonino lay in bed, listening to the sounds coming from the bathroom, where Roberto was clearly having his shower. He heaved himself out of bed, and reached for some clothes, and went to the part of the one room studio that served as the kitchen to make coffee. Last night he had drunk the best part of two bottles of the red wine that had come from the Mattarella agriturismo, and his head felt a little bit fuzzy as a result. But coffee would fix it, and soon he and Roberto would be on their way to Catania.

Roberto emerged, and Tonino nodded to him, indicating the coffee. Before taking the cup, Roberto put his arms around Tonino and kissed him. For just a few seconds, from Roberto's point of view, the embrace and the kiss were perfect.

'Save it for someone else,' said Tonino, rudely and roughly pushing him away. 'You will be seeing her this afternoon, or tonight, won't you?'

'Gabriella? Yes,' replied Roberto.

'I need to ask you something,' said Tonino, now more conciliatory. 'You have spoken to your mother? To Petra? It is just that I have not heard from her since she was here.'

Roberto admitted that he had spoken to his mother and sisters.

'What did Petra say? About her trip to Palermo?' asked Tonino, a touch more eagerly that he had intended.

'She enjoyed herself. Didn't she tell you that herself?'

'She didn't. I just wondered if she had said anything to you. She liked the hotel?'

'Yes.'

'It was nice of your mother to let her come here.'

'Well, she is seventeen, isn't she?'

Tonino scowled. He knew what that implied.

They were soon on the road to Catania, Tonino on his motorcycle and Roberto on the back of it, with the dirty laundry. They were at the gallery at a little past eleven in the morning. They both went up the stairs to where signora Grassi lived with her husband and the new child. Roberto knew that the signora would want to see him, and he was always interested to see the signora at home, to see her husband and to see the way Tonino interacted with them. As they sat around the kitchen table, he saw how respectful but distant he was with his father, and how different he was with his mother and the child. He did not care for the father, but the mother was a different matter entirely, he loved her, and he loved the little brother. With her he was sweet and gentle, and his usual demeanour was gone. He was no longer bad tempered, surly or aggressive, as he so often was with Roberto. Now he just wanted to please, he was a child again, the carapace of adulthood cast aside.

His mother looked at him sadly as he sat there with his little brother on his lap.

'To have a child you do not see,' she said, not for the first time.

'I have seen her, Mama, I have seen her twice. But I know what you mean, I have not seen her enough. I have tried to see her more, but the mother does not want to see me.'

'And the idea of having a daughter whom you do not see growing up,' continued his mother.

'Mama, I know I did wrong. I explained it all to Papà, well not explained, confessed. He was angry with me, and he told me it was my fault, and he did what I would do if I were a father and my son misbehaved. He was right to do so. Papà understands it was an accident, and I hardly know Emma Santucci, so it is not surprising that she does not want to see me.'

Signora Grassi sighed. The revelation that her son was a fornicator was painful to her. Of course. her husband had told her only what she needed to know, but that was painful enough. Her little boy, having sexual intercourse at the tender age of sixteen, with a girl he hardly knew, was something she found hard to accept. It angered and saddened her. The fact that her husband had given Tonino the taste of his belt seemed only right. But if her husband had been here when the boy was growing up, perhaps this would not have happened.

'I can't help feeling,' said the signora, 'that this Emma Santucci is not a good girl.'

Tonino sighed sadly. His father looked uncomfortable.

Roberto spoke, knowing that this was why he was there.

'Signora, Emma Santucci is a nice girl, but it is just that she is unconventional, not like us.'

'You told me she had green hair!' said the signora, to her son, accusingly. 'Why on earth my sweet son should go with a girl with green hair, I just cannot understand it.'

'Signora,' said Roberto. 'She is unconventional, and I am sure one day she will dye her hair back to its normal colour. She is a student; she is, well, radical; she says she is an atheist, but her mother is not like that, and she will soon realise the error of her ways. She just needs to get used to being a mother. And Tonino says she really loves the little girl. Her brother Beppe is one of the nicest people you could ever meet, and a very good friend of Tonino's, though we have not told Beppe about the paternity of the child, as he is still young, still sixteen. The Santuccis are rich and perhaps do not do things the same way we do…'

'You mean they look down on us,' interrupted the signora.

'No, no, no, signora, it is not like that at all. Beppe looks up to your son, he really does, and well, it is my hope that Emma will eventually come round, and then with Tonino being such a good friend of Beppe, then maybe the rest of the family will accept it. But, of course, she has not told any of them, not told anyone who the father is, but she will want to, I am sure. And Tonino loves the child so much.'

'Well, of course he does. He is a good boy. But this girl, this Emma, she has a mother, for goodness' sake,' said the signora. 'What on earth does she think about this?'

'According to Beppe, not that we asked him - he told us - signora Santucci finds both her daughters, and her eldest son, rather difficult to understand,' said Roberto.

'Well, I think that if the signora Santucci could meet my son, she would soon come round to my way of thinking,' said signora Grassi.

'Mama,' said Tonino, 'not everyone thinks I am the little prince that you think I am.'

'Oh Roberto, tell him, tell him that I am not wrong, please,' said the signora in appeal.

'You are not wrong, signora. Tonino is a good Sicilian boy. I know it. He has a great heart when he lets it be shown,' said Roberto, a touch pointedly, seeing Tonino look up at this. 'Emma Santucci does not know how lucky she is. The little girl will have a wonderful, has a wonderful, father.'

Tonino looked at him.

'You have all forgotten that I have a girlfriend already,' he said suddenly. 'Your own sister. And here you all are marrying me off to someone who won't for the most part speak to me.'

'You may not have a girlfriend when she finds out,' said Tonino's father.

This was undeniable. They all sighed.

'Petra is just the sort of girl for you, just the sort of girl you should be going around with. And she is Roberto's sister,' said the signora unhappily.

'She is just the sort of girl that I have been going around with,' said Tonino. 'And if all goes well… I mean…'

It was an insoluble problem. How could he continue with Petra when he had a child with someone else, a child Petra did not know about, and one conceived when he was officially Petra's boyfriend? It would be a lot for Petra to accept. But hiding it from her did not seem either kind or practical, at least for much longer.

'You have ruined your life,' said signora Grassi, in despair. 'But the little brother is your friend?'

'Yes, Mama, he is, and after Roberto, my best friend.'

'Well, that is something,' said the signora. 'And thankfully you have Roberto too,' she added with a smile.

Roberto stood to take his leave. Tonino saw him to the door, shook his hand and thanked him, and they agreed to meet up later that evening, with Petra. He went down to the square with the monument to Cardinal Dusmet and sent a text message; after waiting for a reply, he set off up the via dei Crociferi, towards the flat where Gabriella lived and would be waiting for him.

His time with Gabriella was delightful. He loved the smart flat, so different to what he was used to. He loved the comfortable furniture, so much nicer than anything he had known in his childhood or even now. The softness of the bed and the sheets, the softness of herself. The initial ardour over, they spoke: her latest gardening project, his life in Palermo, which she claimed was a much more interesting city than Catania.

'And how is little short arse?' she asked, as she always did. 'What?' she remonstrated. 'Tell me. You know how I love to know about him; almost as much as my brother does. How is signora Grassi's little treasure?'

'Pretty damned worried, I would say,' said Roberto. 'His father gave him six of the best for getting Emma pregnant; his mother is very upset that her son, despite having a nice girlfriend, my sister, went with, as she puts it, a bad girl. He wants to be recognised as the child's father, he seems quite obsessed with the child; but he is also worried that if the bosses find out, they may be furious, and that Emma's family might be furious as well, and come after him. There is a lot to gain, but a lot to lose.'

'I think he did it deliberately,' said Gabriella. 'It is a way of getting on, isn't it?'

'I think it was a mistake. In fact, I know it was. He met her at a party at her house, where he had come to deliver the cocaine, and she led him on, and he forgot to take precautions. He doesn't think that deviously. He was just having a casual time with a girl, that is all, and he had had her before. He remembered the date because it was between Christmas and New Year, and when the child was born nine months later, he knew what that meant. I am not surprised at him, but I am at her. I mean, she should have got rid of it. That is what usually happens. No one would have known.'

'You mean, you would not have known, and Tonino would not have known. But Emma would have known, wouldn't she?'

'Yeah, but.... All this fuss would have been avoided. It is going to come out, you know, and there will be an almighty row. I mean, she can sleep with whom she wants, and she has done, and how, but she is Santucci's daughter, and her father and her brother and her cousin might just get some silly ideas into their heads.'

'Oh. poor Tonino, he is so sweet,' said Gabriella sympathetically. 'His mother must be so worried. You don't seem so concerned, I must say.'

'He should have been more careful,' said Roberto. 'He told me he was a bit drunk, but that is no excuse.' He smiled at Gabriella. 'Let's not talk about him,' he said, leaning over her, kissing her, and feeling his blood rise.

It was four in the afternoon by the time he got home to the flat his mother and sisters inhabited by the Ursine Castle. He was kissed, asked how he was, told to surrender the dirty washing, informed that the clean stuff was on the sofa, and that there were several things for him to take back waiting for him in the fridge. His two elder sisters, Luisa and Cosima, were there, and his mother was telling him that she had got the money direct to her account, as she did every month, as if this were necessary, for she did not quite believe in the way money could be sent over the internet. Only Petra was absent, and he sensed trouble. The two elder sisters, who were clearly in on some sort of secret, smirked. His mother looked embarrassed and a little hurt. Petra, he was told, was in her bedroom.

He found her there, in the room she shared with her sisters. It was a small room, with two bunk beds and another single bed, and a narrow window that looked out onto the courtyard. It was stifling in summer. His mother had the other bedroom; he himself had slept on the sofa in the living-room. Petra was on the bottom bunk, looking sulky.

'I see this room has been painted,' he observed, which was true.

It was the wrong thing to say. The whole flat had been painted of late, thanks to the money sent from Palermo, money somehow associated with Tonino. Clearly, mention of the new paintwork was an unwelcome allusion to Tonino, and Tonino was the problem.

'Has Mama told you?' asked Petra. 'Has she sent you? Does she want you to persuade me?'

'You had better explain,' he said.

Petra had always been his favourite sister, and he was patient with her. Of course, as his favourite, his mother would rely on her to be amenable to his advice, and him to prevail on her to take it.

He listened. It concerned her recent trip to Palermo to see Tonino. That much was clear.

'He said he thought you liked it all,' he said.

'What does he know?' said Petra with sudden fury. 'He never hears anything I say. He never communicates. He never understands. He is so secretive. I can't stand it any longer.'

Roberto put his arms around her.

'Look, I know him better than most, I know what he is like, so you do not have to explain. He isn't good at expressing himself. His mother is very nice, a very good person, but he, well, he is a bit rougher than most, you know? He is a typical boy from Purgatory. As for Mama, when our father abandoned us, things were very tough. When I met Tonino, when you met Tonino, he was very kind and generous. We could not have done without his help. I got a job because of him.'

'Will you lose your job now?' she asked with a trace of anxiety.

'No, not at all. It is just that I am trying to explain why Mama is cross. I will try to reassure her. I will reassure her. Tonino is my friend as much as yours, really. I have known him longer. Leave Mama to me. I will make her see reason. If you no longer like Tonino, there is no more to be said.'

'He was horrible to that waiter in the restaurant,' said Petra. 'If you had seen it, you would understand.'

'I didn't see it, but I do understand.'

'He's violent,' she said, almost in a whisper. 'He made me frightened.'

'Look, you won't see him again. I promise.'

He had arranged to meet Roberto with Petra outside the Church of the Holy Souls in Purgatory at about six that evening. When Tonino saw him approach without Petra, he knew that something had happened. Roberto seemed subdued, almost ashamed, the bearer of bad news. It was swiftly told. Her mother had told her she was foolish, she was ungrateful, she was putting the family at a disadvantage. But Petra had withstood this onslaught, and Roberto had, after some time, got his mother to calm down. Petra had seen him provoke the son of the owner of the agriturismo. She viewed him as a troublemaker, a criminal, a bully. She had decided that she did not want to have anything more to do with him, and she told her brother that he ought to do the same. This, Roberto reported, while Tonino listened in silence.

'A troublemaker, a criminal and a bully,' said Tonino. 'Well, she is not wrong, is she? Do you agree with her?'

Roberto shrugged.

'When I told you that you had been a fool with Emma, your reaction told me all I needed to know,' he said.

'Having a child can only be a good thing,' said Tonino. 'You should try and understand that. That is my daughter you think I should have disowned, or worse. Anyway, are you leaving me too? Following Petra's advice?'

'Don't be stupid,' said Roberto. 'Petra suggested it, but I am not doing what she wants.'

'Why not? Perhaps you should,' said Tonino, gloomily, half-jokingly.

'I follow my own way,' said Roberto, with a touch of defiance.

'Is she giving back the bank account?' asked Tonino.

He had been paying cash into her account for years. It had to amount to a considerable sum by now.

'Yes, she is,' said Roberto. 'She said she would. In fact, she gave me the passwords, the card, everything.'

'That is really useful,' said Tonino, perking up. 'I may not have a girlfriend, and Emma does not want me, but I do have a very useful additional bank account.'

But someone had seen them from across the square. It was Assunta di Rienzi, and with her two young women, her nieces, Isabella and Natalia.

Because of the general collapse into irresponsibility of the Santucci family, Traiano felt that the work before him was immense. This was particularly marked on the Monday morning when he made a late entry into the office after the week-end he had spent with his brother and sister-in-law. It would take at least two years, Traiano had been convinced, to work out exactly how the system worked, and here he was just over one year in, and still not mastering it. It might even take longer still, thanks to the employees of the family, depending on whether they were prepared to be co-operative, even if surly and truculent, knowing that withholding information could lead to nasty consequences. Under the suit, they assumed, or so he hoped, was a gun, or a knife. In truth, they were wrong about that. He had given up going about armed, just in case he should be stopped by the police and arrested for carrying an offensive weapon or unauthorised firearm. But he did not need to go about armed, for he could rely on his fists, a sharp kick from his feet, a broken bottle, a chair leg or whatever weapon came to hand. Not that he wanted to do that often. Most people, he hoped, would be eager to co-operate.

The Mattarella case was an encouraging sign.

The Santucci business, headquartered in the viale della Libertà, was divided into two clearly defined but interlinked parts, which were called the black and the white: the illegal and the legal. On the surface, the Santucci enterprise was devoted to import and export. It sent olive oil, wine, cheeses and citrus fruits to America, the old-fashioned way, by ship, to New York. The goods were sent in containers and were packaged for sale in the United States. The wine went in huge tankers, as did the olive oil, and their marketing was the responsibility of several friendly firms in America. In return, by the same ships, came what Sicily needed from America, which was certainly not delicious things to eat. (The food the Americans ate, it was unbelievable!) Coming the other way were cars, not complete cars, but in parts, parts which were then assembled in various factories in Sicily; which sort of cars, and what quantity, were determined by demand, and many of the car showrooms in and around Palermo belonged to the family as well, so they could, at both point of supply and point of sale, strangle the factories if necessary. And with the cars came the white gold supplied by the Americans, who in turn got it from further south; the white gold that so many people craved and which made the family rich.

Or had made the family rich. But the truth was that for the last decade or so, profits had been levelling off.

Pandering to human weakness, this was the usual path to monetary success. The exports and the imports came through the port of Palermo, which for decades had been dominated by employees of Domenico and Lorenzo Santucci and their antecedents. But things had changed, and all was now done by containers, which on arrival were immediately driven to all parts of the island of Sicily. But the people who handled the containers and oversaw their arrival and dispatch were still a family monopoly. Indeed, containerisation had made smuggling easier, as there were now so few people employed in the port compared to the past when ships had to be unloaded, and warehouses stacked with goods. No one asked awkward questions about the contents of some of the containers. Because they could, if they chose, close down the port (a nuclear option that had never been tried but was always possible), the nominal authorities left them alone. Luckily, like gold, cocaine was easy to shift around. One particular marked container arrived at regular intervals and was taken to a different place in Palermo or nearby each time. There, the contents, usually car parts, were unpacked, and the important matter extracted for retail and export to various towns in Sicily, such as Trapani, Agrigento, Messina and Catania, which acted as central distribution points, from which the whole island was covered.

There was no 'factory' as such, no fixed place where the material was divided up for resale; it changed constantly, depending on which container was the marked one.

With so many criminals on a relatively small island, the chances of friction and conflict were high, so it was here that Calogero di Rienzi had made the surely very sensible decision to do the opposite of diversification. He and the Santucci people would control cocaine and the other people could divide the remaining spoils between them. Calogero's father had started out by renting squalid rooms to prostitutes, but that was all in the past now. Calogero was a respectable property developer, and had cut his ties with that sort of thing. The girls and the boys could be left to the people in Messina, and Agrigento, and Trapani; the weed could be administered from Agrigento, brought in from North Africa. Others could specialise in heroin, or extortion. Naturally, they all did themselves favours. Thanks to his interest in building waste disposal, Calogero's men could make inconvenient corpses disappear forever. Thanks to the men who distributed the cocaine, those who misbehaved could expect to be punished, and foreigners who wanted to muscle in would be dissuaded. A fearsome reputation kept the house in good order.

The various accountants who worked in the office had been able to show Traiano the files, the paperwork, tell him about the suppliers of wine and olive oil and lemons, and about the places where the cars were assembled and where they were sold, and Elena was able to help him interpret all this information. Soon he had a map of Sicily in his head, seeing all the places where the family had interests. He would go out to these places, often accompanied by Tonino, and sometimes in the school holidays by Beppe as well, to visit the vineyards and lemon groves, talk to the farmers and landowners; Renzo had been visibly bored by this, on the few occasions he had come with him, but Traiano found it interesting, and Beppe loved it, you could see. In late summer or as winter advanced, it was revealing to see where the products were coming from, what sort of harvest was expected, how the weather would impact on the amount produced. There had been years, he was told, when extreme cold had meant that little olive oil had been produced and there had been a spike in prices. Of course, all these things, once the backbone of the trade, were now mere makeweights for the import of white gold. On several occasions, he made a point of taking Beppe with him to visit lemon producers, given that the boy had an almost pathological interest in the subject of lemon cultivation. Gradually, slowly, he began to drop certain suppliers and find others, in the search to improve quality; after all, if they were to ship the stuff to America, they had better make sure it was worth shipping. He greatly enjoyed the cheese tastings, and began to see that there might well be a market in America for luxury goods from Sicily. In time, he would have to go to New York and look for clients there.

At first, he noticed the natural reticence, indeed the dislike, that was directed at himself and Tonino as outsiders from Catania. But this hostility gradually dissolved after the initial contact, and he saw that the people slowly warmed to himself and to Tonino. They asked about don Antonio, but only for form's sake; they sensed, the few who had met him, that don Renzo did not really care about them, and they returned the compliment. Much to the surprise and pleasure of Traiano, the lemon growers loved Beppe, and the older ones remarked that he had something of his late grandfather in him. Traiano hoped they were wrong about this.

Traiano saw these field trips as a welcome interval from the office and as a way of repairing the relations that don Antonio had let slide. The suppliers, who were on the whole gentle souls, came to like don Traiano, who had a certain easy charm about him when he chose to show it, and who never gave himself airs. In this, he was a marked contrast with don Antonio who had never come to see them in recent years, and who had acquired the reputation of being standoffish and unpredictable. Their dealings with him had been fraught in some cases, and where smooth in others, there had always hung the threat that things could go badly wrong. But don Traiano reminded the older suppliers of the time before Antonio, the time of the two Santucci brothers, down to earth characters. He never smiled, but he was personable, and he listened and seemed interested in the products. Renzo, by contrast, for the few who met him, made them remember all the reasons for disliking the Santucci clan, and preferring the new man, even if he were a foreigner, a Romanian, the scum of Catania or the son of a prostitute. There was something not exactly likeable about him, but they could do business with him and wanted to please him.

But the Mattarella case revealed that these charming people could be sly cheats as well. He knew that he had to decide about the Mattarella case. What was needed was to give the suppliers a collective jolt. That was clear. In that way, and perhaps that way alone, one could look forward to a gradual increase in the quality of the material exported and a corresponding increase in demand and in profits from this entirely legal business. A good dose of fear was needed. True, Mattarella senior had handed over 51% of his business; in so doing he made the second step, what would happen after the father had vacated the scene, that much easier. But that was far in the future.

But the Mattarella case had another aspect, and that was what the younger Mattarella had said about Simone Rota and his uncle. The other part of the business that he knew he had to look at carefully was not just the quality of what was leaving the country but the quality of what was coming in. On these trips of inspection, visits to the port, he was accompanied by Muniddu, a man he trusted, and sometimes by Tonino as well. Just as the suppliers had been cheating them for years by selling them shoddy goods, the port, he felt, was the one place where thefts might happen. But he need not have worried. Containers arrived and containers left without interference. If interference was happening it was at the places where the cocaine was prepared for the local market. He worried that the weight of cocaine that arrived in the port and the weight of cocaine that left for various parts of Sicily might not correspond. Cocaine was worth more or less its weight in gold. In the Middle Ages, when gold was currency, unscrupulous people had either adulterated it with base metals, or clipped coins, or rubbed them across counters in shops; and it was the same with cocaine: a little bit here, a little bit there, and one could build up quite a fortune. Some discrepancies could perhaps be explained away by miscounting or accident. But, if what the younger Mattarella was telling them was true, what if there was a uniformly consistent discrepancy? Matteo Rota and his friends were perhaps supplementing their pay by skimming. At least, he had always suspected someone was skimming, but now there might be definite information from Rota the nephew as to who was doing it.

His feeling was that they should wait and see, and that there was no need for precipitate action. The various suppliers, he had been able to tell when he had first met them, were usually nervous of him. He had taken this as a sign that they had something to hide, but he had had no intention of confronting them. Rather his intention was to let them worry until someone, somewhere, broke ranks. That was the police method, shake the tree, wait, see what fell. His guess was that under the neglectful regime of don Antonio, it had seemed only natural to the ones who dealt with the cocaine that they could take advantage of the situation and take a little for themselves to sell quietly on to friends. It had never been officially allowed, but it had perhaps been tacitly agreed as one of the perks of the job. But now there was a change of management, and this leaking away of money, this unofficial tax, had to stop, as they must surely realise.

He expected that someone eventually would break cover.

Ever since his entanglement with the law over the supposedly stolen picture, he had had a fear of electronic surveillance. This meant, in effect, that every email, every telephone call and everything on paper in the office had to be 'white', the sort of thing that the police could read. Anything 'black' was to be discussed face to face and then only in circumstances where there was no possibility of electronic surveillance. For the purposes of security, he judged that the office and his own home and his car were bugged by the police. Moreover, strangers were to be treated with the utmost caution, in case they were wearing a wire. This level of paranoia, he thought, was a useful discipline. He judged it unlikely that the police were listening to his domestic life, the sound of cooking and children and blaring television. But if they were, he was rather pleased that they would have to sift through hours of noise, none of it useful.

'Black' discussions were carried out in two places. At midmorning every day, he would visit a series of bars for a cup of coffee and a cornetto. He would tell the receptionists on the front desk where he was going, in case anyone needed him, and then, if anyone did, they could approach him in the noisy bar at one of its busiest times, and there, under the cover of the noise of conversation and the cappuccino machine, whoever needed him could have a whispered conversation. The bar differed every day, and there were at least a dozen of them, which made surveillance impossible. This way, anyone who wanted to see him could do so without the risk of making an appointment.

His other ploy was to go to the gym that the Santucci family owned behind the Politeama, and have a swim at three every afternoon. This too was an excellent ruse as there was no possible way that anyone in the pool could overhear conversations, nor was there any chance that anyone in the water could be wearing a wire. He chose three in the afternoon for these expeditions because this was the time when the place was deserted. The person on the door always expected him, and nodded him through, and also knew not to stop others, all known by sight, who might be going through for a swim with the purpose of speaking to the boss. Just who these people might be, or their names, or what they looked like, the person on the door deliberately did not know.

Like a man with a fierce dog standing in front a woodland in which some terrified and hunted creature had taken refuge, Traiano waited for the animal to break cover before unleashing the hound. His patience would be rewarded, he hoped. Today, when he went into the gymnasium, he found Tonino Grassi waiting for him. They did not speak, but Tonino waited for the boss to change into his swimming things and then followed him into the pool.

'Well?' he asked.

'I saw Simone Rota,' said Tonino, the attack dog. 'I waited for him outside where he lives and approached him. I invited him to go for coffee with me. He had no choice, as I had a gun. We spoke.'

Traiano considered this. He looked at Tonino.

'Are you telling me…..?'

'I threatened him with the gun, told him he had to co-operate, and that it would be worse for him if he did not. I held the gun against his leg under the table.'

'And did that have the desired effect?' asked Traiano, knowing what the answer was going to be. 'It usually does.'

'Boss.....'

'Yes?'

'He made a demand, boss.'

'He made a demand? I thought we made the demands, not people like him. And what was this Rota's demand?'

'To meet you, boss.'

'Well, he can't. He can speak to you and you can speak to me. That is how it works.'

'He refused to speak to me. He says he can only speak to you.'

'He has got guts,' conceded Traiano. 'That worries me. You threatened him, and he was not frightened. He called your bluff. He has guts, you seem to lack them. It is your job to terrify people when they are not co-operative. To get them to co-operate. You have failed.'

'Boss, I will give it another go. I know where he lives. There are lots of things I can do.'

But Traiano was not confident of this. He felt annoyed, and he felt the desire to tell Tonino to get out of this pool and to go and force Rota to cooperate. He was not used to this sort of failure. But he hid his annoyance. They swam another length, and came to rest once more.

'You were in Catania? All well? Your parents, the new little brother?'

'Not so new now, boss, but yes, all well.'

'Elena got a phone call from her sister saying that she had met you, and that you and Roberto met the boss's daughters. How did that go?'

It was a casual question, but he saw that the answer would be awkward, judging by Tonino's silence.

'You never see those girls in Palermo, do you? They are not part of your social circle. There's a reason for that, you know. According to Elena, according to Assunta, you spent some time with them. The parents were out to some dinner, but to be frank with you, Assunta let you associate with the girls because she likes to annoy her sister-in-law. These girls are being protected, being groomed, for higher things. They don't want the girls to end up like Emma Santucci. I know I am spelling it out for you, and you must already know this, but it is important that you do not forget it, unless you want a bullet in your head.'

'Sure, boss, I understand. No offence taken. Meeting them was a pure accident. It is unlikely to happen again.'

'How's Petra?'

'Over.'

'Oh.' He forbore to ask. 'What I really want to talk to you about is Angela. Emma's mother. The one you made a grandmother. She wants to meet you. I said I would arrange it. Whenever Angela has a difficulty, she comes to me. I am glad you have broken up with Petra. You see, Angela has plans, with which you will want to co-operate, I think.'

Tonino listened to what was outlined without protest.

Rubbish collection was a major concern in all Sicilian cities, and perhaps in Palermo more than others, and in the area around the Corso Calatafimi perhaps most of all. The street off the Corso, where Simone Rota lived with his mother and sisters, a few blocks away from the much better street where Muniddu and his family lived, was particularly squalid, piled high with uncollected refuse, and filled with giant overflowing bins. To one of these, Tonino knew, a member of the Rota family would have to come at least once a day, with a sack of rubbish, to deposit in the bin or next to the bin. He had no intention of watching for the members of the family as they went about this dismal duty, but rather he employed a child to watch the door and see who came out, a child moreover to whom he gave a detailed description of Rota, and whom he paid to be attentive and keep up this watch for a week. It was after a week that he discovered that there was a pattern: a member of the family, usually the son, but sometimes the girl, came out and dumped the rubbish at about 8.30pm every night, presumably after the family had had their supper.

He was there that very night, after his meeting with the boss. He had decided to strike at Simone Rota. He knew what the sister looked like as she had been foolish enough to put her photographs all over social media, as had her brother. Roberto had looked it up for him. Whether Rota himself or the sister came down, he was prepared. The spot was ideal. The dustbins were a short walk from the front door of the apartment block, and near the dustbins was a narrow, ill lit alley round the side, which was a dead end, and ideal for his purposes. Indeed, judging by the detritus that littered the ground, it had been used for various nefarious purposes: the place was full of used syringes, and there was a very strong smell of urine, underlaid with that of faeces. He was there in good time for 8.30pm, and hoped that this night of all nights would not be the night they had no rubbish to bring out. He felt the knife in his pocket, always the more terrifying weapon. If it was the girl, he would pull her into the darkness and threaten to rape her, telling her to send her brother down. The humiliation he had suffered because of Rota – he grew hot at the thought of him walking away from him – made him want to humiliate Rota in return. He would do whatever was necessary from that point of view. He had to restore his reputation with the boss.

Luckily for the daughter of the family, it was Simone Rota who came down at a little past 8.30pm to dump the rubbish. As he was doing so a plastic bag was placed over his head, and he was dragged backwards into the side street. He was flung against the wall, and, panicked by the bag over his head which impeded his breathing, he was powerless to resist the strong fist that began to systematically punch him in the ribs. Eventually Rota slid to the ground, whimpering in pain. Tonino tore off the bag, and let Rota get his breath back.

'Now I am going to break the rest of your ribs,' he announced quietly, kicking him in the side. 'And next time I will rape your sister. So you had better treat me with respect, and tell me what you know.' The kicks came again and again. 'Next time I will break your knees or your ankles and then kill you. You need to co-operate. And as soon as you decide to do so, come and find me.'

He kicked him again and again, powerfully and methodically. Then he walked away having no intention of telling Rota where he was to be found. Let Rota stew.

Rota stewed for seven days.

A week later Tonino saw him, looking both frightened and worried, in the street outside the gym. He ignored him, went in, changed into his swimming things, and headed for the pool. After ten minutes in the water, he noticed that Rota had followed him in. He rested at the shallow end. The place was relatively full of people, of children, and their splashing noise. This was not the quiet hour that don Traiano favoured.

'So you managed to find me here?' he asked.

Rota looked relieved to be addressed.

'Antonello Mattarella told me that you would be here at about this time; that you told him so.'

'Good. So, you want to save your life. You are not stupid after all.' He looked at him. The bruised ribs were not in evidence. 'I want all the details about your uncle. Verbally. I do not want anything written down. And if we like what you say, you will be rewarded and we will overlook your initial stupidity.'

Gradually the story emerged. Simone Rota was twenty-five. He was the archetypal good Sicilian boy. His father was dead, and he was a graduate student, and he, his mother and his sister relied largely on the generosity of his uncle, his late father's brother. This uncle had arranged a holiday job for him. He had been told to ask no questions and keep quiet about what he saw. The job was very simple. It was driving a minibus, and making several pick-ups in the Palermo region, then depositing the people at sometimes a car assembly plant here, or a car assembly plant there. It was boring, negotiating traffic, and involved a lot of waiting around, but the pay was excellent, and he needed the money. Because he was his uncle's nephew, the men trusted him, perhaps trusted him too much. When they were in the bus, they spoke, perhaps forgetting he was there. He gradually pieced together what it was they did. They were a team of six, and they worked around the clock in shifts, and their job was to cut up, store and then distribute the cocaine to the dealers, who arrived on motorcycles. They were the ones who saw to the division and weighing up of the goods, and for years they had been skimming. But recently they had stopped. They had been convinced that no one could notice the amount skimmed off, it was so tiny, merely a matter of a missing ten grams there, a missing hundred elsewhere, and so on, though it all mounted up. But now they were sure Trajan Antonescu suspected, and so they had ceased. They had been worried by the activities of Trajan Antonescu; they knew he was checking up on suppliers. They had heard of his attack dog, Tonino Grassi. They feared attracting such attention themselves. Uncle Matteo had been sufficiently worried to warn his nephew Simone to say nothing, should he be asked by anyone. Uncle Matteo was frightened that one of the team would break ranks.

'But he trusts you?' asked Tonino.

'Yes, of course. I am his nephew. Family is everything.'

Tonino nodded, and Rota continued with the story. Uncle Matteo was still concerned, and his colleagues too, some more than others. One or two were panicking, and his uncle was doing his best to steady their nerves. But they had been worried since the time when two employees of the family had ended up in the harbour, three or four years ago, and divided about what to do next. They had all made considerable fortunes in cheating the family over the years; some suggested that they should approach don Traiano, apologise, and give him a suitcase full of five hundred euro notes to pay back what they had taken. Perhaps if they gave him a million, or two, he might be prepared to overlook the offence. If indeed it were an offence. After all, they had been doing this for years, and it had made their fortunes, and custom had, in their eyes, the force of law. What was of long standing was of right. But others were convinced that this would be the height of folly. To offer compensation would be to admit guilt, and to admit guilt would be to invite punishment. At least one thought that, if they were found out, now would be the time to flee, before it was too late.

'How do you know this?' asked Tonino.

'They are all friends, and they all meet up regularly. I am often there, as I know their children. Big parties, you know. Me and my sister very rarely go anywhere else. I overhear whispered conversations; I see worried looks. This has been going on for more than a year now. They are frightened of Trajan Antonescu, worried about him, but they do not know how frightened they ought to be. They are sometimes panicking, sometimes philosophical, sometimes confident, sometimes talking about leaving Sicily.'

'You overheard the figure of one million or two million?'

'Uncle Matteo owns a house in the countryside and was talking of selling it to raise cash. The others too. One million or two million were figures I heard mentioned. In that they were asking, how can we raise one million or two million in a hurry?'

'That means they can afford at least three. Maybe more,' said Tonino. 'Let us hope your uncle and his friends do not discover we have been talking, that you have been listening. Give me their names, all of them.'

Simone listed six names. Tonino listened carefully.

'This will stay strictly between us, Simone. Understood? If anything leaks out, it could be bad for you. Your mother, your sister, I am sure you are fond of them, and do not want anything bad to happen them, let alone yourself. What do you think my boss and his boss could do for you?'

Tonino looked at him. He saw the desperation in his eyes. Of course, the family lived off the uncle and he had just betrayed the uncle. But more importantly, the uncle's income would soon be no more.

'What?' he asked.

'I want to finish my doctorate soon, then I must find a job. Until now, it has really been my uncle who has kept me and my mother and sister afloat. He has been generous, I suppose, but also very mean, considering he is so rich. He could have made us an allowance, a monthly payment direct to the bank. That would have helped, it would have taken away the constant worry. But he preferred that I should have to go each time to see him and more or less beg, and then he would give me whatever he felt like giving. Sometimes much, sometimes little, so we never feel secure. He is manipulative and unkind.'

Tonino considered.

'There is a charity in Catania that gives pensions to widows and orphans. They helped my mother a great deal, they still do. Two hundred, three hundred a month, whatever, it arrives directly into your account, no worries. I can speak to my boss, and he can arrange it. We have arranged that sort of thing for lots of people. If this goes well, you will be rewarded with a nice pension for your mother. And then later, you want to get a job? We can help with that. What sort of job?'

'I want to get a job in the art world. Those jobs are very hard to find, unless you know someone. I don't know anyone. My professor is not very helpful, as I am not his favourite student. A job in conservation, in the Superintendence of Fine Arts, in an auction house, that sort of thing. I need an introduction, that is all.'

'There is someone we know. Someone who deals in paintings. He knows people, who know people. We can call in a favour for you,' said Tonino. 'We know people who know people…'

'Would that be Ruggero Bonelli?' asked Rota.

'Ah, you have done your research,' said Tonino.

He saw the Rota was both clever and hungry, desperate to get on.

'I have merely read the papers. I know that Ruggero Bonelli sold this painting that may or may not be by Mantegna to Trajan Antonescu,' said Rota. 'A painting that may or may not be stolen. It is quite a story, and it is embarrassing for both Bonelli and Antonescu, isn't it? But a personal introduction to signor Bonelli would be a great help. He knows lots of people in the art world, I am sure, and a word from him could get my job applications at least looked at. Without that sort of recommendation, I stand no chance. I am a nobody. But he has got a lot of influence.'

'I am sure he has,' said Tonino. 'You have got ambitions. I admire that. You want to get on. I understand that. It is hard when you have brains, but, because of various things, you just find doors shut in your face. Well, Ruggero Bonelli could open doors for you. And I can open the door to him. You have been helpful so far, and if that is what you want, if the boss agrees to it, you can have it. Obviously, you think he can be useful to you, and you are best positioned to make that judgement. How clever of you to realise that Bonelli knows don Traiano. What else do you know about Bonelli?'

'That he is clever and well connected, that is all.'

'I will speak to my boss. In the meantime, we may need you again. If I do, Antonello Mattarella will pass on a message. I should warn you that you may have to wait some time. Now run through those names, the names of your uncle and his friends again, to check I have them right. It would not do to make a mistake.'

Traiano listened to the names with great attention; Tonino could tell that he was memorising them. He made Tonino repeat them several times, to assure him that there was no mistake. Then he repeated them back to Tonino.

'You have not written this down?' he asked.

'Of course not, boss.'

'You were generous with your promises,' said Traiano more to himself than to Tonino. 'Meeting Bonelli, and getting him a job when he finishes his degree, and a nice pension for his mother. Oh well, promise what you want, as it is all academic. He seems to trust you? Yes? Good. He is unwise to do so, but it suits us, doesn't it? Naturally, we can leave no loose ends when this operation is over. Understood?'

'Of course, boss. I knew that.'

Just close to them, the cappuccino machine made its terrible noise.

'We will use Simone Rota. He has given us valuable information. Those names. That is important. There's money to be made here, a great deal. I am surprised that Simone asks for so little to betray his uncle and his uncle's friends.'

'What about the two Mattarellas while we are at it?'

'Your desire to kill people is commendable, and understandable. You do not like the younger Mattarella because you think he is an arrogant bastard, and so he is. You do not like the younger Rota, for the same reason. Both made you look stupid. But there are more important things than personal honour. We need to think ahead. Do not touch the Mattarellas, at least not for now. They paid us half their business, and we let them off. They paid the fine, they cancelled the debt. Matteo Rota and his friends will see that as a useful template. They will think that they can buy their freedom, their forgiveness. And right now, they are nervous; they are panicking. We will leave them to stew for that little bit longer. Then we will strike. As for the younger Rota, you can tell him that it will be arranged, but he has to be patient, and in the meantime he should get on with his studies, finish his doctorate and not do anything to arouse suspicion. We will strike later, and we may need him to help us. We will play a long game. OK? In the meantime, keep him happy.'

'Yes, boss,' said Tonino.

'What?' asked Traiano.

'When the time comes....'

'When the time comes, there will be a big share for you. Trust me. And I mean big, in the hundred- thousands. More than you have ever made in a single throw of the dice.'

'Thanks, boss.'

'Now, you go and wait for me outside, while I stay here for a few moments. And I will be using you to keep in contact with Simone Rota. Remember, let us not give them what they want right away, but keep them guessing. Ah, look who is here.'

Beppe Santucci had come into the bar and was looking for Traiano, his eyes questing, lighting up when they saw him. The boy came up to Traiano who extended a cheek to be kissed.

'Aren't you at school?' he asked.

'They gave us the day off,' said Beppe. He turned to look at Tonino, and smiled, and kissed his cheek. This was how he greeted all adults. 'I got bored at home, so I came to find you, and the people in the office told me you were here.'

'I have to go back soon. Unlike you, I have to work,' said Traiano good naturedly. 'Actually, I do not. Today is the day when I have to go and meet your mother, and your sister.'

'Marina?'

'No, Emma.'

'Where are you meeting them?'

'We are going to Emma's flat.'

'We? You mean me too?'

'I meant Tonino. You can come too.'

'Why is Tonino coming?'

'Tonino will explain,' said Traiano.

Angela Santucci looked at her daughter Emma with a mixture of affection and distaste. She was a disappointment. Her eldest son was very plain, her younger less so, though still plain; but Emma, if she had wanted to, could have been a beauty like her sister Marina, but instead had opted to dye her hair green, tattoo herself, have multiple piercings, wear the most awful clothes, and then, worst of all, put on a huge amount of weight. But eventually, Angela reflected, one came to accept that some people would never change, and that the only thing to do was ameliorate their mistakes. One could not reform Emma, it was far too late for that, but one could perhaps help to make her worst excesses less damaging. It was a sad admission, this sense of despairing defeat, but it was something she had learned in her charitable work with the poor, with the drug addicted; the poor usually stayed poor, and the stories of the drug addicts did not usually end well.

She had bought the flat Emma lived in. It was a rather sweet and picturesque place in the historic centre of Palermo, close to the via Alloro. Moreover, she had hired the maid who cleaned it, and the babysitter who helped with the child. The place was clean and tidy, the child seemed well cared for; there was a pile of books on the table, all philosophy, which was Emma's subject at the university, which was reassuring, to think that her studies were progressing. She allowed herself a glance at one: it was *The Critique of Pure Reason* by Emmanuel Kant. That was nice to see. Emma saw her looking at the book, and because any sense of surveillance annoyed her, felt a stir of resentment. Her mother noticed this and sighed.

The truth was, Angela saw, that her dream of having a happily married daughter and a nice son-in-law was in fact just a dream. Emma was never going to find, let alone be attracted by, or marry, someone nice. But what she had been told about this Tonino was reassuring; though she knew she was looking for reassurance, and perhaps hoping to find qualities that were not there. She had been filled in. Traiano had told her about Tonino. He was short, not handsome, looked like a boxer; but girls seemed to like him. He was hardworking, ambitious, in the family business, loyal, discreet and willing to please. He did as he was told. He was not educated, but he could read and write, he had some conversation. When it came to religion, which mattered so much to her, Traiano reported that he was very traditional, and that he took his mother to Mass every Sunday in Catania. Traiano had known him since he was five or six, and he was a 'good Sicilian boy'. None of this was ideal, but it could be a lot worse, she reflected. She was pleased to hear that he was devoted to his mother. He had had another girlfriend, though chastely, and she was now off the scene. All considered, it was not too bad.

The other person she had mined for information was her son Beppe. Until Traiano had told her, she had had no idea that Beppe knew Tonino. She reflected that she was so busy that she really had had no time to monitor Beppe's friendships, and she had been accustomed for a long time now to his giving no trouble, but being a boy who could be trusted. She was a little surprised to hear that Beppe had met Tonino at the wedding of don Renzo, if not before, in Catania, and then afterwards at the house of Muniddu, and that they went to football matches together, and to the sports club as well. It was an odd choice of friends that her son had; but she put this aside, and asked him what Tonino was like. Beppe's endorsement of Tonino was warm but hardly enlightening: he was, he told his mother, very nice.

'No, no, no,' Emma was saying very crossly. 'I have been saying no for three months. When will you understand that no means no? I am not a Catholic. It would be hypocrisy of the highest order to baptise my daughter.'

'And what does the father think?' asked Angela. 'You may not care what I think, and what I am going through, having my first grandchild brought up as a pagan, but what does he think? I imagine he would agree with me.'

'You don't even know him, and what he thinks is nothing to do with you or with me. I don't care what he thinks.'

This was spoken with venom.

'A father has rights, as does a grandmother. And by the way, who pays for all this?'

'The family, you, I suppose,' conceded Emma, less venomously than before, as if sensing that money would be her weakest point.

As indeed it was. She had a taste for low company and a passion for Enlightenment philosophy (Kant was her favourite) and though a diligent student, was filled with dread at the thought of having to get a job. Intellectually curious, she was also profoundly lazy, much relieved to have the babysitter and the maid. The family money situation was, as she was only too aware, in flux. Sandro, with the support of Marina, was challenging the will of their grandfather, which left everything to Beppe. She had calculated, realised where her interests and where the probable outcome lay, and switched sides. She was not disputing the will, which undermined Sandro's case. On the contrary, she supported Beppe and her mother, and she entrusted herself to their generosity. Too bad both of them were fervent Catholics who wanted the child baptised.

The doorbell rang. She was not expecting anyone, but rushed to release the buzzer, not caring who came up; anyone would be better than being stuck here with her mother. It might be the babysitter, back with the baby from their walk in the park by the sea, but she was vaguely aware that it was still too early for this.

'Are you expecting anyone?' her mother asked.

The door was open, and in walked Beppe, followed by Traiano, followed by a young man in a suit, a young man with a boxer's face.

'How lovely!' exclaimed Angela.

Emma felt ambushed. She was, for a few moments, speechless with rage. She watched her child's father being introduced to her mother by the Romanian. She watched the way he made himself agreeable and humble to her. The way he made himself charming. The way the Romanian smiled. The way her mother looked so damned pleased with herself. She felt herself hemmed in. Beppe came and sat next to her, smiling. He it was, who, much to her surprise, dealt the coup de grace.

'You are an Amazon,' Tonino said.

Emma was not quite sure what he meant, whether this was a reference to her warrior qualities, her monumental arms, breasts, buttocks and legs, or a reference to the dense rain forest between her legs which he had spent a delightful time exploring, lost, but not looking for any way out. Whichever way, it was a compliment, and she enjoyed it. Defeat had its consolations.

The others had left. The babysitter had returned and been told to take the baby for another hour's airing.

'What made you change your mind?' he asked, after kissing her, like a man coming up for air.

'Seeing you in your suit. That appealed to me. A thug in a suit. Nice.'

'That was don Traiano's advice. "Wear a suit," he said.'

'I never knew that you and my brother Beppe were such friends.'

'I suppose we are. Did he put in a good word for me?'

'He said you were a very nice boy, and one of his best friends, and he wanted you as a brother-in-law,' she said, omitting the important part, that if she did not co-operate, she would, when he came into the fortune, be cut off without a cent. 'He likes you.'

'I like him. He was a little shocked just now when he found out about you and me and the baby. He thinks it is a sin, and we had better repair the damage. Do you want to marry me?'

'I think so. In so far as I want to marry anyone. You annoy all the right people. I like that.'

He giggled.

'Maybe I do. But those who annoy me generally don't do it very long. I like your piercings,' he said.

'You do?' she asked.

They had stopped in the piazza Sant'Anna, just by the modern art gallery, in the pretty irregular square, to have something to eat, to discuss the strategy.

'On the whole, I am pleased and grateful to you, don Traiano,' said Angela Santucci. 'He is not what I would have chosen, but he seems willing to learn. Some things we cannot change, like his appearance, but there may be improvements in other fields.'

Angela had always loved a project.

'What is wrong with his appearance?' asked Beppe, in the middle of wolfing down a huge sandwich.

'Well, he is a bit short,' said his mother.

'Shorter than me, yes, but the same height as Emma, I think. The baby is cute.'

'I hope to God it is his,' said Angela, thinking of this for the first time.

'I looked into that, signora, as did he. It is most definitely his,' said Traiano. 'He is a bit rough, but he may polish up nicely, and he is very family minded. He was very upset when she would not see him, would not let him see the baby.'

'Well, I am grateful to find him, as you say, very traditional, and as shocked as I was that she didn't want the child baptised. Now I suppose we need to ask who will be the godfather.'

'Me,' said Beppe, pausing in his sandwich. 'I told them. They agreed.'

'We will have to have a nice church for the baptism. But it is best if they choose that. After all, we must not interfere, must we?' She considered. 'Emma has disappointed me, but this may well prove to be something good. I hope you will not disappoint me,' she said, looking at her youngest, now finishing his sandwich and licking his fingers.

'I never will, Mama,' said the boy.

'He is a good Sicilian boy, signora,' said Traiano, placing a hand on Beppe's shoulder. 'And a very good boy,' he added, meaning that Beppe was sexually innocent, indeed sexually ignorant.

'We are meeting tonight, aren't we?' said the signora. 'Beppe and I will be there, not the others. And you will be there?'

'I will. We will all be there. It is perhaps best not to tell don Calogero about your new prospective son-in-law just yet. He knows him, and it might be best coming from Tonino himself. You know what he is like. He likes to think everything is his idea, that it all originates from him…'

'I understand, I understand,' said Angela.

She did too. She had been dealing with these sorts of men forever.

Chapter Three

It wasn't a party as such, just a little gathering, that was how Anna Maria put it, a little family gathering, with the emphasis very much on family. Because children were to be present, it was in the early evening, and not expected to carry on until late. It was, according to Anna Maria, an 'at home'. The last baby, Romano, now two years old, was there, his nanny, the faithful maid Veronica, Romano's two elder sisters and his two elder brothers were all at home, and the number of children was augmented by Traiano's three, as well as by Beppe. Present too were Renzo and Elena and their child. Anna Maria had never really liked parties with hordes of children, but she was now determined to enjoy this one, given that circumstances had placed her in the midst of just such a horde. The boss's other sister, Assunta, and her husband, the fatter than ever Federico, had both come from Catania for the occasion. She had insisted on that invitation. And she had gone further: if both of her sisters-in-law, to whom she had never been particularly close, were to be there, that meant her mother-in-law must come too. And there she was, the Black Widow Spider herself, her thunderous presence dominating the drawing-room, her observant eye taking in every detail of Anna Maria's flat, so very different from her own. But the Widow had recently changed allegiance, as had her daughters. Before, they had seen Anna Maria as an interloper, not one of them; now she was an ally. There had been a tectonic shift. None of them were stupid; they knew what had changed.

Alfio was not there, and neither was Giuseppina. They were in Africa, and Elena had been warmly pressed to visit them there, as she had always been close friends with Giuseppina. But it really was not possible, with a young child, or so Elena thought. Renzo her husband wanted to go, she knew, and would, perhaps, if Traiano went with him. Perhaps they ought to go, as a business trip, more than anything else. Assunta and Federico had been, as they were unencumbered with children. The place was paradise and, as befitted paradise, the cooks were Sicilian, all imported, as was the food. White sand, palm trees, tropical breezes, it was like in a book. And what a beautiful hotel, and an effortless flight, as the place had its own landing strip, and you were decanted from one plane to another with the minimum of fuss. She had visited the orphanage that was run by the nuns, Italian nuns, of course, which Giuseppina patronised, and all the children were so sweet. It was clear that Alfio was doing a wonderful job, with the help of Costantino the Serb, along with the Swiss manager under them.

But the way Assunta mentioned Alfio's name gave the impression that Alfio was not perhaps the most popular of men with her, her sister, or the Black Widow Spider. She gave Traiano a knowing look. He stared back blandly. He looked over towards Renzo, who had not been following, and who, he knew, hated Alfio with a passion, holding him responsible for the death of Gino.

Alfio was, to Traiano's annoyance, someone who had been promoted to the very utmost of his abilities. The African job was huge; it was a hotel and a resort, with direct access to Europe, with no red tape to ruin things with regard to import or export of goods and people. It was an enterprise that was underpinned by the goodwill of the people at home, who blessed it, by the Islamic terrorists who had guaranteed not to touch it, and by the local government, which had guaranteed a similar hands-off policy, indeed given them carte blanche. All of this had had to be negotiated, and all of this cost a fortune in pay offs. But the real idea was to use the resort as a loss-making money laundering operation, a place into which dirty money could be sunk, and a place for training the Sicilian Foreign Legion, as it was called.

The women, the Black Widow Spider and her daughters, disliked Alfio for a particular reason that had nothing to do with business. They disliked him because he had pushed himself forward and used two women to do so; first, his wife, the former sister-in-law of the boss; and second his cousin, Gino's widow, Catarina Fisichella. She had been a sharp girl, and as soon as Gino was dead and buried, she had disappeared from the scene. Of course, her child, Tino, had not been Gino's but the result of her fling with poor dead Rosario, so they resented that, her having Rosario's child and then taking the child away. But if Catarina was sharp, so were they. Assunta and Elena were accountants, and their mother the sort of woman who could smell wrongdoing at a distance of several kilometres. Somewhere, buried in the accounts, was evidence of regular payments to Catarina, they were sure, though they had looked and found nothing; but all that meant was that they were very well hidden; which in turn was evidence of a reason to keep them well hidden. Catarina was surely being paid, and had been paid to go away as well, but where? In their minds the conspiracy grew and grew. Someone must know where she was, what she was doing, how she was living, and that person, they suspected, was the Romanian.

The Black Widow Spider had told all this to her great friend signora Grassi, who had nodded in understanding, tutted, and said nothing. She in fact knew, she had seen the envelopes, she knew her son delivered them to some secret address. But she said nothing.

The one person who might have been able to track down payments was of course the banker, Anna Maria, and the one person most nearly affected, if indeed her husband did have a secret paid woman. Anna Maria sensed, whenever she saw her mother-in-law and sisters-in-law, that they brimmed with secrets, but she did not want to know. She understood her husband: he was an ambitious man, a beautiful man, but a cold one as well, a very cold one. She was pretty certain that he was not having a love affair. He was not the type to love anyone, apart from his children. He certainly did not love her, though he valued her, he needed her, and she was sure he would never ever part with her. Of course, he was the master criminal, but so was she: and the web of crime was in her head, in her prodigious memory, in the details of all the accounts in Panama, the Caymans, Jersey, Monaco, and other safe havens for dirty money, which she, as if by magic, made clean. She was the mastermind, and he knew it. How nice it was to be necessary, she thought.

The two sisters did not like him, Traiano knew, and the mother of the boss, well, she liked no one at all, so that did not bother him; but he could read their minds. They disliked him because they saw him as the man the boss trusted more than themselves. But how wrong they were, he reflected ruefully. Ever since moving to Palermo, he had hardly seen the boss. The boss's affections had cooled, and his had too. The fact that the boss was using Tonino as his intermediary with Catarina was an added reason for his sense that the boss was slowly dropping him from the inner circle. In return, what had he gained? He had gained the friendship of Renzo, someone who was less clever and less energetic than himself, someone who could be both led and dominated; Renzo's wife knew that, he knew that, and Renzo's wife knew that Traiano knew that, so there was respect between them. He himself felt nothing for Renzo (he wondered if she did) and accepted his intimacy as part of his job. He spoke to him every day, he saw him every day, he ate with him, played squash with him, went swimming with him, went to watch him run his boring marathons, sharing a room with him in various hotels in Sicily and Italy when he flew up to run in the Vicenza marathon, the Rome marathon, or the Venice marathon (that last being almost interesting). There was talk that he would do, in the coming year, marathons beyond Italy, in London, Frankfurt and Paris. It was assumed by Renzo that Traiano would be only too thrilled to come with him. Elena too assumed this, saying that she could not, with the child to look after and the demands of work. Work, as no one needed to say out loud, could easily do without Renzo. People were always willing to do without Renzo, and more than happy to pass him on to Traiano.

It was now necessary for both he and Renzo to speak to the boss, to get him to agree to something. They approached him over the buffet, just as he was helping himself to a smoked salmon sandwich (his wife had this affectation for serving British food). He saw them, one either side of him, and sighed wearily, knowing what was coming, some unwelcome request. He led the way into the other room where the children were, and where there was plenty of noise, which would mask anything people should not overhear.

The children were all enjoying themselves. Beppe sat on a sofa with Isabella at one side of him, and Natalia at the other, and one of the little boys at his feet. He was eating a funny little biscuit covered with cream cheese and caviar, and holding a glass of champagne in his hand. Isabella too had champagne.

'That boy is taking a long time to grow up,' said don Calogero, looking across the room.

'It is about him we want to talk,' said Renzo. 'We want to shut down this lawsuit.'

'Has Angela been talking to you?' asked Calogero.

'No,' said Renzo, 'Though I can imagine what she might say. It is just that this lawsuit threatens to drag on and on.'

'This is Italy, that is what lawsuits do.'

'It is damaging the name of Santucci. Uncle Domenico wants it as well. To shut it down.'

Damaging the name of Santucci was not something that bothered Calogero overmuch. They had asked him this once before. He had refused permission then, enjoying the power of refusal, saying that the lawsuit would soon end, or that Sandro would see sense. Yet, with the passage of time, both of these seemed increasingly unlikely. He looked at Beppe. That Beppe should have the whole inheritance and marry one of his daughters seemed the best outcome. It was perhaps time to give way.

'Sandro is a fool, a troublesome fool. We have been patient long enough. But he enjoys the protection of don Domenico and myself. So, teach him a lesson, send him away, but do not kill him. Understood?'

'Understood,' they both echoed.

There was something else. Renzo explained the situation between Emma and Tonino. Calogero heard this impassively, only raising an eyebrow. Then he said:

'I had already heard about this. Signora Grassi told my mother, and she told me. Signora Grassi is very upset at the way her little boy has grown up so quickly. I feel for her, being a parent myself, though my daughters are my chief concern for now. This news will please the signora. That is good. As for Angela, goodness knows what she is planning. The boy is now the father of Emma's child, that is acknowledged, as it should be. The child needs a father. But if Angela thinks she can polish this rough diamond and make him into a son-in-law… the truth is nothing would surprise me. Angela is always making the best of a bad situation. It is what she does. With a son like Sandro and a husband like Antonio, she made a virtue out of cruel necessity. How do you feel about this?' he asked, turning to Renzo.

'It is a bit of a cheek,' said Renzo. 'But I am not sure how I feel. Not yet, anyway.'

Calogero nodded.

'Tell Tonino to come and see me next week, in Catania,' Calogero said to Traiano.

Then Traiano reported on the Rota case.

'Good work,' said Calogero. 'Apart from this, how are you?'

'Very well,' said Renzo. 'Elena thinks she might be having another.'

'Excellent,' said Calogero. 'You?' he said, looking at Traiano.

'I make a point of leaving the Church before the blessing, boss. At least for the moment. But we have certainly not stopped at three.'

The boss smiled at this.

'Make sure you pass that message on to Grassi,' he reminded them.

After talking to the boss, Traiano found himself near Assunta di Rienzi who was uncharacteristically friendly.

'That nice boy you sent to our office, the student, Roberto Costacurta, a friend of Tonino Grassi, who would have thought he would be so useful? We are seeing him tomorrow here in Palermo. You know we are staying for a few days? A nice little break. We are both so fond of Roberto. Well, we see him a great deal, as he comes over to Catania every weekend. And Tonino Grassi, we have just heard. His mother told my mother, and well, she told me. Tonino told his mother at once, he is such a good boy. But she sounds, if you will forgive me saying so, a little unconventional. I think she is several years his senior, the lucky boy. Did you know?'

'I had sort of heard,' said Traiano, 'But I had not thought it that interesting.'

'You liar,' she said pleasantly. 'Everyone, you included, must have thought that Emma Santucci would never link up with a boy like Tonino; you know, that she was destined for higher things. Well, I think she has made a reasonable choice, as Tonino is so nice. Besides, there is the baby to think of; that is decisive. I don't suppose he will ever move back to Catania. But I can tell this does not interest you. There is another girl to discuss, I feel, one we are both interested in, and one I am sure you know all about.'

'You may overestimate what I know,' said Traiano, knowing to whom this referred.

'No, I don't think I do.'

'You know there are things I cannot discuss,' said Traiano.

'So, you admit there is something to discuss. That there is a secret.'

'Did you ask your father his secrets? Or your brother his? Does my wife ask me mine?'

He sighed.

'I am thinking about the business,' she said. 'We depend on our banker who just happens to be his wife. The widow Fisichella has the potential to derail all that. Has she got a pension from the Confraternity?'

'As Gino's widow, she must have. If she is still alive. She may not be. Does she know?' he asked, meaning Anna Maria. He did not wait for an answer. 'I suppose if you think there is something going on, she will surely begin to think the same way sooner or later. Have you any hard evidence?'

'Our intuition. And he did it before, betraying Stefania with her. It makes sense he would do it again. And the fact that Catarina has disappeared. No one just disappears. It is quite a feat.'

'Perhaps it is something only a man like Calogero can arrange. Calogero can get away with anything he likes. But she may have chosen to disappear herself, for her own reasons. She may have her reasons, good reasons, for not seeing any of us again. I bet she is living in Sorrento or somewhere, enjoying her pension from the Confraternity. Now tell me about Volta, the new mayor.'

'Not so new now. But contracts, contracts, contracts,' she said. 'We ask, we get, and our rivals do not, it is paradise.' She smiled. Then she looked at him severely. 'You need to keep your side of the bargain,' she said. 'You need to keep the money flowing. We are making a fortune, but we are in debt up to our necks as well.'

'I will, I will,' he promised.

He knew of course what she meant. The money from Palermo, from the white powder, was what fuelled the building boom in Catania. The money was laundered by the banker Anna Maria and by lots of clever accountants, and then lent to Catania for property development. Some of it came in raw cash as well which was paid out to casual workers. There were so many ways of laundering cash through construction. But the cash had to keep on flowing, and that meant, in the end, the cocaine had to keep on flowing up the noses of the people of Sicily.

When he had come to Palermo and started life in the office there, and visiting the suppliers, he had had the impression that the legal white business could somehow become independent of the black illegal side. But this was fantasy. The lemons, the olive oil and the cheese were loss makers or at best broke even. The imports of cars and electronic goods and chemicals from America were the same. The whole thing was kept afloat by cocaine. That was the profit maker, the rest was there to act as a cover. There was no future in lemons, or wine, or cheese, or olive oil. The future depended on fixing the problems with the cocaine. Assunta knew that; he knew it; he knew too that she was referring to the way their profits from cocaine were declining.

Beppe, rather shyly, was with the adults, the champagne and the smoked salmon. He had spent some time with Isabella di Rienzi. He had found her a little intimidating and had felt an awkwardness in her presence. He had now decided he had done his duty, and could avoid her for the rest of the evening. He knew there were expectations of him, and he sometimes sensed these and wondered how he would fulfil them, or at least that was the impression he gave. Now he was talking to don Calogero, drinking his very precocious glass of champagne, and not enjoying it much. Don Calogero was asking about his family, his father in particular. What a pity he could not come! Or his brother and his sisters!

They spoke of Emma, and Tonino and the baby. He said that Tonino was one of his best friends, and he was glad that Emma had forgiven him and that they were now together, and that the baby would be baptised at long last. Of course, what Tonino had done was wrong, but he was making up for it now.

They spoke of his father. Beppe gave the impression of very much wanting to like don Calogero, such a wonderful man, who wore his clothes with such ease, who sat on every chair as if he owned it, the man who was one of the most important in Sicily, but he felt defensive as he spoke of his father. Don Antonio was retired, in Castelvetrano, overseeing improvements to the house (which was a fine one) and the garden (which was magnificent and huge). He spent some time sailing his small boat, visiting various historic sites in the vicinity and going for long walks. He had developed an attachment to his dogs, of which he had several. But as he explained all this, he knew that it was what he was not saying that was more eloquent. All these activities covered up the major activities of sleeping and drinking, and, for large parts of the day, on the bad days, doing absolutely nothing at all. Beppe went to Castelvetrano sometimes when he did not have school, at weekends and on holidays, though he preferred to be in Palermo and spend time at Traiano's or Muniddu's. His mother was in Castelvetrano from time to time too, but Sandro, Emma and Marina had not been there for years. And because Beppe kept up with his father out of a sense of pity and of duty, Sandro in particular refused, for the most part, to speak to him.

There was no mention of the court case and the lawyers. Neither of them wanted to speak of that. And what was there to say, except that Sandro was being a nuisance? Though from the way Beppe spoke, you would think there was no court case at all. He lived in a world without lawyers.

Don Calogero spoke of gardens. He remembered the one in Castelvetrano, from the one time he had visited. He spoke of the care and attention he had paid to the development of the Furnaces. He had had a very talented designer work on it, Gabriella Bonelli, and now, thanks to her, the place was like the garden of Eden. It was really so pretty. The oleanders, the bougainvillea, the ficus trees, the lemon trees, the pines, the oaks; of course, the latter needed some years to come to maturity. He should come and see it; and the garden and the trees at Donnafugata. His parents should come too. It would be a nice occasion, in the summer, sometime.

Beppe wondered if his father would ever accept such an invitation. His brother and his sisters had implied that the two men hated each other, and that it was hatred of don Calogero that had driven their father to drink. But the gardens sounded wonderful. He liked don Calogero, if you could like someone whom you feared a little, and he did not feel disloyal in talking to him. In fact, his mother had urged him to make sure he spoke to don Calogero and to his daughters. Why she had done this, he was not quite sure, or that was the impression he gave. He had mentioned it to Traiano, and he too had been thoughtful, then explained. His mother wanted him to have powerful and useful friends, he said. This seemed logical to Beppe. If don Calogero liked him now, that was an investment for the future. Though as the future did not yet exist, and as he could not imagine it, this logical truth made little real sense to him.

Traiano approached. Beppe's face lit up at the sight of him. Traiano smiled.

'My daughters are in the next room, and I know they are eager to spend as much time with you as possible,' said don Calogero.

This hint was to be obeyed at once. He was a good boy like that, always eager to please.

'How old is he?' asked don Calogero watching him go. 'Sixteen? He seems younger. The elder brother, what is he like? I remember him from that party where Gino met his death. He perhaps is not ideal son-in-law material from what I observed.'

'Correct,' said Traiano. 'Sandro is a nightmare. Beppe is the nice one of the family. You see, I take an interest, as you told me too.'

'Do you seriously think that Beppe likes you? He is just looking to the future and trying to secure his share of the Santucci wealth, trying to make friends with the circling sharks. But you would put a bullet through his head without a moment's thought. You almost did once.'

'No, you almost did,' said Traiano, in a low voice. 'You destroy everything you touch.'

'I do not,' said Calogero, with a smile. 'I turn everything I touch to gold, like King Midas. And I have made you rich too, so stop whining. And never forget what you owe me.'

'How could I, when you never stop reminding me?'

'How is my brother-in-law?' he asked.

'I preferred him as a drunk and a drug addict, I sometimes think. Now he is able to be rational, though not very rational, I have to keep him from making mistakes. He is a barrelful of resentments. The men who killed his father, the man who killed Gino….'

'That was an accident.'

'Even he does not believe that anymore. I have told him to let it go. It has been two years, but he cannot let it go. He can hide it, but it is still there, the resentment…'

'Against me?'

'He loves you to distraction, boss, you know that, but even he knows, unless he is completely stupid, which sometimes I think he is, that you gave the word, tacit or spoken, either before or after the event. And as for the one who did it… well, he does not like him at all. And he blames himself, leaving Gino alone… He and Gino… he gets these manias, you know, and even though Gino is dead, he still thinks about him a lot, talks about him…'

'We have a small problem in Catania,' said don Calogero. 'We will need to speak in private tomorrow some time. You and me. But that is enough for now.'

In the other room, Beppe drew near to Ceccina.

She was holding two-year-old Romano, the youngest child of Calogero and Anna Maria, and discussing points of interest about him with his elder sisters, Isabella and Natalia di Rienzi. Because Ceccina was there, and because her presence gave him an excuse, Beppe approached, no longer frightened to come into the orbit of Isabella and her sister. He was three or four years older than Isabella, but rather frightened of her. Despite her youth, she was confident. Perhaps this was because she was her father's daughter and used to deference; perhaps because her mother was dead, and her stepmother very fond of her. She was at school in Catania with Natalia, and they spent most weekends in Donnafugata, and came to Palermo but rarely. The talk was now all of Catania: their school, their life in the quarter, the way Aunt Assunta was there a lot to look after them, and their grandmother too, whenever Anna Maria had to be elsewhere. They were very fond of Giuseppina, their deceased mother's sister, and longing to go out to Africa to visit her, and longing for her next visit home. Of their grandmother, they were less fond. And Pasqualina, Ceccina's sister, had been there visiting her parents who were now living on the floor below in their old flat, along with her husband and baby. It was a pity they had only stayed for a week. The two girls paid a lot of attention to Ceccina, but to Beppe, they paid none at all.

Beppe was intrigued by the way they pointedly ignored him, and unsure how to react. There had been a time, though it was very brief, and now some time ago, when Isabella had seemed to like him, but she had evidently changed her mind. Girls did. He knew from the example of his sisters that they changed their mind about boys all the time. One moment they were talking of one, the next moment he was forgotten. Well, he had now been moved to the pile of the forgotten. Not that he cared too much; but the phenomenon of the changeability of human emotion interested him. He himself had been given to deep passion when younger and had not thought himself fickle. He had loved his father dearly, even though he realised that his father was difficult to love, but he now could understand how his brother and his sisters had decided so easily, so without struggle, to stop talking to him. He was their father, even if he had become a sad drunk. Similarly, his sixteen-year-old heart, once smitten by love for Ceccina, who was so beautiful, warm and lovely, and by the deepest feelings for Traiano who was so kind to him and such fun to be with, his heart had cooled. Beppe's passions and attachments, which had faded with the years, were now conspicuous only in their absence. He was sixteen but innocent; by his age, both Calogero and Traiano had been far from innocent, but the world of base desire was unknown to him. He knew that his brother Sandro slept with his girlfriends, and his sisters slept with their boyfriends, and clearly Tonino had slept with Emma, because he knew where babies came from, but he knew too that these partners kept on changing; he understood that the married couples he knew slept with each other, obviously, but this was something about which he had very little curiosity.

Though she was younger, Isabella was rather different already. She knew about sex, she thought about it, and she felt the yearnings in her soul for sexual intimacy. That she had very fleetingly found sweet innocent Beppe so attractive she now regarded with scorn; her tastes were now more adult. Beppe was a child; she was leaving childhood behind. Thus, she was leaving Beppe behind, and regarded him now with dislike, as he reminded her of the childhood she was so eager to slough off.

In other ways too, Isabella had advanced beyond the state where a boy like Beppe might attract her. She had noticed - she was now old enough to notice - that people deferred to her. At school, she was treated as a special case, being the daughter of don Calogero di Rienzi. From infancy, she had, when walking through the streets of the quarter in Catania, seen the way people stopped and spoke to her father, seen the way these walks had assumed some of the quality of a royal walkabout, some of the trappings of a triumphant progress. Her father was important because he was rich, and she was important because she was his daughter. Moreover, she knew that he had not always been rich, but had become rich through his own efforts, and people respected him for that. His father, the grandfather she had never known, had died when he was sixteen, just nine months before she was born. (She had been shocked to learn quite by chance that she had been born when both her parents had been seventeen. She could not comprehend that anyone should want to be a parent so young.) Her father had inherited and transformed the wealth he had come into; then he had married someone even richer than himself, Anna Maria. Money made you important, she could see that. Beppe's family was rich, which was the only reason anyone paid him any attention. Anna Maria was richer than her father, and that was why he treated her with a certain wary deference. Whether they loved each other, she had never considered; the idea that they might have passions was alien to her. Her own passions interested her, to the exclusion of all else. She was her father's favourite, her stepmother's favourite, her three younger brothers, Renato, Sebastiano and Romano, adored her. And if Natalia, still a little girl, was jealous of her, what did she care about that?

Her childhood had been, ever since the death of her mother, unsettled. For a start there had been that dramatic moment at Catania airport when their mother had been shot dead before their eyes by the lunatic boy Enzo. Years had passed since then, but the memory persisted. One moment all had been calm, happy, even exciting, their return from America. Then it had all gone wrong: the single shot, the shouting, the screams, the children being rushed away, and the arrival of the police. Then the procession of substitute mothers, their grandmother, their Aunt Elena, their Aunt Giuseppina, and finally, the beloved stepmother, Anna Maria. As for the murder of their mother, that had puzzled Isabella, and like so many others, she had assumed that Enzo, the mad boy, now locked up in a hospital for life, had really intended to shoot their father and missed. It had impressed her that people might want to shoot her father; she felt sorry that her mother had been the innocent victim of this; but because Anna Maria was so important a figure, she felt no real sadness for the loss of her mother.

One thing was certain. With all these people looking after her, living sometimes in Palermo, sometimes in Catania, sometimes in Donnafugata, with her father so busy, surrounded by aunts and nannies and a stepmother, she felt no constant adult presence in her life, and little stability. In other words, life was not boring.

Calogero di Rienzo and Trajan Antonescu were standing outside the Opera House, in the middle of a busy crowd. To passers-by they looked like two old friends who had met by purest chance, but the meeting had been set up last night. Calogero listened carefully while Traiano explained what was in hand, while he outlined the Mattarella case, and the case of Matteo Rota.

'You should leave Mattarella and his son alive for now at least. It will reassure Rota. In fact, Rota must think you are not going to kill him, as you have not killed them yet. With every day that passes, he thinks the danger passes as well,' said Calogero.

'My thoughts exactly,' said Traiano. 'If we squeeze them for cash, allow them to think they can buy their lives…'

'Make sure it is cash, that way it won't be traced back to us…'

'And once they have paid, then we will get rid of them,' said Traiano. 'I was thinking your landfill site. That way, if they disappear, people will assume they have just fled.'

Calogero nodded.

'Who will do it?'

'Maybe Tonino. He is keen. He has done well so far. He can get in a bit of help, of course. Muniddu can advise. There is no need to get the anyone from Catania involved.'

Calogero nodded again.

'Two thirds for you, one third for me; and you pay Tonino and whoever you use out of your two thirds. These people have been cheated us for years. We are the only dealers in this particular commodity in the western world who have been making a loss. Well, not quite a loss. But this nonsense has gone on too long. I am glad you have found it out at last. They deserve to be made to pay back what they have stolen, and the ultimate price as well. Leave Renzo out of it. There is no need for him to be actively involved. Though makes sure he gets a cut. The nephew, is he trustworthy?'

'I think so, boss. He resents his uncle. He has asked a pension for his mother.'

'Promise him whatever it takes,' said Calogero. 'After all, he will not outlive his uncle for long, will he, this affectionate nephew?' He thought for a few moments. 'When are you thinking of moving against Matteo Rota and his friends?'

'Easter,' said Traiano.

'Good. Holidays are always best. People are not on their guard. By the time people realise they are all dead, no one will remember them ever having been alive. I leave it all to you.' He looked at the Opera House for a moment or two. Traiano sensed that he wanted to say something more. 'We need to get this operation on track, we need the money. As you know, I am in debt, as the Furnaces have yet to start making a lot of money. As soon as the money comes in, we plough it back into some other venture. Something perfectly legal, I mean. Tell me, have you heard of this new drug, fentanyl? It is a pill, synthetic, no growers. We have had some brought over from America; they use it for the troops. Our contact in the American base, the same one who provides that other pill that Gino was so crazy for, the Major, you call him. The thing is that there has been a bit of trouble. This fentanyl causes quite a few deaths. There have been one or two in Catania and as it is a new thing, every death gets reported in the papers, as if it were a case of bubonic plague. Some of the doctors seem to want to start a crusade over this. It has panicked Volta. A couple of people die, and he thinks we are going to turn into Scotland, Scotland with sunshine, that Catania will be like Glasgow. Of course, Volta is sensitive. He was elected to restore law and order. He did so. Now fentanyl arises and threatens to wreck everything. Of course, the money would be nice, but if the Palermo operation gets back on track, we are no longer so desperate for money. People like cocaine, it is clean, but fentanyl.... Our guys like it, but if I tell them to stop, there is a good chance they will sulk. But we cannot afford to alienate Volta. They know that. The cocaine needs to take up the slack provided by the fentanyl.'

'Understood, boss. When can we replace Alfio?'

'Ah, the question that Renzo did not dare raise last night. East Africa is very beautiful. I hope you will go there soon. On holiday. A holiday with an ulterior motive. You can visit the orphanage that the Confraternity supports. Oh, how cross dearest Giuseppina was to discover that the orphanage into which we pump millions had very little to show for it. She said that the money is being stolen; well, it is, but by us, not by the Africans, and not by the dear nuns who run the orphanages. We have made sure that the sweet little children get a little bit more than heretofore. She has no children, and therefore an African orphanage where so many children need love is ideal for her. And he… he has been very busy speaking to the people who take their orders from the Gulf. The Islamist terrorists have met Alfio and the man Omar and we have the guarantee that there will be no more terrorist attacks, in our vicinity at least, as the terrorists never attack their friends.'

'Are we their friends?' asked Traiano incredulously.

'Of course. So I am told in Rome. We provide them with certain things they need, and they in turn will always leave us alone. Have there been any terrorist attacks on Italian soil? Of course not. They need us. We can give them the things they need without arousing suspicion: safe houses, intelligence… Their targets are outside Italy, so it need not bother us. And anything we own is safe. Anna Maria, when she deigns to talk to me, is very keen on our African project. The place has potential. Potential as a luxury resort, and potential for laundering tons of money. The checks they make in Africa are not very rigorous, and we have good contacts at the heart of the government. If something were to happen to Alfio, I think Giuseppina would stay there, to be near the orphans. But we need Alfio for now. And he is in partnership with Costantino, don Carmelo's bastard, so he might have something to say about it all. We do not want to disturb things at this early stage. Explain that to Renzo.'

'Boss, I have done, and will again. But one day….'

'It may come to that,' he said shortly.

'Have you brought me some cocaine?' asked Sandro sharply, opening the door of the Santucci villa, seeing Tonino on the doorstep.

'A little present, yes,' said Tonino easily.

He was invited in. He knew, because he had checked with Beppe, that neither don Antonio or Angela Santucci were in Palermo at present. Antonio was in Castelvetrano, as usual, and Angela had gone off to Turin for a conference on some Catholic topic, something to do with don Bosco and helping young people who had lost their way. (Now he was potentially her son-in-law, he was determined to try and know a bit more about the saints.)

The Santucci villa was a large, ugly and expensive building, surrounded by a high wall and a profusion of bougainvillea, which, even in late January, showed a few remaining blooms from summer. The family employed a gardener, and everything showed the loveless care of hired labour. Inside the house, all was marble and leather and modern art on the ground floor. The father had for the last two years been permanently away, the mother more or less the same. The house had an air of disorder and neglect. They went into the kitchen. Clearly Sandro had only just got out of bed. His feet were bare, and he was wearing a pair of jeans and a very crumpled tee shirt. His sister, Marina, was nowhere to be seen. He had the feeling they were alone, which was exactly what he had wished.

'There is something I want to tell you,' said Tonino.

'I know there is, I have heard,' said Sandro, carefully making two lines of cocaine on the granite of the kitchen work surface. Tonino waited for him to snort it down, knowing that conversation would have to wait.

'Oh, that is so good,' said Sandro, as the drug took effect.

He prepared two more lines, and swiftly consumed them.

'My mother told me,' he said at last. 'What I wanted to say to you is that I am not happy with you or my sister Emma. I have not been happy with her for a long time. First, she took their side in the court case, or at least failed to take my side. Then she got herself pregnant and refused to get rid of it. Now she reveals the worst of all, that she has been seeing you and you are the father. I have found you very useful as a supplier of cocaine, and I am grateful for that, but you are not the sort of guy I want my sister to go out with, and certainly not my dream brother-in-law. Is Emma crazy? Having a child with a drug dealer, a thug and God knows what else? I mean, that time two years ago in the Grand Hotel, she wanted to sleep with a gangster to try and find out what it was like, but then to repeat the experience, and now to say she is thinking of marrying him? And then there is the matter of your personal attributes. You are a short-arsed troll. And it gets worse.'

Tonino gave him an amused and questioning look.

'You may fool my mother, which is not so hard, and you may fool Emma, and I am surprised at her. But you do not fool me.'

The word that came out next was a dialect word, an ugly one, one he knew the meaning of himself, but had never much used. He was surprised that Sandro even knew such a word.

'You insult me,' said Tonino in an even voice, knowing that he should not allow himself to be provoked.

He looked at the kitchen counter behind Sandro and saw a rolling pin and an empty wine bottle.

'I am telling the truth, which perhaps you do not like. Deny it if you can. I have no objection to drug dealers or to men who like that sort of thing. But I do not want such people in my family, father of my niece, boyfriend or husband to my sister.'

'That is your opinion. But Emma is the one who decides, not you. You should mind your own business.'

This calm response infuriated Sandro further.

'I will not be told what to do by you!' he shouted.

'Don't let it get to you. And let me tell you something. I have not just come here to give you your cocaine, but a message as well. Very soon you are going to be far away. Don Renzo and don Traiano have had enough of you and they have decided that you should leave Sicily. You can go anywhere you want as long as it is the far side of the straits of Messina. And you drop the case over your grandfather's will. It has gone on long enough. It's embarrassing. You have got a week to leave.'

For a moment there was complete silence.

'And if I don't?' asked Sandro quietly.

'There will be consequences you may not like.'

'My cousin Renzo, and that Romanian,' said Sandro with contempt. 'That little shit Beppe has done this. Why on earth are you listening to him? Look, I will pay you well, you know him, drop him off a cliff for me.'

'Then the inheritance passes to the Church. Clever that. An insurance policy so no one harms Beppe. Look, you are not wanted on voyage, so get out while you can. Or the person to be dropped off a cliff will be you.'

'I am not frightened of them or of you,' said Sandro. 'I am going to go to my father and speak to him. I will speak to Uncle Domenico. I will even go to Catania and speak to don Calogero.'

He looked at Tonino with venom. Again, he mentioned that insulting word.

'You should be frightened of me,' said Tonino. 'You are not wise.'

There was silence.

Tonino walked over to the kitchen counter and carefully picked up the rolling pin and weighed it in his hand. Then, without warning, he brought it down on the side of Sandro's head. He staggered, and fell to the floor. Then, holding him down, Tonino whacked him on the ankle, until he could hear the bones break. Sandro screamed in pain. He took out his knife and tore open his jeans at the back and reached for the empty wine bottle. A few minutes later, he was out of the house, his last word being the one that Sandro had used.

'Have you heard?' said Emma, the next day. 'My brother is in hospital.'

'Beppe?'

'No, Sandro.'

'What happened?'

'Broken ankle. He fell down the stairs. And something else as well, but he did not say what. Needs an operation. He will be in for a few days then they will let him out. He phoned me. He said he was in agony and that he wanted my father to come and visit him.'

'But he has not spoken to his father for years.'

'That is why he phoned me. He phoned Papà, and Papà put the phone down on him, not surprisingly. So he phoned me to get me to phone Papà and tell Papà that he must go and see him, that it was urgent.'

'And did you?'

'No. Sandro is a troublemaker. He will have to fight his own battles. I don't want to get involved. He should phone Marina, she always was his best friend. Maybe he has. He can hardly phone Beppe, he was so beastly to him, unless he has no shame. Mind you, he has no shame, I think. Perhaps he should phone Mama, as he is feeling sorry for himself. She will be back soon and rush to his bedside, I suppose. She is too kind. You reap what you sow. But enough about him. Have you ever thought of getting a piercing?'

'Where do you think I should get one?'

'Just here would be nice,' she said.

'I suppose,' she said later, 'I suppose he may have upset someone,' meaning her brother Sandro. 'He is a twit.'

Emma, like Marina and Sandro, was an adult, old enough to know about the nature of the Santucci business and the role played by Antonescu, or so her supposition implied; Beppe, being younger, she assumed, did not know. That was one of the divisions between the four siblings, perhaps the principle one. The elder three hated and despised their own father, in varying degrees; the youngest, Beppe, loved him still. As for their mother, their grandmother and their aunts, they refused to talk about the family situation at all. Any attempt to talk about their father, their late Uncle Carlo, their late grandfather Lorenzo, all three subjects were resolutely shut down by the womenfolk, which caused a great deal of frustration and fury. But they knew; they knew it all; or at least they thought they did. They knew their father had never liked the popular Carlo, and that their father had been forced out by his business colleagues, with the co-operation of his own father and uncle who had effectively given the coup de grace. They knew that their cousin Renzo had benefitted from this, and though it was not logical, they hated him too, even if they hated their father as well. Moreover, Renzo had not really benefitted, because behind Renzo were the people from Catania, his wife Elena, his brother-in-law Calogero, the man Antonescu and this Tonino, the one who did things, though what things one could not be sure, for Antonescu. This Tonino with whom she, Emma, was now in bed, which changed everything.

She, with her elder two siblings, understood, but at the same time, they did not understand, she knew. The whole thing was terribly complicated. Of course, they knew what belonged to the Santucci company: the hotels, the car showrooms, things like that. They knew that their income came from the Santucci group of companies, and that they all had shares in it, all controlled by trusts and trustees, and there was a constant income stream which made them rich; but who really controlled things, and who really wielded the power, this was the difficult question. And in what did the power consist, how it was wielded, that was hard to understand as well. But they knew this: their grandfather's will cut them out, and gave all to Beppe. That surely made a difference.

What happened, according to Emma's understanding, was that Calogero di Rienzi gave the orders and these passed through his sister to Renzo, who acted as titular head of the companies; but that was only one type of order. There were other orders given to Antonescu, which were then passed down to people like Tonino. Thus, there was the protection afforded by nothing being direct. The police might catch Tonino doing something wrong, but they would not catch Antonescu, and they would not catch Calogero di Rienzi, ever. But what sort of things did Tonino do wrong, that was what Emma wanted to know about, though without having to ask. Threats, extortion, breaking people's bones, perhaps more. The two men who had been found three summers ago in the harbour in Palermo, they had worked for the family, and look what had happened to them. Who had done that? But if it were so obvious, why did the police not investigate and make arrests? The police, perhaps, turned a blind eye, or more likely were paid to do so. People needed cocaine, everyone knew that, and cocaine was against the law; but it was a stupid law; so, the law had to be ignored. The police knew that. The law was unenforceable. Same with prostitutes; people needed what people needed. These things would always happen. So, the police let them happen, and let them happen with minimum disruption, with a minimum cost to society, and with a commission to themselves. After all, they all took cocaine and who was harmed by that?

But Tonino, when questioned, said very little about Antonescu and even claimed that he barely knew Calogero di Rienzi at all; he had known him as a little boy in Catania, that was all; so had Antonescu, but neither of them saw much of him these days. Calogero was far too important, thanks to the new wife, the new children. He had married her, they were all sure, for her money, of which, they assumed, there was a great deal; and not just her money, but something even more valuable, her contacts, her banking skills, her intimacy with virtually everyone you had never heard of who ran the Italian Republic. He spoke like a man who believed that such information was dangerous, as if he were trained to see nothing and to hear nothing. Emma listened to him with attention but with little interest, and thought of her father, her late Uncle Carlo, her late grandfather Lorenzo, her Great-Uncle Domenico. But she wondered about Antonescu. He was very uxorious, devoted to his wife and children, or so she had heard. People who liked power did not like sex, she opined.

'I like both,' Tonino said, and proceeded to show it once more.

'What do you mean, you broke your ankle?' his mother was asking down the phone.

'Look, does it matter how I broke it? It is broken and that is that, and I am stuck in this hospital, and I need you to come back home.'

'I am in Turin all week.'

'Next week will be too late.'

'Too late for what? You need to explain, dear.'

'I am explaining. It is hard on the phone. You need to come back here at once. I am stuck in hospital with a broken ankle, and I need you. It is urgent.'

'But how can I help? I am not a doctor or a nurse, dearest. What about your sisters and Beppe, and your father?'

'None of them will come near me. You are all I have.'

'Well, that is a new line from you. For years you have made it plain that you do not want me, and now you say you need me, just because of a broken ankle.'

'I am in agony. It is not 'just' a broken ankle. Can't you understand what I am saying?'

'I would be able to understand if you could say it properly.'

He cut her off in exasperation and rage. Rage was what had possessed him since the 'accident'. Rage was an anaesthetic. A week, that bastard had said, a week to get beyond the straits. He was damned if he were going anywhere. Given that he could only hobble, he knew that this was in another, more restricted sense, true.

That weekend, at the very first opportunity, Tonino decided he would present Emma to his parents and, of course, allow his parents to see their grandchild. They drove in Roberto's car to Catania, and Emma and the baby stayed in a hotel, while Tonino stayed with his parents, to preserve the fiction that they were not sleeping together. Much to his surprise, both his parents were delighted with Emma and with the baby. Babies were, he knew, always popular, and his mother had long wanted to be a grandmother as well as a mother; her own younger child was only slightly older than her son's. There was much to discuss about child-rearing between the two women, and Emma was enchanted by the warmth of signora Grassi. As for Tonino's father, he was in awe at the thought of his son possibly marrying the granddaughter of the late don Lorenzo Santucci. When Tonino took her back to the hotel on Saturday night, she was full of enthusiasm for his parents and their warm welcome. On Sunday morning he arranged to collect her in good time for Mass.

This, he knew, she was doing to please his mother, who assumed she would be coming; but he also knew that signora Santucci would be thrilled beyond words that Emma had entered a church, and not for a wedding, funeral or baptism, for the first time since her thirteenth birthday. Emma, as it turned out, was rather pleased with the experience. She was taken aback by the beauty of the Church of the Holy Souls in Purgatory and the wonderful picture of the Spanish Madonna in her nimbus of golden rays and clouds. She did not believe, but beauty always had the power to move her; halfway through the Mass, she whispered to Tonino that they should get the child baptised here, and perhaps get married here too. Afterwards, they spoke to don Giorgio. She had never met such a nice priest before. After Mass, they walked around the square, and people came up to Tonino to congratulate him, to be introduced to her and to admire the baby. Then they went home for a splendid lunch, and after lunch, he took her back to the hotel, and while the baby slept, they made love. Later that evening, she and the baby were picked up by Roberto for the drive back to Palermo. It had been a most successful weekend. He would follow by train or bus the next day, Monday, as he needed to stay behind to see the boss, who was away for the weekend at Donnafugata, but would be back on Monday. Then he went home to his parents to hear them enthuse about Emma, her lovely matronly figure, her sweetness, and her beautiful green hair.

No one came to see him, which made Sandro furious; until someone did come to see him, which made his blood run cold. On Sunday night Renzo came accompanied by Traiano. He was sitting in his chair next to his bed, when they came and picked him up, one either side, and took him down to the carpark, for, they said, a bit of fresh air. The carpark was, indeed, full of patients grabbing a desperately needed cigarette, but they marched him to Renzo's car, opened the boot and threw him in. His voice was paralysed, and as they drove away he was pretty sure no one would hear him cry out anyway.

Three hours later, after a terrifying journey, by motorway and ferry, he found himself turfed out of the car in his pyjamas, on a cold January night.

'If you come back, we kill you,' said Renzo.

His tormentors drove off. He could see in the distance the lights of Messina and knew that he was on the other side of the straits, and that the narrow channel of water separated him from Sicily forever. In his dressing gown pocket, by lucky chance, he had his phone and his wallet, which contained his bank card, thank God. Unsteadily he rose to his feet, his ankle hurting like hell, wondering where on earth he was and what he would ever do.

On Monday evening, Roberto came home to the flat, and realised, from the sounds of shower water in the bathroom, that Tonino had come back from Catania. There were various clothes scattered about the room, and he waited for Tonino to emerge.

'Hi,' he said.

'Last night, when we drove back, all she could talk about was how lovely Catania was, and how nice your parents, particularly your mother, were,' said Roberto. 'Over two hours of it.

She likes you, I got the impression, but she loves your mother. Well, the signora was always a nice person. Everyone likes her.'

'Good,' said Tonino. 'There's that last bottle of red wine from the Mattarella agriturismo. The other ones were really good. Will you help me drink it tonight?'

'Sure.'

There was silence.

'How was the boss?'

'He was very angry. I knew he would be. But not about Emma. He wanted to see me because the week before last, was it, we met up with Assunta and his two daughters. He did not like that one bit. He told me that he did not like me looking at his daughters, well, his eldest one, Isabella.'

'He shouldn't worry about men looking at her, but about her looking at men,' said Roberto. 'She is very forward. Did you look at her?'

'She looked at me…'

'How old is Isabella? Fifteen?'

'Not quite. Two years younger, at least. The boss is getting paranoid about her, and the thought of boys going to bed with her. But I reckon if he wants to keep the boys of the quarter away from her, he is already too late. Despite the dangers, they have been there, or at least one or two have. Don Calogero is so high and mighty, but Isabella will defeat him!'

'You told him this?'

'Of course not!'

'Does everyone else know? That Isabella is not, well, what she should be, not a virgin.'

'A fair few must suspect. And boys will talk. But it is her father's problem. He wants her for Beppe. That is a joke.'

'What did you discuss with Calogero?'

They both sat at the table, the bottle of wine and two glasses between them. Tonino considered. You did not discuss things with don Calogero: you listened to what he said, and you obeyed.

'I told him about Emma, and he already knew all about it. Amazing how he discovers everything. Of course, Traiano told him. And my mother had already told his mother, who had also told him. He said it was a real cheek, me fathering a child with Emma, and I agreed, and I said the damage had been done, and that I had already taken my punishment from my father.'

Roberto heard this in silence. He poured another glass for Tonino, then one for himself.

'But really he is pleased,' said Tonino. 'Me and Emma is an insult to the pride of the Santuccis. Even Emma thinks that, I think, not that we have discussed it. Sandro was furious. Renzo is not best pleased either. God knows what Antonio thinks. Only Beppe is truly happy. The signora is making the best of a bad job, and that job is me. Don Calogero asked about you.'

'Me?'

'And not in a good way either. He thinks they have found out about Enna. To be accurate, that you found out from me, and then you told his sister, your great friend Assunta.'

'What is there for me to find out about in Enna? I know that on the motorcycle you stop there frequently, and go off and do whatever it is you do, while I have a cup of coffee. I have never asked what it is you do. You have never offered to tell me. You must be doing something, but it is your business and not mine.'

'That is what I told him. That you mind your own business, and that you know nothing about Enna, and you would not ask. He believed me. I told him I trusted you.' He looked at the bottle and poured himself another glass. 'This is such a good bottle that I not only want more of where it came from, I want to own the whole place. I might get the company to sell its share in the place to me. Don't you think that would be nice?'

'Very. It is memorable wine,' said Roberto.

'Do you ever think about having a baby with Gabriella?' replied Tonino.

'No, never.'

'Best thing that has ever happened to me. I mean, what is the point of having money, owning a vineyard or an agriturismo, when you have no one to leave it to? I mean, what is the point of it all?'

'I don't think of it that way,' said Roberto. 'I mean, sex is sex, and it's nice, but babies…. They are not my thing.'

'I wasn't there for her birth. But I will be for the next one.'

'Are you already thinking of the next one?'

'Yes, I am,' said Tonino. 'I know my mother would like it very much and so would Emma. By the way, Sandro has gone away,' he added, changing the subject.

'Why?'

'He was made to. He has been told. He won't turn up in court the next time he is summoned, so the case will die. That is the idea. But… I don't like Sandro. He called me something insulting.'

Roberto knew better than to ask what.

'Don't worry about Sandro.'

'I don't. They told him to go away, Renzo and Traiano. But the one who made them do it was Beppe.'

'How?'

'They just knew what he wanted.'

'Telepathy.'

'He gets what he wants, that boy.'

'Lucky Beppe,' said Roberto. 'Lucky us. Are you going out this evening?'

'No,' said Tonino, aware that the only place he might be going was to see Emma. 'I want to stay here.'

'Good,' said Roberto. 'So do I.'

Chapter Four

It was in the middle of February that Traiano decided that he would seek an interview with Matteo Rota. If the whole matter were to be brought off at Easter, which fell on the 20th April, then the preliminary work would need to be done right now.

It was all a matter of money. Rota and his colleagues had been skimming for years, and they had, among themselves, wondered whether one or two million would be enough compensation, which determined Traiano to ask for at least four million. Whereas he had secured 51% of the Mattarella business in the last extortion, this time it would have to be cash, as cash would not leave a paper trail. He knew that raising four million in cash would take time. Well, he was going to give them time. They would have to take money out of savings accounts, sell properties, raise loans, liquefy their various assets. If he gave them until Easter, that would give them the time they needed. He was not being unreasonable, he felt. At the same time, he did not want to give them too much time: he wanted to provoke the right amount of panic.

Of course, as one tackled one's enemies, one did it at their weakest point. There were six of them; and the weakest was certainly not Rota the ringleader. The weakest was, he determined, after getting Tonino to enquire without arousing suspicion, and comparing it with information from Muniddu, whom he also consulted, was a man called Borelli, who was the oldest of the group. According to Simone Rota, the nephew, Borelli was nearing retirement and very nervous that the whole project would be derailed just as he was planning to get out of it. Borelli had children, as they all did, of whom he was fond. Borelli, was, according to Muniddu, who knew the man slightly, a coward. This was useful to know, and he needed Muniddu's help. Finally, Tonino found out, by the simple expedient of asking the undermanager, who knew him and knew who he was, that Borelli liked the bar in the Grand Hotel, and often came with an expensive looking girl in tow, with whom he would then retire to one of the rooms for the afternoon.

On one such afternoon, they visited him. The master key, provided by the undermanager, opened the door of the room, and there was Borelli, there was the girl, and a look of horrified surprise on both their faces, his in particular. Traiano, stood at the bottom of the bed, with Muniddu on one side of him, and Tonino on the other. He looked at the girl.

'Leave,' he commanded.

She did as she was told, perhaps having undergone a similar experience before. She detached herself from Borelli's embrace, and silently and quickly dressed and left, closing the door softly behind her. Borelli stared at the gun that Tonino was holding.

'You disgusting creature,' said Traiano in a quiet and controlled voice. 'You revolt me. You have insulted our boss. Not don Renzo, but the ultimate boss, don Calogero. You have been skimming off cocaine for years. We gave you a job, a good job, and paid you very well, but it was not enough for you or your friends. You were greedy. Now we are going to punish you. And you are going to take a message to your friend Matteo Rota and tell him that he needs to see us as a matter of urgency. He has to make amends. Make sure you tell him that. If you do not, it will be worse for you, very much worse for you. You have a wife and children. We will kill not only you, but them as well. You owe us four million, you dirty thief! We are not going to kill you, so please do not look at me like that. But perhaps, after this, you may wish we had killed you.'

He nodded to Tonino, who took a pillow and pressed it over the man's terrified face. Muniddu sat on his legs to stop him squirming. From his jacket pocket, Traiano took out a pair of garden secateurs. So that he did not get blood on his clothes or hands, he put another pillow over the man's left foot, while he placed one of his toes between the blades of the secateurs, and pressed down hard on the handle with all his might.

'Nice work,' said Traiano, as they left the hotel a few minutes later.

The severed toe was dropped down one of the drains in the via Roma, and the secateurs went into one of the public rubbish bins.

The meeting with Matteo Rota took place a week later in the Mattarella restaurant. The time and the place were carefully chosen. He calculated that a week would be enough to let the enormity of the fate of Borelli sink in. As for the Mattarella place, that was a careful choice as well. Mattarella and his son had sinned, repented, paid compensation, and been forgiven, as Rota would surely understand. They would serve as a confidence building precedent; their example would point Rota and his associates in the right direction.

He brought Tonino with him, just to be on the safe side, just in case Rota tried something; the Mattarellas received them both with obsequious charm, and the very best wine was brought out for them, and there was a long consultation over the menu. Mattarella the father waited on them personally, and withdrew when he saw Rota enter the restaurant. Traiano noticed this. They knew each other, they had consulted.

Rota came to the table and, at a nod from Traiano, sat down. He ignored Tonino. No hands were shaken.

'Thank you for coming,' said Traiano politely. 'Let's place our order. The food should be good.'

At a look from Traiano, Mattarella returned, and the food was decided on. As they waited for the ravioli with butter and sage to arrive, Traiano poured some of the wine. Tonino was completely impassive, and had been instructed not to speak unless spoken to.

'We want to make you an offer,' said Rota levelly.

Traiano raised an eyebrow, while Tonino paid attention to the bread basket.

'We want to cut you in,' said Rota.

Traiano's look invited him to continue, and, feeling encouraged, he did so.

'We know things have changed ever since you arrived,' said Rota. 'That is clear. Don Renzo does not have your energy or your interest in the business. Don Antonio did not look at things too carefully for many a year now, so we have been left to our own devices. And I admit we have taken advantage. I do not see any use in being anything but honest. My friends and I have discussed this, and we have come to the conclusion, or at least I guided them to the conclusion, that you were a person it would be not simply unwise to try to deceive, but futile. We have taken advantage, but not that much advantage. What we have taken for ourselves has been a tiny percentage, less than one percent. So small that no one has noticed it, at least until now. The sort of percentage that could be explained away as natural wastage, caused by breakages, divisions, poor measurements and things like that. When you cut up a cake you create a few crumbs. Who cares about crumbs? We helped ourselves to the crumbs.'

'Indeed, who cares about crumbs?' asked Traiano. 'The answer is that I do.'

'We want to cut you in,' repeated Rota.

'Ah,' said Traiano, surprised.

Even Tonino looked up.

'We know that you are relatively new here, that you are clever, that you are fearless and that you are energetic. We also know that this business is full of sharks. So, we want to be on the same side as you. If we give you a share of our business, in return for being allowed to continue as before, under your patronage and protection, with you guaranteeing our safety and making us immune from interference… the Albanians, the Calabrians, people like that…'

'How much are we talking about?' asked Traiano.

Rota paused. This was the moment of truth.

'It is a very small percentage, but it adds up. In a good year, a couple of million; in a bad year, a million; we divide by six. But we would give you, let us say, a third. So, 300,000 to 600,000 euro depending on how good the year is.'

'This was your idea, or Borelli's?'

'Mine of course. Borelli is a complete fool.'

'Is he?' asked Traiano in surprise.

'Borelli has disappeared,' said Rota. 'He was with a prostitute in the Grand Hotel. There was an altercation, she tried to cut off, well, she managed to cut off, his small toe. He got one of us to take him to a doctor, one of our own doctors, you understand. Then, when he got home, we tried to talk sense into him, but he has disappeared. He has gone to Italy.'

'Will you get him back?'

'Maybe, maybe not. We can do without him.'

'That was some girl who cut off his toe,' said Traiano with admiration. 'Borelli is a complete fool, as you say. And why is he running away? What is he so scared of? Aren't you scared?'

He looked at Rota, a solidly built man in late middle age. Rota stared back. The ravioli arrived. The question went unanswered. They began to eat.

'They say it is nasty losing a toe,' said Traiano between mouthfuls. 'It can make it very hard to balance, to walk, to run. Not nice for a man of Borelli's age. But he should not have been spending his money on prostitutes in the Grand Hotel. If it was his money. Which it almost certainly was not. It is nice of you to offer to cut me in. You made this offer with at least some hope of me taking it. A third of a million in a bad year does not sound at all bad. But you have forgotten one thing. When you talk to me, you are really talking to don Calogero di Rienzi. He and I…. well, I would not betray him for the sums you mention. Of course, you may like to increase the sum, but I would not bother. You seem to have underestimated the gravity of the situation. In a bad year you make a million. In other words, in a bad year for you, you rob don Calogero of a million. And you have been doing this, according to the records, for the last twenty-three years.'

Now he had the impression that Rota was frightened, or at least worried.

'I am not interested in future profits, and perhaps we can come to that in due course. I am interested in past losses and making them good. I was thinking that a mere four million might settle this. I asked for and got 400,000 from Mattarella. (By the way, these ravioli are superb.) I thought your fraud was on a similar level. But I see it is not. Forget four million. That is a sum you would all be able to pay after a few calls to your bank managers. Let us make it something more realistic. Let's make it twelve. Well might you grow pale, Rota. You think I have not checked and have not seen what you own, what you spend. Like all thieves, you became rich and made the mistake of not living modestly. The same with your colleagues. Twelve million from the six of you, that is two million each. By Easter.'

There was silence between them. He looked now at Tonino. The plates were cleared away, and onto the tablecloth Tonino placed an envelope which he took out of his jacket pocket.

'Look at it,' commanded Traiano.

Rota opened the envelope. It contained a series of photographs culled from social media profiles. His children, his friends' children.

'They all look so happy, don't they?' said Traiano. 'Let's keep them that way. You may have to tell them that in the future there is going to be less money for their pleasures, their university fees. Twelve million sounds a lot, but it isn't really, when you consider health and happiness and having all your toes.'

Rota put the pictures back in the envelope and placed the envelope on the tablecloth. Tonino placed it back in his breast pocket. The roast lamb now appeared. More of the gorgeous red wine was poured.

'Twelve million is a lot to raise by Easter,' began Rota. 'I mean banks, selling properties, mortgaging properties, selling investments. Six million by Easter would be possible, and maybe the rest by the summer?'

Traiano pretended to consider this.

'I will speak to don Calogero,' he said at last, 'And I am sure that he will be reasonable. But half now and the rest later…. I think it would be better to have nine now, and the other three later. Nine by Easter, and the rest to follow by the first day of July.'

'Borelli has gone and may never be back. Getting his share may be hard. Could we say eight by Easter and four to follow by the first day of July?'

Traiano considered. Then he nodded.

'OK. On Easter Sunday morning, when all the women are in church, the six of you, well five, minus Borelli, will bring the money to this young man' – he indicated Tonino- 'at a place he will appoint. It will be in cash, in notes of fifty, one hundred and two hundred. We do not like those high denomination notes. Try spending one of those in a café. He will be accompanied by some guys who will count it to make sure it is all there. That won't take long. He will bring a container truck with him, to make sure curious eyes notice nothing. Then you will go home, enjoy your Easter, and start collecting the rest. And then after that, we shall see.'

Rota seemed visibly to relax.

'I would like to meet don Calogero. If we are giving you, him, eight million, I want to know that it is really him we are giving it to.'

'Of course. He is often in the office. I will get it arranged. Just you, or your colleagues as well?'

'Just me, I think.'

'I am sure he will be delighted to meet you,' said Traiano. 'He has discussed you with me a great deal. He will be glad to put a face to the name. Frankly, he took some persuading to overlook your little misdemeanour. Well, I am sure the twelve million will help him get over his anger. Do you know where Borelli has gone?'

'No.'

'Do you expect him back?'

'I don't know.'

'Well, never mind. Wherever he has gone, we will find him. It is not so hard. You can press his widow for the share of the money that he owes. That is up to you. Twelve million, up to you how you raise it.'

A mood of depression had spread over Rota as he contemplated the ruin of his fortunes.

'Cheer up,' counselled Traiano. 'It is only twelve million. You will, by my calculations, have plenty left over. And remember, if it is any comfort, you only have yourself to blame. The accountants were bound to catch you sooner or later. This lamb really is good, isn't it?'

Rota did not stay for the dessert course. Traiano and Tonino were left to savour the zuppa inglese, a particular speciality of Mattarella, on their own.

'Well, boss?' asked Tonino, now judging that he was allowed to talk.

'I would have settled for four. He made a mistake there, offering to cut me in. He thought my greed would overcome my loyalty. Stupid man. But eight, eight is wonderful.'

'Not twelve?'

'Eight. The other four we will renounce. We will not be greedy. They are greedy and so they assume we would never do anything before the entire twelve were in. Now, Easter. I want you to steal one of those refrigerated trucks. Can you do that?'

'Sure, boss. But what about Borelli?'

'The one that got away? He gets away.'

'And Simone Rota?'

'You think his uncle will suspect that he was the traitor, and that it was not some clever accountant that rumbled him?'

'Yes, I am sure of it.'

'Me too. I am sure of it. I could almost read his thoughts as he went through the list of people who might have been speaking to us, and how he was contemplating throwing Simone off a balcony and making it look like suicide. Yes, I am sure that is what he wants to do. But he won't. First of all, we all know that revenge needs to wait. In a year or two, or even five or six, that's when he is telling himself, he will move against young Simone. But not now. To do so now would destabilise things. For the moment, he wants to act as if all were under control. He hopes it is. He really does. When Easter comes, that is when he gets his nasty surprise. By then, it will be too late. So, Simone survives. For the moment. In the meantime, as Easter approaches, Uncle Matteo will treat Simone as he always does, indeed, even more affectionately, to lull him into thinking he is safe. Incidentally, Simone is a bastard! Don't look surprised. Of course he is. He and his sister and his mother have survived because of the uncle; perhaps he was not overgenerous, but who else cared about them, who else helped them out? And how does Simone repay that generosity? He betrays the uncle to us for his own advantage. What a nasty man! He will do well for himself, or so he thinks. You watch. A schemer.'

'You do not like him, boss,' observed Tonino.

'I have not met him,' said Traiano. 'You have. Do you like him?'

Tonino shrugged.

'Well then. Whether we like him or not does not matter. We keep an eye on him. How is Roberto? I presume you used him to get those photographs of the children of Rota and the others? Did he ask you what it was for? No? Good. He is sensible. And by now he will have forgotten all about it.' He changed the subject. 'Aren't you getting married soon? Have you fixed a date? I was married by your age, and had a child. More than one child.'

He smiled at the memory.

'Boss,' he said, 'I am very grateful to you and to the signora Angela. My mother is thrilled. Well, it is what she has always wanted. We are getting the baby baptised in Catania, and don Giorgio is doing it; he has been very kind to us both; and we are getting married there in the summer or just after the summer. Quietly. Emma says she does not want any fuss, just something low key. I am more than happy with that. She likes a quiet life and getting on with her studies at the university.'

'Of course, you are gaining a very rich wife,' observed Traiano with a touch of acidity. 'Lucky you, and lucky for you that she was the sort of person whose tastes led her to you. Sorry, I am not trying to be offensive, but...'

'But with my background, it is a surprise anyone would want me, yes,' said Tonino. 'But signora Ceccina fell in with you, boss, and you were just a kid of fourteen in those days. Not much different from me, either, with a father in jail. I mean, you did well with her, and I am doing well with Emma, so we are equal.'

'So we are,' said Traiano, noticing a new spirit about Tonino. 'You take risks and you want to get on. I like that.'

'You are right, I do want to get on, boss. And as for the money, I have not discussed that with Emma. I know she has some sort of allowance, but I do not know how much. If Beppe has control over the family fortune, as he must do one day...'

'Must?'

'If Sandro is on the other side of the straits and not coming back, and not appearing in court and instructing lawyers in Palermo, the case will be dead,' he said. 'I am not sure how much money Emma has, and I do not want to ask, I do not want to look materialistic or greedy. But more important is the amount I have. That is a bit, but I am reckoning, come Easter, more.'

'You will, you will. Eight million. But it has to be divided up, don Calogero gets his share, I get mine, don Renzo will have to have some, and Muniddu, but you will have yours. Tax free. You can reckon on a substantial sum. Enough to pay for a quiet wedding. Don Calogero gets his usual third, of course.'

'Of course.'

'You have seen him in Catania or here?'

'In Catania. I go most weekends, so I am bound to see him. But now I am with Emma, I may go less often. Roberto goes too, every weekend, so he can take my washing home for me, if necessary.'

'I saw the boss here the other day. I also saw the girls, Isabella and Natalia. Have you seen them at all?'

'We bumped into them in Catania the other day, with signora Assunta.'

'They have become very grand, especially Isabella, who is also very grown up.'

He hoped his own daughter, little Maria Vittoria, would be different.

To Tonino's surprise, don Traiano then asked questions about his family in Catania, about his baby brother, about his mother and how she found having a child in her late thirties, and how his father was adjusting to freedom; how the Bonelli gallery was getting on.

'You know don Renzo is having another with Elena?' he said

'That is nice. Yes, I had heard. So has Emma.'

'They were hoping for it for some time. Everyone is very pleased. A second cousin for your and Emma's baby. You are a member of the family now.'

Tonino looked suitably humble, but it was true. He had, in a sense, outflanked Traiano himself, and he could see that Traiano knew this.

'Of course, don Antonio Santucci will be furious that someone from Catania has nabbed one of his daughters. Sandro as well, I assume. But anything that annoys Antonio will please Renzo. He's always liked you. As have I.'

'Thanks, boss,' said Tonino humbly. 'I never forget who my friends are.'

'How did don Calogero take it?'

'Not well. But he is paranoid about his daughters. That annoyed him more, that I had spoken to Isabella and Natalia without permission; he was perhaps quite pleased that me and Emma would annoy don Antonio.'

'And what annoys don Antonio perhaps pleases his wife Angela,' observed Traiano. 'What a family. As for our boss, paranoid, eh? He wants to protect his daughters. He will fail in the end, of course. They too will find the sort of young men who will annoy him. Indeed, my guess is that any young man will annoy him. And it will be soon. She is a forward girl for her age.'

'I think quite a few young men have annoyed him already, but he hasn't realised it, yet.'

'You mean…..? Oh dear. Poor Calogero. You know this, because…?'

'One can just tell, boss. Intuition.'

'Ah, male intuition.' He considered. 'I can imagine what her father must think, or would think, if he knew. I wonder what her stepmother thinks and what she knows.'

Traiano was thoughtful.

'They have enough things to worry about as it is,' said Traiano. 'I know about Catarina. Were you going to tell me about that?'

'If you know, boss, I do not need to tell you. Besides, I knew that you would know sooner or later, because that man Andreazza organised part of it, as did Costantino, so there were lots of people in on the secret, so I was waiting for you to ask. Costantino would never talk, neither would I, but Andreazza is another matter.'

'Well, I don't need to ask you. But there is one thing I would like to know. Do you take packages of money to her?'

'No, just thin envelopes, containing messages. Not cash.'

There was silence. They both knew what this meant. Even if she were living under an assumed name and receiving money into her bank account, presumably through the Confraternity, or some other way, then that money was traceable, with difficulty, but traceable all the same. Someone would spot it: maybe Elena, or Assunta, or even Anna Maria Tancredi herself. If the first two, they would surely pass it on. It had been secret, up to now, but would not be secret forever. Maybe Anna Maria already knew; maybe that was why she was turning a blind eye or had even facilitated Isabella's precocious sex life, out of revenge.

Perhaps, reflected Traiano, Anna Maria had known about Catarina for a very long time, for he had seen that Calogero's mother and sisters had somehow guessed, and that soon perhaps everyone would know, and there would be a resulting powershift in the Purgatory quarter. The men would not care too much, except one man, Alfio, in far off Africa, who would be pleased to be known not just as the boss's brother-in-law but the cousin of his mistress. But the women would take against, not don Calogero - that was something they could not do - but against his behaviour. The men, the boys, would be grudgingly admiring. As far as they were concerned, the fact that their boss could sleep with whoever he pleased was part of his power, his glamour, his importance. He was simply doing what they wanted to do, and they, for the most part, could not. He was doing what they dreamed of doing. A man with so many children, so many women… It was all they ever talked about, money and sex, and the boss had both in huge quantities. They all basked in the reflected glory of don Calogero di Rienzi.

'Would you like to go back to Catania one day?' he now asked.

'Perhaps. Emma liked it a lot. It all depends on whether we want to be near her mother or mine.'

'They are making a fortune selling those pills. I forget who is in charge of that nowadays. But you were the one who started it. Let's hope they do not muck it up, as it got mucked up here.'

In Calabria, lunch too was proving to be delicious. Oddly, neither Angela nor her daughter had been to Reggio, and it was a nice place too, with lovely views across the straits, with modern straight and clean streets and an efficient one-way system, and excellent food, with good strong flavours, which she liked. It took her mind off her eldest son, sitting opposite her, and her daughter Marina, sitting next to him.

At first, she had been perplexed, dismayed and upset by what Marina had told her about receiving the anguished phone call and driving to Reggio as soon as she could, with as many of her brother's clothes as she could fit into two suitcases, to find him checked into a hotel in just his pyjamas and dressing gown. The immediate crisis thus resolved, Marina had returned to Sicily; now she had returned with her mother and with the rest of the clothes, all of them, as Sandro had insisted.

Marina was angry at the way Sandro had been treated. Sandro too was angry at the way he had been treated, very angry. Their anger was directed at the Romanian and their cousin Renzo, who had abducted Sandro and dumped him on this side of the straits. And their anger was directed at their brother Beppe, who spent so much time with Renzo and the Romanian, and who had had to be behind what had happened to Sandro. All because of the court case. He had stolen their inheritance.

Angela sighed as she ate her beef cooked in bergamot juice. As her two children railed against 'these people' they forgot that they too were these people.

'This is a family quarrel,' she said.

'Well, I did not start it,' said her son.

'No. You did not. It started before you were born. It started, I think, when my brother, your Uncle Carlo, decided that he did not like my husband, his cousin Antonio, and that started on my wedding day or soon afterwards. I am not sure why Carlo did not like Antonio. They had known each other since childhood, but perhaps Carlo decided that Antonio was no good purely because he had the desire to marry me. Carlo did not hide it, and your father, waiting over twenty years, decided he would take his revenge for all the petty slights. And that revenge was the massacre of Favignana. But then he had to contend with Renzo, of whom few thought much. He miscalculated there, not because Renzo is very able, but because he was to arm himself with friends. You see, my dear,' she continued, looking sadly at her son, 'Renzo and the one you call the Romanian could have killed you. But they did not. They had permission to do what they did, but not to kill you. But next time, they will, and no one will be able to help you. Has it occurred to you why you are still alive? Has it not occurred to you that I have protected you, me and perhaps Uncle Domenico?'

'These people....' began Renzo.

'These people are your people, our people. You were born into it; on both sides, you are a Santucci. You take the advantages and you need to play by the rules too.'

Sandro looked too furious to speak.

'I can't believe you take their side, Mama,' said Marina.

'I am being realistic,' she said. 'This is the way it is. We take the money, don't we?'

'Mama,' said Sandro. 'Give me the money that is due to me, and I will go, and they will never see me again. Indeed, you will never see me again.'

'I will never see you again?' she asked.

'You chose Beppe over me, and you let Emma get together with that awful boy from Catania. Actions have consequences.'

'They do,' she agreed, sadly.

'One day they will come for you or those most dear to you, and I shall be far away,' said Sandro.

It was now necessary for them to plan to the endgame with Matteo Rota and his confreres. For this, he would use Muniddu and Tonino, and somehow make Renzo feel he was included, though not taking an active part. They would have to meet and plan. An opportunity arose, which could be exploited: the possibility of another trip, this time to Naples. Beppe wanted to go to the San Paolo stadium to see Naples play Juventus, which was scheduled for Sunday 30th March. He had bought two tickets, one for himself and one for Riccardo, Muniddu's son. The idea was that the boys, being teenagers, were old enough to go on their own, but Renzo had caught something of their interest, and decided he would go too, and found a ticket. Then Traiano announced he would like to go to Naples, because he had never been, and they could make a weekend of it, and it would be a shame not to include Tonino, or for that matter Muniddu. There were no more tickets available, which was no surprise, as Juventus were a great team, but that did not matter, as there were plenty of other things to do in Naples.

The obvious way to go was to fly, which took no time at all; the train was long and tedious, and driving equally so. The flight from Palermo was very short, just an hour, and they arrived on the Friday evening. There were six of them, which meant three double rooms at one of the nicest hotels facing the sea opposite the island of Santa Lucia. The two teenagers usually shared one room, Traiano and Renzo would have shared another as they always did whenever Traiano went abroad with Renzo for one of his marathons, leaving Tonino and Muniddu to share the third. But it didn't quite work out like that as Beppe announced that he wanted to share with Traiano, and Riccardo wanted to share with his father; which left Renzo to share with Tonino. This slightly annoyed Traiano, as it meant the three plotters were all in separate rooms.

From Tonino's point of view, the main drawback of the trip was that none of them could drink, given don Renzo's strict teetotalism; because he did not drink, there was an understanding that no one could drink in his presence, which was a shame. Don Traiano did not drink very much anyway, and neither did the two teenagers, so when they went out to dinner after their arrival in Naples on Friday night, they all drank mineral water, while a cigarette was, of course, completely out of the question. But the dinner was very good, almost as good as Sicily, and they finished the evening at the famous café across the square from the royal palace.

When they returned to the hotel, they sat in the lobby for a while, and then the two teenagers rose to go to bed, kissing the cheeks of each of the adults in turn. Muniddu cautioned his son to brush his teeth, and Traiano did the same for Beppe. After a time, Renzo yawned and announced he would go to bed, and left them. The three survivors looked at each other. Now they were alone, they could talk about the Rota job. There was also the eight million to be discussed. Renzo would be playing no direct part, neither would Calogero, and both would have to be cut in, but eight million was a lot, and there would be enough to go round, Traiano was sure, even after additional expenses. He could sense the way that Tonino wanted a drink, and he called over a waiter, and ordered a bottle of wine. There was a little discussion as Tonino wanted to know what was best, and eventually a bottle of Falanghina arrived, a wine of which Traiano had heard, but of which Tonino seemed to know a great deal. As he took his first sip, he was appreciative. Much better than what the waiter had first suggested, sparkling stuff from the Trentino, which was no better than OK, he said, and bound to be overpriced.

'When you get upstairs, if he is still awake, Renzo will want to talk about Gino,' said Traiano. 'If he does, well, I am sure you will be sympathetic. It was recently the second anniversary. Poor Gino. But Renzo really took it badly, he still does. I mean, we all liked Gino, didn't we, but Renzo, well, to him Gino was really special. You know what these friendships can be like.'

The other two nodded. They did know. One had to be so silent, so discreet, that everyone needed at least one friend as a safety valve. Renzo had had Gino, now he had Traiano; perhaps he would have his cousin-in-law to be; Traiano should have had Corrado, when he saw him, which was hardly ever; Tonino had Roberto, rather unusually, someone on the outside.

'Are those bastards asking questions about the death?' asked Muniddu, meaning the police.

'No,' said Traiano. 'They asked, but no one saw anything, no one at all. They came up against a blank wall of silence. But… Renzo knows, and I know, that it was not an accident. As for the person responsible, Renzo wants him dead.'

He spoke not much above a whisper. He had not mentioned a name, but they knew whom he meant. Alfio. Who else? The man who had murdered his best friend for the boss's convenience.

'One day…' said Traiano. 'That is what I tell him. One day. Same with Antonio Santucci. Of course, we got rid of his son. Well, he was last heard of in Reggio, though he's now demanding a payoff, from what I hear, a shedload of money for the pleasure of never seeing him again. He wants a couple of million, but he will settle for less, I am sure.'

'Are we going to let him live?' asked Tonino quietly.

'Speak to Renzo about that. I think the answer, from his point of view, is no.'

Tonino nodded, and took another delightful sip of the wine. Traiano wondered when the time would come, if ever, when they would have killed all the people who needed to be killed. Perhaps when Renzo was avenged on all those who had profited from his father's death. But by that time, others would have emerged. It was never ending.

'The moment Sandro Santucci puts his nose over the straits of Messina, it will be shot off,' said Traiano. 'I think that is the idea. And if it gets shot off, I am not sure who will be sorry. And I can think of many who would be delighted. Some people are too stupid to stay alive. He may well be one of them.'

'Sandro was always a spoilt kid,' said Muniddu. 'Beppe was the nice one. So was Emma,' he added, nodding to Tonino. 'Beppe and Emma had time for us, the others, not so much. Has Beppe said anything about Sandro?'

They both shook their heads.

'I don't think he has realised anything has happened. I have never heard him talk even about the court case. It will be a relief to Angela when that all goes away,' said Traiano.

'I don't think they should give him a cent,' said Tonino, of Sandro. 'I find it strange that Beppe never talks about it. It is as if he does not care; but I think he does. I mean, he must. All that money. Sandro was never nice to him, never said a nice thing about him, ever.'

As in every family, there were problems, there were tensions, there were discontents, Traiano reflected.

'You don't like poor Sandro,' he observed. 'Oh well, he does not have many or indeed any friends. He's doomed. He has doomed himself. Arrogant little fool! But we all have people we do not like. Some people overreach themselves, don't they? Instead of being grateful for getting away with a minor injury, Sandro is now demanding cash. Indeed, he does not deserve a cent. The people we dislike make things easier for us by being so dislikeable. Whatever Sandro did to annoy you, I understand your disdain for him. Look, maybe you do not need him to come back home to shoot him. Tempting him back would be very tedious. Maybe you could go over to Reggio and pop him there. No one would care; no one would notice. I could guarantee that. But let us leave it for now until we have settled with Rota and his gang. That is the more urgent tidying up. But listen, if I give you Sandro, and square it with anyone who might be annoyed, you owe me a favour later on.'

'Of course, boss. Would that favour have something to do with Alfio?'

Traiano nodded.

'Alfio has pushed himself far forward enough. He married the boss's sister-in-law, and he killed his best friend so the boss could take his wife. My feeling is that Alfio would never have done that, but she made him do it. She was always the clever, ambitious one. First, she seduced Rosario, then she hooked the boss, and has given him another child; she will not be content until she has married him. Living quietly in Enna with the children is not her style. She wants it all, I bet.'

'But he is already married,' said Muniddu. 'I mean, he was married when he met his present wife; but what I mean is that he needs dottoressa Tancredi. He needs a banker. We all do. He cannot afford to alienate her. If he does, he suffers, but so do we. And besides, as she must realise, this woman Catarina, that her man, the boss, has a first-class family, and he now has a second-class family, consisting of her and her children. Those children will grow up to manage the pizzeria, whereas Renato and the other two, the legitimate sons, they will be important people. This Catarina will see that, and that she cannot compete; maybe she will get resentful, but she will also be realistic. She will see what advantages she can gain. She will squeeze him for as much money as she can. But she will not get so resentful as to drive him away or to exasperate him entirely. She will not want to be something she cannot be, namely his wife; she will be content with what she has. The other thing is that Anna Maria, even when she finds out - and she may well have done already: she will accept it for what it is: something that does not threaten her position. I know her. I worked for her. You remember when they used to spend the weekends together at Donnafugata, that summer? She was so beautiful, and him, well, he is a beautiful man. Always so smartly dressed, the perfect shoes, the perfect suit, the ties, the shirts, the cufflinks. But when he stood by that pool just as God made him, showing himself off to the world, my goodness. She was infatuated with all that; but she had been infatuated before, the nephew Perraino, if you remember. She is probably bored with him by now and thinks, if someone else wants him, why not? She knows just how vain he is, and the fact that he has this weakness, that does not bother her, rather it pleases her.'

'I am worried about Catarina's ambition, all the same,' said Traiano. 'After all, she has tasted power, hasn't she, and those who taste power want more. I mean, she will want to advance herself and her – their - children. And there is Alfio behind her. If she marries the boss, Alfio becomes more powerful. But what does Anna Maria think? Does she know? I imagine she does…. In fact, I am sure she does. She is not stupid. Besides which the Black Widow Spider would have made sure she found out by now. But Anna Maria is too clever to give anything away. We all need Anna Maria, as you say, and he needs her more than any of us.'

'And she needs us to make the cash for her to launder,' said Tonino. 'The banker is worth nothing if there is nothing to bank. But if Catarina is getting too ambitious then if something happened to Alfio, that would sort her out, make her think twice, clip her wings.'

'In Africa, they feed them to the crocodiles, don't they? Or so I have heard,' said Muniddu.

'You may have heard correctly,' said Tonino.

But that was something for the future.

As midnight came, and then went, they gradually drifted off to their rooms, in various states of intoxication. Tonino knew that in being selected to share a room with don Renzo, he had been marked out for special favour. He went up, tapped gently at the door, and entered, to find the boss already in bed, asleep. As quietly as possible, so as not to disturb the boss, he got undressed and into bed. Very soon he was asleep too.

Muniddu found Riccardo asleep as well; it was only Traiano who found Beppe awake.

'Hi,' said Beppe, who had been reading a book, looking up as he came in. 'You were a long time.'

'You should have gone to sleep.'

'I wanted to wait for you.'

Traiano went to brush his teeth in the adjoining bathroom, and then got ready for bed. He leant over and kissed the boy's cheek, as expected, before getting into his own bed. He looked at the book. It was a history of Italy, recommended by Rosalia. Beppe was wearing boyish pyjamas, which were decorated with a pattern of cartoon characters.

'Where did you get those pyjamas?'

'I have had them for years.'

'And they still fit?'

'They were big when they were bought for me.'

'Don Calogero asked me a strange question. He asked when you were going to grow up.'

'Tell him 14th August 2016. That is when I will be eighteen.'

'I don't think he meant it like that.'

'He is a funny man,' said Beppe. 'Do you like him?'

'I have known him a long time,' said Traiano, knowing that this was not an answer. 'Are there things you are not telling me, Beppe?'

'I would never deceive you. Ask me anything. I tell you everything. But there is not much to tell, you know.'

'What about Sandro?'

'He has gone. He has gone to Italy. He says he is not coming back. He does not like Tonino anymore, which is strange because he once liked him. He has not been pleasant to my poor mother, or to Emma, or to Papà. It is best he goes. He has caused a lot of trouble. I have nothing against him, far from it, even if he was never really kind to me. I hope he never comes back. It would be better that way. Why are you concerned about Sandro?'

'I am not. I was only worried that you might be worried.'

'I am not. Sandro does not worry me. Neither does Papà. They made their choices, and they need to look after themselves. Poor Sandro, no one likes him, not even me anymore. I gather he wants a lot of money just to go away. That must upset my mother. Are *you* telling me everything?'

'I have the cares of the world on my shoulders. I don't want to burden you. You know, worries about the children, about the wider family, about you.'

'Me?'

'You worry about those you love,' said Traiano.

'Of course. So do I,' said Beppe.

Breakfast was very good. The cornetti were superb, made that very morning. The two boys came down and kissed the four adults on their cheeks, went and helped themselves to food, and joined them. It was all very relaxed. Everyone was now kissing everyone else, and Traiano had made a point of kissing Tonino, which he knew pleased him; moreover, everyone was now calling everyone else by their Christian name, without the honorific 'don' in the cases of Traiano and Renzo. Moreover, the polite form of address had been dropped between them all, and the vocatives 'sir' and 'boss' as well. The atmosphere had become family-like. After they had drunk the last of their coffee, it was time to go upstairs and ring their wives, in the case of Muniddu and Traiano, and his girlfriend, in the case of Tonino. Then it was time to take taxis and go to the Archaeological Museum.

One of the things that Traiano regretted was that he had never been educated. He didn't mean that he had never gone to school, for one could not regret that. Instead of being enslaved in a classroom, he had had the freedom of the streets. Moreover, thanks to the freedom of the streets, he had made lots of money as a teenager and was now, in his early twenties, a rich man, all by his own efforts. One could not regret being a thief, a trickster, an extortionist or a killer, as it had made him what he was, and he was glad to be what he was. Moreover, in the very earliest months of adulthood, he had met his wife, fathered his first child, experienced love in its most complete form. How could one regret that? How could one want to be anything different? But he wished he knew more about the world, not about science and technology, which bored him, but about history and art and geography. He had tried his best to educate himself on these matters, and to some extent succeeded. It had been his idea to come to the museum, and to see the treasures of Pompeii, and to see the Farnese marbles on the ground floor.

On entry, after the chaotic queue for the tickets, they made their way to see the Farnese Bull, which he knew was the largest classical sculptural group extant, and close by, the Farnese

Hercules. These and the rest of the marbles were certainly impressive, and upstairs they encountered a series of rather dull rooms which contained the wall paintings from Pompeii and Herculaneum which were far less rewarding. Traiano felt rather guilty at the way these pictures failed to move him, and the way they were displayed bored him. He was glad to see that he was not alone. Renzo, who was educated, looked equally bored. Muniddu and Tonino looked mystified by the whole experience. Only the two boys seemed fascinated by the whole thing, exclaiming between themselves over the antiquity of the paintings and how, one sunny October day, all this ancient life had come to a sudden end, under a cloud of ash and poison gas, or a tide of boiling mud, or a pyroclastic surge.

'Poor things, poor things,' said Riccardo sympathetically, to himself more than to anyone else.

'It was quick,' remarked Beppe. 'They would not have felt a thing. In Herculaneum, their brains boiled and exploded. They went out like lights. Not a bad way to go.'

'What do you know about death?' asked Renzo curiously.

'Only what everyone knows. Quick is better than slow.'

Renzo laughed.

'You should not think about such things,' said Traiano.

The Secret Cabinet was closed, and there was only all the household rubbish that had been buried by the eruption to be examined. Then, leaving the museum, they took two taxis and ordered the drivers to take them to Herculaneum. There they had lunch, and Traiano was pleased to see that Beppe made a particular effort to sit next to him. The boys spoke of the museum, of the excavations to come, and of the football match the following night. Juventus, in their opinion, was a great team, and as a result, Naples would struggle to beat them even at home; but by how much? And who would score? Beppe was of the opinion that Naples would be crushed. But the most exciting thing, thought Riccardo, would be to see who would score for Juventus. They went through their favourite players: Lichsteiner, Bonucci and Vidal were mentioned with glowing praise. Renzo, who listened to this attentively, hinted at some sort of a surprise, but would say no more. He was pensive, Traiano could see.

Then they entered the excavations. Traiano had chosen these because he had been told they were more interesting than those of Pompeii, and much smaller and less crowded as well, and walking around excavations was tiring, everyone knew. They had the place more or less to themselves, which was pleasant. Gradually, the party strung out. Beppe went ahead with Riccardo, Muniddu was with Tonino, and Traiano hung back with Renzo.

'You're sad,' he said. 'I know you are. I can tell. Well, it is natural, it has only been two years.'

'I never had a friend like him before, and then they took him away,' said Renzo. 'Why won't you let me get my revenge?'

'It is purely a question of timing,' said Traiano. 'Just be patient and trust me. One day, maybe quite soon, we will be able to shed all the blood we want to. On that day, Gino will be truly avenged. One of the pieces has fallen into place. That boy, your cousin, Sandro, you never liked him, did you? I thought not. So, if something were to happen to him…'

'I'd be delighted,' said Renzo.

'It would be good to have him out of the way, I mean definitively out of the way. The only thing is not to upset your Aunt Angela, or Beppe. Beppe is a sweet lovely kid, and my children adore him, and so do I. But he would benefit if Sandro were out of the way. It would be doing him a great favour. Even Angela would be better off, the way he is dunning her for cash, poor woman. The thing is that when Beppe is twenty-one, he will then control what he has inherited from don Lorenzo. I would not be surprised if he inherits from don Domenico as well. But he is amenable, and that is what counts. He will do as you say and I say, and I do what you say too. Things are looking up. Then there is Antonio, another person to be tidied away, and then you are the lord of all.'

'Then there is Calogero,' said Renzo.

'Yes, there is always Calogero. Look, trust me. Keep Beppe close to you. Keep Tonino close to you. Keep Muniddu close. Beppe likes both of them. They bind him to us, and through that child we control everything.'

'But he won't be a child forever,' said Renzo.

'He is sixteen, but he has shown no sign of growing up so far. It was Calogero who pointed that out to me. He is tall for his age, and he is physically advanced but… he has not cottoned on to the adult way of doing things. No sexual interests at all. Oh, they have tried to interest him in Calogero's daughters, but he has never shown the slightest interest in them. But he cannot stay a bachelor all his life, can he? We must interest him in Muniddu's daughter. If we encourage that, Muniddu would be thrilled, I am sure.'

'You think of everything,' said Renzo.

'I try to.'

They were standing in one of the ruined houses – well, not so ruined – they stood in the hallway, viewing the impluvium and the hole on the roof that caught the rainwater; one wondered whether this was in fact an intact Roman house, or had been rebuilt by the industrious Duce at some point in the 1930's. But all that history faded into insignificance against what they had to plan here. The two boys were out of earshot. The four men gathered around the impluvium.

Traiano spoke: 'That is a nice boy you have got there, Muniddu, a real credit to you. You have brought him up well. It is always good to see. And he is studious, isn't he?'

'Very,' said Muniddu. 'We never have to encourage him to work hard. At his books every evening. No distractions. He wants to be a doctor, and why shouldn't he be?'

'He knows about this business of ours? I mean, his two uncles, his grandfather, you…'

'He knows his uncles are away, one cannot hide that, but we have protected him. He knows that I work for the Santucci business and he reads the newspapers and he watches the television, but he never asks questions, so…'

'You know what I think? He is perfect son-in-law material. A doctor, educated, respectable, biddable. Likes sport, and beautiful like his sister. Has he ever done anything bad, have you ever had to beat him?'

'Not much,' said Muniddu. 'He is really good. My father beat me, but then he had to stop, I mean, he went to Ucciardone. But Riccardo is a little saint.'

'That is the old-fashioned way, using a stick on your son. My father was safely locked up in Bucharest, but God sent me another to do that duty. If you displeased don Calogero, you got the belt. You still do. He always tried to make me cry. He hasn't succeeded since I was about eleven. But it is his way of expressing his ownership over his adopted children such as me and Renzo. If he did not beat you, it meant he did not love you. I didn't mind.'

'You didn't mind?' asked Tonino.

'Why should I?' answered Traiano. 'What do you think of young Riccardo?' he asked the others.

'Nice boy. Clever. Lively, very sweet and handsome,' said Renzo.

'Great guy,' said Tonino. 'And I know him well.'

'Perfect son-in-law material. Good brother-in-law material as well,' said Traiano with meaning.

There was silence. Everyone knew what he meant. Riccardo should be the brother-in-law of Beppe, which meant Beppe marrying Rosalia. Everyone was reflective, Muniddu especially.

'Beppe is a good boy, but he clearly needs a bit of encouragement,' said Traiano. 'And we need to encourage him in the right direction. In Rosalia's direction. She is the right age and she is a good girl, isn't she?'

Muniddu nodded. He had thought of little else, it seemed to him now, for the last two years.

'I mean, I met my wife when I was very young, much younger. We had our first child when we were fifteen, but I was pretty wild, I suppose. Rosalia and Beppe, that would be very different. She is going to go to university as well, isn't she? He is a shy boy in that regard, but she would be perfect for him. I mean, he is going to university too.'

'What about don Calogero's daughters? The eldest one, Isabella?' asked Muniddu.

'A nice young lady, I am sure, but a little too sophisticated for my taste, and for Beppe's too, I bet, and not, I hear, though please keep this quiet, all she should be. Beppe is a throwback. If you remember the founders of the Santucci family, two lemon growers just outside Palermo. Tough and strong men who used their shotguns to good effect. Beppe would not like to use a shotgun, I am sure of that, but he would like to grow lemons. He will be so rich; he will be able to do so to his heart's content. Nice. Us, not so lucky. We get our hands dirty so that his can stay clean. But we provide him with everything he needs, and he will be grateful, and the enterprise will continue. Yes, I know, his immediate family do not inspire confidence. Sandro, my God, his father Antonio, but Beppe will not be like that.'

'What he says is true,' said Renzo.

'What do you think?' asked Traiano, looking at Tonino.

Tonino nodded vigorously.

'Rosalia would be a credit to any family,' he said.

'I would be grateful for any encouragement you can give,' said Muniddu.

The Sunday passed agreeably. In the morning, after breakfast in the hotel, they went to Mass at Santa Chiara. The three teenagers went into the body of the Church and followed the Mass attentively, even the tedious sermon: Beppe and Riccardo went to Holy Communion. The three men, Renzo, Traiano and Muniddu, stayed at the back, admiring the architecture, looking at the people, occasionally thinking of God. Lunch followed, and then an exploration of Spaccanapoli. In the evening, they parted, the two younger boys and Renzo to go to the San Paolo stadium to see Naples play Juventus, the remaining three to a pizzeria on the Vomero, chosen at random, which would be noisy and discreet, they were sure. The wine arrived, another bottle of very nice Falanghina. Muniddu and Tonino drank that, while Traiano, who did not like alcohol overmuch, contented himself with mineral water.

'We will be back home tomorrow,' he said wistfully, thinking of his wife, thinking of their very early morning flight. 'Are you looking forward to being married?'

'Very much,' said Tonino. 'It is nice to be stable. And as soon as we are married, it will be time to have another child.'

'What is your daughter called?' asked Traiano.

'Olivia. It sounds foreign, but she was a saint, and one from Palermo.'

'Oh, that is nice,' said Traiano. 'What are the best names for boys in Palermo?'

'Luca?' hazarded Muniddu. 'It sounds Roman but I like it.'

'I like it too. But it depends on Emma, and it depends on it being a boy,' said Tonino.

'You have seen the other family, haven't you?' asked Traiano, suddenly changing the subject.

Tonino nodded. He knew to what he referred. He had seen them. He described them. The little boy who was so obviously the late Rosario's son, not Gino's; and the second boy, called Giovanni, already had the look of don Calogero. The three of them considered these 'outside' children; don Carlo had had several, and they all depended on the family in one way or another. These children would be the same one day perhaps. But what would Anna Maria Tancredi think, when she knew? What did she think if she already knew?

But these were melancholy thoughts. The pizza was ordered; the pizza arrived, and then they began to go over the plans for Easter. The stealing of the refrigerated truck; where it would be parked, the checking of the place for cameras, where the truck would be driven, and finally how it would be disposed of. Only the three of them were to know these details, which made a leak impossible. It was, they all marvelled, the perfect crime.

The two boys came back with Renzo at almost two in the morning. They had been taken to the VIP section of the San Paolo after the match was over, where the home team were celebrating their two-nil victory, for the mighty Juventus had not lived up to expectations. Renzo had arranged this somehow, and there the boys and Renzo had met various players and men in suits. These had greeted Renzo warmly, once they realised who Renzo was, having had his details whispered in their ears by men standing behind them; they made a point of kissing Renzo's cheek. They had listened to Beppe and Riccardo's names, as if they knew they ought to remember them. Both boys were kissed on their cheeks, welcomed to Naples, and asked what they had thought of the match, what they thought of Naples, and what their prognostications were for the next week season. They had listened carefully to what Beppe had to say, and to what Riccardo had to say, and wagged their fingers at them in comic rebuke when they both maintained that Juventus would get its revenge.

The next morning, the boys were not left to sleep late after their excitement of the previous night. But while they dozed in the departure lounge, the four adults discussed business. Because of the obsession, perhaps justified, with electronic surveillance, the business was discussed in low voices, hopefully drowned by the ambient noise of the airport.

In Donnafugata, at the same time, early on Monday morning, they were preparing to drive to Catania, and the sleepy children were waiting in the two cars. The house had been tense with adult disagreement all weekend, and the young ones sensed it. But now, as they were planning to leave, as the children waited for the adults, the tensions had exploded between Calogero and his wife Anna Maria.

In the drawing room, Calogero stood in front of the huge fireplace and said coldly to his wife:

'You must not listen to everything people say. You need to keep calm and prevent people messing with your mind.'

'I need to keep calm?' she asked. 'I am not the one who has let my passions run away with me. I might have done once, but no more. When I met you, for example. They stole your mother's comb.'

'Who did?'

'The magistrates, or people working for them, the ones who have been after you forever. They took her comb, and they took the combs of the children in Enna - your children. And they looked at the DNA and they worked out that those two children are her grandchildren. So don't even try to lie about it.'

'Yes,' he said calmly. 'Well done to them. The eldest child is her grandson. Tino was never Gino's son; he was Rosario's. So, what have they proven? Something that I already knew.'

'Something that you never told me; something that you felt that you could hide from me. The first child may be his, but the second? The second is yours. And the proof of it is that you have been paying her.'

'She is the mother of my brother's son. Of course, I look after her. As for her other child, I deny it. They must have got the wrong comb, or the children both use the same comb.'

'You thought you could hide them away. You failed.'

He had thought this, and certainly he had failed. He was not sure how. Who had spoken? Had Alfio? Or Tonino? Had Tonino spoken to signora Grassi, who had passed it on to his own his mother? He could not have been so foolish. Or was it that awful man Andreazza? Or was it that someone from Catania had seen her there, in Enna, and seen the children, seen the resemblances, which were so obvious, and then told someone who had told the magistrates? Whichever way, this was an emergency. Had they been following him and seen him go to Enna, seen him spend time there, and made the obvious deduction?

'Look, get this into your head,' he said rudely. 'The magistrates want to ruin us. Not me, not you, us, our partnership. Our ability to make money. Money. Please remember that. Money is what counts. It is the only thing that counts in the end. You are a banker. You know that. Everything else is icing on the cake. Remember, I am a tough from the slums of Catania. I wear a suit and nice shoes, but I am a tough and nothing more. Deep down you know that, and you like it. You are in this with me, because you like this.' He gestured to his trousers. 'Just as you liked it with that cretin Perraino. So please do not get moral with me. Put Catarina and her children out of your mind. Let us concentrate on our children, my daughters, my son Renato, our sons Sebastiano and Romano. For God's sake do not wreck things for them. Or for yourself or for me. And may I remind you that you have no right to be moral with me in the first place. I am very angry with what you have done for Isabella. She is thirteen, for God's sake.'

'I acted because I did not want her to get pregnant. Yes, she is young, yes, she needs protecting from her own foolishness.'

'You should have kept a better eye on her.'

'You should,' she shot back. 'But you were spending too much time in Enna.'

'Enna is none of your business,' he said. 'The children, they are your business, and you failed. How many boys has my daughter been with?'

'Ask her!'

'I will, don't you worry.'

'You can't. Have some… dignity.'

'She is my daughter. I can ask her what I like. And if she won't answer, I will ask Natalia. She is the one who told me in the first place, after all, that Isabella was… You have driven a wedge between me and my own daughter.'

'Your daughter grew up, that is all.'

'Don't you see how this makes me look?'

'It is all about you, isn't it?' she said. 'Does it not occur to you that she has acted the way she has because of you? Because you have made her feel so important? Does it occur to you that boys may have found her attractive and wanted to sleep with her because of who you are, to make you look ridiculous? Are you going to give them the satisfaction of proving their point?'

He ignored this.

'Each snivelling teenage popinjay I find out about, I am going to emasculate, do you understand? They may have enjoyed my daughter, but they will never enjoy anyone else again. And if there is anyone who works for me who has done this, I will shoot him dead in the square in front of the Church of the Holy Souls in Purgatory and send him straight to hell. Oh, you think I cannot do that, do you?'

'Actually,' she replied with infuriating calm, 'I think you can do that. You can shoot a teenager dead in the square and no one would ever report you to the police or even admit that they had seen you do it. You have impunity. You can do what you like, but whether that is a wise use of your power, I am not sure. No one doubts that you are a king, my dear, but you have to govern wisely, you have to exercise power moderately. Consider what you are doing and what you are saying. Do you honestly want to shoot your daughter's paramour? How would she react?'

'Has she told you who it is?' he asked.

'No,' she said, truthfully.

He believed her. He also knew she was right. He had to react to this in a deliberate and calm way. Otherwise, he would make a mistake. He considered.

'Look,' he said. 'Let us carry on as normal. I will work out what to do, but not in the heat of the moment. The children are waiting for us. We need to get back to Catania. I promise you; I will work out some compromise that will be to your satisfaction.'

She felt, not that she had won, but that she soon would, and that he was prepared to climb down gracefully. She walked out to her car, grateful to get out of the house, glad to get away from him. As they drove off, the three little boys in the back of her car seemed the same as usual, but the two girls, who were with their father, were both very silent. Isabella was clearly furious, and the object of her anger was Natalia, who had sneaked to her father and broken confidences. Natalia had claimed that she had had no idea that her father had not known, but Isabella did not believe this. Natalia, she was sure, had acted out of jealousy. In fact, it was simpler than that: Natalia had done what she had done because she wanted revenge. She believed, mistakenly, that her sister had enjoyed the man whom she, Natalia, loved. His name was Tonino Grassi.

It was still very early in the morning when their plane landed at Palermo airport. Muniddu drove the two teenagers away at once, to get them to their respective schools without missing more than the first lesson of the day. Renzo got into his expensive car, offering Traiano a lift, which he declined, saying he would go back with Tonino, on his bike.

'So we are agreed then,' said Traiano, as they stood in the middle of the car park, where they could not be overheard. 'Sandro Santucci is doomed. Whatever he did to insult you must have been bad. And Alfio, he too?'

'Yes.'

'There is no urgency. It is not like coffee that has to be savoured hot. And there is quite a bit of preparatory work to be done. You can leave that to me, and I will keep you informed.' Traiano paused. 'Glad to be back?' he asked.

'Yes, boss.'

'Did you miss the baby?'

'Yes, boss, she is sweet.'

'Well,' said Traiano, thinking of his own children and how much he missed them. 'And Emma?' he asked.

'Of course, boss. She is really nice, you know, and I am grateful to you and her mother and Beppe for settling the whole thing. It's just what I wanted, you know….'

Traiano nodded. Then they got onto the motorcycle and went back to Palermo through the heavy morning traffic.

The two discontented daughters were at school; the three sons were happily engaged, and his wife was at her computer in the room she used for her study when she was at Catania, working from home, sending messages, studying the markets, and making phone calls to her subordinates in Palermo, speaking to various clients all over Sicily, as well as various contacts all over the world. As for Calogero, he could not settle. He tried to sit in his study, he tried to walk on the roof terrace, he even went down to the bar in the square to have a cup of coffee, but wherever he went, he took with him a mixture of boiling rage and a sense of defeat.

Oh, how he had loved having Catarina. He remembered the very first time, having her standing up against her bedroom door while Alfio had stood guard at the entrance of the flat, the day after the death of Gino. He remembered that encounter, short, exhilarating, but extremely sweet. And all the other encounters that had followed in Enna, where she had met him, naked at the door of her flat, the child or children being looked after by someone, and he had enjoyed her there and then, against the front door, without preliminaries, his trousers round his ankles. He sighed at the memory. She knew what he liked. And he reflected. She had known too well, and she had manipulated him accordingly. He liked her, he feared her intelligence and her ambition, and he loved the children, but…. He had not wanted this to be known. He felt that now it was known, he had been found out, defeated. He was annoyed with himself. Damn those magistrates, stealing his mother's comb, stealing the children's comb, and then telling Anna Maria. Oh, they were clever. They knew that he could not do without Anna Maria.

In truth, he could not do without Anna Maria. She was essential as his banker. She was the mother of and to his children. She was still very attractive to him, and the thought that she might refuse to make love to him ever again after this troubled him; the thought that she might find another young man troubled him even more. He had to make peace with Anna Maria, though the role of suing for peace was not one he relished. But it was necessary. One could not fight a war on two fronts. If he were to settle the question of his daughters, he needed to get Anna Maria on side. He could not have her undermining his position with the children.

He knew he ought to act before the girls came home. He put his head round the door of the room in which his wife was working. She was at her computer and gave him a brief look. He took this as encouragement, and entered, sitting down to wait until she should stop what she was doing. After a few moments, she took her eyes off the screen and the keyboard, and looked at him, waiting for him to speak. He knew that the words he came out with now would be very important.

'I will send her away,' he said at last.

'Where to?' she asked.

Her voice was even. She realised that this was the nearest thing she would get to an admission of wrongdoing, to an apology. And she was wise enough to recognise that this cost him a great deal, to admit defeat, to make concessions like this. She knew too that she should be gracious in defeat.

'Wherever she wants, somewhere on the continent, or even beyond the Alps.'

'What makes you so sure she will go?' she enquired with frightening calmness.

'The money. And of course, I will promise to be good to the children. You don't object to that, surely?'

'I object to it a great deal,' she said. 'But they are very young, and it is not their fault, I suppose. I don't want them meeting my children until they are adults, and I don't want them having your name. And as for the money, perhaps I should oversee that.'

'Perhaps you should.'

'And don't you go anywhere near Enna. Send Traiano. He has no sympathy with adulterers.'

'As we once were,' he reminded her.

'Yes indeed, but that is no excuse. Her cousin. Get rid of him.'

'Alfio?'

'Yes, Alfio.'

'He is in Africa. We need him.'

'We won't always,' she said. 'You can replace him. He put her up to this, I am sure. He needs to be taught a lesson.'

'We need him,' he insisted. 'And he is a continent away. He is out of the way.'

'Oh, very well,' she said, not wanting to push it. 'And what are you going to do about Isabella?'

'I shall talk to her. I may send her away to school, in Switzerland or somewhere. Maybe England. We did discuss that once.'

'Just talk to her?'

'Yes, just talk to her.'

It seemed to Anna Maria that she had won on almost all points.

He stood. He was wearing one of his expensive grey suits, one she had bought for him. He always looked so attractive in the suits she chose for him, or so she had once thought.

'The girls won't be back for an hour at least,' he said. 'The boys are occupied. Is your work so very pressing?'

She looked at her computer, then she looked at him. She allowed herself a wintry smile. Then she looked at the screen once more.

'I am busy,' she said. 'Ask me again in a few weeks' time. When she has gone wherever she is going, and when you give me details of her bank account. I may have changed my mind.'

Disappointed, he left her.

Traiano had gone to the office and spent the rest of the morning there. He noticed, with displeasure, though not with surprise, that Renzo had not bothered to put in an appearance. His hope was that he would be able to go home for lunch and see his wife and his children, but that proved not to be possible, much as he missed them. He phoned at midday to tell his wife that he would not be home for lunch, but he would try to get away earlier than usual, and that whatever happened, he would not be going out at night. The afternoon ground on, and he began to look forward to his release. But then, at about four, Beppe turned up, fresh from school, and asked him to come to the swimming-pool with him. He was not expecting this at all, but he thought the chance of private conference was too good to miss. Perhaps Beppe merely wanted to go swimming; but perhaps there was something he wanted to say in secret; there was certainly something that Traiano wanted to check with him.

'You're growing up now,' said Traiano a little sadly, as they came to rest after swimming several lengths. 'I mean, soon you may be doing this sort of thing with other sorts of people, not me. What I mean is, you're sixteen, and when you are twenty-one you are going to have control over a lot of money.'

'Do you know how much?' asked Beppe casually.

'You have not asked?'

'I think they told me when my grandfather died, but I have forgotten. Anyway, it is five years off. What difference will it make, asking about it now? I suppose the people who control it know what they are doing and will not lose it all.'

'It is what is called a blind trust. Your grandfather set it all up most cleverly. People you will never meet, and who do not know you, are looking after your assets, and you have no say in it at all. I believe the assets are all controlled by bankers in the Cayman Islands and Panama and places like that. How much it is, well, I have been told in the region of three hundred million, but just how much it is, no one knows exactly. It won't be much less than three hundred million. It is good that you should know that, because….'

'So I can beware of fortune hunters?' said Beppe. 'But all my friends I have now are the same friends I had before grandfather died. And those who did not like me before, still do not like me. I mean Sandro, he never liked me; grandfather leaving me all this money just made him dislike me more. It didn't change anything.'

'Sandro was a fool with his court case, because the terms of the trust were impossible to break. I think he now wants to squeeze your mother for cash, as he has failed elsewhere.'

'Mama is very soft hearted, so she will probably give him something. But that will be self-defeating. He will only want more in the future. Even a mother can lose patience when you spend your entire time asking for money. Papà lost patience with him a long time ago.'

'And you?'

Beppe considered. This question, they both knew, was important, and a lot depended on the answer.

'He burned his bridges with me long ago,' said Beppe eventually. 'I know who my real friends are. You are, so is Tonino, so is Muniddu and so is Riccardo. And Renzo, of course. I will follow your advice in everything. You know I will.'

'Well then, you are growing up. If you want my advice…. What do you think of Isabella di Rienzi?'

'I don't like her. You may well ask why. I mean, she is very nice, and all that, but I do not like her father. She comes attached, doesn't she?'

'So, you have thought about these things, then. There's no shame in not liking Isabella. We were talking….'

'About me?'

'Of course, about you. I was thinking that the right girl for you is someone like Rosalia. You are friends with the whole family. It makes sense. She has attachments, but of the right sort, I hope. She is a good girl, and you are a good boy.... It would be nice for you both. You need a nice girl to go around with. It is sort of expected. When I was your age, I was married and had two children. Obviously, I was different, an early starter. Look, I am thinking about your education. You will go to university, so will she. She will be a good companion for you; it will give you prestige. I mean, her family are ordinary, which is a good thing, but she is the sort of girl people respect, and that would add to your reputation. Sandro was always meeting the wrong sort of people. You must not be like Sandro. You need to remember your roots, and people like Muniddu's family, they are the sort of people you spring from.'

'I thought that your job was to persuade me to do what don Calogero wanted, rather than what was best for me,' said Beppe.

'Calogero and I do not agree on everything,' admitted Traiano.

'No, you mean, Calogero and you do not agree about me,' said Beppe.

'Not just you. Sandro as well, and Alfio,' said Traiano.

'I understand what you are saying,' replied Beppe. 'We agree on Sandro. There's no danger of me being like Sandro. I do not want my mother to be bothered with Sandro anymore,' said Beppe quietly. Then he added: 'As for Rosalia, I have always liked her. I will take your advice in everything, you know that.'

After the swim, he went home at long last, pleased to be with his wife and children. But it was only to be the shortest of respites. There was a message waiting for him, which Ceccina had received from signora di Rienzi, the Black Widow Spider. The boss expected him the next day in Catania.

The boss was at home; his wife, Anna Maria, was in her study, not to be disturbed; the girls were all at school, and the three little boys were with the Black Widow Spider. It was this latter person who opened the door to him and managed a ghost of a smile, a conspiratorial look. That was the first warning he had of the magnitude of the disaster that he was to confront. The boss's mother had always loathed him, now she seemed to be conveying, in that way she had, which never relied on words, that they were both on the same side in this matter, and Calogero, by his behaviour, had lost all right to have allies.

He found him in the study. He bent over to kiss his cold cheek. The place looked untidy. The sofa had been slept on, he could tell, and the master of the house banished from the marital bed.

'I need you to sort something out for me,' he said.

'Something or someone?' asked Traiano. 'I do both, remember?'

'It adds up to the same thing,' said Calogero irritably. 'I want you to go to an address in Enna and see Catarina and tell her that she has to leave Sicily, that I wish it, and that for her good and the good of the children, she will do so, without delay.'

'That is an easy message,' said Traiano. 'Should not be hard to deliver. But to enforce, that is a different matter. When she says no, what do you want me to do?'

'You persuade her,' said Calogero.

'You rate my powers of persuasion very highly,' said Traiano.

'Do I have to persuade you to persuade her?' he asked. 'I am surrounded by women who won't do what I want. Are the men going to act in the same way?'

'Why don't *you* go to Enna and beat Catarina into submission?' asked Traiano.

'Don't be ridiculous. Why don't I just beat you?'

'You always were a man for simple solutions,' said Traiano. 'Do these simple solutions work? This is a disaster of your own making. You set up a mistress, and what a mistress. You think no one will ever find out, but someone has. You killed Gino, rather got Alfio to kill Gino, then took Gino's wife. Oh, I know you hid her away and yet they found out what you were doing.

And then they must have told your wife, your mother, and now, or soon, everyone will know. Did you honestly think you could get away with it? And Catarina of all people, why her? I think I know the answer. She belonged to someone else, so you had to have her too. And that someone else was not Gino.'

'Are you trying to provoke me?' asked Calogero sourly. 'No one knew; it was watertight. I think those magistrates have set spies to follow me. That is how they found out. They stole the children's combs, for goodness' sake. And sent the results of the DNA test to Anna Maria.'

'I almost feel sorry for you. But why should I, why should I bother to help you? Of course, you are counting on the fact that I have never liked Catarina. But all the same, do you think it bothers me that you do stupid things? No, what bothers me is that you want me to do stupid things for you; you want me to clean up your mess. If you had listened to me, or consulted me, this would never have happened in the first place.'

'Yes, that is exactly what I want. I want you to clean up my mess. There is a lot of mess to clean up.'

'There must be. You look dispirited. By now, normally, you would have pushed me to the floor and attacked me with your belt. So, I get to speak to Catarina. You do realise it goes further than that. She has Alfio behind her. He put her up to this, or she backs him, one or the other. You will need to deal with her and with Alfio too.'

'Alfio is far away,' said Calogero dismissively. 'He is doing good work. He can be trusted not to misbehave.'

'Still. Let me talk to the Serb next time he is here: Costantino. Perhaps we can work something out.'

'Speak to the Serb, by all means. See what can be done, but…'

'But what? asked Traiano. 'Alfio has to be dealt with. She will never back down, because Alfio is behind her. She thinks you care about Alfio, that the rest of us are frightened of him. You have got to give me Alfio in return for this. You know you have. And we owe it to Gino, and we owe it to Renzo.'

'You are stupid,' he said without feeling. 'We owe Renzo nothing. And revenge is a very childish project. We should leave Alfio alone. Besides, there is Giuseppina to think of.'

'Never mind her, what about me?' said Traiano in exasperation. 'I am the one who constantly has to pacify Renzo for you. And you deny me the means to do so.'

'What I am hearing is that you do not like Alfio, a man on another continent, for God's sake. Alfio has friends, don't forget.'

'No. He has no friends. He just has one friend. You. And you need to give him up. And what use is he to you? He procured you your mistress, Catarina. Well, if you are giving her up, Alfio needs to go as well. She will appeal to him. He will protest. Neutralise him.'

Calogero was silent. Traiano knew he was thinking. After a time, he spoke.

'You made a mistake with Catarina, a mistake that could damage us all. You need to correct it now. If you had ever thought to speak to me before this, you would not be in this situation now. I will make Catarina go away. Trust me. But you have to allow me to get rid of Alfio. He did the unthinkable when he murdered Gino. He must be punished. And when we punish him, he takes away the guilt of Gino's murder. He, not you. You will be absolved.'

'You will make Catarina go away?'

'Yes. Leave it to me, boss.'

'As you wish,' said Calogero at last.

He had been forced into a corner, first by his wife, now by his lieutenant. It was a bitter defeat.

'There is something else.'

'Ah,' said Calogero bitterly. 'You surprise me.'

'Sandro. He has not learned his lesson. He is being a nuisance. He will always be a nuisance. He is annoying his mother, he annoys his cousin, he annoys me, he annoys Beppe. He has seriously annoyed Tonino. We taught him a lesson, or tried to, but he has refused to learn.'

'Who are you asking for? Yourself, or Tonino? Or Beppe? Surely not Angela?'

'All of them. I mean, all of them will benefit, but it is really Renzo and Tonino. Tonino in particular. I don't know what happened, well, I can guess, some boys' quarrel, but Tonino wants to kill him.'

'No,' said Calogero with decision. 'Absolutely not. Are you aware of what you are asking? Sandro is a worthless boy and I do not care whether he lives or dies, but he is exiled from Sicily and that is enough. We are never going to see him again. Besides, we must not antagonise his father or his great uncle. If you think his mother would be better off without him, maybe she would, but I doubt she would see it that way. Are you mad? Are you in love with killing for killing's sake? If anything happens to him, I will be seriously annoyed. Do you understand? Renzo will just have to restrain himself and be content with the death of Alfio. And who the hell does Tonino Grassi think he is? He has the cheek to sleep with that girl Emma Santucci, and then the further cheek to get her pregnant, to get in with her mother and her younger brother, and now he is proposing to kill Sandro. Why exactly? His father gave him a good whipping for getting the girl pregnant, and he clearly did not whip him hard enough. Do you understand me? That boy needs reining in, and if he thinks just because my mother and his mother are friends, my father and his father were friends…. Well, he is presuming too much.'

'Boss, boss…. He is a nice boy. He's clever, he is ambitious, he is able, and he is ruthless. He just has a grudge against Sandro, that is all.'

'That boy has traded off the fact that my father knew his father, and that his mother knows my mother. I thought I had left people like that behind.'

'People like that includes people like me,' said Traiano sourly. 'You are paranoid.'

'I am not. Tonino is in danger of losing my favour. As are you.'

'OK, boss. Now tell me exactly what I have to offer Catarina.'

She was not pleased to see him, that was for sure. She had found him waiting for her as she came home with the children, glared at him and told him to wait. When he was let up into the flat, he saw that she had put on some make-up in the meantime. But the little boy, Tino, who had such a look of his father Rosario, was glad to see him, and came and sat on his lap unbidden, a little to his mother's chagrin, he thought.

'He is missing his father,' she said.

'The one he calls father? It was him who sent me.'

'I assumed as much. Why else would you come? I doubt you would dare come without his permission.'

'You are not pleased to see me,' he observed. 'Why should you be? We have not seen each other for quite some time, since Gino's funeral, in fact. I am, as you will have guessed, the bearer of bad news. His wife has found out. She is not happy.'

'She should have been a better wife to him,' said Catarina.

'She has been an excellent wife to him, looking after the children, giving him two sons, and, above all, looking after his money. Any man can get a wife; but getting such a skilful banker is not so easy. Anna Maria Tancredi provides services that neither you nor I can provide. You need to appreciate that, my dear. He cannot do without her.'

'How did she find out?'

'The agents of the state told her. They stole a DNA sample from his mother and from your children, which proves they are related. We think they followed him here. They must have thought that they had hit the jackpot. They wanted to make trouble, and they have succeeded. But the simple truth is that, at the very least, she has to be pacified. You have to leave Sicily.' He held up a hand to stifle her objection. 'You really do. It is her minimum demand. He will continue to give you what he gives you monthly for yourself and the children; he will continue to be generous. But only on condition that you live somewhere else. You could be comfortable somewhere else, I am sure. Rome, Milan, Florence, Turin, so many lovely places where you could have a comfortable life. Or even abroad, in England or Germany. Anywhere, just not here.'

'No,' she said.

'My dear Catarina, I know it is a disappointment, but think of the money and think of the future, if you do not lose his goodwill. You have a pension for life. He is not cutting you or the children off. How often do you see him anyway? Once a month?'

Her face became truly venomous as she looked at him. How often did she see him? Once a month? If that. Before she had become pregnant with Giovanni, he had come reasonably often, like King Solomon visiting one of his concubines, to lie with her, to do the deed, and then, getting his breath back, to pull up his trousers and reach for his car keys. But how much time had she ever spent with him, how much time had he spent with the children? He came, brought them presents, but then always had to be off somewhere else, somewhere more important. Tonino would come on a Sunday evening and indicate the day and the time he was coming; she would wait anxiously; he would come, then go, and it was as if he had never been there, leaving the mere ghost of memory behind him. This was not his house, let alone his home. She doubted he had spent more than 30 hours in the flat since she had moved in two years ago.

'Look, the children have a future, don't ruin it for them. And think of yourself. If you refuse to go, and he cuts off the money, how much have you got set by? Oh, I know, your cousin Alfio will always help you. Dear Alfio, the teenager who once made love to you and has never got over it. You can get him to do anything for you, can't you? But if the boss cuts you off, would Alfio risk his wrath by helping you out? One of the things we know about Alfio is that when the boss asks him to do something, he does it. As Gino found out to his cost. If the boss asks us to do something, we all do it. Me, Alfio, and you as well.'

'You know what I want,' she said. 'For him to leave his wife, marry me and legitimise these children. He will do it eventually. He just needs to grow a pair of balls and stand up to her. Why should that old woman dictate to him?'

'Even if he were to leave her and marry someone else, there is no guarantee that someone else would be you, Catarina. I mean, he keeps you here, but has he been showing a deep desire to spend more time, indeed all his time, with you? I doubt it. I know what he is like. I saw him with Stefania. He was so indifferent to her. Why should he be any different with you? It is the children he cares about. You know that. He is your lover, but not much of a lover, I am guessing.'

'You take pleasure in the misfortunes of others,' she said.

'Actually, I do not. I am not a naturally cruel person. I see no point in it. I am just trying to get you to see sense. Enna is nice, and this flat is beautiful, and I love the view, but you must be bored here, surely, waiting for a man who hardly ever comes by? Let me tell you this. Go away, and who knows, he may come and see you again in future, he may be grateful, and maybe one day he may be free to see more of you. He will always want to do the right thing for the children. He loves children, his own children. These ones, who give him so little trouble, he will love all the more. There is all to play for. Do not alienate him.'

'No,' she said.

'You prefer to starve?' he asked. 'You prefer the children to starve?'

'How we live is none of your business, and you do not need to worry yourself about that,' she replied. 'Not that I think you do. You have no understanding of how the human mind works. You seem to think that I am in his debt. That he comes here, smiles at me, and departs, and that I should somehow feel grateful. Now he calls in my supposed gratitude.'

'Oh, you were doing him a favour, were you, and he seduced you? That is nonsense. You were angling for Rosario, then when he died you decided Gino would do, but at the very first opportunity you looked elsewhere and you looked higher. Most women, all women, would love to sleep with our boss who is a beautiful man, a powerful man, and, in the right circumstances, a very generous one. Thank God it was me whom he sent, because I may not care about your future, but I do worry about this little fellow. Ah Tino, if only you could understand what your mother wants to do to harm you.'

Tino, fortunately, was now asleep. But at the sound of his name, he woke up and yawned. Traiano kissed him.

'And we have not forgotten the role your cousin Alfio played. Of course, Calogero sleeps with whoever he wants, and that he chose you was his choice entirely. He is not so weak a man as to be manipulated. Your cousin wanted to sleep with you himself, but he facilitated the boss having you all the same. What a man! You never considered him, did you? Well, he was your cousin, and infertile, but what a family you are.'

'You insult me,' she said bitterly.

'It is the truth. Do you realise that Gino had friends, one friend in particular, and that he will blame you and Alfio for Gino's death?'

'That was an accident,' she said sullenly.

'It was no accident. And don Renzo will not be quiescent forever. He might even come after you. But only if you do not have a protector. A woman on her own, and one who has offended don Calogero, is vulnerable. Really, my dear, you have only got one friend. It would not be good to lose him.'

'I am Sicilian. These children are Sicilian. Sicily is their heritage. Why should we be exiled?'

'Of course, of course,' he said. 'But it would not be a permanent exile. The children will grow up and come back and claim what is theirs, and be given it.'

'They would come back as strangers,' she said sadly. 'I refuse to disinherit my children. Go back to him and tell him that. Tell him he is a coward to have sent you and not come himself.'

'Oh, I admit he is a coward, not with men - with men he is brave - but with women. He trembles before his mother and his sisters, and of course, before Anna Maria. Perhaps you are right. He needs to realise that you are a force to be reckoned with, that you are a stronger player than her, and that offending you is the bigger risk. As you say, he needs to stand up to her. But she is the banker, she is the wife, she is the mother of two of his children and stepmother to the other three. The children adore her. She has allies. Her mother-in-law and her sisters-in-law are all solidly behind her, believe it or not. Wives command loyalty, it is the way it has always been. If I go back and say that you refuse to co-operate, you refuse to budge, well, it is possible he may offer you something more, more money perhaps, some assurances about the future, but what would that be worth without his goodwill? That is the real treasure you have. His goodwill. It is what I have, and sometimes I have to do unpleasant things for him, but I do them, even if I find them difficult. You need to be rational; you need to be practical.'

There was silence between them.

'Is Giovanni asleep?' he asked.

'Yes,' she replied. 'I will get him soon.'

'I am so glad to see this little one,' said Traiano, looking at Tino. 'He looks so like his father, I think. He was my best friend, you know. How I miss him. Do you miss him?'

'He was a nicer person than all of you,' she said.

'Yes, he was. He was born in the wrong place. If he had been born somewhere else, even a few streets away, he would have a had a long and happy life. But Purgatory stifled him. Poor Rosario. I loved him. He was beautiful. I miss him still. And I want to make sure all goes well for little Tino.'

He smiled at the child.

'Do hear from Alfio?' he asked, by way of conversation.

'I phone him from time to time.'

'And Giuseppina?'

'Not her, no. She is too busy with her good works in Africa to talk to me.'

'Shame,' said Traiano. 'Maybe she knows about you and her husband. Some people should be more forgiving. Perhaps one day people will forgive you. But if you do not go away, they won't. I don't think he is going to raise his offer, you know. Calogero is very stubborn sometimes. He did not say to me that I could make a better offer on his behalf. I don't really have any other inducements to offer. Have you been following the news from Catania?' he continued. 'As you know, Volta is our friend and we helped him get elected. Now he is elected his chief concern is the next election and the one after that. Volta does not want Catania to be awash with these synthetic drugs, oxycontin and fentanyl. He is going to start a campaign against both and blame the American bases. A tack to the left, you might say, which will be popular. We need Volta. Incidentally, the Americans do not mind, as they are quite happy to scale down their bases in Sicily. Because of this, we are not going to increase our distribution in Catania for the moment. But we have other things to do. It is at a delicate stage. The one thing we do not want right now is our boss getting divorced, or his banker ruining everything. We need everything to be as smooth as possible. We are making a fortune here in Sicily and abroad too. Alfio is playing a big role in that with Costantino, don Carmelo's illegitimate son.

If someone were to say that you were stubbornly staying here, in defiance of the boss's express command, it would not help Alfio. Now, I know he loves you, and you love him less, but you must want him to carry on, mustn't you? If all this comes out…. Don Renzo is particularly unforgiving. You may have forgotten but, unlike you, he was besotted with Gino.'

'Who are you threatening to kill?' she asked. 'Alfio? Me? The children?'

'You exaggerate,' he said softly. 'We do not harm women or children, which perhaps makes you think that you have the licence to do what you like. But that would be a bad thing. Why not get Giovanni?'

She rose.

'Tino come with me,' she commanded.

The boy looked at his mother.

'He likes it here,' said Traiano. 'Don't you trust him with me?'

After that, he went back to Catania, to report on his failure. The boss was furious. Furious with him, and furious with Catarina, as he knew he would be. But there was something else about the boss that he noticed now. He was worried and he was nervous. For once he had encountered someone whose egotism and stubbornness matched his own. Traiano was not displeased to see this. He was not displeased either that the first stage of the negotiations had failed.

'Maybe she wants to hear it from you,' he said. 'Maybe she refused me so you would go up yourself.'

Calogero dismissed this with a wave of his hand.

'We could kidnap the eldest child. Just for a bit.'

'How dare you even suggest that?' he said. 'None of our children would be safe. Are you mad?'

'Then the thing to do is to call Alfio back from Africa and get him to speak to her. She might listen to him. Give him a chance to explain things to her, and if that does not work, take severe measures, not against her, but against him. He is the real reason for her stubbornness. He has put her up to this. he is ambitious, he has been using her, he has been manipulating you, now it is a chance to bring him to heel.'

'Alfio is here for Easter, I believe, or shortly afterwards,' said the boss. 'You can go now. Go back to Palermo, speak to Anna Maria, and let her know what I have planned for Catarina, as best you can.'

The next day, he called on Anna Maria in the evening, after her work. Veronica admitted him and showed him into the drawing room. He waited briefly, and then Anna Maria appeared; she was wearing her glasses, a sign that she was working.

'I was expecting you,' she said.

'I hoped you would be. I was in Catania earlier, but I must just have missed you. But I am glad I have caught up with you. I did not ring to announce my coming, as one never knows who is listening in. Well, we do know. If the agents of the state were following the boss to Enna, stealing his mother's comb, stealing the children's combs as well, they are surely listening to our phones.'

She nodded. She pressed a button and on came some sweet music.

'He wrote it here, you know,' referring to the composer. 'It is *Parsifal*. I see you do not know it. You should. It certainly soothes one in difficult times.'

'It certainly drowns out conversation,' he said. He came and sat next to her on the sofa, to speak confidentially in a low voice. 'I have seen the young lady. I delivered his message, that she has to leave Sicily. She refuses to go. She is very stubborn. The cousin, Alfio, is behind her, I am sure, and Calogero thinks that as well, I think. He is coming after Easter and we will get him to speak to her. Get the sponsor to pull the rug out from under her. That may work. Or if he and she think they are in a strong position and refuse to budge, I know what we do next. We get rid of Alfio. Then she collapses and she goes to wherever we send her. Renzo wants Alfio out of the way. He has reasons, reasons to do with the late Gino, the big fellow from Agrigento. Without her cousin Alfio, she is nothing.'

She listened in silence.

'I find my husband's behaviour unforgiveable,' she said. 'When the holidays come, I suppose we will all be in Donnafugata, but it will be difficult until all this is resolved.'

'We will resolve it, we will,' he said softly. 'It matters to me as well. I will get rid of her for you, whatever it takes. In the meantime, if you could tell me something…'

'Ah, of course.'

'Angela Santucci and I are such great friends. I gather she is paying off Sandro, who refuses to leave Reggio until all the money he can extract from her is safely in his account. I don't want to press Angela for details, but how much does he want?'

'There is no upper limit to his desires,' she said. 'Angela has been keeping me informed, as I am the one who has to find the money for her. Sandro is not a nice boy. Very selfish. Beppe is different, I know. The truth is that Angela has given him as much as she can. She has assets she can get her hands on, and those she cannot. I mean, she inherited a bit from her father, but most of that is tied up in property that it would be unwise to sell, and this boy wants cash. She has transferred almost two million to him. Well, not to him, at least not yet. I insisted on that. It is in an account sitting in Switzerland and it will be his when she says so; and when she says so is when he stops being so unreasonable and accepts that that is all he is going to get. At present all she wants is a bit of peace. He is driving her mad. So is Marina, who takes his part. Of course, Beppe is no trouble, and Emma, well, Emma, she is getting used to. Apparently, this boy she has is not as bad as she feared. He is short and ugly, but very attractive, she says, and Emma, God bless her, is no beauty, at least she was not when I saw her last. You like this boy?'

'Very much, yes. Perfect son-in-law material. Will always please his mother-in-law; devoted to his own mother and goes to Mass every Sunday.'

'Well, a nice change from Sandro. Frankly, that relationship has broken down. He has been furious for the last two years about don Lorenzo's money going to Beppe; and I can tell you in confidence that he will be even more furious when don Domenico dies. Every penny of that is going to Beppe. Those two old men are, were, in don Lorenzo's case, not stupid. Oh yes, Beppe is a sweet child who is not interested in money; perhaps that was crucial; everyone else looked too greedy and there is nothing more off putting and unattractive than greed. But they could hardly leave it to Beppe's father, could they? Or indeed to Beppe's brother.'

'And you will look after this vast fortune on Beppe's behalf?'

'Of course,' she said, smiling. 'Beppe is swimming in a pool full of sharks, not that he knows it yet, but don Lorenzo knew it and don Domenico knows it, but, and this is only a guess, they thought that you and Calogero would look after Beppe and pick off the sharks one by one.'

'We will, we will,' said Traiano.

Chapter Five

Easter was coming.

Don Calogero di Rienzi had decided that he would spend the holidays with his wife and children at his wife's house in Donnafugata. It was such a lovely time of the year, and the countryside, to which he was largely indifferent, would be at its most beautiful. Besides, the tennis court, for many years neglected, had been recently repaired, and it would be nice for him and the two elder children, Isabella and Natalia, to try and play tennis in the pleasant weather, not cold, but not too hot either. He himself could not play tennis very well, but the girls were keen, and he thought it a noble avocation, a useful accomplishment. The three boys were all crazy about football, and there would be plenty of space for them. This would keep the children busy and provide him and his wife with a little peace.

And so they would decamp for at least a week, he and his five children, his wife, the nanny, and Veronica, both of whom the children adored; and of course his sister Assunta and fat Federico would have to come at some stage, and possibly even his mother, and his other sister Elena and his brother-in-law Renzo Santucci as well, perhaps, which was not quite what he wanted, as it had been in Donnafugata that he had first made love to his wife, and it was in this same place that he hoped to repair the relationship.

Relations were cold, but they were not quite as cold as they had been. He hoped that things might return to normal. It was, he felt, not quite a vain hope, at least not yet. He was on the back foot, on the defensive in the domestic war, though there had been a truce of sorts, as they had hardly spent any time together in recent weeks. She had been in Palermo, working, and he had been in Catania, with the children, also working. The question of Catarina and her children hung over them. Catarina was still there, refusing to budge, refusing to be cast off, and Anna Maria would never be pacified until she was somewhere over the straits of Messina. But it was taking time. Anna Maria was not very understanding about this. Maybe she had a point: in the past he had always extracted compliance from everyone, and swiftly. Now Anna Maria was defying him, and so was Catarina. He could feel power and prestige and respect slipping away from him. He was the almighty boss who could not command the obedience of a former shop girl in Enna. One who was financially dependent on him to boot. He had not cut her off financially, not yet anyway. But Alfio would come, after Easter, perhaps, and he would sort it out. He relied on Alfio. And if Alfio failed, that would be a solution too. For Alfio was under sentence of death.

He felt nothing for Alfio at all, though he had known him all his life, and they had in fact been at school together, not that that counted for much, as neither of them had attended school very often after a certain age. The death sentence he had conceded troubled him for other reasons. First of all, if left to himself, he would never have conceded it; he felt that it was a concession wrung from him by Traiano, at the behest of Renzo, and that while it might suit his subordinates, it did not suit him. It was an act of weakness. He felt he had given way and done so against his better judgement. After all, Alfio was loyal, completely loyal, for he had no other friends apart from his boss, and he had shown he would murder his very best friend for the boss's convenience. But that had been a mistake, he now saw, and he reproached himself for his weakness, his vanity, in wanting Catarina. The world was full of women; why had he allowed himself to be tempted by Catarina? But of course, he knew why: she had had the child, Tino, and now she had another, his own, Giovanni. The children were paramount. If only Anna Maria could see that.

Just as he valued social peace, as it enabled him to make money, he was also beginning to see that domestic peace had its charms. How he wished now that he had never met Catarina. He had not foreseen her constant demands. Unlike the men he knew, this woman was not frightened of him. Her endless discontents had been hard to handle, and the only way to do so had seemed to be the constant stream of favours, which merely deferred her complaints rather than resolved them, as the current impasse now proved.

He had given her a flat in Enna, and paid for it to be beautifully furnished, at considerable expense, but of course, none of this compared to the splendour of the three houses that he shared with Anna Maria. Two of those were Anna Maria's exclusive property, he had pointed out, though this seemed to make little impact. Besides, Anna Maria was his wife, another fact that, once pointed out, had only seemed to annoy Catarina the more. It was precisely because she was the wife that Catarina could not be, that he had to compensate Catarina for her inferior position, she had claimed. But to his mind, her position was deeply privileged. She had a nice house, two lovely children, and he visited her whenever he could and made love to her: what more could any woman want? Of course, she had wanted to be the wife, but that was the one thing she could not have.

She had claimed she wanted to be his wife not for her own sake but for that of the children. The children, his nephew Tino and his son Giovanni, needed to have his surname, and she wanted to be Catarina di Rienzi. He had been adamant that she could not. He would see her usually on Wednesdays, in the middle of the week, and these conversations would take place after they had made love. Those sessions were, he was prepared to admit, from his point of view at least, intoxicating. She knew how to please him, and he was satisfied by that; but there was always a quid pro quo, and he felt some remorse now over the way he had been so generous. She had even demanded that he make a new will, in case something happened to him.

Nothing was going to happen to him. Of that he was sure. But this idea of the women quarrelling over his corpse, of Anna Maria and Catarina facing each other in a dispute over who got what, and whether the children were in fact his own or not, and whether they had any rights, this whole idea was one that he would rather not face. What indeed would happen after his death? He hoped by then that all the children would be grown up. But he remembered his own father's unforeseen demise, and how he had had to correct his will post mortem, with the help of the lawyer Rossi. What would Giovanni inherit; what would Tino inherit? The only person who could really ensure they were treated fairly was Anna Maria. She controlled the money. He was at her mercy, so were they. It was urgent he pacify her.

And yet he did not entirely blame himself for this situation. True, he had chosen to set Catarina up in Enna, had chosen to father a child on her, had chosen to sleep with her. But why not? Didn't all powerful men have mistresses? Didn't all powerful men have illegitimate children? Didn't don Carmelo have thirteen children in all? Hadn't don Carlo left behind numerous half-sisters and brothers for Renzo? He too was not meant for monogamy, not meant to be restricted to a few children. It was unreasonable of Anna Maria, who was after all twenty years his senior, not to see that.

His mother and his sisters, they knew about Catarina as well, but that they knew did not bother him overmuch. After all, he was the boss, he could do what he liked. And if he broke the rules, it was the proof that he was above the rules. Indeed, he made the rules; the rules did not bind him, they bound others. Besides which, it was good for his wife, powerful as she was, and his mother and sisters, who exercised a different sort of power, to know that they did not control him, that he was his own master. The existence of his mistress and his parallel family was his declaration of independence from the women. He had always found women a challenge, for they could not be overawed by men; the first such had been Anna the Romanian prostitute; but now he was approaching thirty, it was clear to them and to himself that he would do what he liked.

Doing what one liked, and being known to do what one liked, was enjoyable. People looked at him as one who could do as he pleased, and admired him for doing what they themselves would have liked to have done, if only they had dared. At least that applied to the men, most of whom had never had their way in the manner they had hoped and dreamed of. The women were different, more critical, but they had learned to keep their opinions to themselves.

He had never been promiscuous when young, and had been faithful to his first wife Stefania until he had met Anna Maria; Anna Maria was twenty years his senior, and it was to be expected that he should stray, not because she was no longer attractive, but because she was now past childbearing, and he wanted more children. And that really was why he had been so tolerant of Catarina, because she could give him children. Of course, her children, and the children of his two marriages would be brought up differently but, in the end, he would be just and fair, though that was a long way ahead.

But Easter was coming, and he would be in Donnafugata for perhaps two weeks. It would be enjoyable, restful, and at the same time challenging: for he knew he had to conciliate Anna

Maria. He had to make love to her again, to reassure her that she was the wife, she was the banker, and Catarina had been no more than a diversion, though, as they had a child, something he had not quite admitted, but not been able to deny either, that diversion was clearly someone with a stake in the future. He had given a great deal to Catarina from his own resources, and now, he knew, he had to convince his wife that none of this mattered compared to what he had given her. If he gave to Catarina, he had to give to Anna Maria as well, and give more.

He had several schemes in his mind. The most obvious was to re-enchant the marriage via the bedroom. Then there was the project to remind her of how he was now a great man, and she a great woman, thanks to their complementary skills and interests; he would fill the house with guests and she would see him shine; he certainly did not doubt his own powers of persuasion.

In the household of Muniddu too, Easter was assuming an additional importance. Riccardo, who was fifteen years old, and a studious boy, noticed that the atmosphere was tense, and that there was something he was not being told. He wondered what it was. Moreover, this tension affected both his parents and his sister, which was strange. It was as if they were all plotting something and keeping him out of the picture. Of course, he was only fifteen, and there were certain things that they never discussed in front of him, ever, certain subjects that were rapidly abandoned when he came into the room. He knew, for example, that they had been discussing Roberto, whom he knew, Tonino's friend with whom he shared a flat, but he did not know what they were talking about. He had asked his parents, and they had looked annoyed. He had asked Rosalia, and she had told him it was not important. He asked Tonino, and Tonino told him not to ask. Eventually he had asked Beppe, and Beppe had told him all that he knew. It seemed that Roberto had had some 'bad news', and the bad news consisted in the fact that his girlfriend, not that she was really his girlfriend, Gabriella, the sister of Ruggero Bonelli, was pregnant. It was a bit of a scandal as she was much older than him, and he had been lucky to have been noticed by her in the first place. Or so he had heard. Apart from that, Beppe seemed to think the matter uninteresting. Riccardo thought it, by contrast, fascinating. First Tonino with Emma, and now Roberto with Gabriella; what a world!

Riccardo's social life was restricted to school, his football team, going to church, and the family circle; the world, he knew, was something he was not supposed to know about; and the same was true of his sister. Their parents were very affectionate, very protective, but one could still find out about the world; the world had the habit of entering into even the most sheltered environments. The family unit, his mother, father, sister, little Emilio, Tonino and Beppe (who were always with them, who counted as family, whom he viewed as brothers) was a fortress against the world; the uncles, aunts and cousins lived in similar, if allied fortresses. But he was fifteen years old, and he knew; he encountered others on the staircase of their block of flats, on the pavements of the Corso Calatafimi, in the market, in the shops, at church and at football;

he encountered others at school, pupils and teachers alike. He saw the wariness, he saw the irony, he saw, though this was hard to imagine, the fear that sometimes crossed their faces. He knew that his family was not like other families. He knew his sister knew as well, though the subject had never been mentioned between them. But one could tell she knew too.

There were so many signs. His father worked as a chauffeur, but had so much more money than a chauffeur should make. His uncles too all had worked for the Santucci family, members of whom he had seen on several occasions: first don Antonio, and now don Renzo and don Traiano, regularly and frequently. He had been fascinated to spend that weekend in Naples with them, to observe don Renzo and don Traiano up close; he had been flattered and excited to call them by their names, to use the informal mode of address, to kiss their cheeks; the football match had been incredibly exciting, but what had followed, when they had gone to the VIP lounge and seen the players close up, that had been even more astonishing. For a moment, it had made him feel the most important person in the world. It had been intoxicating; at the time he had felt numbed; the memory was still fascinating. But to Beppe and his cousin and don Traiano, this sort of thing was normal.

The encounter with the men in suits after the match had fascinated him too, and he had asked Beppe about it, and who they were, but Beppe's answers showed no real curiosity about why any of these presumably important people should want to meet them, or vice versa. They were friends, he assumed, of his father, or his late Uncle Carlo or his grandfather, don Lorenzo; they were family friends, but no more, very vague acquaintances. In fact, Beppe showed little curiosity about anything, or the interior life of anyone. He would have loved to discuss all these people who were, after all, in the newspapers from time to time: don Renzo, sentenced to a period of rehabilitation for his cocaine addiction; don Traiano, because of the court case about a stolen picture. But he knew he was not supposed to ask. No one had told him that he was not supposed to ask – he just knew. Besides, for Beppe, these were uninteresting matters, and he, Riccardo did not want to come across as overcurious, as prying, or worse, as innocent. One needed to keep quiet and observe; that was what he had picked up from his father, not that Muniddu had said so. He had had the distinct impression that his father Muniddu was rather showing him off to don Renzo and don Traiano, showing him off as the model of a good Sicilian boy.

Well, he was a good Sicilian boy. Sometimes at school they asked him questions, the other boys and the girls too, and the teachers. He wanted to be friendly, but he knew he came across as guarded and defensive. (A good Sicilian boy was always discreet.) Yes, he knew members of the Santucci family; he had been in the same room with them. Don Antonio's younger son was a friend of his. But that was all. No details were forthcoming, for he knew no details, though undoubtedly there were details to be known. He noticed that some of the boys were impressed by the fact he knew these people.

He got on well with the other boys in a sort of manner. He was good at football, he was good at lessons, but he had no friends, for he was shy, he was awkward, he did not talk much, and he found almost all social encounters excruciatingly embarrassing. If someone spoke to him, he would frequently break into a sweat. If he found himself near a girl, even when she did not look at him, he felt his cheeks glow red. He had been told he shared his sister's good looks, though he did not quite believe it. It was only at home that he ever relaxed.

He loved his father, and feared him a little too. He knew about his uncles in jail, and he knew too that he must never speak of this or anything else that strangers might find interesting. He knew that he had to say his prayers at night, and that he had to go to Mass on Sunday; both things he did most willingly. He knew that he had to keep away from girls, who would 'distract' him. He had a pretty vivid idea of what such distractions entailed, but he realised that his shyness was safeguard enough against that. He was told very sternly, that unlike Tonino, great friend as he was, he must not make a girl pregnant outside of marriage. Considering he had not even kissed a girl, he considered this an impossibility.

He assumed that his mother spoke to his sister in similar terms, though he had no idea what she might have said. Like him, she was under pressure to do well at school. But he could also sense that she was being pushed in a certain direction, just as he had been in Naples. This good Sicilian girl was, he could see, being pushed, slowly but clearly, at least to him, towards Beppe. The other day, they had all decided to go down to the Corso Calatafimi and walk to the via Maqueda to buy ice-creams, but it had been made clear to him by both his parents that he had to stay behind to do his homework.

There were clear signs too that this Easter was somehow important and different. At Easter, there was always a big lunch, but this year his mother had suggested to his father, in his hearing, that they have the big lunch on Easter Monday instead. He had at once been alert and noticed that his parents did not want to discuss this in front of him. He wondered about Easter, what was planned, what was happening, what it was he was not meant to know or notice. And then, just before Easter, as soon as the school holidays began, Beppe and his sister departed on a little trip to Cefalù. Everyone was tight lipped about that too.

They were just going for the day to look at the Cathedral. Riccardo knew what was really happening, though; Beppe and Rosalia were both sixteen, and this was some sort of romantic encounter. Cefalù was a beautiful place, so what better place than there for one's first kiss? The only thing was this: Beppe had not shown the slightest interest in Rosalia before now, despite having known her for years. And not just Rosalia; he had shown no interest in girls at all. But if he were to show any interest in girls, Rosalia would be the best place to start. But why should she be interested in him, except as a friend? He knew Beppe well, but he could not conceive any girl wanting to kiss him ever.

His sister, he imagined, went to Cefalù like a maiden going to her execution, or some virgin about to be chained to a large rock as a propitiatory sacrifice to a sea monster. He was not correct at all.

Beppe held her hand as they sat together on the train in silence, and perhaps casual observers might have thought they were a sweet young couple, very much in love. As she felt his hand in hers, Rosalia sensed something that she had not felt before. He was nervous, diffident. His hand betrayed a lack of self-confidence. This was a new insight into his character, she saw; he was eager to please her, but not sure that he would be able to please her. Moreover, he wanted to please her in order to please others. The way he looked at her as well; this too betrayed nerves and uncertainty, and she saw that he was relying on her to get him through the ordeal that awaited them. He needed reassurance. She felt sorry for him. She had expected to feel sorry for herself, but she saw now that both of them were subjects of a destiny they had not chosen.

She liked Beppe; he was her brother's best friend; she did not want to make things difficult for him, far from it; and she wanted to please her parents. They both thought Cefalù a very nice place. One went through an arch, and one came to the medieval wash place, where the stream debouched into the sea. She had not been to Cefalù before, and she was enchanted. She saw that this pleased him. He had chosen the place himself, he said, he had wanted it to be special. He looked somewhat apologetic as he said this, as if to convey that he knew he was asking a great deal by imposing himself on her. And she had a glimpse then what their relationship would to be like, and she saw the decades stretch ahead of them; she was destined to be the strong one, to dominate him. Or so she thought.

There by the gurgling water they kissed, a little uncertainly at first, with more confidence later. He looked relieved once it was over. The first hurdle had been passed.

After lunch in one of the best restaurants in the place, they had walked through the old town, admired the cathedral, and then walked the length of the beach, before taking the train back to Palermo. His cheeks still had that heightened colour to them.

'Did you enjoy yourself?' she asked.

He took this as a reference to the mosaics in the cathedral, the undoubtedly highlight of the place. He was about to mention them, when it occurred to him that she meant something else.

He smiled. She sighed. He looked at her.

'What university do you want to go to?' he asked. 'I mean here, or abroad?'

She was a little taken aback by this. She had expected something more. Either a discussion of the kisses, and a declaration of love, or perhaps the one question that troubled her more than anything, her family, his family.

'I want to do history, and I would later like to do research into Sicilian history, so perhaps here, Palermo, perhaps Naples, the Frederick II, but they say that Rome is best. But for research, one has to go abroad, and that means England. All the best universities are there. What do you want to do?'

'Well, agriculture. But I would not go abroad. All the people I care about are here. And I have been abroad enough as it is; only recently we were all in Naples seeing the football, but I don't want to leave my mother for a long time, or my friends. And the sort of agriculture I want to study, citrus cultivation, that is best done here where the lemon trees grow.'

'That is the family business, isn't it, lemons?'

'Lemons, yes, but also other fruit, and cheese and wine, and now it's expanding into Sicilian luxury foods, dried tomatoes, pistachio paste, almond paste, things like that. I go to the office a lot and I hear all about it. Traiano shows me things. It is good for Sicily that people should associate us with delicious things to eat and drink. Of course, we import things as well, cars, chemicals, things like that. That is profitable, but we are aiming to beef up the exports. Sometimes I go with Traiano and Tonino, and we taste cheese, and those bottled artichokes, you know. It's very interesting. Tonino is an expert on wine, did you know? He has even bought a vineyard.'

'I did know that. When he comes round we only serve the best for him. My father makes sure of it. Are you happy about him and your sister?'

'Yes, very. He is very nice. He will make a very good husband. He is very family minded. I know he is a bit short, but you can't have everything.'

'He is short,' she agreed. 'So many Sicilians are. You're not. You know, two of my uncles are in jail, though it is never talked about. Tonino's father did fourteen years, didn't he? And don

Traiano's father was in jail in Romania. Don Renzo was arrested for drug use, wasn't he, and Traiano has had legal trouble with a picture, hasn't he?'

'I know about all that,' he said, 'though they never talk about it, as they don't want to worry or upset me. You forgot to mention my uncle Carlo, who was murdered with several of his friends, and those two whose bodies were found in the harbour, who must have known your father. I remember my uncle, but I was very young, and it is not that I have forgotten him, it is just that these things recede. He was a bit wild, a bit rackety. He did some very bad things.'

'Like what?'

'Well, as a teenager, I heard, he robbed a petrol station, for a dare, you know, and they had some difficulty keeping him out of trouble for that. When he was older, he had lots of affairs with women, and had lots of children, I mean, not with his wife. And Renzo too was wild. He used drugs, and he drank far too much, like my father. But now he is reformed. He does not smoke or drink, and he runs marathons. He keeps fit. But I am not wild at all, you know. I am a bit boring. I would not want to do any of the things Renzo or Carlo did. I want to be ordinary. As for that court case with the picture, I think that is them trying to make life hard for him. It will be sent to the archives soon, you'll see. Traiano is so nice; he and Tonino and your brother, are my best friends. And Renzo too, of course, and your father. I love them all.'

He was stuck, it seemed, in the world of childhood; he had no conception of the world of money, or ambition, or feuding, or sexual desire. But he was surrounded by affection. Why should he have awakened into the adult world? She herself knew about the world, even though they protected her from it. But she knew. She knew, for a start, that her parents were socially ambitious for her and her brother. And that this sweet innocent boy represented the height of their ambitions.

She liked him, but she was puzzled by him. As for her parents' ambitions for her, she saw how tired her mother was, the way she worked so hard, looking after Emilio, cooking, cleaning and shopping, the constant making do; and she saw the way her father was, always tired when he came home. To be married to a very rich and very pleasant man, who loved lemons, would that be so very bad?

As the train drew in to the central station of Palermo, the people stood up to get off, and when they were alone, they kissed again.

Everything was arranged. On the morning of the Saturday before Easter, Tonino and Muniddu went to receive their final instructions, to go through things one last time. Both bosses met to play squash early in the morning every Saturday, and they had been told to be there to meet them, just in case. In fact, there was nothing to go over; the trap was set; the only thing was the handing over of the money afterwards. On Sunday, don Traiano would be at Donnafugata as the guest of don Calogero, and don Renzo would be there too. So, when Tonino had the money, he was to take it to Donnafugata and hand it over; then what was left, his share and Muniddu's share, he could take back to Palermo. The two of them, don Traiano and don Renzo, and their families, were going to the very long, and frankly very boring, Easter Vigil at the Cathedral, led by the Cardinal; then they would go home, grab some sleep, and then drive to Donnafugata for lunch. They would be in the public eye, they would make sure of that, all day long, while the business part of things was concluded by him and Muniddu. The two of them trusted them. Tonino nodded, to show they were right to trust him. This conversation took place outside the squash court. Then they met Beppe. He was going later that morning to Castelvetrano for Easter, with his mother, and had come to say goodbye before he left. Renzo planted a sweaty kiss on his cheek; Traiano hugged him.

The two bosses left them to get showered and changed. The two younger ones were left outside the changing room, in the foyer of the sports club, while Muniddu went home.

'How long are you going to Castelvetrano for?' asked Tonino.

'The whole week, me, Mama, and Marina. She thinks the place is boring, but a good place to read, and she needs to do reading for university. But I will have a nice time. I like it, because of the garden, and the lemon trees. My father says he will take me sailing, if he feels up to it. But to tell you the truth, I would not have minded getting invited to Donnafugata. I have been told the gardens there are magnificent. I would love to see them. But Papà can't stand don Calogero, though I always found him very nice. Renzo's going, Traiano's going…. Have you been?'

'Never,' said Tonino. 'I don't get invited to places like that. Though I would like to see it, I must say. It must be nice. We will be in Catania. My mother and Emma get on so well. I gather you are seeing a girl?'

Beppe looked pleased and embarrassed at the same time.

'How was your trip to Cefalù?' asked Tonino.

'It was very nice. Have you been? You should. The mosaics at the cathedral are very nice indeed, the town in beautiful, and we walked right round the bay. The food was good too. Yeah, I really had a good time.'

'We can trust him?' asked Renzo, above the sound of the shower water.

'Of course we can trust him. I have known him since he was six years old,' replied Traiano. 'He has done a lot for us, hasn't he? Just as we can trust Muniddu.'

'I have known him since I was six years old,' said Renzo. 'The thing is, he and Muniddu, they are very close, and what if they decide to run off with the money?'

'Run off, where to? There is nowhere for them to go. And they can hardly take their families with them, can they? Don't worry. The boy is a good Sicilian boy, and he needs the cash and he needs us because we will put him in the way of making much more. And don't forget, you can't run off with eight million. Eight million is useless without a banker to look after it for you and to turn it into money you can enjoy. Eight million sitting in a cellar, wrapped in clingfilm, is useless.'

Renzo nodded at this reference to the essential nature of the services provided by Anna Maria.

'How do you think Easter at Donnafugata will be? She knows, doesn't she? She must resent it. It might make for a very icy atmosphere. Elena is furious. She takes Anna Maria's side.'

'Ceccina too. But Anna Maria herself is a businesswoman. Her marriage is a business partnership. She won't let feelings get in the way of profit. But at the same time, when it comes to betting on him or her, I bet on her.'

'And Isabella as well. I gather there is trouble there? Elena has heard, Assunta has heard and their grandmother has heard too. Says she is not a good girl. But she is quite big now, isn't she?'

'Don't. Poor Calogero. His children are growing up, and if they all know, and you and I know, who does not know? He must feel the humiliation. And he has got Catarina to deal with,' said Traiano. 'He will be distracted.' He leaned over towards Renzo and reduced his voice to a whisper, not that anyone could hear. 'The boss has given his permission with regard to Alfio.'

'At long last,' said Renzo, his narrow eyes lighting up with satisfaction. 'When can we do it?'

'He is coming over here after Easter, I believe, but... let us speak to Costantino. He might be able to help. He might be most willing to help. There is no hurry.'

'What made him change his mind?' asked Renzo.

'I told him you wanted it. I wanted it too.'

Renzo nodded.

'About time,' he repeated. 'But what about my cousin Sandro?'

Traiano was silent.

'He does not want him touched. Your great-uncle Domenico, and your Aunt Angela, it seems they guarantee keeping him alive.'

'Well, I want him touched, and so do you,' said Renzo with decision. 'I will tell Calogero so. Besides, Sandro is my cousin, not his. I decide. I will speak to him. I will tell him. He will change his mind. We can deal with Sandro after Easter. I think we can do that without consequences. My cousin Sandro is just a footnote. It is just a case of making sure my Aunt Angela doesn't mind too much. And even if she does... The bigger fish is Alfio.'

'We are meeting Costantino at noon, don't forget.'

'I am in no danger of forgetting,' said Renzo.

'They are taking their time,' observed Beppe. 'I suppose they have secrets to discuss. I wish you were coming to Castelvetrano.'

'It was nice of your mother to invite me, but Emma decided she preferred Catania.'

'I am sure you will have a great time there,' said Beppe.

The two men emerged and joined them. Renzo kissed Beppe absentmindedly on the forehead; he smelled of shampoo. He looked at Tonino, then looked at Beppe again.

'Is it the case you are now seeing a girl?' he enquired with a touch of irony.

'Yes,' said Beppe.

'You can tell us all about it over breakfast,' said Traiano. 'And we can tell you about playing tennis. They have done up the tennis court at Donnafugata; that was what we were talking about and why we are a little behind schedule.'

At noon they met in the milling crowd outside the Opera House. They had not seen him for a long time, but the Serb, Costantino, was unmistakeable.

Traiano spoke.

'Thanks for meeting with us. I know you are busy seeing your wife, your father, your children. I know you do not have much time, so we will get to the point. We want to ask a favour. We want to talk about don Alfio.'

The Serb grunted.

'There is a problem here that might well be solved by don Alfio himself, if he can solve it. If he can't, then, well, he becomes a problem, and we would want to do without him. We have spoken to don Calogero, and he understands our position. Alfio is coming over to Sicily after Easter for a bit. If he never returned to Africa, how would you feel?'

'Delighted,' said the Serb.

They nodded. They shook hands, and they parted. The groundwork had been laid.

The meeting place on which they had decided was the via Francesco Crispi, and the time four in the morning. The road was one of the ugliest in Palermo, alongside the port, and wide as well and, at that hour, deserted. They had chosen a place on the road where there were no street cameras – Muniddu had spent several hours checking this – and they had given the men precise instructions as to where they were to come – to the small refrigerated vehicle that had been stolen for the occasion, and which was parked at the right spot on the via Crispi from early evening. Muniddu and Tonino were there at ten to four, as it was not right to turn up too early, and they were able to spot at least two waiting figures in cars; they had arrived on foot. It had been a tense evening so far, though not because of the operation in hand. Tonino had spent the afternoon and evening with Emma, and Roberto had come round as well; then they had all had dinner together, and then he had gone home, only to be woken by Muniddu at about three, not that he had slept much. Roberto, luckily, by then, had departed for his mother and his sisters in Catania.

It was now four in the morning, and they approached the small refrigerated vehicle, and as they did so, five men did the same, their shadows materialising in the darkness. Tonino opened the door of the vehicle and they all got in. It was crowded. Nothing was said. Muniddu and Tonino were careful to take the places near the entrance door, while the others huddled on the bench at the sides of the vehicle furthest from the door. The five cases were slid along the floor to them. It took some time, but the money was checked carefully. They knew how to do this, and they had specified what the eight million should look like. It amounted to eighty thousand one-hundred-euro notes; this was divided into five separate packages of sixteen thousand notes each. Each of those amounted to sixteen carefully bound bundles of a thousand each. So, it was necessary to check that the five cases were there, that each case contained sixteen bundles, and that each bundle contained a thousand notes. They proposed only to compare bundles and to sample a few. The men, Rota and his associates, watched the checking of the money, sure that they would not be allowed to depart until it was all done. Tonino took his time, while Muniddu looked on, his gun on his knee, ready to use it. Then, just when the checking of the money seemed interminable, just when tension was turning to boredom, Tonino gave the signal, a look to Muniddu, and all was done in a second. Before the others could react, they leapt up, exited the vehicle, and slammed the door shut tight, and bolted it. A moment later the vehicle was in motion, the only indication that something was amiss being the hammering on the door coming from the inside. But the streets were empty, and there was no one to hear. They were soon heading east towards the motorway and the province of Catania. Meanwhile, the hammering was becoming weaker, whether as despair set in for their passengers, or the refrigeration and lack of oxygen began to do their deadly work.

There were cameras along the motorway to Catania, everyone knew that, so Muniddu and Tonino both adopted baseball hats with large peaks as they drove, and both wore pairs of glasses, made out of plain glass, as they both had perfect vision. The journey was long and boring and they spoke little, and by six they had made it to the former quarry that belonged to don Calogero, and where much of the spoil from the Furnaces project had been dumped. A silent man opened the gates to the plant, and they drove in. They were not there very long. Parking the vehicle, they approached the back door and discovered that the five men inside were no longer conscious. In the intervening two hours the freezing cold and the lack of oxygen had had their effect. While the man on duty looked studiously away, they took the bodies one by one and threw them into the quarry. When that was done, Muniddu got into a truck laden with building debris and with a few instructions from the man on duty, emptied the contents onto the bodies, which were soon obscured. Then, once they had transferred the bags of cash into the cab of the vehicle, they left.

The roads were still quite empty, it being Easter Sunday morning, but they were in no hurry and they could drive at a leisurely pace. They stopped eventually at one of the motorway service stations outside Enna, right at the geographical centre of Sicily. Here, as arranged, a car and a motorcycle were waiting, with their keys taped to the back of the wheels. There were enough people around to make the sight of two men getting out of a refrigerated truck look unremarkable; and even if someone saw the luggage being transferred from the truck's cab to the boot of a car, no one would have commented on it. It was an everyday scene. Then Muniddu drove the truck away. Tonino settled down in the car to wait, having first bought himself a cup of coffee.

Returning to the motorway, Muniddu turned left at the next junction and then, having memorised the route, found the road he was looking for; a very narrow road that wound its way through the mountains, and through the trees, shadowing the motorway below. The place was easy to find, at a bend in the road. He stopped the truck at the side of the road, got out, opened the rear doors, and pushed the vehicle slowly over the edge into the bushes and trees. It would be weeks before anyone noticed the abandoned vehicle, and it would be even more time before the police took an interest, and by the time they did, and by the time the vehicle was recovered, if it ever was, it would be useless for forensics.

The truck gone, he then turned back to the road and began to walk. He was only a hundred metres or so from the motorway service station where he had left Tonino. The walk was precarious, and involved climbing fences and scrambling down slopes, but within thirty minutes he was there, tapping on the window of his car to alert the boy. That done, he took the motorbike and headed towards Palermo. The car, which belonged to Muniddu, was Tonino's to drive to Donnafugata.

He had been told to arrive at Donnafugata at eleven, which was the hour of Mass, when the signora would be in church along with the children, and when the boss would be alone. He had never been to Donnafugata before now, and of course he had no phone and no navigational device, but he had studied and memorised the map, and though he was not particularly used to driving, he was confident that he would be there on time. Indeed, he was early, and he drove past the turning to the house, and then waited before returning. At eleven exactly, he parked in front of the grand front door, as he had been told to do so. Traiano was waiting for him. He got out of the car and they shook hands.

'All went well?' asked Traiano.

'No problems, boss.'

Traiano nodded. There was no need to say more. Together, they went to the boot of the car and unloaded the five bags of money. Then he instructed him to drive the car to the garages, where it would be out of the way, while he waited for him. Then they went into the house, Traiano leading the way. The house was the most splendid he had been in, ever, but he had no eye for the antique furniture, the paintings, the silver, as they hurried upstairs to what he assumed was a spare bedroom. The bed had been stripped back to the bottom sheet, and it was here that they laid out the packages in silence. There were eighty packages in all, each containing one hundred thousand in one-hundred-euro notes. They were laid out like bricks, eight by ten, all correct, and a few were tested to make sure that they contained one thousand notes. It was quite a staggering amount of money. Neither of them had ever seen anything comparable. While they were doing this, don Calogero entered, still in his dressing gown, and smiled at the sight of so much cash. A moment later don Renzo followed, dressed, holding a cup of coffee.

'Happy Easter,' said don Calogero, to himself more than to anyone else.

Now it came to the division of the spoils. They had talked of this before, but each knew that whatever had been decided in the past could be undone now, if don Calogero saw fit. And he did see fit. He was thinking of his wife, his banker, now heedless in church, unaware of this latest haul. He surveyed the money, and took sixteen of the bricks and placed them in one of the bags which he handed to Renzo. He did the same for Traiano. They thanked him and, with a nod, they were dismissed. Then, left alone with Tonino, he set aside another sixteen bricks for Muniddu, which was carefully put in a bag. Tonino watched with nervous anticipation, unable to take his eyes off the remaining money, the three million or so still left on the bed.

The boss went to the bedroom door and checked it was closed. Then he turned and looked at Tonino.

'So, that is Muniddu in the millionaires' club. He deserves it. And so do you. It makes you into the ideal prospective son-in-law, doesn't it?'

'Hope so, don Calogero,' said Tonino.

'There is sixteen, one point six million, for you. A nice start to your married life. Of course, Traiano may ask you to help pay off the people at the quarry. They may require a little bonus for getting up so early on Easter morning. And I am sure you will be generous to your parents, won't you? But still, after giving away a fair amount, there will be plenty left. I know you are always kind to your mother. She is my mother's old friend, and we owe her something considering what she had to put up with when your father was in prison. I don't want you to go to see Catarina again or take her any more messages. Do you understand?'

'Understood, boss.'

'Now pack up the money, yours and Muniddu's, and put it in your car. It will be safe there. Perhaps less so in Palermo, which is a den of thieves, as we both know.'

He did as he was told and prepared to leave. He made his way to the car and stowed away the two suitcases containing three million two hundred thousand euros between them. He discovered that Traiano had followed him, bearing a cup of coffee.

'You probably need a cup of coffee,' he said. 'We do not want you falling asleep at the wheel on your way back. He was fair to you? He gave you what you expected?'

'Yes, boss. More than I expected. He even remembered my mother, which was nice of him.'

'You need to think what you can do with the money. The best thing is to invest it with the signora. When you are back in Palermo, call in at her office and ask to see her. She can turn a million in cash into the sort of stuff you can use. You can buy a house, for a start. She knows what to do. Speak to her. And you need to make a will, leaving it all to Emma and little Olivia, as you are not married yet, just in case something happens.'

'Sure, boss. Could you show me the garden? Beppe speaks of the lemon trees here, and I would like to see them, and I am not sure I would recognise one if I saw one.'

'I'll show you the lemon trees,' he said. 'You must have seen a lemon tree before now. And when you do, you will have something to talk about with Beppe.'

They walked up to the lemon trees.

'I gather there is some trouble with Roberto and Gabriella,' said Traiano.

'He said I was the fool,' said Tonino. 'But now he is the one who is not looking so clever.'

'Still, if she has him, then it is a step up for him, isn't it?' said Traiano. He looked around. There was no chance anyone could be listening. 'We are going to take care of Alfio. The boss said yes. But as for the other one, he is not so keen. The mother, the great-uncle, you know, they might all object. Besides he is not important enough to get rid of, is the impression I have. Not worth the trouble.'

Tonino was silent.

'I know you do not like him,' said Traiano. 'But the boss… you could appeal to him next time you see him. As far as I am concerned, the man is the dirt under our shoes. Don Renzo is going to speak to the boss again. So, it might just happen.'

Having examined the lemon trees, they walked back to the garages, and after shaking hands, they said good bye to each other and Tonino drove away.

At about quarter past noon, they all came back from Church: Anna Maria Tancredi, the five children, the nanny. By this time Tonino had departed for home. Of course, Tonino had never been there, as his was a secret mission.

Chapter Six

It had been a good Easter from the business point of view so far, thought Traiano, but from every other aspect, it promised to be disastrous.

Tonino had left the house before Anna Maria and the children got back from Mass. However, they had passed his car on the road, and it was clear that Isabella had spotted him, and so had Natalia. The latter, a forward girl for her age, just like her sister, approached her father to ask why Tonino had been there. Her father, thinking that telling the truth was probably the least tiresome option, told her that Tonino had come to deliver a message from Palermo. This did not interest Natalia at all. What interested her was Tonino, the boy she was so precociously in love with, and who had been stolen, she was sure, by Isabella. The two sisters had not spoken to each other for weeks. The two sisters, if the depths of their mutual loathing were to be taken seriously by themselves, would never speak to each other again.

That Tonino had come and gone without stopping to say hello, hurt Natalia; but this sense of neglect was balanced by the idea that he was perhaps avoiding Isabella, and that was why he had left before their return. He had a girlfriend and a child and was getting married, so why would he even want to meet Isabella, if he could possibly avoid it? Isabella's thoughts ran along a similar path: Tonino had paid attention to her once, but then ceased to do so as soon as something better had come along. She remembered the short muscular boy; she did not care about him one little bit anymore; but she did care that he did not care about her. It was insulting. She looked upon him as an enemy. And her sister loved him, that was obvious. The sister who had betrayed her to her father, the sister who had to be taught a lesson.

That all was not well over the lunch table was clear; once could sense that in this large gathering there were three happy little boys, two very angry girls, and a somewhat estranged husband and wife. The presence of Renzo and Traiano, and their wives and children, was not quite enough to mask that all was not well.

Anna Maria cornered him over coffee in the drawing room after lunch.

'Has he asked you to speak to me?' she asked.

'No. Not yet. I am sure he will soon. Catarina is being stubborn. So that means that things will enter a second stage of negotiation after Easter, when her cousin returns. He is the one behind all this, you know. Both she and he have overestimated their position, if you ask me.'

'I am glad to hear it,' she said. 'This is not just personal, you know. It is business as well; in fact, it is business first and foremost. We are rich, but we cannot have this outsider and her children making claims on our money. My children come first. We cannot tolerate rivals.'

'Well, don Carlo had lots of bastards, and so does don Carmelo. Have they made any trouble?'

'No, but there may come a time…. How is Renzo?'

'Pleased. She is having another one, as you know. We spend a lot of time together. He's exhausting. So much energy. All that running and physical exercise. I think he wants to play tennis this afternoon. Ever since he gave up his bad habits…'

'How is Beppe?'

'Very well. He is seeing a girl, at long last. Muniddu's daughter.'

'That is about his level. But when you consider he is going to be so rich, he can choose whoever he likes, and no one will question it. He is a strange boy. Of course, Calogero wanted him for his daughter, but that is not going to happen now. She is rather more grown up than Beppe.'

'I heard.'

'And that I got the blame?'

'I heard that too. But… I wanted to talk to you about Ruggero Bonelli. I know he would like to meet you. I think you should meet him. He's an expert on art. I can't remember if you have visited his gallery in Catania… He is the one who got me that ill-fated Madonna by Mantegna that has caused me so much heartache. I have been told that he has now got a portrait of Lady Hamilton by, he thinks, Angelica Kauffman. It is a very pretty picture, and I thought you might like it. At least you might like to view it before anyone else does.'

'How clever you are, dearest Caravaggio,' she said. 'I would love an Angelica Kauffman, and I would love a picture of Lady Hamilton. But I am not sure I am going to Catania again in the foreseeable future.'

'Well, I could ask him to come over to Palermo with the picture to show it to you. I gather that there are no questions of provenance, if you know what I mean. It is just a generic portrait of a lady, but Bonelli is sure the subject is Emma Hamilton.'

In Catania, Roberto's lunch with his mother and sisters should have been so enjoyable. The food was good, they were all relaxed and enjoying the holiday, talking about what they might do tomorrow on Easter Monday, perhaps go up Etna, perhaps go to Taormina. This sort of conversation, they knew, was all thanks to him, thanks to the money he earned; and that was thanks to Tonino; and it was ultimately thanks to don Calogero di Rienzi. Petra, Roberto's youngest sister, had been a little upset when she and Tonino had ceased to be friends, but she had recently found someone else, a fellow student, or he had found her, so it was now possible to speak about Tonino without any tension in the family circle. They were curious about Emma, about the baby Olivia, about the forthcoming nuptials. She was from a very important and rich family, for whom Tonino worked, and it seemed to them incredible that Tonino should have ascended to such heights and be marrying such a girl. He had to explain that she was no ordinary young lady of a rich family. She had dyed her hair green, and she had multiple piercings, and she was not skinny as all rich girls were, far from it. She had got pregnant partly to rebel against her family, and decided to marry Tonino for the same reason. And if her mother liked Tonino it was because he was so polite to her, such an obvious good boy, so amenable, and he now went to Mass to please the mother-in-law to be, though Emma was an atheist, although Tonino had persuaded her to get little Olivia baptised. Signora Santucci was making the best of a bad job, hoping that Tonino would polish up a bit, which, she was sure, he would.

'If only he were taller,' said Roberto's mother sadly.

After lunch was over, they all went for a walk, and about five in the afternoon, he left them to go and call as arranged on Gabriella, something that he had been dreading all day, and which he had to get over with.

He wasn't, he knew now, the good Sicilian boy he had always thought himself to be. Of course, he adored his mother, he loved his sisters, but in certain respects, unlike Tonino, who was a good Sicilian boy, he had failed and failed badly. For the last two years, ever since that weekend in Enna, he and Tonino has slept together; ever since they had shared the flat together in Palermo, once a week, sometimes more, Tonino had got into bed with him, muttering 'Any port in a storm' under his breath, feigning, perhaps feeling, complete indifference. He too was expected to feign a similar indifference, and he had maintained the outward show of it, but in truth he had wanted to say the forbidden words of love and affection, but knew he could not, that this was against the rules, that this was something a good Sicilian boy could not say. During this time, they each had had their alibi: he had been sleeping with Gabriella, and Tonino had been going around with his sister Petra, and sleeping with, among others, Emma, from time to time. Then everything had changed. Emma had accepted him; he had become hers, and he had become the child's recognised father; and he had sensed that Tonino was lost to him. But what could one say? Tonino would retort that he was not lost to him, because he had never belonged to him. And the truth was, he had not belonged to him; but he had wanted to.

As for Gabriella's most unexpected pregnancy, that too revealed to him that he was not a good Sicilian boy. He had not told his mother and his sisters about that. He was hoping he would not have to.

He went up to the flat with heavy steps and found the door open. She called to him from the kitchen, where she was making tea. He didn't like tea, though he had never told her this, but he knew she liked it. The tea made, they went into the sitting-room, and sat down amidst all the beautiful furniture.

'Happy Easter,' he said.

'Did Tonino come with you?' she asked.

'No. He is with Emma in Palermo. They are coming tomorrow.'

She poured him a cup and passed it to him. He could sense that everything was wrong; well, it was; he sensed perhaps that she had guessed what he had come to say. He took the cup and had a sip. It tasted like poison.

'Have you had time to think of what I said?' he asked. 'About your....?'

'My pregnancy,' she supplied. 'I have. I have thought about it, what you said. I have thought of little else.'

He waited for her to continue. He carefully placed the cup on the coffee table in front of him, lest he let it fall. He felt the blood had fled from his face.

'The answer to your question is no,' she said.

'I am not ready to be a father,' he replied. 'I mean, I am too young, I am 24. It was not planned, maybe if it had been planned, but…. Maybe in a year or two, but now, not now. I am not explaining myself very well. I can't explain.'

She nodded.

'You have explained yourself well enough,' she said.

For a moment, he felt a blessed wave of relief. He thought for a moment that she had, after all, listened to him; she had gone and done it over the last week; she had gone to hospital and got rid of the child. But as he looked into her eyes, he saw he was mistaken, and he quickly looked away again. He felt ashamed. She should not have put him through this.

'I am not surprised,' she said. 'I calculated that was what you were likely to say. It is true. You are not ready to be a father. You are younger than me, much younger than me. We both have very different expectations and desires, don't we? You are twenty-four, I am thirty; actually, I am thirty-three. I lie about my age. You are not ready to be a father. But I am ready to be a mother. In fact, I may never have another chance.'

'I can't support you, I can't support a child,' said Roberto.

'I am financially independent.'

'No, what I meant was I do not want a child, not now, perhaps not ever. If you go ahead, you go ahead without me.'

'I go ahead,' she said. 'Without you.'

'Without me,' he echoed. He took a nervous slurp of tea. 'You are making a mistake. It would be better to, you know, end it while you can.'

'It is my child. I know it is yours too, but do you begrudge me the chance to have a child?'

'You planned this,' he said, not as an accusation, but more as a statement of fact.

'Yes,' she admitted.

'And you knew I would not be happy to be used in this way,' he said.

'You have not been badly treated,' she said.

He stood up.

'Right now, I feel I never want to see you again,' he said.

He left the room, and a moment later she heard the door close behind him.

The first working day after Easter, he had a lunchtime meeting and had decided to have it in a very crowded trattoria in the middle of the city; the food was good, the place was noisy, and there was no possibility of the conversation being overheard or the place being bugged. He did not book, and he had commanded, well, suggested to Ruggero Bonelli to meet him there at 1pm. The message had been sent via his wife and signora Grassi. Sure enough, as he knew he would be, Bonelli was there. He had arrived at the table a few minutes before one. Bonelli arrived at one exactly. He stood to greet him, and they shook hands. This was to be an important meeting, they both knew that; after all, why would he have asked to see Bonelli and expect him to come all the way from Catania, and asked him in so clandestine a way, if it were not important?

They sat at their table and looked at their menus. Half a litre of the house red was ordered, along with the lasagne, to be followed by veal cutlets. These were the necessary preliminaries. It was not necessary to get down to business too soon.

'You came by train?' he asked.

'Bus. It is only two hours. The train takes forever. Driving and parking is a nightmare. The bus is always best.'

Traiano nodded.

'You read the paper on the way over, I expect? You saw the news yesterday evening? Nasty business.'

'Very. It seems to be a confusing case. A young man shot dead in the street by a passer-by, quite casually, no one saw him, and the young man's uncle has disappeared as well. The uncle being an employee of your firm for many years….'

'Yes, it is confusing. The uncle must have done it, don't you suppose? At least, everyone will suppose so. I think it must have been a quarrel about money, don't you think? The nephew, this Simone Rota, was dependant on the uncle…. He leaves a mother and a sister, and they will be very short of cash. I think our Confraternity might help them. I will speak to Calogero. Incidentally, I want to talk to you about Calogero. But before we get to that, that young man Roberto Costacurta, what is he up to these days?'

'You are asking me? He lives here, doesn't he? I am surprised you don't know. He has finished with Gabriella. He did so just a couple of days ago, on Easter Sunday itself. It is all a bit confusing. I don't think he has behaved very gallantly. She had told him she was pregnant; he was not happy about it, and he walked out on her. She is going to have the baby all on her own. That is her decision. She says she is better off without him. Maybe she really feels she is, or maybe she is making the best of it. Who can tell?'

'I am glad for her. Having a child. That is something that will bring her joy. And she has you to help her. He would not have made a very good husband, you can be sure. He is the sort of young man who really only thinks of himself.'

'I am aware that we have you to thank. After all, we met him through you. His father walked out on his children, and now he walks out on Gabriella. But he is much younger than her, and so we should have expected it.'

'I think he likes older women,' said Traiano. 'Some men do. I might have a word with him, to let him know that I do not approve of his ungallant behaviour, to keep him on his toes. Consider it a favour, in return for numerous favours you have done me in the past. I owe you a great deal. This court case over the not stolen picture which is not by Mantegna…. I love that picture and I want it back. I do not want to admit to myself that it has brought me ill fortune. But it is not the never-ending court case that I want to talk about.'

The lasagne arrived. There was a pause in the conversation. The wine was poured and so was the mineral water.

'Do you think the police will make any progress with this Rota case?' asked Bonelli. 'I mean, is that another court case you will have to face sooner or later?'

'The dead young man? Or the disappearing uncle and his disappearing friends? Or the connection between the two? No, I don't expect them to make much progress. There is no case. No case that could possibly bother me. The young man was killed, we know that, but it remains mysterious. Goodness knows whom he upset. I assume the uncle, as generally I do not like coincidences. The uncle killed his nephew and then vanished; he presumably planned to vanish, and killed the nephew to tidy up a loose end. His disappearing is more interesting. As you pointed out, he worked for us, and he and five of his close colleagues have vanished. I believe they have found the cars, all parked near the port, and say that this shows they have gone off to Italy by ferry, or somewhere else, Malta, or even Tunisia. Moreover, according to the reports on the television, the wives and families are all distraught, as the uncle and his friends monetised all their assets, or as many as they could, before going, so that means they are not coming back, I think, and their wives believe the same.'

'Men don't just vanish,' said Bonelli.

'No, they don't. They are in Italy somewhere, or further afield. The Balkans, where I come from. When you want to disappear, you go to Kosovo, or Macedonia, or maybe Serbia. People are hard to find there. But why are you so bothered? Do you think this affects us? It does not. Look how well our business is going. I mean the pictures. You and I are doing well. You are doing well because of me. I hope you are not regretting our association?'

'Not in the least.'

'Good. It would not make sense for us to fall out. Our interests coincide. And I am sure you can be discreet. How much money did we make last year, you and I together? Well, you and I and Pasquale Greco and don Calogero? A lot, I know.'

'I gather not everything is well with don Calogero,' said Bonelli.

'What have you heard? I never listen to gossip, but I would like to know what people are saying.'

'I am always suspicious when people ask a question when they already know the answer. His daughter is causing trouble, is she not? It must be troubling for him. And then his own affairs have come to light.'

'Everyone seems to know,' observed Traiano. 'Poor Calogero. He lives in dread of his past. The whole idea is to leave that past well behind. He wants his daughter to be rather different to the girls he knew when he was young. He didn't marry Anna Maria Tancredi because she was one of the richest women in Sicily, indeed the richest, and one of the best connected in the business world. No, he married her because she is from the upper classes, or rather his idea of what the upper classes look and sound like. But a dog returns to his vomit. Everyone knows about his mistress and the children. Gabriella probably knows all about it; Roberto does, who gets it direct from Assunta. But I suppose Anna Maria needs him and he her, so… But they have not really spoken much for a long time,' said Traiano. 'But she can tell you that herself, as she has come back to Palermo early on business,, and we are invited there for coffee after this.'

'We are?'

'Don't sound surprised. She wants to make a few investments, buy a few pictures, and she needs someone to scout them out for her. She loves the idea of the Angelica Kauffman, by the way. She owns several things that are priceless. She has a school of Murillo Madonna, did you know, to which she is very attached. But that need not impress you. She wants to buy some more things, to start to collect. We talked about it as Easter. Boldini. You love Boldini, don't you? We all do. And I know she loves Boldini too. I live in Piazza Ignazio Florio, and you know that Boldini painted his wife, and that was his masterpiece, and it hangs, where….?'

'In a hotel. Last time it was for sale it made eight hundred thousand euro.'

'Which is not very much. Next time it comes up for sale, she will want it, I can guarantee. We discussed it. Was Boldini the greatest artist to work in Sicily?'

'No, that was Caravaggio. Or some would say Antonello.'

'I would say Caravaggio. You know, a couple of years ago, I did a little tour with my wife and children. We went to the museum in Messina, and we went to Syracuse, so that means I have seen every Caravaggio in Sicily. All four of them.' He saw that he now had his attention, in a way that he had not had it before. 'Yes, all four of them. What would you do to see the fourth one?'

'Anything, anything,' said Bonelli.

At that point the main course arrived.

'I love the sound of your desperation,' said Traiano. 'All I will say is that you need to make a good impression this afternoon. She has it. But don't say I said so. Let her tell you.'

'She has….?'

Traiano was pleased to see that Bonelli was breathless.

'The missing Caravaggio, *The Nativity with Saint Lawrence and Saint Francis*,' he said easily. 'Yes. Win her confidence. If she likes you, if she trusts you, she will confide in you. Make her confide in you. She wants to, well, sanitise it. I think you will like Anna Maria. She is fifty, but very beautiful, very charming. She likes younger men. Someone I like and trust needs to get to her before someone I may not like or trust does. You will do. And she will be grateful to me; and you will make sure she is grateful to me. Oh yes, I know what you are thinking: a bullet in the head from her husband. True, it is a risk. But you do not need to worry overmuch about him. He has a lot of worries right now, chiefly her. He fears and respects her. And he would not want to make a fool of himself by shooting you. And if he shot you, who is to say someone might not go round and shoot her, the mistress, or their child? No, I foresee a profitable relationship for you both. Tell me, can it be done?'

'What? Putting *The Nativity with Saint Francis and Saint Lawrence* on public display? The most famous stolen picture in the world? Sure, why not? There must be a way. One can claim that it is in fact a reproduction, or an eighteenth-century copy, worth a few thousand euros. One can get a restorer to alter it slightly, put something in the background, so it does not look like an exact copy. Why not?'

'Just don't disappoint me. You will be kept busy. For a start, every time a Boldini comes up for auction, you and she are going to fly there and bid. Oh, what fun you are going to have….'

'I can just imagine. The richest potential client in Sicily. But the other thing, me jumping into bed with her, that cannot be done.'

'Why not?' he asked, puzzled. 'She is gorgeous.'

'You will need to find someone else for that,' said Bonelli. 'She likes younger men, you say? Well, it ought not to be hard.'

Traiano nodded. He understood.

After lunch was over, and they were expected at her flat at 2.30pm or thereabouts, they walked the short distance to where she lived. And he took him up, introduced them, and after a cursory cup of coffee, left them, citing business. Ruggero Bonelli, by contrast, said that he had the rest of the day ahead of him, and nothing in particular to do.

After he left them, he decided to walk to his gym and have a swim, which was something he always did at about 2.30 in the afternoon. He entered the building and waved to the man on the door, who nodded back. He was in the changing room, always deserted at that time, when Tonino came in.

'How are you? I was hoping to see you. How is Emma? How was Easter Monday in Catania? How is Olivia?'

'All well, all very well.'

'Great,' said Traiano, tapping his nose.

A few minutes later, Tonino joined him in the pool; they both came to rest at the deep end, holding onto the side.

'It was easy,' reported Tonino. 'I knew his movements. He always came down to put the rubbish out at about 8.30. I thought that maybe as it was Easter Sunday, he would not, but he did. I called his name, and pop, pop. There was no one around. Then I got back on my bike and went home and me and Emma and the baby went out to dinner.'

'You washed your hands?'

'I went home first and had a shower and put my clothes in the wash.'

'Excellent. They will blame this on the uncle and his friends. They have discovered their cars; perhaps they think they have taken the ferry as foot passengers, or that they just want people to think that. Whichever way, they will be scratching their heads. Listen, you will need to see the signora about your money. Leave it until next week. This week, she is distracted with an errant husband and with matters of her own. Have you seen Roberto?'

'This morning, yes, he has gone to work. I saw him go. Has he done anything wrong?'

'So, you do not know? My wife told me all about it. He's made Gabriella pregnant and walked out on her. That is one thing he has done. Not very gallant. What did he say to you?'

'That it was not his idea, that he does not want to be a father, that he is too young. That he felt she had trapped him.'

Traiano was dismissive of this: 'I was fifteen, you were seventeen when Emma had her baby, and we were both delighted. And he is what? Twenty-four? Too young! He is a boy from the slums like you and me, and he seems to have forgotten his origins. Someone should give him a good whipping. But that, luckily for him, is not my responsibility. He's educated, he is certainly very handsome, but he has got above himself. He thinks himself above Gabriella now, does he? Well, what a high opinion of himself he must have. The mother and the sisters brought him up like a little prince, no doubt. The father left the family, and this is the result. A boy like that needed regular whipping. But, you know what, Tonino?'

'No, boss, but I hope you are going to tell me...'

'When I meet someone with a weakness, I try not to feel angry or disapprove, rather I try to work out how I can exploit that weakness, how I can use it for my own advantage. Did you ever hear of a person called Fabrizio Perraino? You were young, and he has been dead at least four years, maybe five or six. Perraino is someone we owe a great deal to. He did not mean to help us, but he did. He was a very unpleasant man, to me personally, and to Alfio and to Gino. I cannot quite remember why we got rid of him now; he was Anna Maria's nephew and her lover; he was getting out of the swimming pool one day at Donnafugata and his aunt noticed how grown up he had become, and…. Well, enough said. Then he had a bust up with Carmine del Monaco. Now this was a long time ago, because I was very young, and I was taken by my mother and Turiddu to have a pizza at Carmine del Monaco's place; it was the first pizza I had ever had, and I was about eight at the most. Turiddu was checking the place out. You and I cleared out his grave, remember? Anyway, by that time the signora had lost interest in Fabrizio because Carmine had broken his jaw in two places, and when they fixed his jaw they left him with a lisp, so from being a very attractive man he became a very unattractive one. Why am I telling you this? Ah, yes. The boss knew about Fabrizio, and decided – well, he did not, she did – to be Anna Maria's lover. You see, that was her weakness, goodlooking rough young men, who are over full of themselves. Well, he exploited that, and or she exploited him, whichever way it was. So, you see what I am thinking? Your friend Roberto strikes me as being selfish, ambitious and ready to sleep with anyone who will help him. Now, that is a weakness, but we can use him. We took Fabrizio away from his aunt; it is time to provide her with another Fabrizio.'

'Don Calogero would not like it,' said Tonino.

'Well, it has not happened yet, and it might not happen at all. But let us see, shall we? Will Roberto play ball?'

'He would think of the danger, I am sure,' said Tonino. 'The danger of don Calogero finding out.'

'To think of the dangers is always wise,' said Traiano. 'But if we think of only the dangers, only the risks, then we would never do anything. I mean, did you think of the dangers and the risks of sleeping with Emma?'

'Boss, I did that because I could not help it.'

'I am sure you did. And it didn't turn out badly, did it? You have done well. I speak with some knowledge of this. I am the son of a prostitute from Romania; you are an ugly short arse from Catania, but now you have a daughter, you are marrying the daughter of Antonio Santucci, and you are gaining a mother-in-law who adores you. Your status, your standing, has greatly improved. And you have one point six million under your bed, don't you, as well as lots more stashed away elsewhere. You even own a vineyard and you can converse well on wine, what grape, what bottle to buy. Tonino, you are well on the way to becoming what the English call a gentleman. It is, as in my case, a miraculous transformation. You and I have both risen so far…. Who knows how far we may rise further?'

He could see Tonino thinking.

'Put the idea into Roberto's head. I don't care how you do it. Just do it. Appeal to his lust and to his ambition. He has plenty of both.' He paused. 'And do we really care about Calogero getting angry? How much do we really care about upsetting Calogero, eh?' He smiled. 'You see how putting Roberto in Anna Maria's bed helps us both, if we are the ones who put him there?'

'It is going to be an important week,' continued Traiano. 'Everyone else is still on holiday or relaxing after a holiday, but we have work to do. Come to Piazza Florio at seven tomorrow, on a motorbike. Bring two helmets. Make sure the bike cannot be traced, so steal one. Bring a spare set of clothes and bring the gun you used on young Rota. We are going to use it again.'

It was easy, so easy. Tonino knew, because he paid attention, he always listened, that Sandro always slept in late, until about 10am, being the lazy man he was; and he knew too the location of the small guesthouse he was staying in; he had chosen a small place to be discreet, and also to save money, until his mother should pay up; and he knew, because Emma had mentioned it, that at about 10.30am he was usually to be found in the next door bar having coffee and pastries and making phone calls and sending messages.

Traiano and Tonino arrived in plenty of time and waited, choosing a spot with a view of the door of the guesthouse and the next-door café. They sat near the bike under a tree, in deep shade, where the cameras, if there were any, would not be able to pick them up so easily. They were wearing non-descript clothes, and had adopted the usual disguises. Taking off their helmets, Tonino put on the same glasses he had worn on Easter Sunday, and the same baseball cap; Traiano was wearing a pair of aviator shades and a bandana over his dark curly hair. After a time, spent in silence, they saw him come out of the guesthouse, and walk the few steps to the café. He was not looking up, but studying his phone. They allowed him a bit of time to order his coffee and choose his pastry, and then Tonino started the engine on the bike, and put on his helmet. Putting on his helmet as well, Traiano walked to the bar; without hesitating, he walked in, saw Sandro, still studying his phone, standing at the bar. He aimed for the heart and the head. He hit the target both times. The noise of the shots was completely deafening, almost stunning. The other people in the bar threw themselves on the ground. There were whimpers, not screams. He did not drop the gun. Outside, the bike was waiting. He jumped on the back and they were away at speed, towards Villa San Giovanni and the ferry. At the ferry terminal, they dumped the bike, and then they threw away the helmets, the gloves, the jackets they had been wearing. Just with their rucksacks, they got on the ferry, and after about quarter of an hour, it set sail. In mid-channel, Traiano threw the gun overboard. The rest of their clothes they changed in the ferry's lavatories, and Traiano thoroughly washed his hands, so by the time they arrived in Messina, they were unrecognisable from the men that had been in Reggio.

In Messina, they parted. Tonino took the train to Palermo, and Traiano took the train south, to Giardini Naxos. There, Renzo was waiting with his car and drove him up to Taormina. He saw Renzo's questioning look and nodded. Renzo smiled with relief. At the top of the hill, in one of the most luxurious hotels owned by don Carmelo, the Serb was waiting for them.

Costantino, the Serb, greeted them warmly; hands were shaken; a bottle of champagne appeared; Renzo politely refused and asked for mineral water; Traiano allowed himself a sip. The atmosphere was polite, conversational. They hardly knew each other, but they knew of each other's reputations; they looked at each other with guarded respect.

'How does it feel to be back in Sicily?' asked Traiano.

The Serb looked pensive.

'It is nice to see my children. I have two. They are great kids, teenagers now. My wife, well, she is a good woman, but ever since our son was born, she lost interest in being a wife. It sometimes happens. She is devoted to the children; I miss them, I don't miss her; but we respect each other. She is a good Sicilian girl. She too is a relation of don Carmelo. It is a big family, as you know, a very big family. Her father and don Carmelo are cousins.'

'So, you are her second cousin,' said Renzo.

Traiano noticed that he said 'don Carmelo', not 'my father'. There was a story there, he could tell. How old was don Carmelo? Mid-fifties at most. And Costantino was about forty, he thought, though strong and very fit, the sort of man who was always taking exercise.

'How is don Carmelo?' he asked.

'I believe he is well,' said Costantino. 'We have had a few business meetings.'

'And your family in Africa?' asked Renzo.

Costantino did something surprising. He smiled broadly.

'The twins are getting big. We are very happy indeed. Both children are extremely beautiful, like their mother.'

He took out his wallet, and showed them a photograph. They exclaimed in admiration. Renzo took out a photograph of Elena and their child, and Traiano also showed his family photograph.

'Your eldest is how old?' asked Costantino.

'Seven. I had him young,' he said with a smile.

'The things we do, we do for them,' said Costantino. 'My African children are a little disadvantaged, as they are illegitimate, and they are half African and, perhaps worse, a quarter Serb. But I intend to give them a good start in life. Some people do not like Serbs. Just like they do not like Romanians. We are at a natural disadvantage. But your children are half Italian, aren't they?'

'They are Italian. They cannot speak the language. I can, my mother taught me, but…'

Costantino nodded. He looked at Renzo, and took another sip of champagne. So did Traiano. There was silence. Traiano caught Renzo's eye. The latter made an excuse and got up, to go and look at the view.

'You trust him?' asked Costantino.

'Yes.'

'He's a Sicilian.'

'So is my wife; so are my children; so is my stepfather. Yes, I trust him. He's actually a nice guy. A bit stupid, a bit without direction, but I have brains and direction for two. Besides, he loves me a lot. But I know what you mean; we are both, you and I, in a sense, outsiders here. That is why I need him. I will never be at the top, but he can be, and I can be behind him, if you see what I mean. He's useful cover. He loves me and, if I tell him to, he will like you too.'

'Would you like to be at the top?'

'What sort of question is that? Of course. Wouldn't we all? People who say they would not, are liars.'

Costantino looked at him.

'You are Balkan scum, if you don't mind me saying, and so am I. Your mother was a prostitute from Iasi, I believe?'

'That is general knowledge,' admitted Traiano.

'We have things in common, and interests in common,' said Costantino. 'My mother was working here as a chambermaid when she was sixteen. She came from Niš, a summer job. She went home pregnant, with me. The owner's son, as he was then, don Carmelo, well he wasn't called that then, took advantage of her.'

'What exactly do you mean by that?' asked Traiano.

'You know what it means. You may even have done it yourself. It is very common. He forced himself on her, he raped her. Not just once, but several times. Then she went back home, with me inside her. Her parents, her relations, made a big fuss, made representations, but don Carmelo's father, my grandfather, was not interested. They sent some money. Maybe they gave Carmelo a good hiding, telling him not to be so stupid again. He was young, big for his age, entitled, thought he could take what he liked. They told my mother's family that she must have led him on, and that if she were raped, why did she continue sleeping with him? Anyway, I came back here when I was sixteen or so, made myself known; they gave me a job. Once I had done the DNA test.'

'Your mother?'

'By that time, she had married, had more children, but not much money, I wanted to help. Well, I have worked hard for don Carmelo; I married his cousin's daughter, I am his eldest child, but I remain his teenage embarrassment, the Serb, the one who is not one of us. His legitimate children do well, are respectable, the eldest studying particle physics in some American university, but I am the one who takes out the rubbish. I have never met them. The other illegitimates, they are all fully Italian, and he favours them above me. That is one reason I was so keen to go to Africa, apart from making lots of money, I was so keen to get away.'

'I never liked don Carmelo,' said Traiano slowly. 'Who controls his wealth?'

'The lady you know so well. Anna Maria Tancredi.'

Traiano marvelled. Costantino had been thinking of this for twenty years, and now the parts were falling into place. He saw Renzo hovering in the distance. He beckoned him to come over. Renzo resumed his seat.

'We want Alfio Camilleri dead,' explained Traiano. 'He killed our friend don Gino, whose death you will remember, two years ago. It is not simply a matter of revenge. It is a considered decision, as it ought to be. Alfio supplied his cousin to the boss, and she has given birth to a child, his child. The boss's wife is furious, as I am sure you can understand. When Alfio is killed, she will be grateful; the dottoressa always helps her friends. Getting rid of Alfio will persuade the cousin that the game is up for her. Besides, Alfio is ambitious. We can do without that. Now you, Costantino, have given us to believe that you can do without Alfio in Africa.'

Costantino considered.

'He is not a bad guy, but he thinks too well of himself. He is constantly interfering. We have those people you sent us, Omar and his people, and we have a lot of Serbs, really tough fellows. These people have been in wars, and they know about fighting. Alfio has nothing to teach them, he just annoys them. And the wife, she is nice, but she doesn't associate with the other women. My African girl resents that. Sometimes you have to muck in with the others. The hotel is breaking even, flying people in and out; well, it is a lovely place, and it helps us to launder tons of cash, I am sure. But the real money is coming from the boys, Omar, the Serbs, the Sicilian Foreign Legion. You have heard of land invasions? People come and occupy property illegally? We turn up, surround the place, use our guns, and well, the land invasion is over. It solves a massive headache. And when the government cannot trust its own troops to do something, well, we do it, and they are grateful. The amount of disorder in our little corner of Africa has decreased markedly in the last three years. Ok, it is not nice work. Perhaps we are the disorder now, but we are the disorder of whoever will pay us. When we go on a mission, Alfio says he feels unwell and can't come. The man is a coward. And there are a few things the Africans do that he thinks are uncivilised. Well, life is uncivilised. The whole thing would run better without him. But does your boss agree?'

'He has agreed,' said Renzo. 'We spoke to him and he said yes.'

'Don Carmelo may be retiring soon,' said Traiano to Renzo, 'and Costantino taking over. If that happens, well, it is sort of linked. Costantino can do us a favour, and we can do him a favour, using our influence with Anna Maria when the time comes.'

'Give me the word, and he will be dead by nightfall,' said Costantino. 'You will stay for lunch, won't you?'

They both accepted the kind invitation.

'By nightfall?' asked Renzo.

'The other Serbs hate him. Omar doesn't care for him. While I am away it would be best, I think. One phone call. From here to there. I can speak to one of the Serbian boys. They would do it at once.'

'How can you speak to one of the Serbian boys?' asked Traiano.

'Satellite phone,' said Costantino. 'Immune to wiretapping.'

'Do it,' said Traiano.

Costantino got up, and left them.

'How was Reggio?' asked Renzo, when he was gone.

'Exactly as it should have been. No worries. He was looking at his phone, when, well, pop, pop. That was all. Why ask? Are you worried he may not have had a good death? He was a worthless person, no one will be sorry, not even his mother, or at least not for long.'

'What about the boss? Calogero?' asked Renzo.

'Bit late to be worrying about him now, isn't it? Anyway, I thought you were the boss? He was your cousin, not Calogero's. Tonino and I did what you told us to do. Oh, I know, we had our own reasons, but… Don't worry about Calogero. He has enough to worry about. This business with Catarina, that hole that he dug and I have to rescue him from. Calogero needs to learn a bit of humility. He has made a few mistakes too many. He should never have allowed Alfio to kill Gino. This will teach him a lesson. And relax: no one is going to get over-excited by the death of someone as unimportant as Sandro.' He looked at Renzo. 'Sandro's dead, Alfio will soon be dead. Isn't that what you always wanted? Just trust me. And there's no progress without a few people falling by the wayside. You wanted revenge. Well, enjoy it. Not that it is simply revenge. It is a material advantage to us. One less annoying Santucci. One less boring rival like Alfio.'

Costantino returned, and they began to think about lunch.

The news of the two murders was heard with annoyance and grief in certain quarters. There was not much co-operation between the police forces in Sicily and those in Reggio; they heartily disliked each other, but there was some grudging sharing of information, and it was eventually realised that the gun used to shoot Sandro Santucci and that used to kill Simone Rota was the same gun, unquestionably so, though this took some time to establish as forensics were notoriously slow; but it eventually became clear that this was the same murder weapon and probably the same murderer, who had crossed their straits, as if to confuse them all, as if to make things deliberately difficult. Then of course there was the Santucci connection: one victim a member of the family, though estranged; the other a temporary employee, the nephew of a longstanding employee, now disappeared. Rota senior and his friends; Rota junior, and Sandro Santucci; it seemed clear that they were all involved in the same plot; and the search for Rota senior was intensified, but of him and four of his missing friends, there was no trace. The only person they were able to find was the man with the missing toe, Borelli, who was hiding in America, and whose extradition would take months, and who was considered too far away to have had anything to do with either the Palermo shooting or the Reggio killing. But the man with the missing toe might hold the key to everything, particularly as he too was a former Santucci employee.

There were a series of police interviews. They came to the offices in the viale della Libertà. They looked, interestingly, at the accounts first, at the records of payment to Rota and his friends. They looked at the bank accounts of the same; they worked out just how much these men were worth, and wondered what had persuaded them to monetise as much as they could and disappear. They conducted a thorough search of the Santucci building, looking for the money, but found nothing. They raided Renzo's house, and found nothing there; they raided Traiano's and found nothing there either. They knew nothing about Tonino, and thus did not raid him. But the money, which was so hot, was all stashed in various cellars belonging to faithful old ladies in Catania or had been deposited with Anna Maria. The financial police called on her, and looked at her recent transactions until their heads ached. They saw the huge amount of money that whizzed around the globe faster than they could catch it: Panama, the Caymans, Bermuda, Jersey, New Zealand, Malta; all belonging to a variety of charities of the most unimpeachable honesty.

The two magistrates who had been working on the Calogero di Rienzi case for years dusted off their files, looked at the new ones and decided that they would come down to Sicily and speak, not to the banker, not to the hardened criminals, but to the softer end of the family, namely to Angela Santucci, the mother of the murdered boy, to the boy's father, to his sisters and to his surviving brother. Silvio Pierangeli and Chiara di Donato thought they had a chance with them.

They tackled the signora first; she was often in the north of Italy, and they decided to approach her in Turin, where she was once more attending a conference on drug addiction and its attendant social ills, and the rehabilitation of drug addicts, which was being organised at the shrine of don Bosco. Turin was such a lovely city, and it would be nice to spend a few days there. They booked into the signora's hotel, and discovered, only when they had done so, that she was accompanied by her nephew Renzo Santucci. It seemed that this young man had, at his aunt's request, come with her, to give a speech at the conference about his own rehabilitation from drug and alcohol addiction.

The signora was at Mass at 7am at the shrine of Our Lady of Consolation, and they decided to ambush her there. She was alone, following the Mass devoutly, unaware that she was under surveillance. They kept their eyes on her, not allowing themselves to be distracted by the splendour of the church. They both felt sorry for her; a woman who had lost a brother and now a son, seeking consolation from the Mother of God, no doubt. She was an attractive woman, better looking than her sons or her nephew, they both thought, having studied the photographs. She was expensively but modestly dressed, her understated elegance hiding the huge care taken in selecting her clothes and her shoes. She wore a black lace mantilla and a single strand of pearls. She was in the act of taking off her mantilla outside the Church when they approached her.

'Signora,' said Silvio. 'We are staying at the same hotel. We would love to join you for breakfast.'

They mentioned their names, and they showed their identification. She looked around her, realising that she was trapped, that there was no escape, but she suppressed the momentary feeling of panic.

'Of course,' she said.

It was a short walk to the hotel, and when they had settled down at a table in the dining room, she asked them:

'Are you investigating my son's death? Because I have already spoken to the police about that,' she said.

Her voice was subdued. She said 'death' rather than murder, as if the incident in the bar in Reggio had been natural causes.

'Other people are doing that, signora,' said Chiara. 'We are looking not at the facts, but the facts behind the facts. We have seen the transcript of your interview. It seemed that your son had a troubled relationship with his father.'

'Oh yes.'

'And the autopsy report showed us that he had sustained a broken ankle some weeks before his death,' said Silvio.

'If you want to resurrect family quarrels, well, it is true. My husband has been a very difficult man for a long time; my son was not an easy boy. The two of them did not get on. They frequently quarrelled. Sandro wanted to leave home and never come back to Sicily again. There was also, as I am sure you have heard, the quarrel about the inheritance. Sandro felt aggrieved, poor boy: his grandfather did not love him; his father did not love him. It was hard for him to be a Santucci, you know; it was hard for him to express deference to these men; and to his cousin Renzo. My son was naturally non-deferential; he was insubordinate. He upset people; he would never do as he was told. He was a little bit wild. My brother was like that, but he was a different character altogether. I think Sandro, in a strange way, felt crippled by his antecedents, knowing he would never live up to them.'

'Ther are lots of difficult men like that,' said Silvio. 'But the idea that someone should shoot him dead for being difficult, that is outrageous.'

'I suppose it is,' she said. 'Most outrageous.'

'And yet you do not seem to be outraged, signora,' observed Silvio, with a touch of acidity.

'Do you have children, sir? Then you will know that quite often they refuse all advice. But it is worse than that. There is something more than contrarian, almost satanic about them. You remember the rebel angel, who said 'I will not serve'? I am afraid I saw it coming. He did not, I am happy to say, so his life was not overshadowed. He thought he was immortal. Most youngsters are like that. They rarely think of death; I think of it all the time. Sandro was an atheist, or so he told me, mainly to upset me. But he was not really an atheist. He himself wanted to be in the place of God, to command. But he did not have the character to do it. If he had been born into a different family, a less rich family…. The last few weeks of his life he spent phoning me every day asking me where the money was, hoping to squeeze enough out of me so that he would never have to work. I monetised everything I could, but it was never quite enough for him. He was so angry…. It quite broke my heart. Angry and frightened. I begged him to go away, but he would not listen. If only he had gone away…'

'Signora,' said Chiara, 'I do sympathise. I have children of my own, and so does Silvio. Children can be difficult, sometimes impossible. Do you have any idea who might have broken his ankle, who might have shot him?'

'I do my best to ignore those thoughts,' she said. 'But I have the feeling you are going to tell me.'

'A pin does not drop in Sicily without Calogero di Rienzi giving it permission to drop,' said Silvio. 'The murder of a member of the Santucci family would have had to have had the nod from him. Though he would not have been the prime mover. That would have been someone closer. Calogero hardly knew your son, after all.'

'I know what you are trying to do,' said Angela. 'You are trying to drive a wedge between me and my family. You are trying to make me distrust Calogero. I will accept that Calogero could not save my son. But that he initiated it, I will never believe.'

'Then who did?' asked Chiara.

She made no reply.

Her nephew now approached, bearing a cup of coffee and a brioche.

'Auntie,' he said, bending to kiss her cheek. 'Sorry I missed Mass, I will try harder tomorrow, or perhaps go this evening.'

He looked questioningly at the other two.

'The magistrates,' she explained.

They flashed their identification. He sat down. His aunt quietly got up and left, admonishing him that the first conference was at nine.

'Are you here to tell me who killed my cousin?' he asked.

'Do you really want to know?' asked Silvio.

'It is not hard to guess. He was killed in revenge, over some stupid quarrel, maybe it was to do with this young man, Rota, who was shot near the Corso Calatafimi. He was quarrelsome, you know. He provoked the wrong person. That is all. It happens week after week, in nightclubs and bar after bar. Tragic, but not uncommon.'

'You liked your cousin?' asked Chiara.

'He was my cousin. He drank, he took drugs, it's so sad for Aunt Angela. It is one of the reasons she does things like this. I used to drink and take drugs, but not anymore. Pity that Sandro could not follow my example.'

'You are right,' said Silvio. 'He offended someone. When we find out who, we find out who killed him, in all probability. But there was something we particularly wanted to ask you, sir. Of the people who were at your bachelor party, three are now dead: Gino Fisichella, Alfio Camilleri and Sandro Santucci. Remarkable, don't you think? Oh, and we know exactly who was there, as following the death of Gino the police came and took statements from everyone, and arrested you and Sandro.'

'Well, it was very annoying to be arrested a week before my wedding,' said Renzo, 'But in retrospect, it was my salvation, as I was forced into rehabilitation, and since then I have not touched a drop of alcohol or taken any drugs. Sandro, as I am sure you will know, refused to co-operate, and look at him now.'

'How well did you know Alfio Camilleri?' asked Silvio.

'Not at all well. He was there because he was Gino's friend and they were inseparable. Gino was married to his cousin. Gino was my inseparable friend too. That was why Alfio was there. But I have not seen him since, really, because shortly afterwards he went out to Africa to help with this hotel business. What happened there I do not know, but can imagine. They did not like him, clearly. Africa is a violent continent. It was some sort of quarrel. You need to speak to the wife, she was there, but what this sad event three thousand miles away has to do with me, I cannot tell.'

'Did you know Rota?'

'The uncle or the nephew? Neither. I would not even have recognised them on the street. Completely unknown to me.'

'Rota and his friends were all extremely rich,' pointed out Silvio. 'They monetised everything they could and fled. We cannot trace the money.'

'I bet they drove it over the border to Switzerland. They will all turn up somewhere, then you can ask them,' he said flippantly.

'They are dead,' said Silvio.

'Then someone else has their money,' said Renzo. 'I am sure your accountants are on to it.'

He smiled.

'I have to go and get ready for the opening of the conference at nine,' he said, rising and leaving them.

They decided that they would go to the conference, as they had come all this way to Turin, and it would be interesting to hear what the signora and her nephew would have to say. They entered the building with little difficulty, after showing their identification. The opening session was extraordinarily tedious. A prelate read out a message from the Pope; a local bishop from an unimportant diocese in Piedmont gave a talk about the necessity of moral revival, which was warmly applauded; a professor of sociology gave a disquisition on how drug and alcohol addiction were not the root cause of Italy's ills but the symptoms of Italy's ills. His manner of delivery was dull in the extreme, but they both found themselves nodding in agreement. Then there was a blessed break for coffee, and then at 11am, signora Santucci had the stage.

It was clear from the atmosphere in the conference hall that what had passed were largely preliminaries, and that this was the one talk everyone had been looking forward to. The atmosphere had changed. But both of them were slightly disappointed, for the talk she gave was essentially the sort of thing that one presumably heard at every meeting of the association for the friends and relatives of the addicted. The damage done by drugs and alcohol…. It was all a bit boring.

'I like her pearls,' whispered Chiara.

'Yes, they are lovely. You don't really notice them, but they give off an aura. In those statues in Spain, doesn't the Madonna of the Seven Sorrows wear pearls?'

'Her son was just murdered. Don't be so cruel.'

'She is milking it for all it is worth,' said Silvio. 'Her hypocrisy is breathtaking.'

Someone turned round and gave them a look.

'She is covering for someone,' said Chiara.

'The nephew?'

'Who else?'

'Could she be that fond of him?' asked Silvio, the disbelief showing in his voice.

Signora Santucci spoke of her work with drug addicts and the foundation that she worked with in Palermo. She stressed something that surprised the two magistrates: it wasn't enough to talk of drugs, drugs alone were not the problem, one had to talk of the people who took them, and one had to meet and befriend these people. There was a little swipe at the forces of law and order. Arresting people was largely a waste of time; putting them in jail was no cure; each person had to be treated as a person in need of medical and, above all, spiritual help; for drug addiction was a disease caused by what she termed emptiness of soul. The rehabilitation took place in a community of former addicts where people could rebuild warm and authentic relationships with each other; sometimes these were the very first such relationships such people had ever had. There was not much philosophy behind this, she said, but a mere recognition that men and women were empathetic human beings and needed each other. She noted that drug addiction, and suicide as well, were much higher among males than females.

None of this was very enlightening, thought the two magistrates, without having to say so to each other. Then Renzo Santucci got up to speak. It was clear that he had given this talk before. He spoke of how he had become a steady drinker by the age of fourteen, and a substance abuser soon afterwards. This was entirely his own fault. What made him change was the experience of losing his best friend just before his wedding, the man who should have been his witness, who, under the influence of drink and drugs, fell off a terrace and died of exposure. This led to his arrest for the offence of being under the influence of cocaine, and the shock of that and bereavement led to a vow never to drink again or to take cocaine again. He was happy to say that he had maintained this, not through some inner strength, for every day was a test, but thanks to the support of his wife, the thought of his baby son, the thought of the child to come, and the strong support of some family members, and the companionship of his friends, who were always there for him. He had also taken up long distance running, and also helped his aunt in her work, with fundraising and raising awareness of the problem of addiction. The years he had spent as an addict and an alcoholic were horrible empty years, he said. He now had rebuilt his life.

After this, they escaped the conference Hall and went for an early lunch.

'Well?' asked Silvio, deferring to Chiara's superior understanding of psychology, something he did not always trust.

'Renzo,' she said, 'is an addict. Once it was drink and drugs and maybe other things. Now it is running, and self-flagellation in public and the company of Antonescu, and perhaps other things. The poor man has been punishing himself since he was fourteen years old. He is tall, he is rangy, he is not attractive, he is somehow not together, if you see what I mean; the boy who was born to great wealth but knew he did not deserve it; the boy who was born to deference and knew he did not merit it. A very unhappy man who is not up to the position he holds; which in fact he does not hold: he is the titular head of all of this, and Calogero is behind him, holding him up, as the aunt was today. I imagine he likes and values the aunt, but her regard for him would be more practical.'

'You mean, she allowed her nephew to kill her son?'

'That, I admit, does not make sense. We need to look deeper. We need to go back to Sicily.'

But her heart sank as she said this. So did his.

They had already examined the transcript. They had examined it so often that they virtually knew it off by heart. They had, of course (both Calogero and Traiano were right about this) listening devices on all their phones and in the offices and in some of their houses, but none of these ever produced anything of great interest, indeed of any interest at all. Calogero had his residences regularly swept for devices, and men who came to read the meter or deliver packages were always rigorously supervised. There was no chance of getting a listening device into his flat in Catania or his wife's flat in Palermo, or the house in Donnafugata. They had listened to phones, but none of these conversations had been worthwhile. They had listened to the mobile phones of the women, but these were conversations to do with cooking, shopping, children and clothes; very occasionally one of the men would use his wife's phone, but these were very short messages about meeting for drinks, meals, or conversations that invariably took place in crowded outdoor spaces where they talked and walked. The huge volume of calls that went in and out of the Santucci offices and the Tancredi office were all innocent. They had introduced a mike into the changing room of the gymnasium in Palermo, which was a public place, and listened in to the conversations that happened there at certain times, such as early afternoon and Saturday morning. These were more instructive, but hardly enlightening, in that they only told them how much they did not know. They identified the voice of Traiano, that of Renzo and that of the young Santucci, and someone else who they did not know – frustratingly these conversations were fragmentary, as the speakers kept on moving around, and they did not always use each other's names. But these were the voices that recurred. The fourth person who was there often was a friend of the young Santucci, but it was confusing because sometimes there was a fifth voice as well. They had tried to place a listening device in one of the shower heads in the shower room, but this was impossible; everything they tried got very damp and failed to work, and besides, could pick up nothing because of the thundering shower water.

Then there was the Enna conversation, which was, compared to all this dross, pure gold. In fact, two Enna conversations. Catarina, living under a false name in Enna, with her children, had not thought that the man who came to fix something with the electricity was an agent of the police; and credit to the Enna police for taking the initiative. Most of it was complete rubbish, even what was caught when Calogero visited: conversations about children. But there had been the conversation with Antonescu that had been interesting and thrown some of the internal dynamics of the group into sharp relief. The mistress was hated by the wife, of course, that was to be expected, but by Antonescu as well, that was clear. She was clever and determined, and thus all the more of a headache. Well, they had set that up, thanks to a sharp-eyed off duty policeman seeing Calogero in Enna, and watching where he went, and what they had set up was paying off.

But the important conversation had been between Catarina and another woman, not Catarina and her lover. It had alerted them to a wide range of possibilities. Until then they had not realised that Alfio Camillieri was dead, or that this might be intimately connected with events in Sicily.

'If you had not pushed him, this would not have happened,' Giuseppina said. 'He made love to you when he was fourteen, you rejected him, and he spent the rest of his life trying to impress you.'

'My dear, Giuseppina, please believe me that it is not my fault that men want to make love to me. We were young and foolish, and I should have pushed him off. He was my cousin after all. But I cannot for a moment imagine that what happened almost twenty years ago had an effect on the rest of his life. If anything, he pushed himself, he pushed me. He pushed me into the arms of Calogero. I never wanted Calogero.'

'You never wanted Gino, you mean.'

'That is unkind. You know who it was that I wanted, the one they wanted for you. Rosario. I would have been a nice lawyer's wife, but it was not to be. Now tell me, what happened to Alfio?'

'They killed him.'

'They?'

'He went for a walk along the beach in the evening, as he often did, and he was shot at point blank range. When he did not come back, I went to look for him, and found him dead.'

'Poor you.'

'First they shot my sister, then they shot my husband. You get used to it.'

'Do they…?'

'No. They know nothing. It could have been an intruder. It could have been a grudge killing; they are common in Africa. Alfio was not always as nice as he could have been to the employees. The thing is that they wanted no publicity, as that would be catastrophic for the business. The whole thing is based on the fact that the hotel is safe. So I brought his body back, and buried him, and it was as if he had never lived.'

'Are you alright financially?'

'Of course. Calogero has been generous. Or at least the Confraternity has been. I am very well off. As I am sure are you, my dear. When Calogero creates widows, he always makes sure they do not suffer financially. Of course, if I were to kick up a fuss, it would be a different story.'

'You are speaking as if you are sure that Calogero killed him.'

'Of course he did. Who else?'

'But why?'

'Because he cannot kill you. So, he sends a message. He kills your cousin, as a warning to you, to do what he wants. You have been stubborn so far, now maybe he hopes you will be less stubborn. He hopes you will do what he says.'

'You're saying that Alfio's death is my fault?' she asked.

'You know I am right. He will not be defied. You need to leave before he kidnaps the children.'

'He would not harm his own children.'

'She would. They are not hers.'

'I will go to Lecce,' said Catarina. 'Will you tell him that? Is that why you came, to carry messages from him?'

'He will be pleased.'

This conversation had yielded something very important: that the murder of Alfio Camilleri had been ordered by Calogero, which meant in all probability that the order had been transmitted electronically. Once the date of the death was ascertained, it was necessary to look at all incoming messages received by the hotel switchboard in the preceding period. The traffic of calls from Italy was heavy, it being an Italian hotel. They had not been eavesdropping on the hotel lines, but they could obtain the records, after repeated requests from the local phone company via Interpol. On the day before Alfio's death, several numbers that had been in contact from Sicily looked interesting. These were from a variety of mobile and fixed line phones in Sicily, all of which were clients, prospective clients, suppliers, or friends of guests, bar one. This was from somewhere in the east of Sicily, made from a satellite phone, a brief call made at lunchtime Sicilian time on the day of the death. What passed on this call, they had no way of knowing, but they could guess. At least now they had a time and a date for the suspect call that authorised the death; and the certainty it had come from Sicily, from somewhere north of Catania.

None of this was evidence, of course, but they knew it was intelligence. It was, to say the least, infuriating that they could not pin the satellite phone down to a more precise location, or find out who the owner was. Had it been Calogero? Or had it been Antonescu and Santucci? Had it been the Serb, present in Sicily at that very date and phoning home in Africa to have some house cleaning done before his return? They inclined to think, as Catarina and Giuseppina assumed as a matter of course, that the order had come from don Calogero as it could have come from no one else, so powerful was don Calogero.

But why would Calogero want to dispose of such a trusted deputy? The cousin of his mistress to boot? The magistrates were mystified, but saw clearly that the answer lay somewhere in that conversation between Giuseppina and Catarina, the transcript of which they read again and again, until their eyes grew weary and their heads ached.

He had always known that one day an enemy would appear, and that enemy would present a very clear threat, one that needed to be dealt with, decisively and firmly. Now he sensed the enemy was close, almost in view, and he felt what he had always suspected would be the case, that the enemy was someone very close to him, someone who had made alliances with people less close to him. Having experienced absolute power, he now felt that power was growing weak. It was his own fault. He should never have alienated his wife. He had made repeated efforts to be reconciled with her, because he knew he needed her. However, the latest news, that Catarina was going to Lecce with the children, had not had the effect he had hoped for. Anna Maria had seemed almost indifferent to it, remarking firstly that Lecce was far away, a broad hint that he ought not even think of visiting her there, and that Lecce was a nice city, a good place for a permanent exile. What a mess.

But there were other messes. The second was the mess of the death of Sandro Santucci. He did not care in the least, personally, but this was a major headache strategically. He had given his word to the late Lorenzo and to his still living brother don Domenico, that no harm would come to any member of the Santucci family, that he would hold back the instinct of revenge that Renzo doubtlessly harboured. Well, that had not happened. He had said that Sandro was not to be harmed, but they had ignored his instructions. They had thought that he did not care about Sandro, which was true, but he cared about being defied, and he could imagine who had defied him.

The third and much bigger mess was the death of Alfio. Of course, he had given his permission for the Alfio job, but it was surely understood by everyone now that no one harm could have come to Alfio without his permission. Giuseppina, his former sister-in-law, the sister of his first wife, the children's beloved aunt, had come to him, and, from what she said, made it clear that she held him responsible for her husband's death. He had not denied it, because to deny he had authorised the death would be to admit that he was no longer fully in control. So he had let her accusation stand.

He knew too that Giuseppina could be satisfied, could be brought round, and that her accusation was rather like an insurance claim. He was responsible for Alfio's death, so he must compensate her, and that he accordingly did, making her the recipient of a huge pension from the Confraternity. He was sure she would come round. She cannot have been so very happy married to Alfio, he imagined, who could not give her children. In a year or two she would meet a nice man who could. And hadn't Alfio married her simply because she was his former sister-in-law, hadn't it been ambition that had driven him? But the next husband might be similarly influenced, he reflected.

The death of Alfio had clearly dislodged Catarina, for which he was grateful, though he had no intention of breaking with her completely. The children were too important to him. He would keep her at a distance, and one day perhaps call her back. He had no intention of divorcing his wife in favour of Catarina. He loved his five children too much, and he certainly did not love Catarina in the same way, if at all. He just wished that his wife could understand that: he did not care for Catarina. He cared for the children.

In the meantime, it was necessary to reassert his authority.

The first to be summoned was Traiano. They met in Palermo on Monday morning in the Santucci offices and descended to the street to talk where they could not be heard. They stood outside the Politeama.

'Explain what happened to Sandro Santucci,' commanded Calogero.

'I shot him,' said Traiano.

'So I imagined. Why?'

'He was being a pain in the neck with this court case. So, we made him go abroad, to Reggio. He carried on being a pain in the neck. He was cruel to Beppe. Renzo wanted him dead. So did Tonino. I am not sure why, but he said something to Tonino that Tonino took offence at.'

'Tonino should grow a thicker skin,' said Calogero. 'Tell Tonino that I will see him one Monday morning in Catania, without fail. Make sure he gets the message. Did I ask you to shoot Sandro?'

'No. Renzo did; Tonino helped, he was the other one on the bike. I did it. And I did it because I knew lots of people wanted him dead, and no one cared if he stayed alive. It was a favour to Renzo.'

'And Alfio, was that a favour to Renzo too?'

'It was a favour to you, boss. It is neat and tidy that way. Renzo is calmed by getting revenge for Gino; and you, you get rid of Catarina. She got the message, I believe. But it was something else as well, boss. It was a favour to the Serb. He didn't like Alfio; the other Serbs were the same; and the Africans too.'

'And why are we doing favours for the Serb?'

'Because he wants to get rid of don Carmelo, take over, and he needs us to clear up the financial mess afterwards to make sure he gets a controlling interest. Anna Maria will be crucial. But because we got rid of Catarina, she will help.'

'And what do we get out of the Messina operation?'

'A sizeable chunk.'

'I never liked don Carmelo. But the Serb, he sounds a nasty man.'

'But he is our nasty man, boss. Thanks to me.'

'Thanks to you. Who is going to hit don Carmelo?'

'The Serb and other Serbs. We just stand back and watch.'

'His own father,' marvelled Calogero.

'He raped the mother, so that is why the Serb does not like him. And he has never treated Costantino fairly. These people, they have long memories. Luckily, Costantino trusts me because I am from the Balkans too.'

'So, what will we get?' asked Calogero.

'To be negotiated after the passing of don Carmelo.'

'Is Anna Maria talking to you? She is not really talking to me that much,' said Calogero.

'I can talk to her, boss. And we shall be the richer by a controlling interest in one of the hotels. Perhaps the one you spent your honeymoon in.'

'That was a lifetime ago,' he said. 'Go back to the office and send me my brother-in-law.'

'I want you to know that it wasn't me,' said Calogero. 'I gave my word, and I kept my word. Some other people stepped out of line.'

'Whether it was you, or it was them, or whether it was someone else entirely, Sandro is dead,' said don Antonio Santucci. 'He and I did not get along with each other, but all the same, I grieve for his loss. I am surprised that it makes such a big difference to me. He was a source of grief while alive, and now a source of grief while dead.'

There was silence between them.

'Your wife…?' asked Calogero.

'God only knows what she thinks,' said Antonio. 'She never speaks to me. She is very composed.'

'The other children?'

'Marina has taken it very badly. She blamed her mother for not protecting the boy, though I think Angela did do her best to do so. He was hard to protect. Marina has left the country and gone to America. We are paying, naturally enough, as it is all our fault, in her eyes. So, we have lost two children. One day, this may happen to you.'

'It already has,' said Calogero grimly. 'I said to both my daughters I was coming to see you, and they both refused to come. I had hoped they would. My eldest is very grown up now and she resents the fact that I seem to resent it. And my wife, like your wife, speaks to me but rarely, and when she does, says very little. It is good of you to see me,' concluded Calogero.

They were sitting in the study of don Antonio in the house outside Castelvetrano. It was the first really hot day of spring. The afternoon sun was blazing. From the garden one could hear merry voices. One belonged to Beppe.

'I had not expected to see him here,' confessed Calogero, not meaning Beppe, but the boy holding the baby, Tonino.

'They came to show me the child,' said Antonio. 'My first grandchild. I never go to Palermo, so they came here, which is nice of them. I think Emma had the idea of cheering me up. She is upstairs asleep, exhausted, poor thing. But the real reason they came was to show me the child's father. I gather you know him very well.'

'Oh, very well,' said Calogero. 'He is a good Sicilian boy. He is an excellent worker. His parents were friends of my parents. His father went inside for rather a long time. His mother is a great friend of my mother. He is a nice boy. Your Emma's taste is surprising, though. I mean, I thought she was a young lady, instead she has chosen the sort of tough that her great-grandmother must have been married to.'

'Emma was always a rebel. This is her rebellion. But you know, after three generations of rising into the middle classes, it is perhaps time for us to return to our roots. Anyway, I accept that you had no part in Sandro's death. Who then did?'

'Your nephew. Renzo. But the actual deed was done by Traiano.'

'Renzo would never have dared, if it had not been for Traiano. And they did this without asking your explicit permission? Tut tut! The subordinates are getting out of hand.'

'It is not the only thing they have done,' said Calogero. 'They also popped Alfio, or rather got the Serb to do it for them. Though I did allow that, against my better judgement.'

'The Serb, you say? Don Carmelo's bastard?'

'Yes. The very one. He is planning something very big in Messina. But I would like you to keep that quiet.'

'Silence guaranteed, naturally.'

'It would mean a big chunk of his holdings coming under our control, as a reward for providing the services of Anna Maria, and as recompense for sacrificing Alfio. It is very tempting.'

'And you are tempted?'

'If a ripe apple falls into your lap, you do not complain, do you? You take what is offered you.'

'And afterwards?'

'Afterwards can wait,' he said. 'But there will be an afterwards, you will see.'

Emma was upstairs, asleep. Olivia had been sleeping badly in the night, and as a result she needed to get some rest herself. The two boys were in the garden, holding the baby in turns. Beppe was delighted with his niece.

'Are you happy with my sister?' Beppe was asking.

'Yes, said Tonino. 'Very. Getting married, having children, that is what I want.'

'She is a bit unconventional,' said Beppe. 'But so are you. You are well suited. I am very happy with you as a brother-in-law. Mama is very happy with you too. I can tell. I gather you are rich.'

'Am I?'

'The way you carry yourself, since Easter, you and Muniddu. I think the others were rich before you were, but you are now, and you are regarded as an equal. It is good. You are not after Emma for her money; not that she has so much.'

'So, I look rich, do I? I wasn't aware of it.'

'Muniddu keeps wads of banknotes under the spare bed in Riccardo's room. He told me. Not Muniddu, but Riccardo. Where do you keep your banknotes?'

'My mother's place. She has a cellar. In Catania. You are clever.'

'What was it for?' asked Beppe.

'Don't ask.'

'No one ever does ask, do they? I bet Emma does not ask questions. Did Sandro ask questions?'

'Are you sad your brother is dead?' asked Tonino. 'There, questions can go both ways. I bet you don't want to answer that.'

'He was my brother; of course I am sad,' said Beppe.

'Liar. You are no more sad than I.'

'Sad may not be the right word. Should I be grateful to you?'

'Your cousin, Traiano and me, yes. We planned it when you were at the football match in Naples. Muniddu was in on the idea as well. We did it for you. I had my reasons, but we did it for you.'

Beppe looked up at the windows of the house, all of which were open. But they were far enough away.

'Does everyone know?' he asked.

'Everyone who needs to know, yes, everyone who understands these things. That we did it for you, no, no one suspects that. You see, they all think you are a sweet boy. I know differently. You put us up to it, because you did not want your brother getting in your way.'

'I didn't put you up to it.'

'You did. But you did so in a way that could be plausibly denied.'

Beppe was silent for a moment.

'Did he have a good death?' he asked curiously.

'He was looking at his phone with a cup of coffee in front of him, then, pop, pop, and he woke up in Heaven. I suppose he had a good death.'

'He did not have a good life,' said Beppe. 'I feel sorry for him, in a way. I feel sorry for my father. I feel sorry for Renzo. But you, I like.'

'I am glad to hear it.'

'Do you like him?' he asked.

There was no need to mention a name.

'He is the boss… Your question makes no sense.'

'He may not be the boss forever,' said Beppe.

Later, Calogero found them by the swimming pool. He smiled at Beppe; he nodded at Tonino. Beppe was wearing his bathing things, as it was a hot day, and he was contemplating the first swim of the year. His long thin and very hairy legs were exposed; he was half child, half man. As for Tonino, shorter, much more solid, holding his daughter, he was fully dressed, for under his shirt and his trousers were the horrible bruises from the severe beating he had received from the boss for his part in the killing of Sandro. A similar beating had been administered to Traiano and Renzo.

'I thought I would find you here,' he said. 'I need to get back to my wife and children, so I am driving back to Donnafugata, and then later the children will go to Catania, where their grandmother will be, and I and my wife will go to Palermo. So much travelling about. Are you well?'

'Yes, thanks,' said Beppe with a smile.

'Your father and I had a long talk, about everything, about your poor brother Sandro. When you see your mother, do let her know.'

'Of course, don Calogero,' said Beppe seriously.

'We must arrange that lunch at Donnafugata,' said Calogero. 'Now the nice weather is here.' He embraced Beppe and kissed him. 'Tonino,' he then said, 'if you let Beppe hold your precious daughter for a few minutes, you can walk down with me to the car.'

They walked in silence for a moment, through the lemon trees, until they were out of view of the house, and out of earshot of Beppe.

'I have been cleaning up the mess that Renzo and Traiano created, with the encouragement of Muniddu and with your help as well,' he said. 'I beat the pair of them so badly that they bled, do you understand?'

'Understood, boss.'

'I am not sure I can trust you anymore.'

He looked at Tonino sadly.

'What would don Antonio say, if he knew you had taken an active part in the murder of his son? What would Emma say? What would Beppe say?'

'Beppe knows,' said Tonino. 'He does not care about Sandro. He's glad… because of the court case, because of the inheritance.'

'And you did this to please him?'

'Yes, boss.'

'Tell me, Tonino, how is your handsome friend that people make such a fuss about?'

'Roberto is well, boss. He will reconcile himself to Gabriella and to the idea of being a father, I hope. He ought to know that it will be a good idea, in the long run. Gabriella is a very nice lady.'

'And a clever one, picking young Roberto to be the father of her child. Older women are often the best pickers. Look at me, married to a wife twenty years my senior. Listen, Tonino, our mothers are friends; our fathers were friends. Ours has been a useful alliance, though not for your father, though we got him out of jail eventually, but we did look after your mother. You need to remember what is good for you, and good for them, OK? You made a fortune out of this last thing. I made sure you made a fortune. That was your reward for loyalty. Understood?'

'Understood, boss.'

'Is your loyalty to me unshakeable?'

'Yes, boss.'

'Good.'

They walked down to the car, and before the boss got in, as Tonino knew he would, he embraced him and kissed him.

'You will see me again soon,' he said, and departed.

Chapter Seven

The hot weather had arrived; the streets around the Casa Professa stank of decaying rubbish, and on the via Maqueda, the stench of the drains was noticeable. Even near the via Alloro, where Emma and the baby lived, there was an awful smell emanating from the sewers. In the evenings, Tonino and Emma would take the baby out and walk around the cool green space of the Piazza Marina; or else go out and walk by the sea, to try and catch a bit of breeze. At night, Tonino would stay with Emma, the excuse being that she had air conditioning, and he did not, and that one could not sleep without it. He was also useful in helping with Olivia during the night, something he liked doing. And he also liked sharing the double bed, so comfortable, with so much space, and sleeping next to her. He himself, though short, was well built, with a huge chest, and muscular thighs and arms; but she was monumental and beautiful to the touch.

He had to go back to the flat near Casa Professa, from time to time, to pick up clean clothes, to fetch a bottle of wine; coming in one evening, he saw Roberto. He heard him before he saw him. He was singing in the shower. The door was open, and he leaned in the doorway. Roberto saw him with surprise and then a smile. He stepped out of the shower and grabbed a towel, while Tonino looked at him critically. When he was dry, and with the towel wrapped round his waist, he stepped forwards to kiss Tonino lightly on the lips. Tonino was impassive.

'I haven't seen you for a long time,' said Roberto, looking for his moisturiser.

'It has been a couple of days,' said Tonino.

'Still…' said Roberto. 'Are you being kept busy?'

'Night in, night out,' said Tonino.

'And the wedding is when?'

'September, when it is cooler. But September next year.'

'Looking forward?'

'Of course.'

'You like it as much as you like the other thing?'

'There is no other thing,' said Tonino.

'There was for me,' said Roberto.

'Don't speak like that. It is not helpful. Besides I told you…'

'Yes, you did tell me that you had no soft feelings. I suppose I should follow your example,' said Roberto. 'I should try to be as tough as you.'

'Yes, you should,' said Tonino. 'If you want to get on. I thought you did, want to get on, that is. And getting on requires sacrifices. Is what you are doing so very tough?'

'Not tough, no, how could it be? It is just that… I was not in love with Gabriella, and I am not in love with the signora either. You suggested it, and I did it. I feel bad about certain things,' said Roberto. 'It feels insincere.'

'It was Traiano's suggestion,' said Tonino. 'I was merely passing on the message. You did not have to go along with it. But I am glad you did. We all have to make sacrifices. But I hope you do not let her think that for a moment.'

'With her, I am all enthusiasm,' he said. 'Rest assured. She is the best' – he used an obscene word - 'I have ever had. And I have had plenty. When I am with her, even the thought of Calogero putting a bullet through my brain is far away. It comes back at other times. Like you, it is day in, day out. I went round there to deliver that picture for Bonelli, and she was delighted with the picture, and with me. I did my bit as best I could. And I have been doing it ever since.'

He was now looking through his suits.

'Are you going there this evening?'

'Yes. I am assiduous in my attentions, and she in hers.'

'Have you ever been with someone so old before now?' asked Tonino curiously.

'Mind your own business,' said Roberto.

'I hope you call her dottoressa when you are in bed.'

'I do not. I call her signora.'

The Mattarella agriturismo seemed to be a wise choice for dinner. It was some days later. There was little likelihood of them being overheard, as it was one of many restaurants they might have chosen. Besides, on a weekday, it would be largely deserted. The younger Mattarella was alert, the elder was obsequious, when they arrived at about 7pm, and announced they would be having dinner, to give the kitchen plenty of notice. There were two of them, and three more to come.

The third arrived soon afterwards, and went up and kissed Renzo on the cheek coldly, and then the cheek of don Traiano. The younger Mattarella came forward to ask what they would like to drink. Traiano recommended the red that was made in the agriturismo itself, and which was very expensive – but as they were not paying, who cared? Then there was a little discussion about the food. It was amusing to see how on edge the boy was, how the murder of his friend Simone Rota had forced him to grow up and realise what was what. He ordered the food, making it simple, guessing what the other two would like. He guessed as one does when one knows people well.

'This is a nice place,' said Costantino the Serb.

'We own it, so they are very keen to please. Gratifying, I feel. But it is the same with all your hotels in Taormina and Messina, I am sure. When you come in, they all jump to attention.'

'When don Carmelo comes in, you mean. With me, I am just the management, not the owner.'

'That will change,' said Renzo.

'A change that is overdue,' said Traiano. 'Now tell us your plans.'

'August seems the best time,' said Costantino. 'Everyone is relaxed; everyone is off guard, or on holiday, or both. His birthday is on the 3rd, and on the nearest Sunday, he always has a lunch party for his nearest and dearest.'

'You'll be there?'

'I have never been in the past. It is for his cronies, the people he trusts most, the people at the top of the organisation. The people who have to be got rid of in any decapitation strategy.'

'Tell me that this party is on a yacht,' said Traiano, thinking of the massacre of Favignana.

'It is not. It is nowhere near the sea. Rather it is in a mountain refuge on Etna. It is essentially a little house. They use it once a year. It has gas cookers, with those gas bottles, you know? They drive up there with all the food and drink and then they spend their time eating and drinking. I have never been, but it is all his oldest associates; all his trusted people; about a dozen in all. And his sons, his legitimate sons. Then as it gets dark, they drive down the mountainside. People drive them up, leave them, and then come back for them, leaving them alone. A few staff are there to prepare and to clean up afterwards.'

'The gas bottles,' said Traiano.

'I have friends in Serbia who learned what to do in the war. A signal sent from Taormina, and the gas bottles, or what pass for gas bottles, blow up. By the time the police arrive all they find is another crater on Etna.'

'You will be here in August?' asked Renzo.

'Oh yes, another holiday. To see my wife. And to pick up the pieces.'

'You trust these Serbs?' asked Traiano.

'Of course. The one I am relying on is a relation of my mother. Her brother, in fact. You can always rely on family.'

'When don Carmelo and all his closest associates are gone, along with his sons, his legitimate sons, what happens next?' asked Renzo. 'I mean to his property, to the hotels? It is all very well sending him to his eternal reward, but one wants an earthly reward for doing so.'

'One hopes Anna Maria will explain the aftermath,' said Traiano.

At about a few minutes before eight, Anna Maria arrived with her husband in tow. Their air of relaxation was rather forced. The smiles and kisses and handshakes were a little too natural to be entirely so. Anna Maria looked on the Serb with an appreciative eye, seeing a serious man of business. They sat down at table. More wine and more mineral water came.

'If I can speak freely,' she said, knowing that she was the one that everyone wanted to listen to, 'The situation is this. Don Carmelo's business interests are united in one vast holding company, all perfectly legal, and it is this company that pays out dividends to him and to his legitimate children, quite a handsome income all told. In addition, there are other companies in various parts of the world, all impossible to trace, of which he is the ultimate beneficiary. The will is clear: everything goes seven ways, to the seven sons; four legitimate and three not; the girls and the girlfriends and the wife get nothing. I presume the male beneficiaries are meant to provide for the womenfolk. It is unusual but makes things simpler. They inherit the shares in the company; there are a quite a few other bequests, which are one off payments, which needn't bother us. The only really important thing is who gets to control the holding company and the other companies after he is no longer here. Whoever controls the board controls everything. Which means, very simply, Costantino, that after your father is gone, it is important that the surviving members of the board appoint you to run things. Don Carmelo has been very careless. He ought to have realised that a hostile internal takeover is always possible. He should have appointed a blind trust in the event of his death, as don Lorenzo did. That way, no one can touch anything. But as it is, especially if the board members recognise the forceful character of someone like yourself, they will be keen to let you take over, I think. The four legitimate sons are all abroad. As long as they get their regular income, they will be happy enough. I can't see any of them wanting to come back and manage things.'

'The other illegitimate sons?' asked don Calogero.

'They are both kids,' said Costantino dismissively. 'All the secret accounts; all the stuff held abroad?'

'It is well hidden, and I can help you to find it before anyone else does, and well, that is the problem of hiding money.'

'And what it is in it for us?' asked Calogero. 'Given that we ensure a smooth transition?'

'We will sell you one of the Taormina hotels at a knock down price,' said Costantino.

The pasta arrived. Old Mattarella hung around for compliments. The signora was effusive. It was just what she liked. The sauce was exquisite. More wine was poured. The conversation moved to Africa, where Costantino was returning tomorrow, and the sad death of Alfio which, it was good news to hear, had been successfully hushed up and had not damaged business at all. The security at the hotel was superb. Guests flew in directly from the international airport, and the hotel and its grounds were protected by their men, a good twenty of whom were on duty round the clock. Trespassers, said Costantino, were fed to the crocodiles. Anna Maria laughed at this pleasantry, but was assured by Renzo that there was a crocodile farm near the hotel, where the animals were raised for their hides and their meat, which, he had heard say, was disgusting. There were lions too patrolling the hinterland, and no roads to speak of. The only way in was by air, or by boat; it was a perfect enclosed paradise; and the cooks were all Italian, thank the Lord, and supplies arrived every day from Italy in the belly of the plane that brought the visitors. They must all visit, Costantino said. He might even be inclined to sell his share to don Calogero, he hinted. Though leaving Africa would be a wrench, and he was not sure if the mother of his children there wanted to come to Italy. Calogero watched Anna Maria hear this, and thought bitterly that she was tolerant of other men's adultery and illegitimate children, but for her own husband, she made an exception.

The roast lamb accompanied by anchovy sauce was succulent, the potatoes roasted with rosemary were first class, and the peas cooked with pancetta and white wine were delicious: all very straightforward ingredients, perfectly cooked, thought Anna Maria, and it was no shame to eat plainly once in a while, when plain cooking was so good.

After the main course, she felt satiated and said she would take a turn around the grounds, gesturing them not to follow, knowing there were things they might want to discuss while she was out of the room. There were, of course. Sunday 3rd August, where they would all be then, what would look least suspicious. The boss would be either at Donnafugata or abroad; Renzo was sure that he could find a marathon that weekend, somewhere cool, but failing that, they could all book a holiday, somewhere nice, rent a villa with a swimming pool. Traiano wanted to know what could go wrong. Were the bomb makers reliable? Would they be able to plant the bomb without detection? Where would they make it and where assemble it? And what would the reaction be, particularly among the other bosses? Calogero was easy on this point: it was an internal settling of accounts in the Messina province, no more. No one outside of

Messina had any vital interests. They themselves were neutral, and being well paid for their neutrality.

Traiano went out into the garden to see Anna Maria. He found her contemplating the view.

'It used to be so lovely before all the building happened,' she said. 'Though even I am not really old enough to remember it as it was, before the overdevelopment took place. Sad, but that is the history of this island. I am very pleased, by the way, with my new acquisition.'

'Lady Hamilton?'

'Her. Of course. No, but also the man who spotted her. He is a fount of information. He is so well informed, so cultured. I intend to make full use of his expertise. We are going to visit a few galleries. I mean beyond Sicily. It is time to spend some money, to invest in art. It makes sense but it is also a good idea financially. And.... He can help with the Caravaggio. It may need some expert advice to stop it deteriorating. And he may have some ideas on how it can be displayed.'

'I am glad he has won your confidence,' said Traiano. 'Won't Calogero be jealous?'

'My husband will have to keep his feelings to himself,' she said crisply. 'It will infuriate him. But he will have to learn to put up with it. As far as I am concerned, there are a lot of things he has to learn to put up with from now on.'

The next morning, in faraway Milan, Chiara walked into Silvio's office.

'There is trouble in paradise,' she announced. 'This police report says that there is a spike in the street price of cocaine in all Sicilian towns. Interestingly, if you look at it, the further the towns are from Palermo the greater the spike. But even in Palermo, there is a spike. You know what that means?'

'Of course I do. It means there is a shortage of supply. That means either the incompetent police have made a huge haul, or else our friends in the San Lorenzo crime family are having problems with the suppliers.'

'I have checked,' said Chiara. 'There have been no notable hauls of late. But I said a spike: the price is already returning to normal. The problems with supply were temporary, and they began to happen just after Easter. Now you don't have to be Sherlock Holmes to work out what this means.'

'I am not Sherlock Holmes. But you are,' he said.

'The glitch in supply was just that. Moreover, the prices started to go down, starting in, can you guess where?'

'Palermo?'

'No. Catania. What has happened is this: they have changed their centre of supply. It was Palermo, now it's Catania. And what happened at Easter? These six men disappeared. They were the distributors. They have been replaced, and replaced with people Calogero di Rienzi can trust, people in Catania, in the Purgatory quarter.'

'A clever move. The Purgatory quarter is impenetrable. Worse than anywhere in Naples. A real rabbit warren of cellars, tenements, blocks of flats, all with escape routes over the roofs. He owns a lot of those properties. They will use the empty ones, clean up, then move elsewhere. What a nightmare!'

'Another thing,' said Chiara. 'He and his wife are more or less living apart. She is in Palermo during the week, and he is in Catania with the children, and they meet most weekends at Donnafugata. But they are not sleeping together. Even though he exiled his mistress, at her behest.'

'How the hell do you know that?' asked Silvio, with admiration. 'You have been going through the laundry, or what?'

'I found a handsome young policeman,' she said.

'That is a real find. I love handsome young policemen, but they are generally only to be found on television. Most of the ones I see in real life are ugly as hell.'

'Be serious. This one is a friend of the niece of Veronica the maid. Veronica adores him. I adore him, even though we have not met, but I have seen photographs. He's blond. Like a Viking.'

'That will go down well in Sicily,' said Silvio.

'He met this girl, and when he realised who the aunt was, he began to take notes. That is what he has discovered. The thing is Veronica is very discreet, but she has never liked Calogero. Never thought him good enough for the signora. Like a lot of domestic servants, she is a snob. So, she has been saying all is not well in the marriage with a degree of satisfaction. But nothing more, nothing about the business. She is loyal. By the way, she likes Antonescu, or so he assumes, though she has not mentioned his name, and she loves Antonescu's wife. Real down to earth people. But she does not like the signore as he gives himself airs.'

'He certainly does.'

'Finally....'

'There is more? I am full of admiration.'

He sighed. He knew what was to come next, another fruitless trip to Sicily. Well, the weather would be nice, he was sure. He looked at her. Like himself, she felt guilty at the way they had failed to protect their star witnesses: the woman Bednarowska and her son Paolo. With her, the duel with Calogero was personal. It was with him too, he supposed, but he was older, more tired.

'You know I said she was protecting someone, Angela Santucci, I mean. It can only be one person. Someone killed her son. She protects the one who killed her son, or who at least gave the order, or with whom the idea originated. She is protecting the other son. It cannot be anyone else. Think about it. You wouldn't, as a mother, protect anyone else.'

'The other son is, what, a teenager?'

'Weren't they all, when they started?' she asked.

'Yeah, but, this boy is from the nice part of Palermo, for goodness' sake, he goes to a private school, doesn't he?'

'You are showing your prejudices,' she said.

'What about the sister in America?' he asked. 'Marina?'

'I have thought of that. She is in New York, and going to that university when the time comes.'

'Colombia?'

'No, the other one. Fordham. There are two,' she said knowledgeably. 'We know all about her from the transcripts of the telephone conversations. She hates the little brother, she really does.'

'Don't all girls hate their little brothers?'

'Most. But that is not the point. She hates him; she now hates the mother; she has long hated the father; and she has fallen out with her sister Emma, because, she says, they were all complicit in Sandro's murder. All. See what I mean? She also says that the boy hangs out with all the wrong people.'

'Any names?'

'Antonescu. Muniddu, their former chauffeur and his family. And the guy who supplies, or supplied, Sandro, and I presume her, with cocaine. But no name, just a lot of insulting nicknames: short arse is the only one I can bear to repeat.'

'Short arse means someone short, right? Good luck in find a short drug dealer in Palermo.'

'He is from Catania, she says that. And she accuses her sister Emma of being in love with him.'

'So: short; from Catania; deals cocaine, and knows Emma Santucci,' said Silvio appreciatively. 'That might narrow it down.' He paused. 'If you think we have enough to go on…'

'I think we do. We leave tomorrow,' she said crisply.

'Well?' asked Tonino.

It was Monday, late afternoon. Roberto had just come in from the office and put his jacket aside. He was sitting at the kitchen table. They had not seen each other for some time. Roberto had spent the weekend in Catania where he had been trying to conciliate Gabriella, following the advice of Tonino, advice, he imagined, that had come from higher up. One had to conciliate Gabriella, because, at least in part, one had to keep Bonelli happy.

'How was it with Gabriella?'

'It is getting better,' said Roberto. 'Obviously, I upset her, so she is getting her revenge, making me suffer. The baby is beginning to show, and she looks well. I can't say I am thrilled by the prospect of having a child, but, well, I can see she is. Maybe, when the child is born, I will feel better about the whole thing. My mother, oh God my mother, she is furious about it. Furious. And my sisters have taken her part. I am ruining my life, tying myself down.'

'That is ridiculous,' said Tonino.

'That is what I tell her. I am twenty-four, old enough to work, old enough to have a child, and Gabriella is thirty-three, for God's sake, old enough, and has plenty of money. Maybe my mother just can't get used to the fact I am a fornicator. Well, it is a bit late for that now. Thank God she doesn't know the truth or can't imagine the truth. But she has a point. I am depressed. In her eyes, if I meet someone else, and want to get married, I have to explain why I already have a child, and who with and how often we meet. Oh dammit.'

'You don't need to get married,' said Tonino. 'Having a child with a mother you are not married to is the perfect excuse. Having a child adds to your status. Besides, what about the signora?'

'The signora,' he said, feeling less depressed. 'The signora is dynamite. She is twice my age, but she is dynamite. Have you ever been with a woman who is dynamite?'

'No. I don't think I have,' said Tonino.

'Gabriella does not want me in her bed anymore, I am relieved to say, not that I ever thought I would say that. I don't think I could manage both of them at the same time.'

'The boss, what does he know?'

'He knows that his wife is spending time with Bonelli, who does not like women. So, he is more or less happy. I am providing the things Bonelli can't. He does the art advice; I do the sex. We are careful. She sends me a message, and I go to see her at lunchtime in her flat. He is never there; he is with his children in Catania in the week. I must say, being a gigolo is quite an exciting life.'

'It is important that we keep her happy,' said Tonino. 'Important for you, and for me too.'

'I am trying my best,' he said, smiling. 'What?' he asked.

'The signora is going to invest my money for me. That means I am going to buy a house here in Palermo. We will need to start looking soon. That will take time. But I will keep on this place, and you can live in it on your own when I am married to Emma.'

'You are young to get married,' he observed. 'No one could accuse you of throwing your life away, though. I mean, I understand why you are doing it, but is it what you want to do?'

'Sure, why not? I mean, it is what people do, isn't it? Marry, have children. I aways wanted to do both young. No point in waiting. It was an accident with Emma, but a happy one. One day you will look upon Gabriella in the same way.' He looked around the flat. 'Have you been tidying up?' he asked.

The place was a terrible mess. The table was strewn with empty bottles, empty packaging, old magazines, and other bits of detritus. The floor was strewn with discarded articles of clothing, waiting to be gathered up for the weekly trip to Catania. But the mess was not quite as he had remembered it. The thing about mess was that you accepted it, and after a time no longer noticed it. He was not sure now why he had noticed the mess.

Silence descended between them. They had not sat like this for weeks. They had barely seen each other. Tonino was more or less living with Emma, and Roberto was either in Catania or with the signora. Nor would they see much of each other in the future, both of them felt. This was it, the end. But it had been something while it had lasted, thought Tonino.

'There is one last bottle left of that red wine from the Mattarella place,' he observed. 'I know you like it. We might not have another opportunity to finish it.'

Tonino went to fetch the wine, two clean glasses and the corkscrew. Emma was expecting him, but later that evening, at about eight. Beppe and Rosalia were joining them at Emma's flat. In the meantime… He put the bottle and glasses on the table, finding an uncluttered space, and then wrapped his arms around Roberto.

'Oh, get lost,' said Roberto, but did not push him away.

Two hours later, Tonino left his own small flat, walked past the Casa Professa, and took the narrow street to Emma's much larger and more recently refurbished flat near the via Alloro. He had a key, he was expected, and he felt a slight tremor of excitement as he went up. At this moment, the baby was usually asleep, and he found her waiting for him.

'Did you see the police car in the square?' she asked. 'It arrived at about three this afternoon and has not moved since.'

'I was too busy thinking about seeing you,' he replied. 'Shall I go and see if it is still there?'

He got up and went to the window. To his surprise and his dismay, the car was still there, and a policeman was looking up at the window, and their eyes met. He swiftly withdrew.

'I saw them. They saw me,' he said, as he withdrew into the room once more.

'What can they want? Why are they there? You know Mama and Renzo were questioned by the magistrates when they went to Turin? They were sort of ambushed.'

'Well, let us hope they don't barge in and ambush us right now. Not that I care.'

He took her in his arms and kissed her.

'Are you getting used to the piercing?' she asked.

'I think so. Are you?'

'Oh yes,' she replied.

Beppe arrived at eight precisely to find the baby up, the babysitter arrived, and Emma and Tonino, spruce and smart and waiting for them. Rosalia was with him.

'Why is there a police car in the square?' asked Beppe. 'Are they spying on you?'

'It is quite flattering,' he said with a smile.

To his surprise, the car, or a different police car, was there when they returned to the house, and when he left the house, having spent the night there, in the morning. He wondered what their game was: to watch him, to make him feel nervous; to hope he made a mistake? But no, it was none of these things, for as he walked the short distance between Emma's house and his own, he felt a hand on his shoulder, and knew even before they said it, that he was under arrest.

Beppe was at school, in the middle of a chemistry lesson, a very boring one, when the headmaster of the school came to get him. He was taken, rather apologetically, to the headmaster's office, where a man and a woman were waiting to see him. The headmaster sat behind his desk and looked concerned. The man and woman spoke. They were friendly and introduced themselves as Silvio and Chiara.

'We have come to tell you about the progress of the police investigation into the murder of your late brother Sandro,' said the lady sympathetically. 'Obviously this has been a very difficult time for you.'

Beppe nodded. He supposed it had.

'Were you close to your brother?' asked Silvio.

'We were brothers,' said Beppe. 'He was older than me. So we did not spend much time together, but he was my brother.'

'How did you feel when you heard he had been killed?' asked Chiara.

Beppe considered what to say. Why were they asking about his feelings? Of what importance were they?

'I was very upset, but I knew I had to do everything I could to make things easier for my mother and my father.'

'Do you know who did it?' asked Silvio.

He shook his head.

'Do you?' he replied.

'Yes, we do,' said Silvio. 'But getting proof is difficult. Can you remember what you were doing on the weekend of 30th March?'

Beppe shrugged.

'You went to Naples.'

'Yes, of course. Naples beat Juventus two nil at the San Paolo. We were there, myself and Riccardo and Muniddu. It was great fun. And the others were with us: Tonino, Traiano, and my cousin Renzo.'

'That was the weekend when the adults plotted the murder of your brother. Were you aware of this?'

'No. I was not, and I doubt what you say is true. Why should they want to do that, they of all people? What could they possibly have against Sandro?'

'Indeed,' answered Silvio. 'Had Sandro any enemies?'

'None that I know of,' said Beppe. 'I do not want to say anything that may incriminate my friends.'

'They are your friends, are they?'

'Of course. I have known Muniddu for a long time, and I go out with his daughter. I have known my cousin Renzo all my life. I have known Tonino for two years, and he is my sister's boyfriend. I have known Traiano for longer. They are all my friends. I do not want to speak to you anymore. Headmaster, can I go?'

'Not so fast, young man,' said Chiara. 'If you are determined to be obstructive, then we have certain weapons in our armoury we can use against you. You were there in Naples, with them. Do you want to be arrested for conspiracy to murder? So, you had better sit down and co-operate. If you and your friends are innocent, what have you or they to fear? Look, we know you are young. We know that you did not like Sandro, that he was a bully, and that he was standing between you and the considerable inheritance from your grandfather. We also know that Tonino hated him, and that Muniddu, whose daughter you go about with, feels very protective of you, as does Traiano Antonescu. We know all this.'

'Tonino and Sandro were friends.'

'Your brother had a mobile phone, and he spent lots of time on it. Lots of conversations, lots of texts, passed between him and Emma and Marina. Some poor policeman had to listen to the lot, and here are the transcripts.' He tapped a file. 'Do you want us to read out the choice bits? To hear what Sandro said about you?'

'Spare me. I can guess.'

'He says that you wormed your way in with your grandfather, with your mother's connivance, in order to get him to change his will.'

'Untrue. My grandfather was free to leave his money to whoever he chose. He chose me, not Sandro. Sandro never went to see him.'

'He says you are a liar and a cheat and a hypocrite.'

'Not very original.'

'He says that you were, and I quote …'

The headmaster winced at the quote. Beppe laughed.

'He says that you had a taste for very low company, like Muniddu, his children, and Antonescu and Grassi.'

'Sir, I am surprised at you,' said Beppe crisply. 'Muniddu is a very respectable person, and so are his family. The same goes for Tonino Grassi and for Traiano. They are very nice people. Why shouldn't I associate with them? My brother Sandro was a snob. Do you understand that? Sir, I am not sure what social class you imagine I come from, or which you come from, but the truth is that here in Sicily we are all equals. It is not like England where everyone wants to meet royalty or dukes or counts. Here we are all one people. Now, I know that you are going to say that Tonino's father was in prison, but that was not his fault. And Rosalia has uncles in prison, but that is not her fault either, or Riccardo's fault. These are my friends, and I am not ashamed of them.'

'Tonino Grassi kept your brother and sisters supplied with cocaine,' said Chiara.

Beppe considered.

'My cousin Renzo was a cocaine addict, but he now campaigns against addiction, along with my mother, his aunt. Sandro, I am afraid to say, was not a good boy. But I have no reason to think that he was supplied with drugs by Tonino. They were just friends.'

'It is strange you should think that,' said Silvio, 'because the transcripts make plain that Sandro only tolerated Tonino because he was his supplier. He loathed him otherwise, as a lower class, common little crook. He was particularly angry with your sister Emma for sleeping with him and having his child and giving him what he termed a meal ticket for life. The terms he used are revelatory. Short arse.'

'He is short. So what?'

'And this word.'

He showed him a sheet of the transcript where a sentence was highlighted.

'That is what your brother said to Emma, upbraiding her for her relationship with Tonino. Look at that word there. I don't even want to pronounce it with a lady in the room. Do you know what it means?'

The headmaster looked alarmed and leaned forward to see the transcript, which Silvio passed to him. He sighed more in sadness and in anger, and passed the sheet of paper back.

'That word is banned in our school,' he said. 'If a boy utters that to another boy, he gets suspended, and he had to do a lot of apologising and explaining to get let back in. I am surprised someone from a good family like Sandro, one of our former pupils, knew this word and would use it to his sister.'

'Well?' asked Silvio.

'As the headmaster says,' replied Beppe, 'It is not the sort of word that I would ever hear here or at home. I can see that it is an insult.'

'A very particular insult.'

'It is a word that is used by Catullus,' said Beppe. 'The Latin version of the word.'

'Catullus poem 16,' said the headmaster, who was a classist. 'In particular line 2. Though I doubt that Sandro had the literary allusion in mind.'

'My brother certainly knew how to insult people,' said Beppe.

'And Tonino Grassi knew how to avenge an insult,' said Chiara.

There was silence.

'So, he went and shot my brother for calling him a homosexual?' asked Beppe. 'That is ridiculous.'

'A particular type of homosexual,' said Silvio.

'You do not know Tonino,' said Beppe.

'Oh, we do,' said Chiara.

He felt uncomfortable for the first time in the interview, and began to think longingly of the chemistry lesson he was missing.

She opened the file and placed a photograph of Roberto in front of him. It was taken from his identity card.

'That is Roberto,' he said. 'If you think…. He has a girlfriend in Catania, and she is having a baby. If you think…'

'Do you understand what makes people want to sleep with each other?' asked Silvio.

'I really must protest,' said the headmaster. 'That is not a suitable question for a boy of his age.'

'He is sixteen. He is old enough to commission his own brother's murder. He is old enough to answer the question.'

'You are both delusional,' said Beppe evenly.

'People often tell us that,' said Chiara.

'Riccardo is a very good friend of mine, and so is Tonino, but we never discuss these sorts of things. It is not right, not decent to do so. I know that both Roberto and Tonino have children, but I am not privy to details of their relationships. I do not ask about those sorts of things.'

'That is a lie,' said Silvio. 'You might like to look at this.'

He passed over another transcript. Beppe looked at it, and realised that it came from the changing room at the gym. The conversation had taken place last week.

'You were there,' said Silvio.

Beppe felt severely embarrassed.

'What you were talking about was this, let me remind you,' he added, pushing a photograph towards him.

He glanced at the photograph and looked away. The picture told him one thing: they had arrested Tonino. Who else, he wondered?

'Tonino told us he had had a piercing. Renzo made a few vulgar comments. He asked Tonino to show it to us, but quite rightly he refused. He said only two people had seen it, Emma and Roberto. Emma is his girlfriend and he shares a room with Roberto, they live in a one room flat, so there is very little privacy, and Roberto may well have seen it, but that does not mean…'

'So, you had no idea that Tonino, your friend, was sleeping with your sister and his friend Roberto at the same time?'

'He was not, and there is no evidence that he was,' said Beppe. 'He clearly slept with my sister, but he and Roberto are just friends.'

'Except your brother Sandro did not believe that, and Tonino conspired to murder Sandro because of it; because of the truth of the accusation. And you profited by it, because you wanted him out of the way. As did Trajan Antonescu, as did Muniddu, as did your cousin Renzo.'

'That is quite a conspiracy,' said Beppe. 'Do I look like the sort of person who would commission my own brother's murder?'

'Murderers come in all shapes and sizes,' said Chiara. 'Some are young and sweet and innocent looking. That makes them all the more dangerous and frightening.'

'Sir, signora,' said Beppe with extreme politeness. 'I understand your theory entirely. You attribute to me an almost satanic cleverness and ability to manipulate others. But there is no evidence, is there? Now, may I go back to chemistry before the class finishes?'

The three adults nodded. They watched the boy leave.

'Well,' said the headmaster wryly. 'As he says, you have no evidence.'

'Thank you for allowing us to interrupt your busy day,' said Chiara. 'No, we have no evidence, at least not yet. But one of them will crack, you will see.'

'And do you think it will be Beppe Santucci?' asked the headmaster.

'Well, it might be,' conceded Silvio.

'He comes from a long line of them,' said the headmaster. 'The father, the uncle, the grandfather, the great-uncle, and their father before them. He is the inheritor of many generations of not co-operating with the forces of law and order. Though, I have to say, unlike his brother Sandro, who was a very difficult young man, Beppe has always been a model pupil.'

They wished him good morning and left.

That evening, they were in the Carabinieri barracks just next to the New Gate into the city, a nice quiet place, all things considered; at this time of the evening, deserted. They sat looking in on what was happening on the other side of the glass.

'I want to see my lawyer,' Tonino was saying.

'You saw him earlier,' said the first of the policemen. 'He was sent by your friend don Calogero di Rienzi. But we think you probably don't want him to hear what we are going to play you.'

'Where did they get him from?' asked Silvio. 'Have you ever seen eyelashes that long? He reminds me of my son. And the plucked eyebrows. My goodness.'

'I think they do this sort of thing, this sort of case. They have experience at it. I prefer the blond. I didn't know you got such nice blonds in Sicily. It makes me jealous of my own daughter. If I were her age, that young man would not be going home tonight; he would be coming to my hotel room, for intense questioning.'

'Oh, shut up!' said Silvio.

In the room, they were listening to the tape. It was the usual stuff: grunts and groans and sighs, and repeated calls on the Holy Name.

The tape was paused.

'That is you, isn't it?' asked the blond one.

'You bastards! You bugged my girlfriend's bedroom. Well, it is embarrassing but it is not criminal.'

'Correct,' said the other. 'Embarrassing, but not criminal.'

He pressed play once more. More grunting, more groaning, and this time low voices. Tonino sat through it all impassively. After about twenty minutes it stopped.

'It is fake,' he said at last.

'No, it is not,' said the one with the eyelashes. 'The microphone was placed behind the grille that closes off a ventilation shaft, right under your friend Roberto's bed. There were two people in the flat at the time, yourself and your friend Roberto. The tape is a long one, but that is clear; your voices are heard before the sexual act, and after it. And it is pretty obvious what sort of sexual act it was. I mean, some guys like other guys, some guys like girls and other guys, but no one really wants their friends, their relations, to know what exactly it is that they like. I mean, I would not want my mother to hear what I get up to in my bedroom, which is nothing similar, but...'

'Leave my mother out of this,' said Tonino.

'That is exactly what we hope to do. I am sure she is a very nice lady, and she has already had enough trouble in her life. We wish her and all Sicilian mothers well. We revere Sicilian mothers. And Roberto, he has a mother as well, doesn't he? I don't think he would like her to know. And sisters. And a girlfriend, as do you,' said the blond.

There was a long silence. No one spoke.

'I want to see Emma,' said Tonino.

'Ah,' said Silvio.

'At last, at last,' said Chiara. 'How many years has it taken? Now we have a crack!'

They let him sweat for several hours. Chiara and Silvio went out to dinner, trying to keep their excitement to a minimum. It was quite late when they returned to the barracks. They watched what unfolded from the other side of the glass.

Tonino was sitting at the table. Emma came in. Tonino stood: the embraced, they kissed. The embrace was long.

'Where is Olivia?' he asked.

'I took her round to my mother,' said Emma. 'I could not think what else to do. I will bring her next time.'

'If there is a next time,' he said bitterly.

He nodded towards the window, to signify they were being watched and overheard. He saw that she understood.

'What are you in for?' she asked.

'Everything they can think of, and a bit more besides. Association with a criminal organisation is the major one. Drug possession and intent to supply. And conspiracy to murder.'

'What evidence have they got? I mean, they came and got me just after I had gone to bed, and they are taking the flat apart, but…'

'They searched me,' said Tonino. 'That is why I am dressed like this. They took away my clothes to test them for traces of cocaine. They subjected me to a full cavity search. They took swabs, and a blood sample. But I know I am clean. The lawyer says I just have to sit tight, and they will have no choice but to release me. The only evidence they have got is something Sandro said on the telephone to Marina and to you, claiming that I supplied him with cocaine. But is that evidence? I think not. Sandro made things up.'

'He certainly overdramatised things,' said Emma. 'Even when he was a little boy.'

'They are saying that Sandro and I did not get on. But that does not mean that I killed him, which is what they are trying to get me to admit to.'

'Admit to nothing,' she said. 'Sandro was never an easy character; I see that now. He quarrelled with everyone.'

'I know.'

'They have been listening to Sandro on the phone for weeks, months. It was interesting to see how much he loathed and despised me, what names he called me! And poor Beppe as well. Well, I sort of knew it, but it was still a bit of a shock. Sandro was crazy. I don't think any judge would listen to him. If he is dead, can what he said be used as evidence?'

'I am not sure. I think so.'

'A lawyer would know,' said Tonino.

'They have arrested Renzo, Traiano, and Muniddu,' said Emma.

'So I assumed. They will get nothing out of any of us. There is no evidence.' He keened forward and placed his lips very close to her ear. 'Try not to react,' he whispered. 'They have a tape of us in the flat.'

Emma was impassive.

She whispered back: 'Does that matter?'

Tonino did not answer directly.

He whispered again into her ear: 'They have tapes of me and Roberto in my flat. Embarrassing tapes.'

She considered this, and then whispered back.

'Sandro told me all about that, to try and shock me. But I am unshockable. I knew. Like Sandro, I had guessed. It doesn't matter. I matter. Olivia matters. Do you think you would mind if the world knew that you like a bit of the other, as well as girls?'

'Damn,' said Silvio to Chiara, unable to hear a word.

'Don't worry,' she said.

'I do mind,' said Tonino, whispering in her ear once more. 'I mind very much, can't you see? It would make me look ridiculous. That is the worst thing. Ridiculous. And you would not look good either, though less bad than me.'

'Do people still care?' asked Emma. 'I don't. Why should anyone else?'

'I do,' said Tonino. 'I have got to think about my mother, my father, my little brother, all the friends; I have got to think about you.'

'I am open minded. Maybe they are too.'

'You don't understand. I am not open minded, whatever that means.'

'Do you really care so much about what other people think?' asked Emma sadly.

Tonino looked at her uncomprehendingly. This whole business was based on what people thought of you. If people thought you were ruthless, but kind, harsh but also fair, brave and uncompromising, then that was good. They respected you; they obeyed you. But if they thought you had a weakness, and this was a weakness, your reputation was gone.

'What are you going to do?' asked Emma.

'What they ask,' said Tonino.

'Think about it, let them wait,' counselled Emma.

'Can I trust you?'

'If you cannot trust me, who can you trust?' asked Emma. 'I love you. Don't you see that? We have a child.'

'I love you too. I want what is best for our daughter. Would you leave Sicily to be with me, and never to come back?' he asked. 'That is the offer they will make. If I tell them everything. A new life somewhere else, but we could never come back, never see our families again.'

'And you would live a normal life?' she asked.

'What is a normal life?' he asked. 'But yes, I would get a job, get qualifications, live a normal life. I would get away from all this, we would be married, have more children, have a life. We would get away from Calogero. We would escape.'

'Did you kill Sandro?' she asked, no longer whispering.

'No, I did not. But I know who did.'

Even though they were behind glass, and invisible, he could almost sense the way the magistrates were leaning forward in their seats as he said this.

'A new life,' she said. 'That is something that very few are ever offered. Most of us are condemned to repeat the old life over and again. A new life is an offer too good to refuse. It means redemption. Where?'

'America, Australia, Lombardy, somewhere far away. Would you come? With me? With our daughter?'

'Yes,' she said.

There was another embrace, longer than the first. They kissed once more. They stood up, and he looked round at the window from which they were being watched. Turning his back, he adjusted the tracksuit he was wearing and made love to Emma in front of them.

'That is some boy,' said Chiara.

'It is not her, it is the baby,' said Silvio. 'That is who he really cares about.'

Emma left, and they took him back to the cells. They left him to stew there until midday the next day. He knew they would. The boredom was part of their plan, he could see that. And they were giving him time to think, time for the facts to whizz around inside his head, to see if there was any way in which the facts would fit together that would somehow save him. But there was not. He was sure that Traiano would throw him to the dogs if he knew about Roberto; he was sure that the boss don Calogero would do the same; he suspected Calogero would be very glad to get rid of him; they all would.

It struck him that none of them had ever really liked him or valued him for himself. For fourteen years, they had let his father stew in Ucciardone, even though he had supposedly been a friend to the Chemist of Catania, Calogero's father. For fourteen years, the first fourteen years of his conscious life, they had left himself and his mother to live in poverty eking out a meagre existence with a very thin pension from the Confraternity; his mother had supposedly been a friend of signora di Rienzi, but they had not treated her well. He had carried messages for them; gaining a euro here, a euro there; he had sold drugs for them; he had beaten people up for them; he had killed for them, and what was his reward? He had been paid, and paid well, but did they like him? Did the boss, did Traiano, did don Renzo, did Muniddu? He remembered the death of the Polish woman and her son Paolo; he had certainly helped save the day then; he remembered the murder of Rota and his associates, and the Rota nephew. So many killings, and what for? He remembered the sadistic beatings from Traiano, and from Calogero. They had used him.

He thought of his mother and he grew tearful. He would have to go away, and unless she came, he would never see her again. She had his father and his baby brother; would she and they want to come to some place to be hidden away? He feared not - how could they? Would she, still less his father, approve of what he was going to do? He doubted that as well. And if they took you and hid you away, in some place like Rome, in that miserable flat where Beata and Paolo Bednarowski had met their end, wouldn't they find you in the end? Didn't they always find you? Hadn't they found Paolo and his mother? Of course, Paolo had been a horny twelve-year-old boy, sending messages to that girl, and that had given him away. Paolo had not listened, so it was his own fault that he had been found. He, if he had to go into hiding, would be careful, but a whole life stretched ahead of him, being careful, and his heart sank.

But there was one comfort. He would not be alone. Emma would be with him. Olivia would be with him. There would be comfort in exile. She had said she would come, and that showed, surely, that she loved him. And the thought of being with her, and the comfort it gave, proved that he loved her, did it not? Going away would not be the terrible dislocation that it might otherwise have been. He had never seen the world, and there was another world out here: there was Italy, until now only glimpsed from a train window and a hearse window, apart from that trip to Naples. There were the lands beyond Italy, places he had heard of, seen on television, but could barely comprehend. There was too the possibility of a normal life, a new life, unlike the life he had been born into; there was a chance of being born again.

But to get a job, to work alongside other men, to be told what to do, to be an ordinary person, to be a bricklayer in Dusseldorf – one heard about people leaving Catania for just that purpose – how would he like that? How would Emma like that? If he were to come home, tired, every evening, bad tempered, with some paltry but hard-earned sum… But there was of course the money. If he were to go away, to disappear, could he take the money with him? One point six million for the Rota job; the other sums he had hidden away; that would be enough to ensure he did not have to work too hard.

He thought of the money, the one point six million stashed away in Catania, the two or three hundred thousand that he had invested in the flat and various bank accounts. Could he really live without all that money?

'Nice place you have got here,' said Traiano. 'I had passed it on several occasions, but never been inside. Nice hotel. Great food. I was expecting you. Familiar company.' He opened the pizza box that they had brought him. 'Good, you remembered. I like green olives and I can't stand black olives. Now where did I last remark on that? Was it at home? Was it in the office, or in the car? Was it in the gym? Or was it all of those places? You love listening to other people's conversations, don't you, spying on people. Do you listen to me in bed with my wife, talking to my children, talking to my friends? Well, I hope you do and feel sad: because I am sure no one loves you; you don't have any marital relations to speak of; your children do not care for you, if you have any, which I doubt, and you certainly have no friends. You just have the fog and rain of Lombardy, which you so richly deserve. At least one good thing comes out of your spying: green olives not black; that and the fact you know how happy and prosperous I am and how completely innocent all my conversations are.'

'Which is why, when you plot murder, you go to Naples, under the cover of watching a football match,' said Silvio.

'You strike me as very angry,' said Chiara.

'I am being harassed by the forces of law and order, when I have done nothing. How would you feel, signora? Mind if I start?' he asked, taking a slice of pizza.

'The case against you is very strong,' said Silvio. 'We have everyone from that weekend in custody.'

'What, including the children?'

'No, not the children. We have spoken to Beppe Santucci, though. We showed him the transcripts that we showed you.'

'Your case is as weak as water,' he said. 'Please be reasonable. Your transcripts show that Sandro Santucci hated us all and insulted us all. It does not prove we responded like for like. I know his father, I know his mother, and his cousin is my best friend. For their sake, we ignored Sandro's insults. His poor mother, she knew he was very difficult. So did his sister Emma. He *was* very difficult. A spoilt rich kid. His mother and brother are very upset he is dead, but their grief will be tempered by the knowledge of just how difficult he was. You are trying to say that because Sandro says all sorts of nasty things about me in your transcripts, that I must have killed him. Well, it does not work like that. I am a Romanian by birth, and my mother was a prostitute; but after a time, you get used to being called a Romanian and the son of a whore. So what? I mean, look at you two. You eat disgusting polenta day in and day out, but when you are reminded of it, you just shrug it off. You have heard it all before. Well, so have I. You think I murdered Sandro. Well, I didn't.'

'Then who did?' asked Chiara.

'That is not my job, but your job, to find out. You cannot attribute every unsolved murder in Sicily to me and my friends. But let me ask you something. How many young men were killed inside or outside nightclubs in this last year, all for very silly reasons? A good dozen, I should think. Sandro was entitled, he was rude, he was mouthy. He went to nightclubs, and there he might well have insulted someone of his own age who took it upon himself first to break his ankle, and second to follow him over the straits and kill him. The clue is in Sandro's character. I did not have anything against him.'

'We know you did it, and it is time for you to confess,' said Silvio. 'It really would be good, you know. You are fond of your wife and children, and if you ever want to see them again, I mean if you ever want to be free in the near future, you ought to confess before someone else gets their confession in, and dumps all over you, leaving you carrying the baby.'

'Mixed metaphor,' said Traiano, taking another slice of pizza. 'Do you think Muniddu will crack, or Renzo or Tonino? We are friends and we stick together. You, by contrast, have no friends, and worship that mummified corpse, the Italian Republic. You are idol worshippers, not Catholics. Anyway, you cannot keep me in here forever; you have to charge me or release me; and to charge me, you need evidence. Of which, as usual, you have none. When are you going to let me see my lawyer?'

'You really think that don Renzo won't crack under strain?' said Chiara. 'He strikes me as the weak link in your chain. He's fragile. The guilt of killing his own cousin must be a burden to him.'

'I agree. Which is why he would not do it. And Muniddu, he used to drive Sandro to school when he was a little boy. Come on. It's tantamount to killing puppies. And Tonino, who is going to marry Sandro's sister? He killed his future wife's brother? Don't be ridiculous.'

'And Beppe?' she asked. 'Was he so fond of his brother?'

'Do you think a brother would turn against a brother like that?' asked Traiano.

'Yes, we do,' said Silvio. 'Who killed Rosario di Rienzi?'

'That case was solved long ago. The guy who tried to steal his computer. Poor Rosario. He should have let him take it.'

He smiled sadly.

'You are wasting your time,' he said.

Muniddu, they knew, was a tough nut to crack, so they did not bother. They decided rather to concentrate on Renzo. But here they came up against something they could not understand, namely his fear of his aunt. Renzo was adamant that he had had nothing, nothing at all to do with the death of his cousin. He revered his aunt, and he would never, ever, have hurt one of her children. It was no less than the truth. The disapproval of his aunt was something he could not bear to live with.

He explained his total innocence. The trip to Naples was merely to see a football match, nothing more. He had been in the company of two teenage boys the entire time. Nothing untoward had been discussed, and he was aware of no such discussions. On the day his cousin was murdered, he had been in Palermo all morning, at the office, where numerous people had seen him. Moreover, he had no motive to kill or harm his cousin. The court case did not concern him. It was purely between Beppe and Sandro, who got their grandfather's money. He had nothing to do with that at all. As for his friends, they were innocent too. Muniddu, he had known almost all his life. Tonino was a good boy, as his aunt could attest, as Emma could attest. Traiano was a good man too.

They returned in the afternoon to Tonino.

'We want to talk to you about Rota,' said Silvio. 'Matteo Rota and Simone Rota, uncle and nephew. One disappeared with four friends on Easter morning, the other was shot dead near the Corso Calatafimi soon afterwards.'

'Were there witnesses?' asked Tonino.

'The cocaine distribution for the whole island of Sicily has been moved from Palermo to Catania, has it not?' said Chiara.

'Has it? How should I know?'

'You were one of those who cleaned things up at this end, terminated the contracts and the lives of Rota and his friends. Then you tidied up the loose ends, by getting rid of young Rota,' said Silvio. 'Didn't you?'

'You keep on asking me things to which I do not know the answer,' he said. 'What are you offering me in return?'

'Immunity from prosecution,' said Silvio.

'And a one-way ticket to Australia?' asked Tonino.

'They have used you and exploited you. They have taken advantage of your youth and your poverty, and your lack of education,' said Chiara.

'But for one of the downtrodden, I have done well. Tell me about Beata Bednarowska and her son Paolo. Where are they now?'

'Have you been to Rome?' asked Chiara.

'Only to the outskirts. I went once to the shrine of Our Lady of Divine Love. But that is all. With Traiano. You see, we are friends. You want me to betray my friends for the benefit of a state I do not believe in, and which cannot protect anyone, not even Paolo and his mother. It is not much of a bargain, is it?'

'Look,' she said. 'Tell us the whole story, and they go straight to jail, and they will never be seen again. We have them all under lock and key and they will never be free again.'

'Do you have don Calogero under lock and key, by any chance?'

There was an embarrassed silence.

'I want to see Roberto Costacurta,' he said.

There was a garden at the back of the barracks. There was a high wall topped with menacing signs and razor wire, which meant no one could get in and no one could get out. It was here, as evening fell, that he was taken. The two policemen who had played the tape for him conducted him to the garden, and one of them offered him a packet of cigarettes and a lighter. He walked around smoking a pensive cigarette. A few moments later, a door opened, as Roberto joined him.

'Just keep in sight,' said the man with the eyelashes.

'How are you?' asked Roberto.

'Ruined,' said Tonino glumly. 'They have everything on tape. You, me, everything. They played it to me. You know what I am like. Any port in a storm. Not one for soft feelings. But try explaining that to them. I am telling you this, in case they create trouble for you.'

'For me?' he asked.

'Gabriella, the signora, your sisters, your mother…'

'But I am a nobody. They don't care about me.'

'They can blackmail you, and force you to work as their spy, to tell them what you know, to find things out.' Tonino looked over his shoulder to check that the two policemen were out of earshot. 'You have access to the signora.'

'What are you going to do?' asked Roberto.

'Go to jail for twenty years, that is always a possibility,' he said gloomily. 'Or else immunity from prosecution and a new life in Australia or somewhere. Is this garden bugged?'

'There is too much background noise and if we keep walking around and do not speak in loud voices we should be alright.'

'Which would you choose? Ucciardone? Or Australia?' asked Tonino.

'Australia. They have got good weather there,' said Roberto. 'Why not? But have they got any evidence against you? I mean, evidence of crime?'

'Do they need evidence? Evidence of crime? They have enough to destroy me in the eyes of the others. But never to come back? Never to see my mother again?'

'Never mind your mother, what about Emma and the baby?'

'They would come with me, but my mother would not, of that I am sure. She has my father; she has my little brother. She would never betray don Calogero.'

'And you would?' asked Roberto.

He sounded shocked.

At that moment, he knew he wanted to get away. Australia, wherever it was, sounded like paradise. He wanted to get away from Sicily, he wanted to get away from Calogero; but, to his surprise, he wanted to get away most of all from Roberto Costacurta. He wanted to run away from the humiliation of once having loved this man.

'Why not?' he said quietly.

He did not look at him as he spoke. Roberto understood. He was going away, in his mind he was already away, without him. Without needing to be told, he knew he had deluded himself. He had assumed that Tonino had wanted him, but could not admit it, least of all to himself. Perhaps he had; but he wanted him no longer.

Then why had he called him? This question was soon answered.

'The money,' said Tonino. 'You have control of the bank accounts. Keep that. It may be that I will ask for that money in the future. I may need it. You are going to be well cared for, by the signora, aren't you? The flat is yours. Keep that. Now listen, there is one point six million, in cash, in various cellars in Catania. I want you to put that into your accounts, bit by bit, and send it to me, bit by bit. I am trusting you. Can I trust you?'

'How will I get the money? How will we communicate?' asked Roberto.

'I can write to you from Australia, at the flat, and give you details. As for the money, it is in three different locations in Catania. Three old ladies whom my mother calls auntie. Two of them are her aunts. You ask my mother about them, you go round, you collect on my behalf. They know, they won't be surprised. But you take it bit by bit. It might take years.'

'One point six million would be a nice start in Australia, or anywhere else for that matter,' said Roberto wistfully. 'I will wait to hear from you. You can trust me. Is this good-bye, then?'

'Maybe, maybe not. I don't know when we will meet again.'

Roberto looked towards the two policemen, who were not looking in their direction. He took Tonino's cigarette and threw it away. He leaned forward to kiss him, but Tonino turned away. The two policemen were now watching, one smirking, the other frowning. Tonino made an obscene gesture in their direction.

Roberto sighed.

'Where will you go?' he asked.

'That depends on Emma, I suppose.'

Roberto nodded.

'Are they going to arrest Calogero?' he asked

'If I tell them to.' He lit another cigarette. 'I don't care about Calogero. What about Beppe? I am worried about Beppe.'

'Why?'

'Will they arrest him too? The murder of Sandro was all his idea. I didn't like Sandro and the way he spoke about me. Traiano will do anything Beppe suggests. So will Muniddu, whose daughter he is going to marry. And Renzo hated Sandro because he was the son of his enemy, the man who killed his father. All these together might not have been enough, but Beppe's little push was decisive. Will he go to jail?'

'Sounds like he deserves it,' said Roberto. 'You know, if you are going to betray someone, you have to do it ruthlessly, and not allow yourself any regrets.'

'OK,' said Tonino.

It was time to part. The two policemen looked away. A moment later, Roberto was gone, and Tonino stayed in the garden to have another cigarette.

Chapter Eight

'This is a very splendid way of spending the lunch hour,' said Anna Maria Tancredi.

'I agree, signora,' replied Roberto. 'Do you think this place is bugged?'

'No one ever comes in except members of the family. No man to read the meter, nothing like that. Only people I trust. Of course, they could come in when I am not here, and plant something. But I have the place swept regularly. Are you worried?'

'I don't like the idea of people listening. They could create trouble.'

'Veronica cleans very thoroughly, every day she is here. She would discover something. These arrests, is that what is worrying you?'

'Yes. Does it not worry you, signora?'

'The lawyers are seeing them today. They will try and get them out on bail. Your friend, Tonino, he will get bail. I am sure. He has no previous, has he? And the evidence against him is very weak. Hearsay. Sandro said he was a drug dealer, but that does not mean he was, does it?'

'They might refuse bail to the lot of them,' said Roberto, 'and spin it out and spin it out, as they love to do. As they have done with that picture don Traiano had. Could they drag don Calogero into this?'

'It seems not, he was not at the football match in Naples. That was the great conspiracy, wasn't it? They ought to come clean, that they were there to visit the ruins at Herculaneum and the museum. There was no conspiracy. Someone somewhere has let their imagination run away with them. The whole thing is fantasy. Have we any idea what they are going to be charged with? My feeling is that they will release them without charge, and this is a way of trying to damage their reputations.'

'How is Bonelli?' he asked.

'How is his sister?' she answered. 'The brother is well, and so is the sister, I hope. He is such an expert on art. And you, my dear Roberto, are an expert in another field entirely.'

'I have to go back to work,' he said at last, with considerable regret. 'I am in the office this afternoon.'

She watched him rise and get dressed with longing eyes. Adultery had never been so pleasant.

'Did I ever mention my nephew to you, Fabrizio Perraino?'

'I may have heard the name,' he said, as he buttoned his shirt.

'You remind me of him. Or rather you make me remember how things were when he and I were enjoying life.'

'Your own nephew,' he said, with raised eyebrows, feigning shock. 'But isn't he dead?'

'Sadly, yes. And so, I believe, are those that killed him.'

'You know, I said to Gabriella, 'You never told me your brother was gay,' and she replied 'Well, you never asked.' Isn't that funny?'

'Very,' she said, watching him put on his socks.

He put on his shoes, then bent to kiss her, and quietly left.

As soon as he arrived in the office, Elena Santucci, he was told, was waiting for him.

'What have you heard?' she asked, as he came into the room.

'Nothing,' he replied. 'I was hoping you could tell me something. They arrested him on Tuesday morning, and today is Thursday. I am not sure how long they can hold them without charging them.'

'Oh, they have all these new laws, but our lawyers are meeting, and getting their defence together, trying to find out what they need to defend themselves against. But you know how rumours fly about. I heard that it was all this blasted weekend in Naples, and the death of Sandro afterwards. And I also heard that Tonino is going to be charged with drug dealing. Beppe told me that. He has been interviewed by the magistrates. But that is typical. They go and fill a boy like Beppe's head with all sorts of nonsense, and it creates panic. I refuse to panic. For God's sake, I am pregnant and have enough to worry about. Anyway, you have nothing to worry about, do you? You have never done an illegal thing in your life, have you?'

'That is right, signora.'

'Beppe said that they had been listening to Sandro's phone conversations and reading his messages. And bugging various places.'

'You wonder where they get the time, signora.'

'If they have bugged my house, I shall be very very cross,' she said. 'Anyway, Calogero is quite calm about the whole thing. He wasn't in Naples, he does not like football, thank God. They met all sorts of important people after the match, I gather.'

'Riccardo and Beppe mentioned that to me. What an honour for them.'

He was dismissed and returned to his desk. He did not have to wait long. Half an hour after school ended, Beppe was there. They went out to a noisy bar, as noisy as possible.

'Rosalia's mother is very upset,' said Beppe, 'and so is Riccardo, so is Rosalia. Their father has never been arrested before now, and with two uncles in jail, they know what this may mean. I am going over there later. The lawyers are coming to try and calm them all down. You can come if you want, as you are Tonino's closest friend. You may want to pass on any news to his mother.'

'Of course, of course.'

'And the lawyers want to speak to me about what happened on Tuesday, when those magistrates came to speak to me.'

'What did they say?'

'That they had been listening to Sandro's phone, and that he said some very bad things. That he said Tonino supplied him with drugs. That he called Tonino very bad names. And that the four of them - Tonino, Muniddu, Traiano and Renzo - decided to do away with Sandro that weekend we were all in Naples. They also had a microphone in the gym changing room. They showed me a transcript. It was pretty embarrassing. We were talking about his piercing.'

'Oh that. Hardly illegal. Well, make sure you leave it there, the microphone or whatever it is. There must be lots of noise there. That will annoy the hell out of them.' He paused. There could be no microphone where they were now, they both knew. 'I was there yesterday, I saw Tonino.'

'And?' asked Beppe, tonelessly.

'He is going to tell them everything, I think. I got the impression that they were negotiating; what he would say; what he would get in return. They will arrest don Calogero soon. You need to warn him. And they are coming for you. Tonino told me that the one who gave the push, that is the word he used, to ensure that Sandro was done away with, was you. You persuaded them. So, you are in danger.'

'Why are you warning me?' asked Beppe. 'Aren't you supposed to be his friend?'

'He has lost his head,' said Roberto. 'He needs to be stopped. Before he does really grave damage. You need to speak to don Calogero.'

Beppe considered. He nodded, and putting down his cup, left without a further word.

The atmosphere in the flat near the Corso Calatafimi was dismal. It was clear that Rosalia and Riccardo had been in tears most of the day. Muniddu's wife was more stoic; only the baby Emilio was too young to understand, but seemed to have noticed the depressed atmosphere.

The lawyers arrived. They had been sent by don Calogero, and Roberto did his best to follow what was happening. The lawyers - there were two of them - were confident that the evidence gleaned from Sandro's phone would not be admissible in court. Sandro was dead and could not appear to be cross examined; the phone tapping, they would submit, was illegal, as the police had had no real right to tap Sandro's phone or read his messages as he was not a criminal and not in league with criminals either. What other evidence the prosecutors had, they would have to disclose to the defence in due course, so the defence could prepare itself; and very soon, the four men would have to be charged. On this matter, they were cheerful. They would be charged and released on bail. Most people who were charged with conspiracy to murder were released on bail, and perhaps subjected to house arrest at worst. They would soon be coming home. Then what would happen is that there would be a trial which would drag on for months, if not years, and numerous appeals. There was no murder charge as yet that had materialised; that would be more difficult; but as in the case of the painting of the Madonna belonging to don Traiano, this was really a case of legal harassment.

'Riccardo and I were there,' said Beppe, 'All that weekend in Naples. When the supposed conspiracy took place.'

The lawyers nodded, and told him that one of them, or one of their colleagues, would be with them, if they were questioned by the police.

The lawyers left. Roberto and Beppe were invited to stay for supper. After supper, they watched the news. When the happenings of more local interest were broadcast, they groaned. There was a picture of Tonino, scowling, wearing his prisoner's white jumpsuit, and a report that a 'boy' of eighteen had been arrested in Palermo for the distribution of cocaine.

'They make him look so ugly,' said Rosalia sadly. 'He is not that ugly.'

'Poor Tonino,' said Riccardo.

'It is a canary down the mineshaft, a fishing expedition. They are putting his face on the television in the hope that sharks start circling, people come in with fresh accusations,' said Roberto.

'You mean they will do the same with Papà and don Renzo and don Traiano?' asked Rosalia.

'I am afraid so. It won't be pleasant. They want to parade the accused but innocent in an attempt to show they are cracking down on crime. As the lawyers say, it is a form of legal harassment.'

'This is the worst,' said Angela Santucci, 'The worst challenge you have ever faced, don Calogero.'

They were in the drawing-room of his wife's flat. He had decided to come to Palermo to consult the lawyers, to be nearer to the centre of things.

'My husband, safe in Castelvetrano, is positively smirking. I spoke to him on the phone, but I could hear from the tone of his voice… he takes pleasure in your misfortunes.'

'I am sure he does,' observed Calogero.

'So, what are you going to do?'

'Why do you care so much about this? Are you so very fond of my brother-in-law, your nephew?'

'Of course I am fond of my nephew,' she said patiently. 'Poor boy. His mother is going to see him, not that she will be much use. But, much as my feelings as an aunt are involved, my feelings as a mother count more. Beppe must be kept out of this. It would be unthinkable for him to be dragged into court, or worse, sent to some junior jail where he would not survive.'

'I am beginning to think that he might survive quite well,' said Calogero. 'If what I think you are going to say to me is true.'

'He resented Sandro. Sandro was difficult, Sandro was the elder, Sandro was spoilt. Besides, Beppe never had the tendency to pleasure that Sandro had. You may think me strange, but I do not want to lose two sons.'

'My dear Angela,' said Calogero, with something like sympathy. 'If these idiots, Renzo and Traiano, had kept to the rules, and not done this without my permission, then not only would Sandro be alive still, they would not be in jail facing a charge for conspiracy to murder. I have quite a mind to leave them there to stew, to teach them a lesson. But the other thing is this: if you think that Renzo or Traiano or Muniddu – Muniddu for God's sake – will say to the prosecutors 'Oh, it was not us; this sweet little sixteen-year-old put us up to it; it is all his fault!' then you are mistaken. If Beppe led them by the nose, well, I admire him for it; but they could hardly admit it, even to themselves. What fools they have been. Tonino killing Sandro, I understand. A hot-headed youth, too sensitive to insults.'

'Beppe told me, what Sandro had said on the phone about Tonino. Would he have killed him for that?'

'Yes. I think he would.'

'Well, he can't marry Emma now, not after that.'

'True. It would make for an awkward wedding and a difficult marriage. Does Emma know?'

'She will soon.'

'Poor Tonino. Things do not look good for him, do they? He has annoyed you; he has annoyed me… he has been useful in the past. He is the father of your granddaughter.'

'Please do not run away with yourself on my account,' said Angela. 'Leave the poor boy alone. The person that this reflects badly on is you. You cannot run your own organisation effectively. Your subordinates are insubordinate. And so is your wife.'

'If that is the case, I hardly need you to remind me of it.'

'You need to know what people say about you. My husband is a depressive and a drunk, everyone knows. But you, you think you are so important, don't you? And you have taken your hand off the tiller, and the ship is drifting.'

'You sound like my mother,' he said. 'That is a compliment. She, like my sisters, is the embodiment of a tough Sicilian woman. When the men were in jail or dead, the women managed, and they often managed extremely well. I am surrounded by tough and vociferous women: my mother, my sisters, my wife, Traiano's mother, and now you. Well, what do you all want me to do?'

'Your job. Break a few heads, show them you are not to be messed with. Protect Beppe.'

'Maybe I need protection from him,' he said sweetly. 'He takes after his mother, clearly, not his father. Listen, and I have good reason to say this, all is going to be well. And I believe we will have a bail hearing soon. You are panicking. I am not.'

Indeed, he was not.

They had met that earlier morning in the middle of the Palermo Central Station, just as lots of people were arriving. There were cameras there, of course, which might or might not been working, but there were crowds and noise. They had met in front of the departure board, and walked around separately, met again, separated and met again. They had not looked at each other, except to identify each other.

'You have something to tell me?' he had asked. 'My mother said you did. I hope it is good. I did not come all this way or get up this early only to be disappointed.'

'It is very good, don Calogero. You will be pleased to hear it. Tonino is betraying you. I have been told so, and told to warn you. He was at the barracks by the New Gate, but they have now moved him somewhere else, I should imagine, and he is talking to the two magistrates. He is doing so on the understanding of a new life abroad. My sister Emma will go with him. Moreover, he is going to shift the blame of Sandro's death onto me. I know all this from Roberto Costacurta, who saw him the day before yesterday.'

'And this Roberto told you, knowing you would tell me? The snake! Poor Tonino, bad judgement on his part. A lesson for us all. I wonder why Costacurta is betraying him to us?'

'Because you have more to give, don Calogero. And maybe jealousy of my sister. And maybe after being so close the two of them are now less close, and he wants to be rid of him.'

'You are a good judge of character. As soon as I find out where he is, I will get rid of him.'

'Forgive me, don Calogero, you may not be able to. You may find yourself under arrest very soon.'

'Is that imminent, do you think?' he said. 'I have come here to see your mother later this morning. Afterwards I shall return to Catania. Let them catch me if they can. But my dear sister Assunta will know where I am. You can speak to her when you want a meeting, when you have something more to tell me. Well done, Beppe; one day…'

And with that, he was gone.

After he had seen off Angela, he took a taxi to the station, leaving his nice car, regretfully, where he had parked it. He was on the next train to Catania and, on arrival, went home, changed out of his suit into more practical clothing, packed a small case of essentials, and then walked the short distance across the Purgatory quarter, to his sister's office. Assunta was pleased to see him, and he gave her brief instructions. He wanted to have the keys of all the empty flats that he owned in the quarter. There were currently four. As other places became empty, he would want their keys as well, and give these ones back. He would sleep in a different place every night. If a message came to him from their mutual friend (she understood him to mean Volta the mayor) he wanted to know as soon as possible. All she had to do was send a message to that effect to the guy on the door of the gym, who was a relation of Traiano's wife and was to be trusted. Then he was out of the door, and gone.

His first port of call was in fact the gym, and the room in the bowels of the earth that the boys met in. It was midafternoon, and there was no one there, so he settled down to wait. He lay down on one of the benches and went to sleep. Not more than half an hour later, one of the boys did come in, and was delighted to see him. They shook hands. He explained something. The place they were using for the processing of the drugs, where was it now? And when had it been moved there? It had been moved just on Monday, he was glad to hear, which meant that Tonino would not know where it was.

'You know one of our men has been arrested in Palermo for supplying drugs to the late Sandro Santucci?'

'My mother and I saw it on television last night,' said the boy. 'It is a real shame.'

'It certainly is. We will meet again,' he assured him, and departed.

He went to the flat he thought would suit him best. There was a bed, thankfully, and more importantly there was a window at the back that led out onto the roof, so that if he had to make an escape, he could do so, with a little difficulty, over the roof tops. There was a rather nice smell of cooking coming from a few open windows, which made him feel hungry. It reminded him that he had missed lunch. Leaving his suitcase, he went down to the square. The Church door was open, and there was the Madonna, glowing in the evening sunlight. He made the sign of the Cross. He was not a believer, but he was superstitious. God did not exist, and there were no laws apart from the law of the human will which was enforced by fear. The Madonna, well, she existed, she had lived in Galilee centuries ago, and somehow her kindness and her love to him, Calogero, extended from there to this little corner of Sicily which was her own. She would look after him. And so would all the people of the quarter, his own people, many of them his own tenants. He turned from the picture, and already feeling himself surrounded by admirers, young and old, made his way to the bar, where he ordered some of his favourite whiskey and shook a lot of hands. People were glad to see him, they always were. They had heard the news about the arrests in Palermo, but they had confidence in the boss; he would fix it; he always had.

As soon as the trattoria was open, he went there, and rather than sit at a single table, he sat at a large table, and very soon a dozen or so young men had joined him, and they had a long, delicious and convivial meal. Afterwards he walked back to the square and to the bar for some more whiskey. He wanted to watch the news. It was as he thought it might be. The first item in the local news was the arrest and charging of Tonino; he was charged with supplying cocaine to the late Sandro Santucci. He was also charged with conspiracy to murder the late Sandro. This news was heard with disbelief, and jeers. Also arrested and charged, with mugshots supplied, were Muniddu (not known in Catania), Traiano and Renzo. The jeers became intense. Then there was a profound silence. A warrant had been issued for the arrest of Calogero di Rienzi – they used the photograph from his identity card – who was being actively sought by the forces of law and order.

Calogero ordered another whiskey. He noticed that the atmosphere in the bar had become one of admiration: he was here, in their midst, not frightened. He noticed that the two traffic cops having a drink at the end of the bar were pretending not to notice him, though they did have the good grace to look embarrassed.

The arrest warrant was for conspiracy to murder, he noticed. The irony! The one crime that he had not committed. The news reported that Calogero di Rienzi, boss of the Purgatory quarter, presumed boss of bosses, was now on the run. At this there was a tremendous cheer in the bar. Boss of bosses, how that would annoy everyone outside Catania. And the last boss of bosses to go on the run, how long had it been before they caught him?

He walked to the empty flat, making his discreet way there under the cover of darkness. He felt that he was going to enjoy being on the run. It was going to be liberating.

'I suppose,' said Traiano, 'that you are getting nowhere with Muniddu, who is pretty tough, I admit, and pretty good at maintaining silence, and not the sort to be intimidated; and that you are getting nowhere with Renzo because he only knows about football and marathons, which don't interest you; and that Tonino is a waste of time, because he is a youngster who knows nothing at all; so here you are with me, again. Well, it gets me out of my cell. So, much as I thought I would never say this, I am glad to see you.'

'Your spirits are buoyant, I see,' said Silvio, 'despite the ever-expanding charge sheet. Let me see. You ordered the deaths of Beata Bednarowska and her son, because they were talking to us. You ordered the deaths of Rota, nephew and uncle, and the uncle's four colleagues. You are the kingpin of all the cocaine distribution in Sicily; you are the man who introduced fentanyl to the streets of Catania. These are token charges of course, because there are other crimes. Rosario di Rienzi, for example; you conspired to murder him with Calogero di Rienzi. You have caused actual bodily harm to numerous individuals.'

'You have witnesses?'

'We do,' said Chiara. 'You used to beat boys with your belt, using the flat side if it was not serious, and the buckle if it was. You beat them in some cases till they bled. Calogero did the same, and worse.'

'Worse?' he asked.

'Yes. It is pretty damning. He is of course on the run. He will escape the country, perhaps, and leave you to take the rap. He is a young man; he has fallen out with the wife; he can go to America. She will make sure he gets his cash, as she does not want to see him again perhaps. The American gangsters will receive him with open arms. He will fly to Canada, and walk over the border, and be in Manhattan before you can say knife. And you will rot forever in Ucciardone. Not a pleasant fate.'

'I agree. Not pleasant. But you know it is not going to happen.'

'You think Calogero is going to come to your rescue, don't you?' said Silvio. 'He isn't. First of all, why should he; what are you to him? You are the sort of person he picks up and throws away. He does not need you anymore. And he is annoyed with you, because you killed Sandro without his permission; you caused trouble. And Alfio Camilleri. You had something to do with that, didn't you, also without his permission. A man like him does not like that. He would be quite content to see the state take you away forever and do his business for him.'

'How long have you both been studying Sicilian customs?' asked Traiano.

'Sicilian customs? We call it something else. It is not folklore, you know,' said Chiara.

'Well, you have been at it, judging by your ages, for some years, but you have learned nothing. Have you ever heard of that Scottish word? Calogero likes that disgusting drink, whiskey, the water of life, they call it. The very expensive stuff. Well, in Scotland they have this word which means a magic mist that comes down on a man in the mountains. The word is glamour. It is now applied to women, but it means the magical quality of a man, a man like King Arthur, a man like Salvatore Giuliano. Calogero has it, and people love him. Such men can do what they want, but they also safeguard their reputation, because their reputation is the foundation of all. They look after their friends. If I spend the rest of my life in Ucciardone, I will suffer, no doubt, but Calogero will suffer more, as the man who failed to look after his own. That would be intolerable to him.'

'Do you love him?' asked Chiara.

'Signora, what a question. How little you know me. I only love my wife and children. But Calogero is family. I have seen him in all sorts of circumstances and I know his strengths and his weaknesses. I have never ever seen him afraid. He is on the run, but he is still in control. You have not frightened him. You can't frighten him. He is not capable of fear. But I know too that his reputation is a carefully maintained stance. Everything he does, he does for effect. And what effect!'

'The hunt for him is on. We shall have him in here soon enough,' said Silvio.

'Are you so sure? Tell me, have you got the police, the army, the helicopters after him?'

'We have.'

'Oh good. You see, the more you try, and the more you fail, the more ridiculous you will look. I look forward to another catastrophic failure of the Italian state to deliver on its promises.'

'We shall see,' said Chiara.

He was enjoying himself. He really was. It was like the old carefree days when he had been a teenager, before he had shackled himself to his first wife Stefania. He was free, no wife, no children, no people around him, moving through the quarter as and when he pleased, dodging the police, and not just the police, but the army, the helicopters, the sniffer dogs as well. It was a huge operation, but it was getting nowhere. The very size of it showed how important it was that they catch him; and it also showed that it was not just the police in Catania that wanted him; it was the entire Italian state; this was a duel with Rome, and it was Rome's credibility that was at stake.

The first night, when he had retired to the empty flat, he noticed a bit of commotion in the street below, shadowy forms, men in military uniform, combat dress, heavily armed, going not from door to door, but to certain doors in particular. The first, though he could not see it, but sensed it from the direction the sound came from, was his own house. The army had broken into his flat, he discovered later, without ringing, actually forcing the door, and then gone from room to room, followed by his scolding mother, and waking his children; then, pursued by the Black Widow Spider's angry shouts and the wail of the children, they had withdrawn, only to go through every other flat in the building, starting with Traiano's parents-in-law in the flat below. There were men on guard at the main entrance, and it was clear what they were doing; women hung out of windows and shouted the news. People gathered in the square and threw coins at the soldiers and spat at them and called them names. The soldiers looked embarrassed, and despite their guns, defenceless. Then they looked frightened and alarmed when, on the other side of the square, someone fired a gun into the air. There developed a chase for the shooter, who fired into the air at various points, and who knew the streets better than they did. As the soldiers chased the shooter, people placed objects in their paths to trip them up.

He was hanging out of the back window doing his best to hear all this, when he saw a teenage boy doing the same, who, by being able to look out of the front window of his flat, was able to report what was happening in the street below.

Eventually, things calmed down. Silence descended. It was now about two in the morning.

'Francesco!' he called softly to the boy.

The boy was not asleep, but poked his head out of the window immediately, thrilled that don Calogero knew his name.

'Yes, don Calogero?' he asked.

'Are things quiet below?'

He went to look and came back a moment later to tell him that they were. He instructed the boy to meet him on the street. A moment later they both appeared at different doors. No one was in the street. He sent the boy wordlessly forward to the corner, and waited for him to gesture him forward. And so they came to the edge of the square outside the Church of the Holy Souls in Purgatory. All was quiet. The bar was still open, as it stayed open all night. The late-night drinkers had mainly gone home, and the street sweepers were not yet in for their coffee. They crossed the square and entered.

'Things were a bit noisy earlier,' he said to the barman, who poured him his whiskey.

'I hardly noticed these things, don Calogero. Here, life carries on as it always does, thank the Lord.'

There were five or six people in the bar and they murmured their approval. Francesco, too young to drink, was given a coke. The boss spoke to him. He asked what the soldiers were wearing. The boy had noticed. There were some with the funny hats with feathers, some with those other hats that had wide brims, some with just ordinary red berets, and some with the sort of caps with a long dangling tassel.

'They are paying us a huge compliment. I think the red berets are the paratroopers; the feathers belong to the Alpini, and the wide brims are the Bersaglieri. I am not sure who the tassels belong to. All these to find one man, and that man me. They seek him here, they seek him there… Look, Francesco. Tomorrow morning, when you can, go to my sister's office – you know where it is – and tell her that the people of Catania no more want foreign soldiers on their streets than they did when the Bourbons used Austrian troops against us. Tell her that she has got to spread this around. She will know what to do. And if she has any message for me, tell her you will take it – verbally mind, nothing to be written down. Tonight, I will be where I am now, but then I will move. How is your mother? She is a relation of don Traiano's wife, isn't she?'

'Yes, don Calogero. They are second cousins.'

'And your father?'

'He is away, don Calogero,' said the boy, slightly crestfallen.

'Ah, well, she is lucky to have you, so big for your age too. You have grown since I saw you last. Listen, tomorrow I will come for lunch, and then you can take me to my new place.'

He went round the bar, shook all the hands, and then disappeared into the night, Francesco acting as his lookout.

Day two of what was later known as the siege of Purgatory, was very interesting. A bald man with glasses and big teeth arrived in the quarter at about nine in the morning, accompanied by the Mayor Volta and various other people in official positions. There had been a lively debate about whether the bald man in glasses, who happened to be the Minister of the Interior, should be guarded by plainclothes police, or by men in uniform, or by armed soldiers. He had decided that plainclothes policemen were best, and that he should try and look as normal as possible, and that anything else would perhaps betray fear, or be provocative. But when he came into the square, he looked vulnerable, and his manner betrayed that he felt like Daniel entering the lions' den. He took up his position on the church parvis and stood in front of one of the RAI cameras that had come with him. He made a little speech: Italy was one and indivisible. There were no 'no go' areas for the forces of law and order. An outlaw, a bandit, a criminal, was hiding in the quarter, the geography of which made it very hard to find him, but find him they would. The Italian Republic would not be defeated by hooliganism and criminality. The people of this quarter and the whole city ought to know that there were no hiding places. Anyone hiding the wanted man would be punished by the full severity of the law. The rule of law was everything. He said all this in an accent that betrayed his roots in Agrigento and his education in Milan.

He only just finished the speech, when he was jeered with cries of 'Bastard!', 'Rome is a den of thieves!', and 'What have you ever done about unemployment?' The plainclothes escort closed ranks around him. The people with him looked alarmed. The atmosphere, at first sullen and hostile, was turning what the newspapers called ugly. The Minister had two things on his mind, namely, getting back to his car, and how these pictures would look on the evening news. He had made a point, and the people here were emphatically proving his point, namely that this sort of behaviour was intolerable. Someone, somewhere, panicked, and overhead the sound of helicopter could be heard. The troops rushed into the square to extract the Minister, which they did with difficulty. Coins and insults flew. Women screamed abuse from windows. They got the Minster to the car, where to their horror, they discovered that one of the tyres was flat, the work no doubt of a very small boy, operating under eye level. The car limped away. People banged on the bonnet. A rubbish bin was thrown. Sirens blared.

An hour or so later, Volta gave a piece to camera in the safety and peace and quiet of the courtyard of the city hall. The atmosphere was serene, his voice was calm, effortlessly projecting authority.

'I deplore the scenes I witnessed earlier today in the square outside the Church of the Holy Souls in Purgatory. It was a grave insult to the authority of the state in the form of the Minister of the Interior. As the Minister so rightly said, there can be no 'no go' areas for the forces of law and order. I have, however, asked the government in Rome, putting the request directly to the Minister before he left us after his all too short visit, to scale down this operation. There is no evidence that Calogero di Rienzi is hiding out in the quarter, and if he is, this is not the way to catch him. Besides, there is no real evidence that Calogero di Rienzi is the fabled boss of bosses. He is known to many as a respectable businessman. Prescinding utterly from that, I want to draw attention to the fact that Sicily in general and its second largest city, Catania, have been starved of funds from Rome, and the huge amount of money being used to fill our streets with troops, which may assuage some atavistic feeling with voters in the north, merely makes us wonder why such funds cannot be spent on schools and hospitals here, quite apart from helping the unemployed.'

In the square of Purgatory, the RAI cameras had stayed and were doing vox pops.

'We don't want alpini and bersaglieri and paratroopers on our streets,' Assunta di Rienzi was saying, doing her magnificent daughter of the people act. 'This is not Northern Ireland. We are not a colony.'

Watching this on the lunchtime news on television, in the relative comfort of Francesco's mother's flat, Calogero laughed. He admired the cleverness of Volta, the man he had helped to become mayor. He laughed at the humiliation of the Minister of the Interior. He felt extremely pleased at the way the people had played up to the cameras.

After the news, there was lunch, and Agata, the mother of Francesco, had clearly understood the importance of her guest. He had of course met her before, through Traiano and Ceccina. She was a very pretty girl, going to waste in this flat. Lucky to have a son, and while the boy was out of the room getting the second course, he enquired delicately after the father of the boy. Gone north to work, had come back regularly, then less regularly, and then not at all. The feckless bastard, thought Calogero. And how lucky for him.

The flat only had two rooms, and when lunch was over – his thanks were effusive, her smiles too, which could mean only one thing – she went to make coffee. He spoke to the boy, asking him to go to the flat he had been using, giving him the key which he should keep and give back to Assunta. He told Francesco to pick up the few items of clothing in the flat and put them in the bag near the bed, and wait for him by the front door, with the bag, keeping a look out. The bag was a sports bag, and Francesco was wearing a football shirt, so he would look natural, and he should act natural as well. He would have coffee and a little rest and be down in half an hour. The boy nodded enthusiastically, so pleased to do something for the boss of bosses.

She was about to light the gas under the coffee when he put his arms around her and held her.

'We are alone for a bit,' he said softly.

She turned around in his embrace, noting that he had already undone his belt.

Francesco was a curious boy, so when he arrived in the almost completely bare flat in the next building, he picked up the clothes carefully, examining them and putting them neatly in the bag. In order to pack well, he emptied the bag's contents, and to his surprise there tumbled out, along with the bare minimum of clothes, a gun, some magazines, and several packages of cash, these being the things that Calogero had taken from the safe at home, the things he wanted no one to find. He looked at the money, all in neat bundles, and hardly dared touch it. There were twenty bundles in all, each of about fifty notes, made up of fifty-euro notes. He tried to calculate how much there was in all, and what fifty times fifty times twenty was. Eventually he worked it out. It was 50,000 euro. That was so much money, it made him tremble and made his mouth go dry. He looked at the magazines. There were two of them, one in what he saw was English, and one in a language he did not recognise, which was Hungarian. His eyes were transfixed by what he saw: statuesque blondes with perfect features whose bodies promised heavenly bliss. He had never seen such perfect detail. He thought he might faint.

'I was always jealous of Stefania,' his mother was saying. 'We were at school together.'

'She was a good girl,' he said, something he had never said when she was alive. 'But she ended unluckily, didn't she? Why were you jealous of her? The big flat, the money, three nice children, all those clothes, all the shoes a woman could want?'

'No. I was jealous because she had you,' said Agata. 'She had this. I never thought I would. By the way, you didn't…'

'I never have, never will. Don't worry. If God sends us a child, no one will be more pleased than me.'

'Well, that is nice of you,' she said.

'Saint Agata,' he said, 'My patron saint. You are the bestower of happiness.'

She giggled.

'I need to get up,' he said.

'But you will come again?' she asked.

'Most certainly,' he said. 'I am on the run, but I will find you. Promise.'

Downstairs Francesco was waiting, alert and watchful, holding the bag, with colour in his cheeks. At a sign from the boss, he walked to the end of the road, and kept a look out. The boss followed him, and then to the next corner and so on. They came to the desired street, and the door to the flat, opening the main door. Inside it, he told the boy to wait. He took out five or six fifty-euro notes.

'I want you and any boys you can find to go and buy as many fireworks as you can. There are shops that sell them on the Etnea; but go to several shops, not just one. Then take the fireworks to the room in the gym and tell the boys there to use them. They will know what to do.'

'OK, boss,' said Francesco. 'Are you coming to our house again?' he asked.

'I hope so. But I am on the run, so it is a different house each night.'

A few minutes later, he was out the door, in search of other boys to buy fireworks. And don Calogero was up the stairs to the next empty apartment, which had a good view of the street outside, and glimpse of the square. He lay down on the bed and slept.

In the city hall, the authorities were meeting, the heads of the police, the army, the people from Rome over video link, and the mayor Volta. The Roman authorities were making it clear that they needed, and expected, what they called a 'win'. So much had been invested in this, that if they were to abandon the operation now, the government would look extremely foolish. The win they needed was the capture of Calogero di Rienzi or the finding of the drug factory which was somewhere in the Purgatory quarter, or preferably both. These were the pictures they needed for the evening news: Calogero in handcuffs being taken away and, or, the drug factory under the bright lights of cameras being examined by uniformed men. The people from Rome insisted that this had to be done; the Minister insisted.

'We have to control our own streets,' they were saying in Rome. 'We have to show we are winning the war against drugs.'

The various military chiefs were speaking. The Purgatory quarter was a warren of streets and alleys, and very hard to police. It was a labyrinth. It was full of hiding places. The helicopter pictures proved this. People could run from building to building over the roofs, if they were agile enough, and they could run from street to street, through ground floor habitations and through various passages between courtyards. The Purgatory quarter was the ideal hiding place. Getting involved in a military campaign there was about as difficult as trying to control some of the more challenging urban environments in the Middle East. They mentioned Gaza, Nablus, Baghdad. The whole strategy was wrong. One needed men out of uniform who could blend in with the resident population and who could act covertly. One needed people who could gather intelligence, who could ask questions, find things out. The trouble was that they simply did not have any counter-insurgency personnel who could do that. They were all men and women with Lombard or Roman accents; no one had been trained to act Sicilian, to pass themselves off as natives. Besides which, the use of non-uniformed officers was almost certainly illegal; if anything happened, if anything went wrong, there might be terrible legal consequences, and the men themselves would be very wary of putting themselves in such legal jeopardy; indeed, the military commanders said, they could not countenance such underhand ways of operating.

Rome's anger at hearing this made them even more obdurate.

The other thing, one of the miliary men pointed out, was that Purgatory was a hostile environment. Our boys, he said, were having to wear their rain jackets to protect themselves from all the spitting and people were throwing coins at them, and other stuff too nasty to mention.

They need to toughen up, said someone in Rome.

We are here all the time, retorted the generals. Your minister came here for one hour and eight minutes this morning, and he is presuming to tell us what to do?

One of the solders coughed. They all looked at him.

'It seems to me,' he said, 'that if the government wants to turn Catania into another Beirut, there is not a lot that any of us here on the spot can do to dissuade them. As our mayor has said,' - he nodded towards Volta - 'these decisions are made in Rome with an eye not on Catania or even Sicily, but the whole country. For decades, people have been saying send in the army, make war on the Mafia, fight the war against drugs. Wars can be fought, though the hard bit is not starting them, but ending them. One has to have realistic objectives. Here, there are no realistic objectives. The drug factory has probably been packed up and dispersed by now, only to be reassembled at some later date. It even may have been moved back to Palermo, or some third city. Calogero di Rienzi has endless hiding places, and making his capture so central is merely setting the state up to fail. He may indeed have already left the city and be in a safe house elsewhere. Trust me, I was in Afghanistan: I watched the British, I watched the Americans make every mistake in the book. We are on day two of the operation. I suggest we get our troops off the street corners right now, and pretend this never happened. Leave di Rienzi where he is, let him hide for the rest of his life; but for goodness' sake stop this pantomime which you are putting on for the voters of the north before someone is killed.'

'Oh,' he went on, over the murmurs of approval in the room and the groans from Rome. 'I know what you are going to suggest. We seal off the Purgatory quarter, which is just about possible, though it would take a lot of men to do that, and we arrest every man or boy over the age of sixteen who comes out, and we interrogate them and only let them go if we are quite sure they are innocent. The method of the Iron Prefect, Cesare Moro; it worked then, it can work now. Well, it won't. There are very few adult men in Purgatory, statistically speaking; you would really have to arrest every boy over the age of ten, for most of the criminals are very young. Now, how would that go down outside Italy? But go back in history to General Filangeri: he merely used the weapon of indiscriminate bombardment. Shall we blow the place up? Even then we may not get the result we need. And I need hardly remind you that that making our respected Minister of the Interior into a new King Bomba is probably not a good idea.'

The meeting ground on. There was a clear division between Rome and Catania, as there always was. The accusation from Rome was the same as ever: that the people in Catania did not want to confront their own problems and take responsibility for them; the supposition was that Sicilians were lazy, stupid and retarded criminals. The Sicilian response was that all their problems were caused by Rome, which did not understand local conditions, or that local problems required local solutions. Volta had heard it all before. He felt the desire to bang his head against some hard surface, the table in front of him, the wall, whatever. Oh, let it end, he prayed, invoking the God in whom he did not believe.

But it was not going to end. It was going to get worse. A man came in with a note, which he presented to Volta. He read it, and felt himself go pale.

'Gentlemen,' he said. 'We have a crisis. One of the troops had just shot a six-year-old boy dead.'

In the room there was complete silence. In Rome, once they gathered what had happened, there was silence too.

Outside, in the via Etnea, the shop keepers were already drawing down their shutters, offices were closing, bars and restaurants were shutting. They knew what was coming.

In the Purgatory quarter, soldiers and police were listening to their radios, looking concerned, and then scuttling like mice back to the via Etnea and their vehicles, heading back to barracks.

In the square outside the Church of the Holy Souls in Purgatory, a young woman held a child in her arms. The sound she made was terrible to hear. Other women stood around her, and some tried to comfort her, knowing that no comfort could be given. There was blood on the cobblestones. The mother's cries were raw, inarticulate, grating on the ear. At some distance stood a crowd of teenage boys. Then an ambulance crew arrived. They approached the mother, and tried to examine the child. She fought them off. They stood at a little distance, unsure what to do. Then a man approached. It was Calogero. He recognised the mother, even though her face was transformed by grief. He stooped to where she sat on the cobblestones, holding the child.

'Annunziata,' he said, with kindness, 'You must take Pierino to hospital. Go with the ambulance.'

She too became silent and looked at him; her eyes focussed on his kind, compassionate, beautiful face. His voice to her was the voice of God. She nodded mutely. Then she allowed herself, still carrying the child, to get into the ambulance, which soon silently drove away.

He spoke to one of the teenagers.

'The father, does he work in the Furnaces?'

'Yes, don Calogero.'

'Find him as quick as you can, and take him to the hospital, tell him, well, tell him that he needs to be at the hospital. Now go.'

The soldiers were gone, the police were gone, and he went to the bar which was still open. His whiskey was waiting for him. The television was on. What they had just seen was now being reported on the news. Already, the words 'tragic accident' were being used. Then the usual talking heads appeared.

'How many more people are going to be shot by the forces of law and order on our streets?' asked a famous left-wing activist. 'This is the worst yet. We remember the young man Carlo Giuliani in Genoa in 2001, we remember those shot in Bologna and Rome in 1977. But they were adults, this is a child. The struggle for justice continues. I call on all citizens to go down into the squares of Italy tonight and protest, in every town.'

The Minister of Defence was not available for interview. He was judging a flower show in Trastevere. The Minister of the Interior was not available; the Prime Minister was not available. The spokesman for the President of the Republic spoke from the Quirinal Palace in Rome. He spoke of national grief and national anger, the need for calm, and the need for a proper investigation before conclusions were drawn.

Volta appeared.

'We are told,' he said, 'that this was a tragic accident. Right now, our thoughts and prayers are with the parents of this poor child. Their suffering must be unimaginable. My hope is the ballistic and forensic investigation into the fatal shot can happen unhindered. We need to determine exactly what happened. Initial reports suggest that a young soldier, startled by a firework thrown at him by some children, fired his gun by mistake, or into the air, and the bullet ricocheted off a hard surface with fatal results.'

Calogero finished his whiskey, shook hands with everyone, and then walked down the road to where the gym was.

The man on the door looked a little startled to see him.

'Should we close, sir?' he asked.

'No. There will be no trouble round here,' he said.

Then he went downstairs. There were several boys and young men in the room. Their faces became expectant when they saw him. They gathered round.

'Some years ago,' he said, 'before Volta became Mayor, there were days when the headline in the news was 'Catania Burning'. Some of you may remember that, others are too young. Well, you know what you have to do. Go out and do it.'

He took out a roll of cash from his pocket. Each boy was given a hundred. Among them was Francesco, the son of Agata. He smiled at him with particular warmth. One of the slightly younger boys was Nino, whose history he knew. Another was Marco, the one they called The Dentist, who had an excellent and terrifying reputation for one so young. He smiled at them all. He was enjoying himself. After they had gone, he left for Agata's flat, sure she would be waiting for him. And she was.

'The Five Days of Catania' was the term that the newspaper and television used for the events that surrounded the death of Piero La Farina, 6, for it was five days before order returned. Other outlets used the phrase 'The Hot Summer of Sicily', for there were disturbances in other Sicilian cities as well. There were protests all over Italy, torchlight processions, vigils, meetings with speeches, Masses, prayer events, appeals for calm, authoritative words spoken by the Pope at the Sunday Angelus; but in Catania, there was chaos: strikes, burned vehicles, and people throwing stones, coins and bricks at the forces of law and order.

During these five days, Calogero moved around the Purgatory quarter with impunity, as the police and army did not dare enter it, lest they be torn apart by furious women, or killed by mobs of teenage boys with knives and guns. He took the precaution of sleeping in a different place every night, lest they try a raid to extract him, but he made no pretence of hiding. At his sister's request, RAI came to interview him on the Church steps, where he spoke of his innocence in the matter of the murder of poor Sandro Santucci, and referred the interviewer to his lawyers, and the simple assertion that there was no evidence at all that linked him to the killing. He also claimed that the warrant for his arrest was politically motivated. The government had failed Sicily in so many ways, but to try and take people's minds off this they had constructed a wasteful, destructive and futile campaign against an organisation that did not exist. The government should leave Sicily to the Sicilians. As he said this, he was surrounded by a crowd of grim-faced people who seemed to agree with every word he said.

All this time, his children were in the quarter, at home, with his mother to look after them, unable, because she forbade it, as it was far too dangerous to leave the house, to join Anna Maria in either Palermo or Donnafugata. There was no school, so they were at home with the Black Widow Spider, their widowed aunt Giuseppina, and Aunt Assunta as well. It was, for them, an unusual and exciting time. From the wide roof terrace, they could hear the helicopters; they could see the palls of smoke from burning vehicles and rubbish containers that that overhung the via Etnea and Terpsichore Square; they could hear the endless wail of police sirens that only grew more insistent as each evening advanced. The younger children, the boys, were merely excited by all this chaos. Because the quarter itself was a calm oasis in all this trouble, their grandmother allowed them to go down to the square in the afternoon and play football with boys of a similar age, under her watchful eye, or that of Giuseppina, or the parents of the late Stefania. The boys had to be protected, and while the Black Widow Spider sat and watched them, the women of the quarter would come and pay their respects. She was most gratified.

Isabella di Rienzi was old enough to know what all this chaos and disorder, and all this attention paid to her grandmother, meant. All of these events had something to do with her father; he was at the centre of everything. He came and had lunch with them every day, and one could see the way he was flourishing, away from his wife, no longer wearing a suit, enjoying his children's company, enjoying, most of all, the power and the storm that he had unleashed.

In the square, while her brothers played football, the two youngest hardly old enough to take part, Isabella looked at the boys, conscious that they were looking at her. She knew them all, had seen them grow up, and many of them were clearly men already, at the age of sixteen or seventeen. She had, as a girl educated in a private school with middle class boys, despised these boys from Purgatory, once upon a time, but now she saw they had their merits, even if they were not conventionally attractive for the most part. She was under her grandmother and aunts' eyes; and under the eyes of her all seeing and all reporting sister, Natalia, but one day, she felt, she would choose a boy like one of these. During the chaos of those days, when she was able to escape the watchful eyes of her family, she was able to take a few of the boys on a test run. The results were satisfactory. It made the Five Days of Catania most memorable in her mind.

The two people whom no one saw was signora Grassi or her husband.

In Palermo, all was, by contrast, quite calm. Every day, Anna Maria rang to speak to the children for an hour. She also spoke to Angela Santucci and to Renzo's mother. These in turn passed things on to Beppe, as did the lawyers, as did Muniddu's family, with whom he spent much time after school. He also got permission to see Muniddu, his cousin Renzo, Traiano and Tonino, from their handlers. He got this by the simple expedient of asking. They said yes, of course they did, because they expected to hear something to their advantage. But he knew that. He did not have to be told or warned about it.

They were all being held in police barracks in various parts of the city. With Muniddu, the conversation was simple: his wife was fine, Riccardo was fine, Rosalia was fine, Emilio was fine; he was doing his best to keep them cheerful, and the lawyers were keeping them informed, and from them they understood that he would soon be released without charge. Muniddu asked about the baby's progress, and was reassured; he asked about Riccardo, and whether he was doing his homework properly, and was told he was; he asked about Rosalia and her homework, and whether she was letting anything distract her. He replied that there were no distractions. Muniddu confessed that the worst thing about confinement, apart from the food, was the lack of visitors, and the boredom. They would not allow him a radio or a television, so he had no access to the news or any form of entertainment. (He was, Beppe knew, not a reading man.) There was no news, Beppe assured him, just riots in Catania, not that Catania interested Muniddu much, as he had never been there. He had spoken on the phone to Anna Maria, Beppe assured him, and she was well, as was her entire family. Muniddu understood. They had not caught the boss. He was glad of it. They ended the conversation with hugs, and on Muniddu's part, tears.

There were hugs and tears with Tonino as well, at the beginning of the interview, at least on Tonino's part. Tonino confessed to being miserable. He was being held in solitary confinement, and the only people he saw were his two handlers. He asked about his mother, but Beppe had no news of her; he asked about Emma and the baby Olivia and was told they were well; he asked about the others, and Beppe told him about Muniddu and his family and that they were well, but gave him no other information. (He had been told not to mention Calogero as a condition of the visit.) Tonino had seen the lawyers, who told him that, very soon he would be sent to a proper jail, that is somewhere like Ucciardone, if he admitted to the drugs charge.

'But why would you do that?' asked Beppe, sharply.

'Anything to get away from here,' said Tonino. 'Nothing can be worse than this. The two bastards I see are driving me mad.'

'But would you want to go to Ucciardone, where your father was?'

'They might send me to the continent, to Rebibbia,' he said. 'I have never been to Rome,' he added sadly. 'They put you in a van and drive you all that way. But maybe Rebibbia is better than Ucciardone. I would only get about two years, maybe. Do you think I killed your brother?'

'Of course not.'

'How is Roberto?' he asked.

'I saw him at the office. He is fine, but worried about you.'

'I believe they searched my flat. That might have upset him. Not that there was anything to find. Did they search Emma's flat? Nothing there either. They have a camera on me in my cell all day, all night, and they never switch off the light. It is torture. The camera is there to stop me killing myself.'

'Would you, would you kill yourself?'

'Maybe,' said Tonino miserably. 'Does Emma think I killed your brother?'

'None of us think that. Not Mama, not me, not Emma. As for Papà, goodness knows what he thinks. But no one really cares about that. Look, try to be brave.'

Tonino nodded. He would try to be brave.

Traiano, when he saw him, was, by contrast, confident and smiling. They embraced.

'I am doing lots of reading,' he said. 'Manzoni. You know I never read it? It's long, but it is good. They have given me books, which is nice, otherwise I would be bored out of my mind. I have also read the whole of the first part of *The Divine Comedy*. You know, *Purgatory*. Are the other two parts any good? No? Then I might not carry on with it, perhaps try something more modern. No radio, no television, but television is always so dull. No newspapers, which means, don't tell me, I know they have probably told you not to, that there is plenty of news that they do not want me to see or hear. Which means we are winning. Well, I am not surprised. I had the magistrates speak to me the other day, they are rather dull people, I have heard them so often. How's Rosalia?'

'Well, very well. I mean she was very upset, so was Riccardo. I have done my best to support them and cheer them up. The lawyers are very encouraging. They have told us that you will all be out soon, and that they won't be able to hold you much longer.'

'I am not sure about that. They have all these things in their legal armoury. When you are charged with belonging to an illegal organisation, it is hard to prove a negative. Now, just because Muniddu is not there, do not misbehave with his daughter!'

'I never misbehave.'

'How are Ceccina and the children?'

'They are well. They know Papà is away; and their grandparents are well, though they have not been able to leave the house or the quarter for the last few days. Isabella and Natalia and their brothers are well too, and they have a lovely view from the roof terrace over the whole city, and they see everything.'

'You know I am in solitary, but I hear things,' said Traiano.

Finally, he saw his cousin. Renzo was pleased to see him. He too was doing much reading. He asked about his pregnant wife, and he asked about the child; he asked about Aunt Angela. He asked about Beppe himself.

'I am not worried about anything,' he said. 'So many nice books to read, and I am doing lots of exercise in my cell.'

'Can you believe it,' said Anna Maria Tancredi, one evening, curled up in bed with Roberto. 'What we have come to? What would Cavour have thought?'

'He would have thought, signora, that he had been right all along, that Garibaldi's expedition should have been stopped, and that Sicily should never have been part of the United Italy of which he dreamed.'

'This is the fifth night of rioting in Catania,' said Anna Maria. 'My husband is quite the man, you know.'

'Signora?'

'No, not in that sense. I mean I underestimated him. I thought he was losing his grip, but now he has reasserted himself splendidly. He had proved himself stronger than all his enemies, and his chief enemy above all. He has proved the utter weakness and incompetence of the state. He has defeated them.'

'What does that mean for me, signora?' asked Roberto, after a few moments.

'Precisely nothing. He sinned with that woman in Enna, and this is his punishment, my pleasure with you. You see, he has defeated the state, but he has not defeated me. I am sure he is having a lovely time in Catania, running around, giving them the slip, making them look foolish, but I am the one person he can never bring to heel. My mother-in-law is not my type, I have to say, but I admire her, because she showed me something important, as did his sister Assunta, as did Traiano's mother, as indeed, in a certain way, did the woman in Enna: he cannot handle strong women. Remarkable. He can defeat the government, but not us.'

'You are remarkable, signora.'

'Yes, I think I am. I was brought up to be so by my father, who had no son. He worked for don Lorenzo and don Domenico. Perhaps the whole history of my life would have been different if I had had brothers, and if don Lorenzo and don Domenico had had any son between them apart from Antonio, or if their cousin Carlo had lived longer. So many silly men. I think Calogero is intimidated by Angela too. But you, dearest Roberto, you are remarkable too.'

'I try my best to please, signora. But I cannot talk about art in the way Ruggero can.'

'Dearest Ruggero, I love him. So amusing and charming, and he knows everything. How is your girlfriend, by the way?'

'You seem very well, signora.'

'I meant Gabriella.'

'Very pleased to be having a baby. But otherwise she has not much use for me. I have not seen her since these troubles in Catania, but we spoke on the phone, and she is fine. She says she watches the riots from her balcony. About twice a day, the troops charge down her street, chasing the kids, and then go away, and then do it again. Every car in her road has been torched.'

'My goodness. The government in Rome must be tearing its hair out. The insurance bill will be huge. By the way, Veronica loves you. She was saying how polite and nice you are. She does not like Calogero at all, you know. Hardly surprising. He is so high and mighty. I do not much like him myself. But he needs to be flattered, and I do admire him.'

'I am glad she likes me. If she did not, she would just tell him all about me, and I would be a dead man.'

'Luckily for you, Calogero has his hands full. And when this is over, he will discover that he has to do as I say. For a dead man, you throb with life!'

Chapter Nine

Two men were there to see him, reported the little boy. He listened attentively, and then went in the direction of his sister's office; he asked the little boy to go up to the office and ask the two men to come down. It was early in the morning, and he was only just out of bed. There was silence throughout the town. Last night, there had been the noise of rioting, exploding vehicles and police sirens. Two men appeared before him. One he knew; the other was a stranger. Volta, the Mayor, stretched out his hand to shake it. The other man was introduced as Colonel Andreazza. He had never met him before now, but knew all about him. He supposed this was meant to be reassuring. After all, Andreazza was a long-standing friend, even if he had never met the boss. But so was Volta, he too was a friend.

He knew they were here to negotiate. He said to the little boy, who was still there, hoping to be useful, handing him a fifty euro note, to keep the change but to bring three cups of coffee and three cornetti to the gym.

'Follow me,' he said to them, and led them to the depths of the earth, the one place, he was sure, that was not bugged.

'Well?' he asked, as they settled, not very comfortably, onto the benches in the changing room, which was deserted.

Volta spoke.

'For five nights, Catania has been paralysed, and for five days too, the police are at their wits' end, the army too, but above all so is the Minister of the Interior. If this goes on much longer, he will be forced to resign. The government has already looks very foolish; there have been questions from the opposition; moreover, the commentary in the foreign press has been unremittingly negative. The reputation of Sicily is suffering, as is the reputation of the government in Rome.'

'And?' asked Calogero.

'They need it to stop and are prepared to do almost anything to make it stop. And you, don Calogero, are the one man who can stop it. I know you are. I am the messenger boy from the Minister of the Interior, whom, I have to say, I like no more than you do. If they had listened to my advice in the first place, listened to anyone here in Catania, then none of this would have happened. But Rome always thinks it knows best.'

Calogero smiled. He waited. Volta looked immensely uncomfortable. The tension was broken by the arrival of the coffee and the cornetti, brought down by the man on the desk upstairs.

'Don Calogero,' began Andreazza. 'I hope you can trust me, and not think I would mislead you. The four men in custody are being charged this morning, and so are you, in absentia. The lawyers will give you all the details, but as they may find it hard to get hold of you, I can tell you now. Tonino Grassi and this man Raimondo, known as Muniddu, are being charged with the rape and murder of Beata Bednarowska and Pawel Bednarowski; the same pair are being charged with the murder of Simone Rota, Matteo Rota and five others. Renzo Santucci and Trajan Antonescu are being charged with conspiracy to murder in the Rota case and in the case of Sandro Santucci, as are you. That is the main part of it. But then there are some separate charges that will need separate trials.'

'What does that mean?'

'Beppe Santucci will be charged with conspiring to murder his brother Sandro, but as he is under age, that requires a separate process.'

There was more, there was clearly more, he sensed.

'They will be charged this morning, and they will be out on bail by lunchtime. That is what the Minister of the Interior and the Minister of Grace and Justice is offering. Then, when these things come to trial, well, we shall have to wait and see,' said Volta, thoughtfully finishing off his cornetto.

Andreazza looked at him. Volta stood up to go. He bent over and took Calogero's hand and kissed it.

'Don Calogero,' he said, 'I wish you good morning.'

He left. They watched him go. Then Calogero looked at Andreazza.

'The offer,' he prompted him.

'When you hear it, you will understand why he left it to me to spell it out. Someone has betrayed you.'

'Oh, I know that, and I know who.'

Andreazza nodded, impressed.

'In a couple of hours, they will all be out on bail. The one who has confessed is Tonino Grassi. But you know that. He has signed a confession, with all the details he knows of. Details about you, don Calogero, which are highly embarrassing. Things that happened between you and him. These things, clearly, must never come to court. This boy is devoted to his mother, and as soon as he is out of jail, he wants to come to Catania to see her. He may never see her again, because after that he will go into witness protection, and then after the trial is over, he gets his one-way ticket to Australia. Or so he thinks. He will be here, today, at about two. Not only is he very devoted to his mother, he is very sensitive to the fact that he has betrayed you, not that he cares about what you think, but he cares about what his parents will think. After all, his father did fourteen years and never breathed a word about the Chemist of Catania, did he? The mother would rather die than say anything against don Calogero, her friend's son. If his parents knew he was a traitor, they themselves would hand him over to you, he fears. At the very least, they would upbraid him and scold him and abuse him. But he wants this to be a nice goodbye.'

'His release is being done without any publicity at all. His handlers will drive him to the mother's place, but they won't go in with him, and they will leave him there for however long he likes, until he asks to be fetched. He will be there from about two in the afternoon until, I should imagine, late evening. You can extract him at any time. This is the offer of the Minister of the Interior, who sees this as the necessary sacrifice he needs to make to keep his job. Like all important men, he sacrifices not himself, but other people, something with which you are familiar, I am sure. Once you have this miserable boy, the entire case collapses.'

'I will need to check that with my lawyers,' said Calogero. 'Can the witness statements of dead men be admissible in court?'

'They do not have as much force as those of the living, do they?' said Andreazza.

'I am grateful to you, Colonel,' Calogero said, with a smile. 'You have helped us in the past, and no doubt you will help us again. We have never met before now, have we, but your reputation goes before you. Tell the Minister of the Interior, or whoever you need to tell, that he need worry no longer.'

He nodded to Andreazza, who got up and left. He was left alone with his thoughts for a little while.

The door opened. In came the boy Francesco, the son of Agata. Calogero smiled at him and beckoned him to approach.

'You are up early,' he said, gesturing the boy to sit down next to him on the bench.

'There is no hot water at home,' said the boy.

He looked at don Calogero with a look of the most intense devotion.

'This whole thing is now over,' he said. 'I will come and see your mother this evening, do tell her that.'

The boy beamed.

'Would you like a little brother or sister, Francesco?' asked don Calogero.

'More than anything, don Calogero.'

'You might get your wish. I am working on it. Meanwhile, tonight is going to be a quiet night in Catania. The fun and games are over. Tell all the other boys. Tell them it is my order.' He took out a hundred euro note and placed it in the boy's pocket. 'Don't lose that. Now, go and enjoy the hot water. And I have something for you to do this afternoon.'

The plan of extraction was very simple. He went to the bar, and had another cup of coffee and another cornetto, in order to work out his plan. There were quite a few teenagers there, and he told them that tonight was to be quiet, and the fun and games were over. They looked disappointed, but he comforted them all with little presents of fifty-euro notes. Finally, he remembered what it was that he had been trying to remember: the cellar in which he had used to keep his hoard of stolen goods, the cellar that he himself had appropriated from Turiddu's father. That was where he had kept the stolen Spanish Madonna. He had the key to that cellar somewhere, he was sure. So he went up to his flat and called out a greeting to his mother as he entered. The children were all pleased to see him, though he had the disappointing news for them that tomorrow they would be back at school. Then he went into the office and opened his desk. One drawer contained a quantity of unlabelled keys. There was a pair that looked as though they might be the ones he was looking for, but he would have to take the whole lot. They were heavy in his pocket. Calling out that he would be back in good time for lunch, he left the house.

Crossing the square in front of the Church of the Holy Souls in Purgatory, he made for the narrow street where Turiddu had lived. In the years since Turiddu and his family had lived there, the street had improved somewhat; it was still narrow, sunless and airless, but no longer strewn with stinking rubbish, at least not usually. Because of the riots, there had been no rubbish collection for five days, and the place had returned to its former state. He arrived at the front door of the building and tried the various keys. He was in luck. He was soon in the dark hallway, in front of the familiar stairs. But instead of going up, he went down. There were the basement rooms, a catacomb of neglect. He thought it was the third door along, and tried that. He had, in the end, to try most of the doors until he found the one he was looking for. A narrow staircase led down to a small chamber strewn with old bits of carboard and newspaper. There was no natural light, and no electric light either; the only light came from the open door, which was metal. With relief, he left the place. It stank of mould and damp. The damp was a new thing. It must come, he supposed, from leaks in the building above.

It was not until three in the afternoon that Tonino arrived. The little boys who kept a watch on the house near the monument to Cardinal Dusmet reported it. When he was in the building, bigger boys took over, quite a few of them, to keep eyes on the door, and on the two minders who had brought him, two plainclothes policemen, one with very long eyelashes, the other a blond. These two were also keeping an eye on the door, though they thought the chances of Tonino absconding were minimal, as he was a dead man walking; and the chances of him being kidnapped were hardly considerable, as no one knew as yet, or so they thought, that he was in Catania, or had even been released.

It had already been a long day. First thing in the morning, Tonino, along with the rest of them, had been charged, and then there had been a brief bail hearing, and bail had been set. This meant he was free to go. Before that, the two magistrates had wanted to see him, in order for him to sign multiple copies of his witness statement, which they had coaxed out of him, and which ran to many pages. There were ten copies in all, and his laborious signature had to be at the bottom of each page, along with the date. The process took hours, and he was anxious to be away. Then, at last, they set off, Tonino and his handlers, for Catania, so he could see his mother. After the visit with the family, the two handlers were to take him to a hotel anywhere in Sicily apart from Catania or Palermo, and settle him there with them in attendance, and they were to change hotel every two or three days. Their cover story was that they were three boys on a pre-wedding trip. It had been promised that at some time there would be five of them, as Emma and the baby would join them. And thus would pass the two or three months – for the authorities were determined to move quickly – until the trial. It was not something that either of the handlers looked forward to. But this was what had been decided; false identity cards, and hotels, frequent moves; the old idea of a safe house or a barracks somewhere was thought too risky.

He was so pleased to see his mother; so pleased to see the way his sudden and unexpected arrival had transformed her face with joy. He was even pleased to see his father and pleased, of course, to see his baby brother. He reflected sadly that he might never see them again, but that his mother would at least have her other child near her to comfort her.

His parents were at a loss to understand why he had been arrested and held in solitary confinement. They simply could not understand it. They did not ask about the charges, for they made no sense either: drug dealing; conspiracy to murder. Tonino's father had done fourteen years for murder through sheer ill fortune; but what had gone wrong for his son? He had friends: don Calogero, don Traiano, don Renzo; well they too had their legal troubles, but why had he not been protected? The only conclusion was that someone had spoken; someone had broken silence.

While his mother cooked in the kitchen, cooked something really special, because he had not had any nice food for some time, his father sat at the table and cursed whoever it was that had broken silence.

'They told me when they arrested me that if I spoke, if I gave them the information they needed, then they would arrange things, they would fix things up. The person they wanted to know about was my friend, don Calogero's father, Renato, the one they now call the Chemist of Catania. They asked a lot of questions about him, even though they did not know who he was. That only appeared later, after his death. There was so much I could have told them. But I refused to say a word, and they let me rot in jail for fourteen long years. But, even though by then his father was dead, don Calogero did not forget me, or your mother, or indeed you. He looked after us, didn't he? Your mother had the pension, and I had the respect in Ucciardone afforded to a friend of the people who counted. No one interfered with me there. I was fine. I took the punishment, just as I had taken the good things. If someone has talked, that person is not a good person, that man is not a man, he is scum, and he deserves to die in agony. And rest assured, they will get him in the end. The government will make extravagant promises, but they will not be able to protect him. Calogero has eyes and ears everywhere. The man who spoke is not only not a man, he is a fool. When he meets his end, he will realise that almost any number of years in Piazza Lanza or Ucciardone would have been better. Do you remember that Polish woman and her son?'

'I remember,' said Tonino.

'They deserved it. May all who break silence end the same way.'

Tonino looked at his father. He remembered growing up without him, then meeting him for the first time when he had gone to visit him in Ucciardone. He had only been in his forties, but he was pale and shrunken, and he had resented him then, and he resented him still. His whole life was in the shadow of his father, wanting not to be like his father, but to be successful. His father perhaps thought he had done the right thing, but Tonino remembered his youth, the lack of money, the way that don Calogero had never really looked after them as much as he could have done. He felt no gratitude towards don Calogero at all. In fact, he hated him.

'And how's that girl of yours? And the baby?' his father was asking. 'Your mother and she really got on. I liked her too.'

'Emma is nice. She is not like the rest of the Santucci family at all. She is more down to earth, less materialistic. I suppose that was why she chose me.'

'Don't be ridiculous,' said his mother. 'You are a catch. You are so beautiful.'

'Mama, I am short. How can I be beautiful and short? Even Beppe Santucci is taller than me, and he is sixteen, and Riccardo, Muniddu's son, who is a year younger than Beppe, is taller than me.'

'The beard is beautiful,' said his mother.

They had not allowed him a razor. He had a week's growth on his face. He wanted to keep it. It was a disguise after all. He tried to think of Emma and the baby, but somehow the thoughts would not come. In Australia, or wherever they went after the trial was over, then perhaps there would be time to get used to the idea of Emma. Right now, she did not seem real. The thought of being with Emma all the time, living with her, and with Olivia, this was something he could not quite form into a coherent thought. They had spent time together in Palermo, but during all that time, it seemed as if they had spent very little time together. They hardly knew each other. They would arrive in Australia as strangers to each other. Was he doing the right thing? He wondered about his parents. They would never see him again. He wondered if they could fit in another secret visit like this one. He would talk to the handlers tomorrow. But this visit had been hard enough to arrange.

'Mama, at some point, Roberto Costacurta will come and see you and ask to get the packages I left. You will show him, won't you? He will send me the money when I ask him for it.'

His mother nodded. Then she went to fetch the pasta.

The two handlers were in the square by the statue of Cardinal Dusmet. The car was there too. They had instructions to leave Tonino with the family, and not to interrupt him. They wondered how long he would be. They were bored stiff. The only consolation was that they were being paid for this job, and paid handsomely. Over the next few months, they would get to know each other well, and get to know Tonino well. It was Tonino they were discussing.

'I feel sorry for him,' the blond one was saying. 'Brought up in the worst part of Catania, his father in jail, no money, no guidance, except from Calogero di Rienzi… If he had been brought up somewhere else, he would have had a different life.'

'Rubbish,' said the one with the eyelashes. 'If he had been brought up in Sweden, he would be exactly the same. I bet you are now going to say that if only he had not been so short, he would never have had to become a mass murderer to increase his stature. Or if he had not been a homosexual…'

The blond sighed: 'Are you sure you are not one too, because the amount of time you spend talking about it? Look, I am not saying he is a nice person, because he is not. I just feel that he is unfortunate, and that we, by contrast are fortunate. A life of crime does not lead to happiness. If only people could be persuaded of that and not make these criminals into heroes. How is your girlfriend?'

'She is great,' said the one with the eyelashes. 'We have been together since we were sixteen. What about you? Do you have anyone?'

'No one in particular. Situation vacant,' said the blond. 'Oh, I would love to go somewhere like London and have a good time, but this is home, and my mother is a widow. Trapani is such a lovely place, particularly in summer. You have been, haven't you?'

'Yes. My grandmother lives in Val d'Erice,' said the one with the eyelashes. 'I suppose when they send us on our tour of the island, we will be able to visit all these places. I suppose too we had better learn some card games.'

They both sighed.

'We should have got something to eat,' said the blond.

'Yes, we should,' said the eyelashes.

There was a hungry silence.

An hour or so later, the blond said:

'What do you think of that?'

'What?'

'That boy staring at us. The one sitting by the monument.'

'Well, whatever you do, don't stare back. This is Catania. He is probably up to not good,' said the eyelashes.

'Too late,' said the blond.

The boy approached, a little diffidently, as if to convey that he was shy with strangers. He had an unlit cigarette in his hands.

'Sirs,' he asked. 'Have either of you got a light?'

Neither of them smoked, neither of them had a light.

'Is there anything I can do for you, while you are waiting?' asked Francesco.

'What makes you think we are waiting?' asked the blond.

'Sir, this is where people wait. Drivers. People, rich people, go into that building there, which belongs to signor Bonelli, the art dealer, and sometimes I watch their cars for them, or if they have a driver, I offer to go and get the driver a cup of coffee or a sandwich or something. I presume you have someone in there looking at paintings with signor Bonelli. They are often there for hours.'

At that moment, nothing seemed nicer than a sandwich and a cup of coffee. He seemed a perfectly nice boy too. They told him what they wanted, and gave him the money, and a few minutes later, he was back with a tray, with two delicious sandwiches, and two tiny plastic cups of the most bitter coffee imaginable, and two bottles of mineral water. The boy then disappeared to take the tray back to the bar.

An hour passed, and when Calogero went to the front door of the Bonelli gallery, he could see that both the handlers were in the car fast asleep. The sleeping drug in the bitter coffee had done its job. He rang the bell.

In the flat, Tonino flinched at the sound of the bell. Before he could stop her, his mother was at the intercom, speaking to whoever it was. He knew who it would be, and he felt himself go pale at the entry into the room of the smiling don Calogero.

'I guessed you would be here,' he said, enfolding Tonino in a strong embrace. 'I knew, as soon as they told me that you were out on bail that you would come here. We paid a fortune to secure his freedom, signora, and it is worth every penny. Goodness, I hardly recognise you with this beard. I thought of growing one myself, but.... It suits you, I think. He is really handsome, don't you think, signora? You do? I knew you would. My mother says the same, and so do my daughters. Then he had to go and throw his lot in with Santucci's daughter, but she is a nice person, I am sure. Now listen, all of you. The good news is that he is out on bail. The less good news is that there are other charges coming down the line. My instinct, years ago, was always to trust people from Catania, people I had grown up with, people whose parents my parents had known. But we had to work with people from Palermo and perhaps that was a mistake. Someone from Palermo has spoken, and they are placing the blame for the disappearance of some people on poor Tonino here. So, we think it best for him to go away for a time, because if he does not, he will be arrested again, and this time no bail. It is for his own protection.'

'Who has spoken?' asked Grassi senior.

'Muniddu,' said Calogero quietly. 'He has done quite a few bad things, and he claims it was not him, but our Tonino here. Look, you will come with me, and we will put you on a boat to Malta. There they will give you a false passport saying you are a Maltese; just keep your mouth firmly shut, as they speak a barbaric language. Then, with that passport, you will fly to London and then to America. We have friends there. Don't worry, it will not be forever, only until Muniddu is in no position to give evidence against you, or against the rest of us, me included. But you are the weak link in the chain. You need to be placed somewhere out of the way. Don't be anxious, signora, he will be safe. But we need to leave soon.'

There were tears, there were embraces, and soon, he was gone, down the stairs, with don Calogero. He felt his legs grow weak underneath him, so that he could barely walk downstairs. He felt don Calogero holding him by the arm, and the cold hard metal of his gun against his side.

'Oh Jesus,' said the blond one, waking up, a moment of calm giving way to blind panic.

He jabbed the other one in the ribs. He groaned. It took some time to make him realise what had happened. Precious minutes were lost, though they both knew that it was already too late. They sprang out of the vehicle and made for the door. They rang the bell. No one responded. The did their best to force the lock. They bounded upstairs, where another door met them, on which they pounded. They forced that lock as well, which made a tremendous noise. Inside the art gallery, they were confronted by signora Grassi.

'If you have come to arrest him, he is not here,' she said in a voice of withering contempt.

Both Grassi parents were taken in for questioning, both said nothing at all. They were confident their son was safe, already on his way to Malta, and the more police time they wasted, the better. They treated suggestions that their son was in danger with contempt.

Their son was not very far away, in a dark, dank hole. He had been placed in a car boot and driven at speed, conveyed into the hallway of a building and taken downstairs. In the corridor that led to the cellars, he was stripped and beaten with belts and given the worst kicking of his life. A door had been opened, and he had been thrown down a staircase. He had been warned that any noise he made would mean no food and no drink. Then the door had clanged shut. Every bone in his body, every muscle, ached, but the despair he felt inside his heart was the worst of all. He had never felt fear, often wondered about it; but now he wondered no more.

Chapter Ten

Beppe was lying on the floor on the gym in Palermo. It was very early on a Saturday morning. From where he was lying, he could see the microphone. He liked to check these things, just to make sure that no one had come in and removed it. But though the microphone was there, they could not be sure that anyone was listening.

'So, where is Tonino?' he asked.

'He has done a runner, cost us a fortune, as he skipped bail, and we had put up the money. Hundreds of thousands, can't remember how much,' said Renzo.

'He was a coward, didn't want to face the interrogations. He was on bail for the lesser charges, but knew bigger ones were coming,' said Traiano.

'Tell me what he did, or what he was supposed to have done?' asked Beppe.

'That is an impossible question to answer,' said Traiano. 'He did nothing. Nothing I know about. What do any of us know about his activities? He was a courier for the business. That is all. He carried stuff back and forth from Palermo to Catania. He was only eighteen, for goodness' sake. A boy. He was totally unimportant. Did your father ever mention him?' he asked, looking at Riccardo.

'Often, often,' said Riccardo. 'He was a good friend of ours. We used to talk about the football. This idea that he dealt in drugs is a surprise. I mean, my parents are very strict and they would never have allowed him in the house if they had known that.'

'How is Emma?' asked Renzo.

'Upset,' said Beppe. 'He went without saying a word. She cannot understand that. She is upset and rather angry. He just left her and the child. I go and see them often. I am the godfather of the child. Little Olivia is sweet. My mother is upset too, because she liked him and trusted him, and now realises that she shouldn't have.'

'Did you like him?' asked Riccardo.

'Very much. You know I did. I am disappointed that he just left. But maybe one day he will be back. Emma and I were discussing it. We both think he has gone to that hotel in Africa.'

Renzo shook his head.

'But that would mean don Calogero would know where he was, and he does not.'

'I had not thought of that,' said Beppe.

Riccardo had dressed and said he would wait outside for Beppe. Beppe, still in his bathing suit, nodded. The two men, clad in towels, went into the showers. He gave them a moment, then followed them.

'Hi,' said Traiano, standing under the powerful jet of water.

'What is he doing here?' asked Renzo, who was covered in soap.

'I invited him,' said Traiano.

'Well, disinvite him. Go away,' he said to Beppe. 'This place is not for kids.'

'I am not a kid,' said Beppe.

'You are,' said Renzo.

'He is not a kid,' said Traiano.

He got out of his shower and walked a step or two to the soapy Renzo. He placed one hand against his right cheek, which surprised Renzo, and then with his right palm slapped him hard on the other cheek. Renzo cried out in pain.

276

'Now apologise,' said Traiano sternly.

'I am sorry,' said Renzo. 'You are not a kid. You have every right to be here.'

Beppe accepted this in silence.

'My lawyers,' he said, 'have told me that as soon as the police locate Tonino, then the trial is back on track. It's scheduled for the autumn, isn't it? Furthermore, if they find Tonino, as soon as they find Tonino, then they will arrest me, and I shall be put in Bicocca.'

'No. Malaspina,' said Renzo. 'Not so very far from the office. Via Francesco Cilea. You would not like it there. You are a soft boy.'

Traiano raised a finger to caution Renzo.

'He is not a soft boy. You are. He has done his bit.'

Renzo bowed his head and nodded.

'In answer to your question, there is no possibility of the police finding Tonino any time soon, before the trial, or ever. The trial, I expect, will be put off, and eventually abandoned.'

'Is he dead?' asked Beppe.

'I accepted don Calogero's assurances that we would never be troubled by him again,' said Traiano. 'Can you accept those assurances?'

'Given that it is don Calogero giving them, I can,' said Beppe. 'Can we trust Roberto?'

'Yes, we can. Tonino betrayed us, but Roberto betrayed Tonino. Roberto knew that in the end, loyalty to us was far more important. Roberto is rock solid. All of us are.'

'They were friends,' said Beppe. 'But…'

'Wasn't Tonino your friend too?' asked Renzo.

'No, he was not my friend,' said Beppe. 'What made you think that? Anyway, he was a traitor. I am glad he can no longer bother us.'

The darkness and the smell, he did not know which was worse; then there was the alternating cold and heat, along with the discomfort of the floor; his only consolation was the thin strip of dim light that came from under the door. He managed to trace the outline of the cellar in the dark and guess its dimensions. It was rectangle, about twelve feet by six. He could stand up, and stretching, just touch the ceiling. His cell was a large cupboard really. He spent most of his time at the top of the steps, where the light came from, the terribly dim light, not natural but electric, which made it impossible to count the days, or mark the passage of time. Sometimes he sensed people outside the cell door and heard whispered voices. These were his jailers, he was sure. He dared not cry out, certain that he would be punished if he did. The kicking and beating he had been given was still with him. The only sense of time passing came from the sound of the plumbing in the building above, which was busier at certain times more than others. These busy times, he thought, marked morning and evening.

After an interval, he thought that perhaps their plan was to starve him to death, for he felt very hungry. Or perhaps their plan was to keep him barely alive, for every now and then, the door opened, and from the blinding light came a bottle of water and a packet of biscuits or some bread. He had always hated biscuits, but in his voracious hunger he devoured them. He thought that perhaps the most rational thing was to shorten the agony, not eat, not drink, but even when he had no food, he longed for it, and when he had no water, he licked the dampest patch of the walls. The instinct to survive was strong.

Ever since he had been taken away by don Calogero and forced into a car boot and then dumped in this oubliette, he had known he was a dead man. His mother would think he was far away, on his way to America, to some safe place. The fact that he had told her to give the money to Roberto, that would reinforce the idea that he had jumped bail. She would not suspect that he was still in Purgatory, in this isolated hell, less than a kilometre from her house. And what about Emma, and the baby, Emma in her warm comfortable bed? Would she wonder where he had got to, what had become of him? Would she care? Had she loved him? He hoped so. It was a slim hope. Could a girl like Emma find him? Would she have the sense to speak to her father, speak to her cousin don Renzo, speak to her brother Beppe, and ask where he was? Surely, they would listen to her, ask questions, find out where he had last been seen with don Calogero? Surely, she and they would not accept the explanation that he had jumped bail and was hiding abroad? But that, he knew, was the most obvious explanation, that this was what they would believe, that Emma, instead of searching for him would assume the worst, that he had left her, that he had run away.

The other hope was Roberto, who would surely wonder what had happened to him, and speak to the police. But how could they find him, in this cellar in Purgatory, a place the police never came to? And did Roberto really care about him, or had he betrayed him just as he himself had betrayed Calogero?

They had not killed him yet. That gave him some hope. Would they spare him? Just allow him to go away? Surely not. He had been so close to them all. His betrayal was unforgiveable. Even he could see that. He deserved death. Why had he listened to the magistrates? Why had he listened to his own desire to run away? Why had he listened to Emma? There was no escaping Calogero, ever. He remembered Beata and Paolo. He remembered Rota, uncle and nephew. He had done those things, and now the same would be done to him. It was justice, he realised bitterly. He could not complain.

Justice was a fact, merely an illusion. Would he have spared any of the people he had killed, or beaten, or mistreated? Of course not. How could he possibly ask for something he himself would never have granted? Besides, to ask, to beg, to plead, that was all wrong, contrary to his dignity as a man, which was the last thing, shivering and starving and in this cellar, that he still possessed. Again, if by a miracle he were to escape, or be rescued, then he would exact a terrible punishment on his tormentors. How could he claim a kindness in which he simply did not believe?

High summer arrived like an unwelcome surprise over the Sicilian landscape, the sustained heat burning the countryside brown. Palermo became stifling as July advanced; Catania became unpleasant. Everyone who could afford it left.

Anna Maria Tancredi went on an art viewing and perhaps buying trip to London, having declared an interest in twentieth century art, and took Ruggero Bonelli with her; Bonelli only stayed a few nights in London, and together they visited the Tate galleries, as well as the famous Wallace collection, which was a little off piste, as Ruggero put it, but so very rewarding. They went to the galleries in Cork Street and the surrounding roads and pronounced everything very overpriced. Then Ruggero went back to Sicily, and Roberto appeared on the scene. There was so much to see and do in London, so many art galleries and museums and parks, and so many different restaurants to try, so many styles of cuisine. He was young, he was so lucky to be staying with her in a hotel on Piccadilly, and when she asked him if he were enjoying himself, he replied in the affirmative. He was so happy, he said, to be seeing the world through her educated eyes.

But he realised that week just how profoundly ignorant and uncultured he was, just how little he knew, just how provincial he was. They went shopping, and he let her choose clothes for him, for she was paying, but more importantly, she had taste. He allowed himself to be passive in conversation, to follow her guidance, for she knew things that he did not. He had been brought up in Catania, not far from the baroque splendours of the cathedral façade, and the historic site of the Roman theatre, and yet, all this had passed him by. Sicily, so beautiful, once the centre of the world, had produced people like himself who knew nothing of the past, and who had no sense of beauty. He was quite shocked, as they walked around the National Gallery and saw all the Italian masterpieces, that these had meant, still meant, so little to him. He had to improve himself; he had to become the sort of person who knew who Veronese was, who knew which century he had lived in, who knew what subjects he had painted and what they meant. He had to be the sort of person who did not feel ill when he ate curry, and the sort of person who understood instinctively that in England, a Garibaldi meant a biscuit, and that Edward VII and Edward VIII were different people. He had to have more knowledge of the language so he could pronounce the words 'Buckingham Palace' without feeling self-conscious. He had to wear clothes that looked and felt natural on him. He had to be able to stand in a room without feeling he did not belong there.

At night, things were easier. He was half her age, but he found her very attractive. He had always liked older women. The bedroom was a place where he excelled. Of course, she would get bored of him, eventually, but that did not matter too much; he was content to live for the present, to enjoy it, to make the most of what was offered. Women adored him, and he liked them. He could see the way their eyes followed him across the hotel lobby, how women, young and old, studied him, appreciated him, drank deep of his tall and well-built frame, his sympathetic eyes, his dark hair, his luxuriant beard. He was certainly handsome, but how deluded they were, he thought, to assume that good looks went with a kind and generous heart.

Generosity and kindness, were these things he had ever possessed? He could not remember. Had he ever felt them? Perhaps there had been a few chinks of light that had briefly illuminated his inner darkness. He had always loved his mother and sisters and hated his father for the way he had treated the family and abandoned them, leaving them so unprovided for. At the same time, being a boy, he had always had consolations that his sisters and his mother had never had. They had had no sexual adventures. They had had no exemption from housework. They had had no deference paid to them as members of the male and privileged sex. And he had not thought this was wrong. He had been quite happy to make the most of the opportunities offered him. There had been numerous girls, there had been Gabriella, and now there was the signora. Each had brought abundant benefits.

But there had also been Tonino, about whom he preferred not to think. That had, undoubtedly, been a thing. That was how he viewed it: a thing. These things happened; boys had feelings for boys, or more accurately a boy developed feelings for a boy who tolerated those feelings and gave him what he wanted. He had, he told himself, merely given Tonino what he had wanted. Or had it been the other way around? Tonino had never said that he had wanted love, quite the opposite. He had denied any soft feelings; Roberto had not believed him, but that was not the point. No soft feelings had been declared, and that meant no reciprocal soft feelings had been solicited. He had betrayed Tonino, he would rob Tonino, and he was certain that Tonino was dead, and that he was at least partially responsible. He had heard that the police were searching for Tonino, but he was sure they would never find him, dead or alive. Tonino was a figure of the past, and soon it would be as if he had never existed. He was already a person who had been swallowed up by silence. Just like Sandro Santucci. Dead people were not spoken about. They were allowed to rest in peace, simply because their memories were troubling.

One person who had difficulty understanding this was Emma Santucci. Perhaps because she was a girl, she did not understand. Perhaps because he was the father of her child. Perhaps because she had lost Tonino on top of her brother, on top of her Uncle Carlo, though that had been years ago, but perhaps she sensed there were too many premature deaths in her family. She was asking questions, wondering where he had gone, and was not quite satisfied, he could see, when they spoke, with the explanations given her, namely that he had jumped bail to avoid prison, that he had gone to America, that he had gone to Africa. Perhaps, this must have occurred to her, he had gone not just to avoid jail, but to avoid her, to avoid the jail of marriage and fatherhood. This thought, he was pretty certain, had crossed her mind, for she had stressed, to Roberto, just how much Tonino had loved the child. Surely, she had said, he would not abandon his daughter?

Perhaps she would pipe down, find some other amusement for herself, and forget Tonino. He hoped so. On several occasions she had come to him, to ask questions, to talk, as she put it, even though this was the last thing he wanted to talk about. She would, he was sure, with her mother's encouragement – for surely the mother knew – let go. He hoped so. And he himself, did he have regrets?

He told himself constantly that he did not. He had calculated, and he had made the right decision. Indeed, there had been no calculation at all, for the decision he had made was the only possible one. How could he have done anything else? How could he, even if he had wanted to, have resisted that temptation? The money had made all the difference, the money had been decisive, and it was because of the money he was so reliant on the signora, who would, when the time was right, administer it for him, make sure he was rich and respectable. He felt only a little regret at the way he was planning to deprive signora Grassi of the money, after all her kindness, but he needed it more. There was also the money too that Tonino had deposited in his sisters' and his mother's and his own bank accounts.

He had no regrets. As he lay in bed with Anna Maria, he banished all thought of regret. And yet sometimes images came unbidden into his mind. Undoubtedly, Tonino had been no beauty, too short, too facially unpleasing, and yet, and yet, he remembered the beautiful things about him, and sometimes, as they walked by the lake in Hyde Park, he would find himself catching sight of boys who reminded him of Tonino, and who have him strange looks as they passed him. Was he going to spend the rest of his life haunted by ghosts?

One evening, they ate sushi. Until then, he had thought the curry they had consumed was the most disgusting thing he had ever tried, but sushi, if that were possible, was worse; cold, clammy, starchy and fishy. He did his best to pretend he was enjoying himself. Every evening, before dinner, she rang the house at Donnafugata to speak to her husband, to speak to Veronica, and to speak to the children.

'The boys,' she said, 'are terribly sweet and are no problem at all. Even if they were to behave badly in future, Calogero will always adore them, largely because they are boys, and bad behaviour for him is not that bad. After all, wasn't he badly behaved once? For him, that is natural. But as for the girls, he does not understand them, their lusts, their sensitivities, their jealousies. That is what we discuss endlessly. He thinks they should just buckle down, do as they are told, behave themselves. He can't understand that that is the one thing they cannot do. Look at Beppe's sisters. Girls are rebellious, at least they are now; boys are biddable. They all adore their father, of course, but with boys that is uncomplicated; girls want so much from their father. I know I did. But you will discover this with your child. Calogero has some silly ideas when it comes to his own children. First, he thought that Isabella might like Beppe Santucci. Now he thinks Natalia might. And all because Beppe Santucci is so rich. He is staying with them. So is Angela. I think Angela sees it as a non-starter. I certainly do. Those girls must find Beppe very dull. He is not interested in the sorts of things teenage girls are interested in. He is not like a teenager at all.'

'I agree,' he said. 'I have observed him. He is not like other teenagers. I mean, he likes football. He has a girlfriend, Rosalia, Muniddu's daughter. He has interests, he is studious, he is very clever, he makes himself agreeable. He is unfailingly communicative and polite. But he is not like other teenagers, largely because he is worth hundreds of millions of euros.'

'When he gets to be twenty-one,' she said.

'Which gives the fortune hunters plenty of notice. Get in early. Try and convince him that you always liked him for himself, that your liking predates his grandfather's death. But he sees through them all.'

'Are they all like that? Even Muniddu? Even Traiano?' she asked. 'All his friends? Even you?'

'No, not me,' he said with a smile. 'After all, what have I to gain from his friendship?'

'You work for the Santucci company, don't you?'

'Yes, but, I have no daughter to marry him off to; unlike Muniddu, I don't have a daughter to push in his direction; a daughter, I might add, that he is very keen to have pushed in his direction.'

'I am sure. He is a nice boy, but not at all attractive, I always thought.'

'No, I meant something else. He is not over-interested in girls. The other one, Riccardo, is, I suspect. But Beppe is not. So having Rosalia pushed towards him saves him the bother of having to attract her himself.'

'Well, there are men who are not interested in girls. People like dearest Ruggero. Is Beppe like that?'

'I doubt it. He hasn't got feelings towards his own sex. He does not have feelings towards the opposite sex. He does not have feelings at all. He recognises the feelings of others, just to exploit them.'

'You are harsh,' she said, with interest. 'He is years younger than you, and he is immature, that is all. He will grow up. You watch. He will be like Angela, kind and generous and full of good works. He will be nicer than poor Sandro, I hope. Are you enjoying your sushi?' she asked solicitously.

'Very much,' he answered.

'When August comes, I will be busy,' she said. 'It won't be a quiet month this year.'

They settled down to talk about the joyous topic of money.

'Of course, you know,' said Roberto, much later that night, when they were in bed together, 'Isabella and her sister may not care for Beppe's company very much, but Calogero, I am sure, likes him, and Traiano adores him.'

At Donnafugata, the talk was of children and babies. The women in the kitchen spoke of children, the three boys, the two girls, belonging to don Calogero, the three children of don Traiano, the one child of don Renzo; so many children. It was, they all agreed, a huge blessing. Other nations would die out, but not them. This talk was fuelled by the advanced pregnancy of Elena Santucci, expecting her second, and the not so advanced and only recently announced pregnancy of Ceccina Antonescu, now expecting her fourth. But the real cause of the obsessive discussion of fertility lay perhaps with don Calogero himself who, taking advantage of his wife's absence in London examining and perhaps buying art, had slipped away to Lecce for some days. Nothing had been announced, but everyone guessed it. He had gone to Lecce to see Catarina, to see his nephew Tino and his son Giovanni, and perhaps to pacify the lady herself. But all of this paled into insignificance compared to what had happened last month when the boss had been hiding from the police. Agata, who Ceccina knew, her second cousin, had, it seemed, gratefully received his attentions, and who knew to what effect? If Agata did have a child, then it would be the third cousin to her own children, Ceccina reflected, and make Agata's son, Francesco, a half-brother to the boss's new child. How would they carry off this new dignity? What would Anna Maria say? How would she react if she found out? Would she find out? And if she did, would she care?

Veronica, who discussed this with Ceccina, who knew Anna Maria best, was of the opinion that she would not care, and that anything the signore did, she would take in her stride. Veronica said nothing, gave away no secrets, but it was clear to the others that she knew something. And what could she know, except that Anna Maria had found solace elsewhere?

Among the men, this too was the settled opinion, that the marriage of the boss and Anna Maria was now purely commercial and political, and no longer emotional. They still had much business to do together, and though there was respect, there was no longer love. With the men, the boss confessed his trip to Lecce, and how cross Catarina was at her exile. He also spoke of the possible other new child to Traiano, who knew Agata slightly, and her son Francesco as well. It was typical of the boss, he thought. He was not a sex maniac, but a power maniac. Another illegitimate child increased his status. He had so much money: illegitimate children were an extravagance he could afford.

His domestic life, his life with his children and his wife, his mother and his sisters, had reached a sort of peace, it seemed. And as for business, that too was very good. Volta did his bit. The properties were bringing in a fortune. Very soon they would expand into Messina and

Taormina, as soon as that was under new management. The only thing was the past insubordination of Traiano, which was not a surprise, and that of Renzo, which was. The treachery of Tonino was worse, naturally, but that was being dealt with.

He was annoyed that they had killed Sandro, not because they had killed him, but because they had done so without asking. And to what end?

'It is his fault,' said Renzo, looking at Traiano accusingly. 'He does everything that Beppe suggests. Beppe controls his mind. And Beppe is only a kid.'

'Beppe is his grandfather's heir and is going to control a great deal, if not everything. When Domenico dies, he will, I am sure, control even more. He may be sixteen, but you can't treat him like a kid,' replied Traiano. 'I am surprised at you. You need to see him as he is and manage him.'

'He manages you,' said Renzo.

Traiano laughed.

'You both deserve a good whipping for your silly squabbling,' said Calogero. 'He is a sixteen and he is not properly grown up, but we will manage him, and we will help him grow up. We do not want jealousy between cousins, Renzo. Trust me, and trust Traiano. We can handle a sixteen-year-old. I have decided to invite him to the picnic on Etna. On Sunday 3rd August. You may remember that day is don Carmelo's birthday, the day he goes up the mountain, and, sadly for him, does not come down again. The day the management in Messina changes; the day of the decapitation strategy; the day Costantino takes over - another Roman Emperor from the Balkans. We will take him with us. I think we shall invite Muniddu as well; he can drive our young friend over from Palermo. But not Muniddu's son. This will be serious. We will see if the youngster is serious or not.'

'You're sulking,' Traiano said to Renzo later that day, while they both sat by the pool, their feet dangling in the water.

'You misinterpret me,' said Renzo. 'I am not sulking. I am just worried. I am beginning to think that we should not have killed Sandro.'

'You agreed to it. You wanted that for years.'

'I know I did. But I cannot remember why I did so. I remember never liking Sandro, and I am not sorry he is dead. I just think that the reason we killed him was wrong. We did it to please Beppe, didn't we? I don't think we should have done that. We should have kept Sandro to be a thorn in Beppe's side, to keep Beppe in check, in his place. As it is… Beppe becomes overimportant thanks to his brother's death, his father's incapacity, his grandfather's generosity and the generosity of his great-uncle to come. And he is sixteen. What will he be like in ten years' time?'

'He will be the way he is now. He is sixteen, you are right. What were you like at that age? Not like him. Me neither. Look, the boy is a boy, keen on his schoolbooks and football. That is the reason I like him. He has the childhood I never had. At his age I had two children and I had already proved myself to be a heartless beast by killing several people who, admittedly, deserved to be killed. Calogero and I together were soaked in blood, that time we killed that man, Michele Lotto, the wild Romanian. And neither of us felt a thing. It was the way we had been brought up. But Beppe is different. He will have a controlling interest in the Santucci companies, but he will do as I say, and as you say, and as don Calogero says. He may think it otherwise, but that is the way it will be. He will cultivate lemon trees. He will be a perfect figurehead, no more. He is a very sweet child, but he is retarded in many aways: intelligent, but loves lemons above all. No usual interests. No soft feelings for girls at all. I mean there is Rosalia, but I can assure you that is simply a friendship, if that. He feels no more for her than he feels for her brother Riccardo.'

'He does not have feelings; that is what worries me,' said Renzo.

Traiano forbore answering. He judged that Beppe did have feelings, for himself, of course. But, for Renzo, he probably felt only cousinly indifference. But if people did not love Renzo, that was not his burden, that was Renzo's. He sighed internally. He spent so much of his time trying to convince Renzo that he was loved.

'I had no confidence that Calogero would listen to me, but I had some hope that you would,' said Renzo. 'I trusted your judgment more than his. This new woman, Agata. Elena knows her a bit. Well, Agata, whoever she is, has done well for herself, just as Catarina did. She has a teenage son, doesn't she?'

'Yes, he is called Francesco,' agreed Traiano.

'I am sure he feels very happy too. The boss making love to his mother and providing him with a little brother or sister, and opening up all sorts of opportunities for little Francesco as well.

Lucky Francesco! Perhaps he does not realise what happened to Tonino, the previous teenage favourite.'

'You are not very subtle,' remarked Traiano. And not very clever, he might have added, but forbore.

'Surely you see what Calogero does not: the danger in Beppe?'

'There is no danger in Beppe,' said Traiano. 'You misjudge him. And as for Calogero spending time with teenagers, as he did with me, he recruits them young, and they want to work for us when they are that age, don't they? There's nothing unusual about that.'

'Is Tonino dead?' asked Renzo.

'I expect so,' said Traiano.

Beppe came to join them. He sat between them, and dangled his feet in the water. He smiled at them both, but said nothing.

'How are the children?' asked Traiano.

'The boys are playing football and the girls are watching a film. But I saw you here and thought that this looked like more fun. What are you talking about?'

'Adult things,' said Renzo. 'About Calogero having a child with this woman Agata.'

'All three of you are having children, then,' said Beppe, without much interest.

'Do you want children?' asked Renzo.

'One day,' said Beppe. 'When I am married. But I am in no hurry. School, university, work, they come first.'

'Well, of course they do, but sometimes people get impatient,' said Renzo. 'How old were you when Cristoforo was born?' he asked Traiano.

'Just fifteen, not that he realises that yet,' said Traiano. 'Yes, some people are, as you put it, impatient. I was one of them.'

'But I am very patient,' said Beppe. He smiled at his cousin and rested his head on his shoulder for a moment. 'Don't be cross,' he said.

Traiano looked at Renzo, and saw the spasm of irritation that crossed his face. But he caught Renzo's eye and Renzo read the warning correctly.

'I am not cross,' said Renzo placidly.

Perhaps, in the end, you could have everything, Anna Maria reflected. She was very rich herself, she was married to one of the richest men in Sicily; she had friends in all the right places, in politics, in the Church, and in the Santucci family; she had the most exciting young lover, who aimed only to please her, and whose long hair, beard and melting eyes were delightful; she had the friendship of Ruggero Bonelli, the most wonderfully well-informed art dealer; she had the joy of five children, two her own, three inherited, when for many years she had thought she would never have children.

She was back from London. The ever-attentive Roberto was with her, and they were about to sit down to lunch; with them was Ruggero Bonelli; it was good to see that these two, so necessary to her in different ways, were able to get on. Well, they had to. They had her in common; and they had Gabriella in common, Ruggero's sister, and the former girlfriend of Roberto, who was about to bring a child in the world, who would call Roberto, father and Ruggero, uncle.

'I have spoken to Calogero,' she said, as they sat down, and as Veronica brought in the first course, a refreshing cold soup, suitable for July. 'Don't look surprised. I had to speak to him. You see, the painting is stolen, is it not? I don't mean stolen from the Oratory in October 1969, though that was the original theft. I mean stolen from the Santucci family, in that they gave it to my father to look after, in deepest secrecy, and then died without revealing its whereabouts. Therefore, it is important that Calogero knows just in case someone like Renzo or Antonio objects. Calogero asked only one thing: that we delay the announcement to the weekend of 3rd

August. What is happening then, I don't know. But it will be a slow news day, and as a result we will get lots of publicity. I am speaking to the Cardinal Archbishop and have told him that I have bought an eighteenth-century copy of *The Nativity with Saint Lawrence and Saint Francis*. I told him it is of the very highest quality, and that the art dealer will bring it to the Cathedral where it can be displayed for the faithful on the night of Saturday 2nd August. We are pretending that the painting has come all the way from Catania, where it was part of the collection of Professor Leopardi, though how he got it, we do not know, though he certainly had it before 1969, we think. Of course, the professor had lots of contacts, didn't he?'

'That is one way of putting it,' said Ruggero with a smirk.

'And then, of course, you will be in front of the cameras to tell everyone that this is a copy from the eighteenth century, of the very highest quality, and you will say you have been researching it for years and are preparing a paper on it; and then after a suitable period the Archbishop will place it in the Oratory though, this being Italy, only after a huge and furious debate about the quality of the picture. But one thing is for sure. I have paid for it, and I will be keeping legal ownership of it.'

She smiled. Very soon everyone would be happy.

He could not understand why they were keeping him alive, but he was sure of this: that it was for no kind or charitable motive. He was being kept alive so that his execution, when it came, would have a greater impact. An immediate bullet when they had first taken him away from his mother's would have been nicer, but now that he was alive, days on, weeks later, he knew that he ought to use the time he had been given well. Sitting or lying in the dark, feeling the heat of summer, and the terrible smell of his own rotting faeces, unable to wash, with little to eat, aware of his long hair and an unaccustomed beard, feeling himself grow thinner and weaker, he was nevertheless mentally alert and occupied.

They would be kind to his mother, his father, his baby brother, he was sure, not because they were kind, but because their reputation depended on it. They would not punish her, his beloved mother, as she was the friend of signora di Rienzi. His mother would be happy, she had her husband, his father, and she had the child. She would wonder about his absence and, after a few years, draw conclusions. She had had a son, and that son had failed, and he was gone, gone forever. And she would accept that.

Emma's rationalisation would be equally convincing, he was sure. She would see him as yet another of the many boys who had made love to her and left her; who refused to commit to a relationship with her or the child. She would see his previous expressions of devotion as fake, and that he was simply a liar, a bad person. Then she would forget him.

One person remained in his mind and that was Roberto. Roberto had encouraged him, then betrayed him, he was sure, and, he was equally sure, stolen the money. He was not entirely surprised. He had loved Roberto, in a way, but Roberto had not loved him. Or had he not loved Roberto enough? And had he overestimated Roberto's love for him? Why should anyone, apart from his mother, love him? Hadn't his expertise with the knife and the gun been an attempt to make people fear him and respect him, simply because he had always known the path to love had been closed to him? He was disappointed in Roberto, just as the boss must be disappointed in him. But he must not disappoint himself: he needed to die bravely, to let them know, in the very last act of his life, that he was not frightened of them, or of death itself.

Occasionally in his dungeon he heard the bells of the Church of the Holy Souls in Purgatory. He had often heard these bells as a very small boy lying in bed late at night or early in the morning. And now he heard them once more. What happened after death? Did one become, as his mother certainly believed, a Holy Soul in Purgatory? Was one judged by God and sentenced to a long spell in purgatorial flames until one was cleansed and fit for the divine vision? It was a comforting belief, this belief that all would one day come right, and that eternal happiness was possible. But he had never believed until now, for even as a very small child, religion had made no sense to him. How could there be some beneficent power in the universe when it was clearly the case that there was not? Had God saved or protected Paolo and his mother? Had God loved Rota and his friends and his nephew? Had God punished the wicked? On this last point he reflected that perhaps he had: God was punishing him, and would eventually punish the others. They would prosper for a time, as he had, and then would come their downfall. Or so he hoped.

The world was cruel, and even though one inflicted cruelty, eventually it was inflicted on oneself. That was only just. Perhaps there was a different way of doing things, but not in Sicily, not in Purgatory, not here.

Eventually the summons came: the door opened, as he knew it must, and he was blinded by the light that he had not seen for weeks. They picked him up, for his legs were weak, and he was dragged along the corridor, up the stairs, and into the hallway of the building, and then out into the street and into the boot of a car.

The car drove for several hours, and when they arrived at their destination, it was dark. He was taken out of the boot of the car and into a house – he had the impression it was large – and taken to a bathroom where he was dumped in a shower, and the water turned on. He heard voices in a language he did not recognise. Gradually he was able to take off his filthy rags and wash himself, aware of a man holding a gun in the room with him. Then the water was turned off, and he was given a towel and a tracksuit in which to dress himself. Finally, he was put into a chair, and another man with a set of clippers cut his hair and removed his beard. From some distance away he could sense the aroma of cooking. He was then taken to a room, and locked in. There was a bed on which he gratefully lay, and shortly afterwards a tray of food, real food. The window was locked and the glass thick; below was an inhospitable slope. Before him was a view of Mount Etna, and he watched the rising sun gradually illuminate the volcanic slopes.

There was to be a picnic on Etna, in a house that was controlled by Costantino; not the same house in which Gino had met his untimely end, but another house which commanded a view of the northern slopes that looked towards Messina. The date was Sunday 3rd August, and they were to be there by noon. The person hosting the picnic was Costantino, the Serb, the son of don Carmelo, though not the son of don Carmelo's wife. When he heard this, and was told that he was invited, Beppe sensed the importance of the event. Muniddu was coming too, and Muniddu would drive him from Palermo. But Riccardo was not coming, and Rosalia and her mother were not coming either. It was going to be five of them: Muniddu, Beppe, Renzo, Traiano and the boss.

Riccardo was most offended at being excluded. He had always wanted to go to Etna, to see the volcano close up. This would be the perfect opportunity. Besides which, he was Beppe's best friend, and the other people there would all be adults, and who would Beppe have to talk to and to spend time with? But it was impossible, his father told him. He next applied to Beppe, and to his surprise Beppe said that it was impossible. He asked why. Beppe refused to answer and told him to stop asking questions. Muniddu intervened and told his son that he was too young for the trip to Etna. Riccardo answered that he was merely a year younger than Beppe, and what difference did that make anyway? Beppe looked displeased at this obvious statement of fact. Muniddu repeated that Riccardo should not ask questions about business that did not concern him. Once more, Riccardo asked how anything that concerned Beppe could not concern him as well.

'You are being stupid,' said Beppe. 'I have my business which I may not wish to share with you.'

Riccardo felt hurt, angered and provoked. There was a table separating them, but he tried his best to launch himself at Beppe. Muniddu grabbed him before he could, and sternly told him to go to his bedroom. The boy did. Muniddu followed his son, and taking off his belt, struck him very hard six times on the back of the legs. Later, Riccardo came to Beppe to apologise. He did so with true humility.

'I know what I did was wrong,' he said. 'You have business that does not concern me. I accept that.'

That Saturday, Beppe went to play squash with Traiano. Riccardo was left behind. Renzo was not there.

'What is happening tomorrow?' he asked.

'We are having a picnic,' said Traiano.

'I mean, what is really happening?'

'Don Calogero is gathering us. He has not told me why. There is one reason, to watch don Carmelo's birthday party at some mountain refuge which we will be able to see from where we are. It will be worth watching. Costantino did us a favour some time ago and we are doing him a favour.'

'What?'

'You don't want to know.'

'You are treating me like a child,' said Beppe.

'Yes, I am.'

'Give me a chance and I will prove myself,' he said. 'Muniddu gave Riccardo a good beating for being cheeky.'

'To his father? That is not like him.'

'No, to me.'

'Ah,' said Traiano. 'Is that what you like: seeing other people suffer?'

'No. That would be stupid. What is the point of that? Pain for the sake of pain? I am glad he was beaten because he needs to learn that he and I have different paths. I am my grandfather's heir; he will be at best my brother-in-law. We are not equals, are we? And where is Renzo? Why isn't he here? Is he sulking?'

'Yes, he is sulking. He feels… well, I don't know what he feels.'

'Oh, I will tell you exactly. He feels he can play second fiddle to don Calogero and to you, but not to me. He feels that his father was my Uncle Carlo, and that makes him special, but he refuses to acknowledge that don Lorenzo my grandfather chose me over him. He needs to get over that. You need to manage him. Isn't that your job?'

'Of course it is, and I do, but it takes time. He needs to be flattered and soothed. He is not very intelligent, you know, and he is very sensitive.'

'Oh, very sensitive, I know,' said Beppe. 'I want you to use your belt on him so that he becomes less sensitive.'

He smiled.

'When you have proved yourself,' said Traiano. 'Right now, you are just an untried sixteen-year-old.'

'I will prove myself at the first opportunity,' said Beppe.

'It may come sooner than you think,' said Traiano.

'So, you know something,' said Beppe.

In the isolated house on Etna, the prisoner, as he thought himself, Tonino, sensed that something was amiss, that something had changed. They came to his locked room and took him to the bathroom, and watched him use the lavatory, and then have his shower, with an alertness that they had not had before. He soon understood; their vigilance was because this was the last day on which things could go wrong. Their eyes were peeled, and along with their heightened nerves, was the sense of impending relief that they felt, he could tell, that this job would soon be over, that today was completion day. Either he was going to be handed over to someone else, thought Tonino, or else this was the last day of his life. He thought he knew which. He had a cold feeling inside, but he was ready. He was allowed to dry himself and then was handed a new tracksuit, but only the bottom part. Again, no shoes. Back in his cell, he listened carefully for noises that might tell him what was in preparation. There were vehicles arriving and departing. There were heightened voices from the garden, and there was some sort of hammering noise, which he guessed was the erection of a gazebo. And there was, just for a few seconds, the sound of an electric saw being tested.

They brought him some food, rather better than the food they had been giving him, and a glass of red wine as well. He realised that this was the final treat for the condemned man. He tried to sip it as slowly as he could. When they came to take away the tray that had had the lunch things (there had been no cutlery, and the wine had been served in a plastic cup) without a word, they had seized his wrists and cuffed him behind his back. He let them do this. He knew what it meant. They, his jailers, had not spoken to him all the time he had been there, and he had not spoken to them. There was no further point in speech.

Then they left him alone. He wondered if tears would come, but none did. He had never had tears for others, and he had none for himself. He wondered if he should ask forgiveness of the boss, or of God, but he knew he could not, as he would do it all again; he himself had never forgiven anyone or shown any mercy to any living thing; why should he expect for himself what he had not given to others?

They would come for him, and they would come for him soon.

They arrived at the house in three separate cars: Muniddu with Beppe, Traiano with Renzo, and the boss on his own, coming from Catania. The caterers had been there, and the caterers had left. There were three Serbs: Costantino and two others, who were not introduced by name, but who came forward and respectfully shook hands. The food and the drink were set on a table under a gazebo, and the view from the garden was splendid. Binoculars had been provided, as if for a bird watching expedition. The mountain refuge at which don Carmelo and his friends were to assemble was some three miles away, but clearly visible. They would be looking at it; but don Carmelo and his friends would have no idea.

Don Calogero drew Costantino aside, wanting to know who the other Serbs were - they were cousins recently arrived from Niš and as such utterly trustworthy – and whether everything was ready. It was all ready: the chainsaw had been tested earlier that morning; the acid was waiting, and the boys from Niš knew how that worked; the prisoner was securely cuffed and held; there was no chance of his running away. Don Calogero enquired if the prisoner knew. The boys from Niš and he had not exchanged a word, but they got the impression that the prisoner knew what was coming; a sort of fatalism had come over him. The prisoner, opined don Calogero, would give no trouble, would co-operate, thinking of his mother, his child, the others he left behind. He would not want to make life hard for any of them. Had the boys from Niš treated him well, he asked. They had, they had, he was assured.

They had a few drinks in the garden, and at 1pm they went into the house to see the television news. A slow news day, and the news from Sicily was the second item on the agenda. The Cardinal Archbishop, the crowds in the cathedral, and Ruggero Bonelli, and pictures of the eighteenth-century copy of *The Nativity with Saint Lawrence and Saint Francis*, which Bonelli, having inherited the picture from Professor Leopardi was giving to the Church on behalf of an anonymous donor who had bought it from him; he had had the picture restored, but it was a copy, he stressed, a very good copy. A snooty art critic from Rome, who admitted he had not seen the picture, except on television, opined that it was a bad copy, and all this was a pantomime. A committee of experts needed to assemble, and examine the picture, and evaluate it properly, which would take years and years. Of course, all this depended on the owner allowing them access…

There were congratulations, and then they went out into the garden once more. The boss drank champagne, as did Costantino and Muniddu. Beppe and Renzo and Traiano all stuck with the mineral water. The food was served, the boys from Niš acting as waiters. Through the binoculars they could see the assembling of don Carmelo's party. It was exclusively male, consisting of don Carmelo's closest collaborators and all four of his legitimate sons. Renzo asked curiously about the sons. They were, said Costantino, the sons of his wife; he himself did not know them. One of them, or maybe two of them, were back from America for the summer. They were in their thirties or late twenties. He had several daughters with the wife, but they were not invited. He had seen them all, but never been allowed to mix with them. There were thirteen children in all, he believed. He was the oldest, misbegotten when don Carmelo was fourteen or fifteen. There were some who were years younger, by a variety of women, five or six more, girls and boys, and of the boys, a couple worked in the business.

They all reflected, as they sat there, eating their food, consuming their drink, on the matter of children and the working of heavenly justice. Don Carmelo was in his fifties, fat, lazy, genial, but he had once been energetic, strong and well built, and as a teenager, accustomed to taking what he wanted. He had raped the woman from Niš, and then expected her to get rid of the child; he had been angry when she had returned to Yugoslavia; but by the time the child, eighteen years later, had presented himself, asking for a job, happy to take a DNA test, he had thought nothing of it. And for twenty years that child, the illegitimate Costantino, has waited. Until now.

They talked of children. Costantino had two with the cousin of his father, the Sicilian wife, and two with the African wife. Traiano had three and one on the way. Renzo had one and another on the way. The boss had three with the first wife, two with the second, and two (more or less) with Catarina; then Agata was presenting him with one, he was sure. So that made nine. He might stop soon. Agata was nice, but Catarina was difficult, though her children, his children with her, were sweet. He asked how many don Carlo had fathered: there was himself and his sisters, reported Renzo, and three or four others, all of whom he knew, all nice people, all looked after.

Silence descended, and with it an air of expectation. They were approaching the moment when don Carmelo and his friends would be sent sky high to heaven or to some other place. They had all arrived. Several cars had been left outside the refuge, all four-wheel drives which had made it up the steep volcanic track. It was time to refill their plates, and wait. Costantino looked at his watch. Two o'clock was approaching. The boys from Niš became attentive and they all looked across the valley at the peaceful scene.

Peace came to an abrupt end at just after two in the afternoon. There was a huge echoing sound, like a crack of thunder, and the mountain refuge disappeared, to be replaced by a pall of smoke and a black cloud of volcanic dust. The windows of the house behind them shook. Then there was silence. After a time one could discern that the cars were on fire. No one at all could have survived. As the dust and smoke cleared, all that was apparent where the mountain refuge had stood was a crater.

Calogero stood and embraced the Serb.

'Don Costantino,' he said.

The others did the same, as did the boys from Niš.

The police were all on the beach or having lunch, and it would be some time before they worked out what had happened. Calogero gave Costantino a nod, and the boys from Niš received a look from their master. There was to be another death that day.

They brought him out, grey faced, painfully thin and undernourished, barely recognisable as the Tonino Grassi they had all known.

'This is the person who betrayed us,' announced Calogero.

The two Serbs held him up. They were impassive. So was Tonino. Only his eyes showed his defiance. He had done what he had done, and there was no apology. Besides, he had not spoken for weeks, he could not speak now. He had forgotten the sound of his own voice. He looked at them all. He hated them, all of them; though not Beppe, who had been his friend. He wondered why Beppe was here. He had heard the explosion, of course, and did not understand it. Calogero was holding a knife; he deliberately did not look at the weapon. He concentrated his sun blinded gaze on the roof of the house behind Calogero. They were talking, but he did not listen. He looked at the distant scene, knowing he would soon be free of this place and free of them.

Calogero was offering the knife to whoever wanted it. There was a moment of hesitation.

'Sure, boss, I will,' said Muniddu, whose job these sorts of things were.

'Thanks, Muniddu,' said Calogero, but did not give him the knife.

'Do you want me to do it?' asked Renzo, knowing this was a test.

'Do you want to do it?' asked Calogero.

'No, he wants me to do it,' said Beppe, before his cousin could answer.

He too knew it was a test.

'Are you crazy?' said Traiano in a furious whisper to Calogero.

Calogero smiled. Beppe took the knife.

'What are you doing?' asked Traiano.

The others were listening, but he did not care.

'What does it look like?' said Beppe. 'Don't stand in my way.'

'Leave the knife. Put it down. Walk away,' said Traiano.

'No,' said Beppe. 'Why should I? I don't want to. I am my grandfather's grandson. Did you ever walk away? And walk away to what? What sort of life would you have had?'

'You can have a different life. With me, it was different. But for you… I had no choice. You do. Do not do this.'

'But I want to. Now get out of my way.'

'Do you know what to do?'

'Every surgeon has to learn his trade starting somewhere,' said Beppe with a smile. 'Give me a tutorial. But be quick about it.'

'Don't look at his eyes. Look at his chest, and see where the heart muscle is moving. Aim for that. Between the ribs. Take off your shirt. There will be blood, lots of blood.'

'I expect nothing less,' said Beppe. He pulled off his tee shirt. He took the knife. He approached the place where Tonino stood, the boys from Niš holding him up, one on either side. He looked for the heart muscle and could see it moving below the thin and emaciated flesh. He did not look at the contemptuous eyes of his victim.

There was, as predicted, much blood. The body of Tonino sagged, and the two Serbs allowed it gently to fall to the ground. Beppe studied it. Then Calogero approached, looked at the wound and placed the palms of his hands in the blood and anointed Beppe's cheeks and his bare chest with the warm blood of Tonino. Beppe was impassive. A few moments later the Serbs carried the body away to the back of the house where there were some trees. There was the sound of the chainsaw.

Beppe received the congratulations of the others. They shook his hand. When he came to Traiano, Traiano embraced him, despite the blood, not caring about his shirt. Beppe received this and laughed, not noticing that there were tears in Traiano's eyes.

Printed in Dunstable, United Kingdom

66520321R00167